ASSET X

A NOVEL

David A. Davies

DAPCON PUBLISHING

Warning: This book contains scenes of violence and strong profanity.

10 9 8 7 6 5 4 3 2 1
Printed in the United States of America

LCCN 2020924256
ISBN 978 0 9974727 3 8

For more information on *Asset X* and the author, visit:
www.davidadaviesauthor.com

Editor: Karalynn Ott
Cover Designer: Dapcon Publishing
Interior Design: Paul Salvette

ALSO BY DAVID A. DAVIES

THE POTENTIAL
MASK OF DECEIT
THE NEXT CELL

A MAN WHO USES FORCE IS AFRAID OF REASONING
KENYAN PROVERB

FOR THOSE WHO PERISHED ON 9/11

ACKNOWLEDGEMENTS

Once again, I have to give the biggest shout-out to my wife Patty for her unending support, love and understanding with this and many more of my projects. Thank you to Stevan Rankic for his insights and his keen eye for detail. Many thanks also to beta readers Tom Abel, Gabe Mason and D.M. for allowing me to get into the weeds without going too far off-track. And last but not least, thank you to my editor Karalynn Ott for her expertise and skill in keeping my writing, something worth reading.

CHAPTER ONE

Djerba, Tunisia, 2002

NISER BIN MUHAMMAD SLOWED THE vehicle down to a crawl to negotiate the hard-right turn. He crunched the gearbox down to second and sweated as he pulled at the steering wheel of the old natural-gas tanker truck with all his strength, silently pleading for it to comply. Within 500 meters he had to turn right again, cautious of the badly parked cars and pedestrians bustling their way in and out of the town center. His cousin, Farouk, sitting in the passenger seat, rivulets of sweat pouring down his face, continually called out potential dangers and obstacles that might hinder their progress.

Rounding the last turn, neither man breathed a sigh of relief. Instead, both sat up straighter and focused only on what lay before them.

Niser began pumping the clutch and grinding the gears back upward, gaining momentum. Farouk checked the mirrors. There was nothing behind them. He glanced over at the speedometer and was encouraged to see that they were finally reaching a good speed. They were nearing their goal. "Allahu Akbar," he began chanting.

There was a slight fork in the road, forcing them to the right again—and towards their ultimate destination. Niser saw the white archway first, and in unison he too began chanting the same as his cousin, both now eager to reach their target and on to glory. The truck raced at 70 km/h; the engine shrieked, begging for another gear that wasn't there. A slight dip in the road increased the motor's whine, topping it out at 75 km/h.

Ahead, a security guard alerted by the monstrous bellowing stepped into the road to stop the incursion. Niser held his right foot down on the gas with all his might and, without even a passing glance at the man, blew right by him. Niser's eyes were bulging and foam was frothing from his mouth as he screamed at the top of his lungs that his God was great—then he finally yanked the tanker hard, right into the compound walls of the blue and white synagogue.

He never saw, or felt, the impact of the three German tourists rolling under the wheels of his truck, nor did he see the tour group inside the compound fleeing for their lives.

He took one last deep breath and looked at his cousin. Farouk closed his eyes and pressed the detonator.

Port Hadlock, Washington State

Chris Morehouse stood in the cockpit of the *Certa Cito*, his feet planted wide apart, hands steady on the steering wheel, and eyes trained on the sails and the wind. The thirty-seven-foot oceangoing sailboat bobbed gently under canvas through the Strait of Juan de Fuca. The seas were calm and the winds were fair—a fitting end to an untroubled ten-day excursion along the shores of California, Oregon and Washington.

When he sighted Fort Worden State Park off the starboard bow, Chris suggested to his crew that it was time to drop the sails and prepare for docking. He would have liked to sail right into Port Townsend Bay, but the narrow stretch of water between the mainland and Whidbey Island about seven miles east as the crow flies was one of the busiest stretches of water in the Pacific Northwest, especially in summer, when it teemed with freighters of all shapes and sizes, ferries, cruise ships, naval vessels and pleasure boats. He wisely surmised the use of the inboard engine was the smartest way to get around the lighthouse at Point Wilson and keep out of the swells of larger craft.

Chris' girlfriend Sandy scuttled down to the saloon to stow away the last of their equipment.

"What do you think Patrick?" Chris asked of his maritime mentor.

"You've got a lovely boat Chris, and you're getting good at handling her—not to forget you have a fine crew." Patrick motioned downstairs to Sandy, and looked below to see if she was listening. "She's a sweet girl that one," he whispered. "You need to get a ring on her finger and stop stringing her along."

"She told you that?"

"If it's plain for this old Irishman to see, it's plain for everyone else, boyo."

Chris knew he was right. Although the three of them had spent nearly two weeks in cramped and generally unromantic quarters aboard the boat, he enjoyed his time with Sandy and was happy knowing that she loved sailing as much as he did. After this trip they'd spend a week ashore, then the two of them, with Patrick's blessing, would set out on their own little nautical voyage. They were ready. Both had taken the requisite licensing and safety courses, and had spent untold hours in dock and on shorter saltwater jaunts, preparing. The current trip under the Irishman's guidance was the final sea trial for the new boat and the adventurous pair. And it appeared that they'd passed.

Even so, Patrick couldn't resist one last bit of advice before docking.

"Stick to what you know, Chris. You still need more hours under canvas before you attempt a long crossing. Don't bite off more than you can chew. The sea will always be there; don't fight it all in one day."

"Anymore clichés?" Chris cracked.

"You know what I mean boyo—and I'm not just talking about sailing the Seven Seas either."

Chris smiled. "Oh, so now you're offering me relationship advice?"

Patrick tied off the last of the sheets. "That's not my job . . . I'm just an old sailor who's been in too many ports. Now kick on your engine before we flounder. I don't want to walk home from here."

"Aye, captain."

The *Certa Cito* puttered along towards Port Townsend, pausing for a minute to let a Washington State Ferry leave its slip at the Victorian seaport. Once cleared, Sandy shuffled forward on the deck and threw out the fenders on both sides of the craft. Chris killed the engine and expertly coasted his yacht up to the jetty. He tried his best to focus on the task at hand, but his brown, deeply suspicious eyes were already busy scanning the harbor, the other boats, and the other sailors going innocently about their business. He may have been on vacation from his job with the US Central Intelligence Agency—the CIA—and at sea he indeed had let his hair down a bit. But now being near land again, his threat-awareness mindset ratcheted up ten notches. He may have looked calm, cool and collected, but his kind, handsome face as always hid his true nature: that of a survivalist. Once on terra firma, everything and everyone would be a threat.

Grabbing a bowline, Sandy jumped onto the tiny Port Hadlock jetty and tied the boat off. Chris held the vessel in place, then threw the stern line out for her to secure.

For the next few minutes, the seafaring trio busied themselves with the motions of packing bags and offloading gear to take ashore. Chris was on the jetty taking a ripe bag of trash from Sandy when his phone rang. He pulled it from his pocket, saw the number, and then looked back at her. She was standing on the boat watching him, both hands on her hips. Her eyes narrowed, her lips tightened, and her posture was as stiff as the deck she was planted on.

Chris turned and marched away. "Hello," he said curtly.

"Hey buddy, how are you?"

"I want to say it's delightful to hear from you Gene, but it's not. You know I love you, but you can't keep calling me like this—people will talk."

"You know this call is being taped, right?"

"I got nothing to hide. It's not my fault you have issues with your sexuality."

"Asshole!"

"Takes one to know one. What's up? You forget I'm on vacation?"

"They've given us an all-hands tasking. You need to get to Paris as soon as possible. You'll receive orders, then deploy from there."

Chris was irritated. The dreaded "they" was the Counter Terrorism Center, or CTC, in Virginia—the supposed end all and be all of counterterrorism for the CIA.

"Gene, I'm in the middle of the Pacific. I told you I'd be out at sea. I won't be back for days."

"Don't fall into that harbor and catch a cold, Chris. You're not getting off that easy. I know you're back."

It didn't surprise Chris that he was being tracked; the deputy head of the CIA's Special Activities Division had eyes everywhere, even in a historic little harbor in the upper-left corner of the country. He spun around to see if he could spot a watcher, then meandered along the jetty. There were dozens of cars in the harbor's parking lot, as well as other boaters, dog walkers, mothers with strollers. It could have been anyone. Someone might have tagged his boat with an electronic tracker or knew of his itinerary. It mattered not, for now. There was something afoot if an all-hands operation was taking place.

"Give me break Gene," Chris pleaded. "I've got plans. Sandy and I—"

"Chris, you know this isn't up for debate. I'm sorry to call you in like this . . . well, not really, but there's work waiting for you. I'll meet you there. And if you want to keep bitching, you can do it to my face. Get on a plane soonest."

"One of these days I really will be in the middle of the Pacific, or the Caribbean, and I won't answer the call Gene. I'm tired of this."

"Don't be stupid—that's not you. Get on a plane, Chris."

The line went dead. Chris had a funky feeling in his stomach. He didn't relish the conversation he was about to have with his girlfriend. Patrick, kit bag over his shoulder, sauntered up to him.

"Everything all right?"

"Could be better, Patrick."

"She's throwing the f-bomb around down below. What did you say to her?"

"Nothing. My job's getting in the way again."

"You got to go back?"

Chris nodded. He wanted to stay; he was ready to have a normal life. But he'd only told Gene a half-truth about being tired of his job. He knew as soon as he got the call that he was ready to go, and likely always would be. He couldn't give up the rush so easily.

"Will you check in on the boat while I'm away?" he asked, despairingly.

Patrick nodded. "I'll even take her out for you, I kind of like her. When are you coming back?"

"I really don't know, Patrick. I really don't know."

They discussed a few mundane details about what they needed for the boat—fuel, water and other sundry items. Then they shook hands and said their goodbyes.

By the time that Chris strolled back to the boat, Sandy was sitting in the cockpit, smoking a cigarette.

"I thought you'd given that up?" he quizzed, surprised.

She ignored him for a few seconds, then shot him a look of derision. She flicked ash into the air, and took a long pull. "I suppose you're off again."

Chris was silent. There was never a good answer, there were no excuses.

"I took time off for you," she said coldly. "We had plans. I have people covering for me—the ranch, the office. It took a lot of favors to pull this vacation together."

"I know, I know."

"You told me you had six weeks, Chris. It's been *two*. It's unfair."

"I'm sorry," was all he could muster.

An awkward silence separated them. Neither could look at the other. Chris for his part gazed down at his feet, not knowing what to say, and not wanting to say something wrong.

She finally broke the impasse. "I'll be here Chris . . . even though I still don't know what it is you do—"

"You don't want to know, believe me," he interrupted.

"Whatever. I know you're passionate about your work, but you'll have to make a choice one of these days. This trip, I mean this whole vacation . . . I wanted it to help you relax, help us. But you can't switch off, can you? You can't let the job go, or let someone else do something without you . . . You choose that life over *us* Chris. It's not right, not normal."

Christ, an ultimatum, that's all I need, he thought.

There was another long pause before she spoke again.

"I can't go on like this forever. I'm tired of you being gone for weeks at a time. You never call, and I never know where you are. I don't know if you're safe . . . You're not helping me, Chris."

"You know I can't tell you where I am."

"Chris, come to think of it, most of the time you're not even here when you're standing right in front of my face. You're always on edge, you trust no one, and you always carry that damn gun! The boat was a way to help us get away from that."

Let her vent, keep your mouth shut, he pleaded with himself. *Don't say something stupid.*

"We don't have friends—except the ones you choose. Other people, other normal people . . . they fear you, Chris. I don't want that; I don't want that for us. If this is to work, you and I . . . you need to change."

Lahore, Pakistan

Chris was feeling cramped and annoyed in the quickly filling room. It was supposedly a safe house, not a conference center, yet given the number of vehicles and human traffic around the area, it would have been easy to believe it was the latter. With forty-plus men jostling for space in a dining room designed for small gatherings, Chris felt like he was being stuffed into a Tokyo commuter train, face-to-bad-breath-face with people he didn't know. He wanted to plug his ears; the noise was becoming unbearable. If he closed his eyes, he could imagine he was backstage in a concert hall surrounded by a passel of choir singers, each trying to warm up for their big operatic performance.

Chris was snapped out of his imaginary version of mayhem when Jon, the senior CIA officer in charge of the operation, jumped up on the dining room table and clapped his hands three times to garner everyone's attention. The din dissipated as all eyes focused on the bearded man wearing traditional Pakistani clothing, now standing a few feet above them. One and all knew that the next few words out of the man's mouth would seal their own futures: his utterance could mean life or death for some, and success or failure for others. Chris felt his jaw head for the floor as Jon looked at his watch, then told everyone else to synchronize theirs to his. Chris glanced over at his colleague and friend Alex Faber, who was equally dumfounded at the request, then played along with what felt like a bizarre World War II movie scene.

After a few seconds of mumbling and grumbling—and even a few giggles—Jon delivered a brief message: the mission was a "GO," the execute time was 0200 hours, and there were no changes to the plan. Everyone in the room nodded, and a few smiled. Chris looked over once again to Alex, whose arms were folded across his chest, but also dipped his head in approval.

Operation Torque, a bold plan to raid fourteen sites in Lahore and Faisalabad simultaneously, in order to capture a senior member of Osama bin Laden's inner circle, was just hours away from being implemented. Chris, along with the horde in the room, shuffled his feet—eager to get going.

Chris Morehouse, a thirty-five-year-old CIA officer and former British soldier, had been in many armed conflicts, from Northern Ireland to Afghanistan. He'd traveled to these engagements by helicopter, by Land Rover, by Toyota pickup and various other such vehicles, but never in a bus. As the miles passed by on the busy Pakistani roads, he dwelled on this latest mission. This new form of transport turned out *not* to be on the list of things he expected to utilize in order to catch terrorists when he joined the CIA. He brooded over the lackadaisical approach to their appearance, and worried that neither he, nor his American colleagues on the bus were in control. It was a Pakistani affair. He mulled over the umpteen number of things that could go wrong. His eyes and ears constantly looking and listening for a problem that would need his immediate attention. He was feeling uncomfortable, his butt itched, sensing something was wrong—but it wasn't because of the state of the aging transport. He thought it strange the Operation Torque participants were deployed on a mission in such a way, but was told, much to his chagrin, that logistically it was the only way possible.

Chris had recently been promoted to the CIA's Special Activities Division (SAD) from working as a surveillance specialist within the CIA's Directorate of Operations. While happy being on such an elite team, he was told from the outset that if he wanted to be involved, he had to strictly follow orders, keep his thoughts to himself, and play nice. Maintaining his silence, Chris squashed his thoughts, forcing them deep into the back of his mind. Operation Torque, meticulously planned down to the exact minute by others outside his sphere of influence, prevented him from trying to second-guess a tactic or throw out what-if scenarios that people didn't want to hear about. Although his team members valued his opinions, the undertaking at hand was greater than any individual's predilections, and the target too valuable to let slip away because someone didn't like his place on the bus. As such, he bit his tongue. He had to remember he was at heart a soldier. He followed orders and his opinions were of no consequence; whereas, dealing with Sandy, he should be doing the opposite.

His job was rendition: the apprehension, detention and interrogation of suspected terrorists. SAD recruited Chris for his expertise as a leader of a CIA deep surveillance unit, as well as his background as a counterterrorist specialist with combat experience. His skills were much in demand. However, as pointed out by his girlfriend, his attitude and brash demeanor were sometimes not.

In the lead-up to the mission, there had been many briefings, tactical planning sessions, and strategic discussions. Some meetings the SAD team were privy to; others they were not. The consensus was that nobody on the team was pleased to be sharing their identities with the Pakistanis—allies or not for the endeavor. Nor were they comfortable discussing their methods with members of the FBI, NSA and other American agencies and contractors drafted in for the operation. They preferred to keep things close to the vest.

The current leg of the plan would drop off mission participants—two CIA officers, an FBI agent, and an officer from Pakistan's Inter-

Services Intelligence Agency (ISI) per team—at various checkpoints in Faisalabad and Lahore. Two large buses and two trucks would be employed to transport the specialized manpower needed for the entire operation. Once these teams had reached their appointed staging points, they would meet up with members of the Special Service Group (SSG), a Pakistani special forces unit, in addition to a force of the paramilitary Pakistan Rangers, who had responsibility for area containment.

In conjunction with this deployment, officers of the US National Security Agency (NSA) had circled the target neighborhoods in vehicles with technology designed to send out an electronic signal keyed to a particular cell phone. These "magic boxes" as the NSA liked to call them, had located the phone that they were looking for—however stymied by the frequent relocation of the phone and its user, which led them to surmise that the target never slept in the same location more than a few nights.

Clearly Operation Torque was a huge undertaking, with multiple moving parts that required concise and expert coordination. There were no real backup plans, save for abort codes that each team could call. The mission objective was stated in simple terms: capture the terrorist Abu Zubaydah. However simple that may have sounded, it was, of course, just the opposite.

The operation's first element was the necessary success of the NSA team in identifying the precise location for the raid teams to hit. Once confirmed, they needed a quick analysis of the site to establish opposing force security measures. Second, there was a need for a secure perimeter with all the tactical tools needed, but without warning the terrorists of the potential raid. A challenging endeavor, considering the constant movement of man and machine in the locale. The final part of the plan would be to gain entry, engage with potential adversaries, and secure the target. Simple on paper, perhaps, but potentially impossible with the numbers of unknowns facing the teams.

The CIA station in Islamabad, designated ICE CAVE for the operation, was in overall command and control, with Pakistani backup support and general oversight. Its bearded commander, Jon, also known as ICE BEAR, would coordinate efforts on the ground with the raid teams. Until Jon climbed on the table at the Lahore safe house, nobody knew that the first parts of the mission were already complete. The NSA magic boxes had a fix on their target, although they weren't 100 percent positive. The brain trust at ICE CAVE, as well as the counterterrorism center in Virginia, projected that there was a strong possibility that Zubaydah was in the Shahbaz Town district in the southwest of Faisalabad, and they gave Jon the green light to proceed.

Chris shifted his Russian-made Makarov 9mm pistol on his right hip, desperately trying to get a little more comfortable on the decidedly uncomfortable bone-shaker of a bus. He wasn't as nervous as he'd been in worse operation conditions; he knew the Pakistanis would be the ones to kick in doors this time. All he was there for was to take out the trash and dump it elsewhere for someone else to bury. As he adjusted his butt in the seat, he strained to look forward out of the front of the bus—just in time to see the lead escort car bust through a tollbooth at high speed. As the bus passed through, he spun around to see the second team bus and follow car do exactly the same, and for a second he thought nothing of it. But then his worry-wart mind took over.

If we just blasted through there, then they knew we were coming. I thought this shit was ultra-tight and nobody knew we'd be here. He looked for a reaction from Alex, a few rows in front of him. Although the interior of the bus was dark, Chris could tell from his friend's uneasy body language that he too was concerned. The small convoy speedily continued on its journey, edging closer to the center of the city. The clock was ticking, and timing was everything.

Chris couldn't settle down. He sat up straighter when he saw the unmistakable blue and white strobe light of a police car passing the bus. *Got to be routine, nothing to do with us,* he reasoned. But his mind sprinted to a dozen what-if scenarios as the police car forced the lead escort to pull over, thus bringing the entire convoy to a stop. Pistols and rifles suddenly appeared throughout the bus and made ready by the Pakistanis. The ISI agent sitting next to Chris pulled out a pistol and pointed it directly at the floor. He didn't draw his weapon, though, as he rationalized there was enough firepower inside the bus to take on an altercation, and if things were to go south, his mind would be on escape and evasion—not waiting to see who the best shots were.

Maintaining their cool, the Americans sat in silence, but each inwardly pleaded for the clocks to stop. Nobody forgot the timing for the takedowns. Everyone nervously checked their watches, and more than a few whispered curses coursed through the vehicle. An FBI agent at the front of the bus called ICE BEAR over his radio to inform him of the situation. The head honcho of the Pakistani contingent stormed off the bus and marched quickly over to the police officers, who were arguing with the members of the lead car. A small shoving match ensued and Chris shot Alex an "I told-you-so" look. He got up, brushing past the ISI man sitting next to him, and leaned over toward Alex.

"How far do you reckon to our drop off point?" Chris asked in a hushed tone.

"Mile, mile and a half. Why, you want to get off this train wreck?" Alex jibed.

"Mile and a half . . . we can make that in ten minutes if we run."

"Let's let this shit play out, Chris. We have some flex time."

"Not enough. If we're here for another five minutes, we're screwed. I don't know about you, but I'm not going to repeat this bullshit again." The fracas was still continuing with the local cops. Chris looked down the aisle of the bus. "I can drive this shed; you navigate?"

"Chris chill out already—"

Another CIA SAD officer sitting in front of Alex caught the conversation. "Sign me up, this is horseshit. We should never have gone along with this shitshow in the first place."

Before they furthered the discussion, the lead ISI officer got back on the bus and instructed the driver to drive on. Chris grabbed a hold of a seat back as the driver wrenched the bus around the still-static lead vehicle and police car. He then squirmed back to his seat. By the time he was comfortable, the voices from the front of the bus became louder. Chris, knowing only a few words of Urdu, couldn't understand the now-boisterous conversations taking place simultaneously between groups of ISI officers. Finally, an FBI agent with language skills solved the mystery.

"Okay! Okay! Enough already." Like a high school teacher on a field trip, he stood and made an announcement in order to quell the racket. "Someone forgot to have money for tolls. Let's forget about it. We have a mission to complete. Settle down, kill the noise."

Chris stared straight ahead. He couldn't believe what he was hearing. It took the CIA eighteen months to track and plan the capture of Abu Zubaydah, and it could all fall apart because someone didn't think to bring a few rupees for a stupid toll road. He turned to look out the window and wondered what else could go wrong—and if it set the mission up for failure. For the umpteenth time, he looked at his watch. The few spare minutes he wanted to save for "in-case-of" situations had dwindled away. He wracked his brain, going over worst-case scenarios. If the Lahore teams conducted their raids before the Faisalabad teams set up, all because of the toll road fiasco, then the terrorist they were trying to capture might have warning of the raids. He wanted to go over his concerns with Alex and the rest of the SAD team. He wanted to tell them that the missing toll road money could have been a ploy by the Pakistanis to allow the terrorists time to escape. But there just wasn't enough time; the bus stopped to drop off the first members of the raid teams.

His thoughts drifted back to the last six months. During that time, Chris and the SAD team had been on multiple raids in Pakistan and the tribal borderlands with Afghanistan, scouting out al-Qaeda operatives with some success. But it seemed to the CIA that most of it was just window dressing, as the missions only captured low-level terrorists, and to date nobody of any actual value was in custody. The SAD team was skeptical of the Pakistanis' commitment, and they were getting highly pissed off by repeatedly hearing the words, "We just missed them." He hoped that he wouldn't hear them yet again over the next few hours.

Despite all of Chris's misgivings, fourteen teams of men in Faisalabad and Lahore moved in on their targets simultaneously at 0200 hours. Chris and Alex patiently waited at site, dubbed TIGER, a three-story pale peach stucco home surrounded by high walls and a solid metal gate. The sound of the special forces' vehicle ramming the gate was enough to wake the dead up within a ten-mile radius, but the tight angle of the street didn't allow for precision, and the vehicle had to back up and ram the gate again, finally forcing the obstacle off its foundation. As soon as the soldiers crossed the threshold into the property, the unmistakable, *klink, klink, klink* of bullets hitting metal permeated the air. Chris, standing in cover with Alex at the security cordon created by the Pakistan Rangers, held his breath and mentally reached for his gun. He knew his rules of engagement and would only draw if an imminent threat appeared. He was sure his partner was thinking the same as new sounds were coming out of TIGER: shotgun blasts from door hinges being blown, followed by automatic fire. Then a loud *thrump*, followed by more fire. A gun battle had ensued. Chris popped his head over the cover of a vehicle to see if he could spot some activity.

Well, we haven't stumbled on a quilting class, that's for sure; this could be it for a change. About bloody time we got one right.

He tried in vain to hear if other firefights were happening at the nearby sites, named SNAKE and EAGLE, but the sound of the explosions and shots being fired at TIGER drowned out any other sound.

"Second floor; it's going to get more difficult as they go up." Alex, the former Delta Force soldier, commented to his partner.

Chris agreed. "I'm guessing this is it. If Zubaydah isn't here, there are going be some very pissed off neighbors."

An FBI agent standing nearby had his hand pressed to his right ear, listening as best he could to his radio, "SNAKE is a dead end, sounds like a few others too."

Bearded Jon appeared around a corner with a senior ISI officer closely following, carrying a cell phone in one hand and a portable radio in the other. The American grinned at the two SAD officers but kept his thoughts to himself and took cover behind a police vehicle.

Chris turned his attention back towards TIGER, and saw, then heard, a loud explosion causing a second-floor window and part of a wall to blow outward toward the street. The rest of the team down below instinctively ducked at the sight and sound, hoping that the debris wouldn't rain down on them.

"We need him alive!" Jon hissed at the ISI man, who immediately got on the radio to relay the information to the soldiers. But the fight intensified, with long bursts of automatic fire.

Alex once again voiced his opinion to Chris. "If they don't maintain forward progress soon, they'll lose the advantage; they need to move forward. There are too many rounds being thrown around."

"If you want to go sort the shit out, I'm right behind you," Chris offered, eager to play his part.

"Wishful thinking buddy. Not our circus, not our clowns." Alex grimaced at the sound of another small explosion. "There's a determined force in there. Just hope there's something for us to process when the shooting stops—and someone in the meantime doesn't feel the need to go meet his maker and invite everyone along for the ride."

Bearded Jon cringed once more at the sound of explosions. When he designed Operation Torque, he was adamant that Zubaydah was not engaged with current terrorist operations, and thus would not prove to be such a pugilist opponent. Now, with the rounds still flying, he realized he might have been wrong.

The initial CIA supposition of Zubaydah was that although he was a confidant of bin Laden, he was only a logistician, a recruiter. But Jon argued that the terrorist acted as a conduit for al-Qaeda's forces as they were being forced out of Afghanistan by American efforts, and towards the safety of Pakistan. His capture would be a major coup for the CIA, which was still reeling from the fallout of the 9/11 catastrophe.

However, all theories aside, the resulting firefight, now in its fifteenth minute, was proof enough that al-Qaeda, while on the run from Afghanistan, was still a formidable force.

"Rooftop!" Alex pointed.

Chris and Jon looked up in unison to see a Pakistani Special Forces soldier drill a terrorist with a burst of rounds at close range. Either the bullets hit a grenade, or the fanatic detonated an explosive device, but the blast was enough to blow the two combatants off the roof, showering the street below with roof debris and body parts.

Jon was shocked; he didn't want to believe his eyes. "My God!" he croaked.

Chris wanted to respond to Jon's astonished outburst, but he kept his mouth in check. He viewed the spectacle for what it was: the price of battle. *What did you expect, you muppet! Butterflies and fairy dust?*

The battle continued, but with less intensity. There were no more explosions, but sporadic shots, coupled with shouting and screaming, came from inside the house. Pakistani radio traffic was, to Chris's ears, a blend of gobbledygook running at full speed; he couldn't translate anything. Clearly though, they were the shouts of men still high on adrenalin. While Chris chomped at the bit to get inside the building, Jon added to the communication mayhem by barking orders over his phone and cajoling the ISI into action.

"We need to get in there Alex," Chris stated.

"Roger," his partner acknowledged, nodding. "Jon, are we clear to go? Jon . . . Jon?"

Jon heard the request and turned to his ISI liaison officer for clearance. The ISI man nodded, which was all the SAD officers needed. They broke from the safety of their cover and made their way to the house. An FBI agent was five steps behind them.

The Americans moved past the broken gate, but then stood aside as two soldiers carried out an injured comrade. The main entry door was hanging off its hinges. Just two steps inside, Chris almost fell over a couple of dead bodies lying on top of each other, face up. The first was a Special Forces soldier, his throat sliced open with a garrote; the second, a terrorist who was missing his face, but still clutching his bloody length of wire. Chris knew it wouldn't take long for the stench of death to poison the air, if not from this scene, then from others that were waiting deeper inside the house. As Chris and Alex crept down a hallway they were suddenly brushed aside from behind by two soldiers carrying an empty stretcher as they rushed up the stairs ahead of them. Neither of the SAD men protested. They'd both experienced combat and knew that the first minutes after a firefight were crucial to get people the aid they needed. The pair continued on their mission, scouring the rooms in the house for their target.

The place was becoming as busy as a *Pac-Man* game in hyper mode, with ISI officers running from room to room, screeching into their radios, and soldiers dragging screaming women and crying children towards the outside of the dwelling. Pakistan Special Forces were cuffing face-down terrorists, while more white Western faces showed up by the minute, trying to justify their reason for being there.

Chris and Alex made it to a room on the second floor where an injured man lay face up on a stretcher flanked by four silent Pakistani Special Forces sentinels, weapons still at the ready, adrenalin pumped and ready to kill again if called upon.

"Is this him?" Chris asked of the four soldiers. None spoke but all four nodded their affirmation. "Are you going to leave him to bleed out, or are you going to help him?" he pushed.

Alex pulled off his backpack and kneeled next to the stretcher. "I'm not so sure Chris. This doesn't look like him, and he's pretty close to checking out. Get Jon up here. I'll see what I can do."

Chris didn't have to go far. Jon was squeezing his way up the narrow stairs through bodies coming and going. Chris got his attention and led him to Alex. By this time an ISI officer had shown up.

Jon too asked the obvious question of the sentinels. "Is this him?" He took a few moments to size up the man on the stretcher.

The soldiers didn't respond this time, but the intelligence officer answered emphatically. "Yes, this is him, we have him."

"He's too big," Jon proffered. "He must be forty or fifty pounds heavier than our guy, and he doesn't look at all like his picture. His hair is wild, Zubaydah is cleaner cut than this." There was a long pause as Jon's brain worked overtime, like a hamster on a wheel. "Alex, what's his status?"

"He'll die soon if we don't get him to a hospital, Jon." He made sure everyone knew why things were serious. "He's been shot in the stomach, thigh and groin. He's losing blood that I can't stop—there's only so much I can do." Alex, his hands covered in the man's blood, continued to shove wads of gauze from the small trauma kit he carried into the man's wounds.

Jon took two steps away and pulled out his phone. He called ICE CAVE and got one of the FBI profilers. "Take a picture of his iris and send it to me," the agent ordered.

Jon leaned over and shouted at the prone man in Arabic, "Open your eyes!" But he would not or could not comply. Chris leaned over to pry open his eyelids, but his eyeballs rolled back in his head. Chris then shifted the terrorist's head over to one side and brushed his hair out of the way. "Take a picture of his ear," he commanded.

Jon squinted his eyes and then tensed up. "What the hell are you talking about?"

"His ear, it's as unique as a fingerprint. Take a picture, send it back. Maybe they can work with it."

Jon obeyed and waited patiently for ICE CAVE to work their technology; the line was still open and on speaker. After a minute, the response they were waiting for came.

"It's him, positive ID." Everyone in the room smiled, including the normally morose Alex, who threw in the obvious. "We need to get him out of here. He'll need a transfusion, and it needs to happen now!"

Chris wanted to get the ball rolling too. "Jon, we need to organize a convoy to the nearest hospital. We'll take two of these guys with us, you get things in motion. We'll see if we can strap him onto this stretcher, bring him downstairs in the next few, okay?"

Under normal circumstances, Jon wouldn't be happy taking orders from a junior officer, but these were exceptional times. He was so ecstatic that if he were asked to do a naked, happy dance on the rooftop, he would have sprinted up there to do it. It was every CIA officer's dream to catch the big guy, prevent cataclysmic events from taking place, and protect his country from harm. Today, with the capture of this man, Jon's dreams came true. He stood there for a minute and soaked in the moment. He'd reached a pinnacle in his career, a feat only met by a few at the CIA, so if an underling wanted him to get a vehicle, he would get the best set of wheels possible and deliver it with a smile.

Alex sensed the buoyant mood. "Don't look so smug Jon, he's borderline. You'll be talking to a corpse if you don't hurry up."

"Let me kill him," a voice interrupted. "It will save us all time, he does not deserve to live." The outburst from one of the Pakistani soldiers shocked Jon. "Say what?" he asked.

"He should die. Why do you waste time to treat him? Let me finish this animal."

Jon stood his ground. "No, absolutely not. This man has intelligence that we need. He will be coming with us."

"He killed one of my best men," the commando continued, raising his rifle toward the injured man.

Chris slowly rose from his kneeling position and got between Zubaydah and the soldier. One of the other commandos shuffled towards him, eyes threatening without words, knuckles whitening around his rifle's pistol grip. Chris knew not to make any sudden movements, and to keep his hands down at his waist; he didn't want to come across as a threat. These were tight confines in which to start a fight with professional soldiers. He didn't want to start something he might lose. He wanted Alex to keep working on their prone captive, and he wanted Jon to go get someone who could order these men to stand down.

He spoke in a soft tone. "Guys, we don't need this to get out of hand. He's coming with us; we need him alive. He has valuable information. I'm sure you can understand that . . . it looks like he'll die eventually anyway—but while he's alive, we need to talk to him."

"There are many more like him. They need to know that we take a life when they take a life," the soldier replied.

"You're right . . . but not this one. The information that this guy gives us may lead us to the next operation, the next raid. There's plenty of killing yet to do, there will be other times for revenge—but not today."

The conversation ended as soon as a Pakistani army officer with what appeared to be scrambled eggs on his peaked cap and spaghetti medals festooned across his chest entered the room. He questioned why the man on the stretcher was still there and not on his way to a hospital, obviating the need for discussions of who should live or die.

Chris wasn't sure if they'd just jumped out of the frying pan and into the fire. The hospital was a mess, with a steady stream of bugs marching across its grimy surfaces, as if on their way to a factory job. There was no air conditioning, so all the windows were open, inviting any airborne bugs who felt the need to join the work party on the ground. Zubaydah, placed in the only available bed in a quiet corner of the hospital, lay on a soiled and sagging mattress, which was causing his bum to reach for the floor. Chris had to look away when he saw a doctor plunge a needle into a bar of soap before injecting their patient. Jon wore a look of pure horror. He turned his attention to Chris and Alex. "You guys stay here with him for now; I know he's not going anywhere, but tie him down somehow. We're getting out of here. I don't want him to die in a place like this, and neither do I."

He marched off looking at his phone, trying to determine if there was enough of a signal for a call. Alex fished out some water from his kit and began dousing his hands to clean off the blood from Zubaydah. He didn't need to worry about a making a mess on the floor. The fluids from his hands merrily joined the other unidentified liquids that were either pooling on or running across the uneven tiles.

Chris reached into his backpack for two sets of latex gloves and some sanitary wipes. As he and Alex finished cleaning themselves up, Jon returned with two FBI agents who brought with them a camera and a fingerprint kit. They had also come to retrieve the FBI's terrorist's evidence bag, mistakenly taken out of TIGER and transported to the hospital. As the agents snapped close-ups of the man on the bed, a cell phone in the bag rang. Jon made a move to pull the phone out, but the senior agent intervened. "You can't touch that, it's evidence," he snapped, grabbing the bag off the bed.

"I need to answer it." Jon countered. "What if it's someone who thinks he escaped and is alive? I need to know who that person is."

"No, you will not touch that," the FBI man reiterated sternly. "We need that for prosecution. Back off."

Jon was desperate. "Are you serious? This call—" The ringing stopped.

The agent held on to the bag tightly. "This is going back to Islamabad with us, then it'll be in the next available diplomatic pouch back to the US."

"You can't do that, this is a CIA operation—we need to get the NSA guys down here and start tracking this thing—" the phone rang again, "give me that damn phone!" Jon spat as he made a move closer to the agent.

"Back off! You have no jurisdiction here. This is evidence from a crime scene; we will use this in his prosecution!"

The phone kept ringing.

Chris rolled his eyes at Alex, who shrugged his shoulders. The Brit didn't want to play diplomat again. The phone eventually stopped. The FBI-CIA argument continued to rage.

The bag found its way to the bed again, and the phone rang once more. Chris stared at the see-through plastic evidence bag and spotted a few credit cards inside, along with some cigarettes, a lighter, a gold ring. The sum of a terrorist's belongings. Chris sat in silence, watching the two representatives from America's top security agencies argue over a phone.

The Central Intelligence Agency's prime mission was to prevent more terrorist acts, and to be successful they needed intelligence. Phones belonging to terrorists were priceless in possibly identifying more al-Qaeda operatives, as they offered more rings or layers to prod, provoke, and pursue. Conversely, the Federal Bureau of Investigation was traditionally happy when they had bad guys in cuffs, on the way to jail, or incarcerated. Unlike the CIA, they were happy to close cases when judges passed down sentences—and to do that, evidence was crucial. The FBI collected lots and lots of grains of sand within their reach to build their castles of evidence; the CIA liked to build their castles from all the sand, from all the beaches, from everywhere.

The argument ended when each of the antagonists stormed off in different directions, dialing numbers on their phones, both shouting versions of "This is not the last you will hear of this! You will regret crossing me, and You are out of your depth!" And the phone kept ringing. Chris daydreamed for a second that the caller was perhaps simply trying to order a pizza and got the wrong number; but he kept his silliness to himself and quietly chewed a piece of gum. He looked over at Alex, who was practicing the discipline that the two phone fighters had forgotten to do: never show weakness in front of a prisoner. Offer nothing, except enough to keep a man alive. Do not speak to him unless you are ordering him to do something. And above all remain silent, passive, and non-confrontational. Chris made a note to himself that during his debrief he needed to let someone know what just happened.

The hours ticked by and the phone calls eventually stopped. Chris noted the time, not that it mattered but he would pass it on to Jon, just in case someone could use a tidbit to paint a picture.

French Beach, Karachi, Pakistan

Mukhtar finally gave up with the phone. He'd called Zubaydah multiple times without success as he meandered out along the shoreline. Alone on the beach, he enjoyed the ambiance of the moment, the light spray of the ocean, the breeze that cooled the air, the feeling of insignificance against the surrounding elements, realizing that the sea was the great equalizer amongst all men.

He stood for a moment in the darkness, pondering the situation while waves crashed endlessly against the shore. He knew that the Americans were stepping up their activities to track his organization, but his sources in Pakistan's government circles were not so forthcoming with their usual reliable intelligence. He thought he had presented enough cannon fodder to appease the Pakistan ISI, who had placated the CIA with meaningless arrests. But as of late, the Americans were baying for blood and expecting results; the hounds were at the heels of his beloved al-Qaeda and he wondered gravely if his ISI informers were succumbing to the pressure and failing him.

For Abu Zubaydah not to answer his calls was strange, but not unusual; however, when he tried alternate numbers that also went unanswered, it unsettled him. Altering some of his plans was out of the question. Some, however, now required acceleration, while others needed postponement, or even cancellation. Countless thoughts ran through his mind, each needing to be analyzed and picked apart for validity and consequence. Unsure of his position and wise to the threat to his own safety, he snapped the flip phone apart and threw the pieces into the turbulent waters of the Arabian Sea.

Faisalabad, Pakistan

Hospital staff eventually took the heavily sedated Zubaydah to surgery to remove the multiple pieces of metal that had lodged in his body. Alex, the SAD team's medic, observed the proceedings in the operating room. One, to watch over the patient and ensure he didn't miraculously wake up and make a run for it, and two, to observe and later report to his superiors the proceedings in case he died on the table.

Wheeled out hours later, the ashen-faced terrorist looked closer to death's door than when he arrived. Alex was still by his side when Chris found the pair in recovery; Alex motioned his friend away from the bed. Chris wanted to know their captive's status.

"How's it looking?" he asked hopefully.

"He's still kicking, but the surgeon can't believe he's still alive. He's never seen someone with so much damage," Alex morosely reported.

"Jon will want to move him."

"Yeah, I know, but it ain't going to happen soon." Alex was talking quietly, trying to ensure that there weren't any eavesdroppers in the vicinity. "They need to make sure he doesn't get an infection before they release him to us."

"That's the reason we want to move him—so he doesn't die in this place from a rat bite. How did the surgery go . . . they didn't use soap again, did they?"

"No, I saw some pre-wrapped things in there, but I tell you what— I've seen prettier bulldogs chewing on wasps than some of that ugly stitching they did."

Chris smiled inwardly, thinking that maybe he and Alex had been spending too much time together for his friend to use one of his own favorite sayings. "I'll make a Brit out of you yet, Yank. Soon as we're done with this malarkey, you and I need have a beer or two in a proper English pub."

"Thought you weren't welcome back there?" Alex chided.

"I might have gotten around that . . . heads-up Jon's heading this way."

Alex filled the senior CIA officer in on the latest medical assessment. He held nothing back, stating the obvious lack of hygiene as being the chief threat to Zubaydah's well-being. He recommended moving him to more sanitary conditions sooner rather than later.

Jon then turned to Chris for his evaluation of security conditions at the hospital, and potential threats to their overall safety. Chris also painted a grim picture. There wasn't a window or door in the whole place that wasn't open to the world. There were dozens of entry points, most of which were difficult to secure. The ring of Pakistan Rangers outside the room that they were in provided some comfort, and the cordon outside the facility looked pretty at the main entrance—but the coverage was loose and sporadically manned in other areas. He also recommended moving their charge as soon as possible, as a determined force to rescue the terrorist would only face light resistance and ease of escape.

Jon kicked around the news for a few seconds and nodded his head. He already knew all this, he just wanted to hear it from men he could trust to tell it like it was. "I'm not going to take anymore risks guys, we can't afford to lose him now. Clearly the longer he stays here, the greater the chance of us losing him to health, rescue—or worse, the Pakistanis wanting to keep him. They lost three of their soldiers during the attack, and took some serious injuries. They're pretty pissed off as we all know . . . so I've asked the Director for support, and he was happy to set things up. We have a Gulfstream IV en route. I don't have an ETA, but there'll be a medical team on board. As soon as it's close, we'll get transported out of here. Your orders haven't changed. Stay with the prisoner until we have him out of the country. Questions?"

———⊶⊷———

Chris darted back down the steps of the G-IV aircraft and shook his head. Alex was readying Zubaydah's stretcher out of the back of the ambulance. "This will not be easy. There are ten steep steps up, and a tight turn at the top. Luckily, they've removed the safety rails. They took a bunch of seats out as well so we can set him on the deck as soon as we go in . . . but it's going to be a bitch."

Before Alex could respond, Jon made it to the back of the ambulance. He looked anxious. "What are you complaining about, Chris?"

"We should've had a better plan than this. Normally we extract guys who can walk on by themselves."

"This is what we have. Make it work."

"Getting up the steps is going to be problematic, that's all I'm saying."

"And I'm saying quit your whining and get on with it. We're going to lose our window of opportunity to get out of here if we sit any longer. The Pakistanis may change their mind about letting him go."

Chris insisted on caution no more, and grabbed ahold of one end of the medical litter. He pulled it out of the ambulance. Alex joined him and grabbed the other end. An FBI agent raced up to one side to help with the load, and Jon, who'd stowed his cell phone in time, grabbed the other.

Chris, in the lead and facing the stairs, got to the first step and balked. "Set him down, we need to talk this through."

"No! Let's not dick around!" Jon screamed. "Get up the goddamn stairs!"

Chris complied but inwardly fumed. *Don't fucking rush me asshole!* His right foot lifted to the first step, then he leaned forward and pulled with all his strength. He only hoped that the three behind him would push and pull their weight. *This is going to go tits up,* he thought, almost in a panic.

As he climbed the steps slowly, he could feel Alex pushing from behind, but the support from the sides was missing. Three-quarters of the way up the stairs, Chris's legs were getting wobbly under the strain. Jon, who had relinquished responsibility on his side of the stretcher, raced back to the side of the steps to offer support, hoping that the FBI agent on the other side would do likewise. Jon grabbed the underside of Zubaydah too quickly, making Chris lose balance. The FBI man was too far away to counter the movement, and Chris's left hand lost his grip under the shifting weight. Jon couldn't see what was happening on the opposite side and he pushed the stretcher upwards, causing it and the patient to slide over to one side. Chris couldn't hold on any longer. Zubaydah, still strapped in to the stretcher, fell face down onto the tarmac.

The commotion reached the medical team on board, who rushed to offer help. Alex, stunned, turned Zubaydah right side up with the aid of the FBI agent. Jon released a torrent of curses. Chris ran down the steps to help. Then an older gentleman pushed everyone aside.

"Get out of my way. I'm a doctor." A male nurse joined him with a medical bag and the pair administered aid to the patient.

Jon shot daggers at Chris for causing the carnage. The Brit wanted to defend himself, but thought better of it. *Don't look at me like that asshole. I told you we needed to talk this through.*

The doctor announced that besides an obvious broken nose, a wound had opened and he needed to get the ailing man on board to treat him. This time, the nurse led a discussion about who would hold what and who would release the load at the proper times.

With Zubaydah finally safely on board, the doctor announced he needed to get to work on the prisoner before the plane could leave. Jon almost burst a blood vessel on hearing the news. He pleaded with the doctor to let them take off, and only realized the seriousness of the terrorist's condition when he saw the nurse and Alex applying pressure to a deep gouge on his right thigh. He looked on with a sense of uselessness. He couldn't let his prized possession die.

"You all need to get off this plane," the doctor ordered. "And shut the door behind you." He pointed to Alex. "This man and the pilots can stay, but the rest of you, off, now!"

Jon, Chris, and the FBI agent followed the order and retreated down the steps to the ambulance, which had still not left. The agent, sensing the tension between the two CIA men, announced that he needed to relieve himself and disappeared.

Chris stuffed his hands into his jacket pockets. He checked his surroundings and looked for potential areas of threat, vulnerability, and safety. Jon strode off, talking loudly into his phone. Chris stood alone, not sure what to do next, but had confidence in feeling that he had done nothing wrong. He continued to scan the area, planning his what-if scenarios. Fifteen minutes later, Jon returned. Chris could tell that he hadn't been off meditating somewhere. He looked red, flustered, and angry.

"You're lucky I've bought us some time."

"Why should I be lucky?" Chris quizzed.

"This is your mess, you dropped him. We would have been out of here by now if it wasn't for you."

"Fuck you!" Chris blurted, then realized he'd overstepped. His temper had gotten the best of him; he immediately was disappointed in himself. He knew that it was the measure of a man if or how he could keep his mouth shut under pressure, or own up to his misgivings.

However, this time he didn't want to look weak or back down. In his mind, his opinion mattered, even if people didn't want to hear it. It was time to stand up for himself.

"Don't go pinning this on me." His tone was firm and confident. "I told you we needed to talk it through. We told you we needed a bigger plane for this very reason. Our team is better prepared for this kind of mission, but we pushed on with your piss-poor planning and shame on us for following your lead. All you do is parachute in with your grand schemes but you forget the details, all the fiddly little bits you don't think are important, when they are, and this is the shitshow we get."

"Who the hell do you think you're talking to?"

"Jon, I don't give a shit. Torque has been a mess. You knew that there would be casualties, yet there was no medical staff standing by to help this guy at TIGER, or anyone else who was injured. What if one of us got hurt, what then? Then that stupid bus ride fiasco, and don't get me started with that hospital, who the hell knows if we picked up some communicable disease while we were in there."

Jon was silent, but his eyes thumped in time with his speeding heartbeat. He didn't know if it was a smart idea to whack the man standing in front of him for being so insubordinate or just let things go . . . for now. Discipline could wait, but the upstart needed to hear a truth. He crept up as close as he could to Chris without jeopardizing his own safety; then he stared into his eyes. "If that man dies on that plane and takes with him information that could prevent the next 9/11, I will make sure people know that you are the one who contributed to his death."

———◦◦◦◦———

It took another forty-five minutes before the plane door opened again. Alex came down the steps and headed towards Jon. Chris made his way over to hear the news. "We're good to go. That doctor worked some miracles in there; he's probably the best I've ever seen.

"He should be, he's one of the top surgeons at Johns Hopkins, a friend of the Director," Jon stated. "Plane ready?"

"Yes, we've got clearance, ready to roll."

As if on cue, the FBI agent with his colleague appeared, bags in hand, ready for a flight.

The group headed to the base of the stairs; Alex climbed first with Jon close behind. The senior officer turned to Chris.

"Not you, the plane's full." Without waiting for a reply from Chris, he carried on into the aircraft. Alex heard the conversation, let Jon pass him inside the plane, and then stomped back outside to his friend. The remark confused him.

"What the hell did you do to piss him off?"

"I didn't call him a prick if that's what you're asking."

"Jesus Christ, Chris, when are you ever going to learn to keep your mouth shut around people like him?"

"Do you know where you're going?"

"Thailand."

"Shall I meet you there? Call you when I land?"

"Chris . . . you've obviously been kicked to the curb; call Gene to see if he can patch things up." He shook his head in disgust. "I got to go buddy, catch you on the next one."

"Be safe, Alex," Chris offered glibly and watched in rejection as the G-IV's door was closed in his face.

CHAPTER TWO

Islamabad, Pakistan

CHRIS MOREHOUSE SAT IN THE back of the bus licking his wounds. He would have preferred to have a "Do Not Disturb" sign pinned to his chest as he slouched down in his seat, trying to avoid all eye contact with the world around him. His anger at being shunned had waned, and his disappointment and self-loathing took over for a while, but his grit and determination to carry on, no matter the odds, outweighed his doubts. During the ride back to Islamabad on the same bus that took him to the raid, he thought about his actions. He wriggled through the superfluous word judo of "should have said this, should have said that" but it was all pointless. He knew he'd screwed up, and he knew that he had to bounce back. His main enemy at this point was simply his hatred of retreating from the battle with his tail between his legs . . . on a bus no less.

He'd lost count of the hours it took the transport to creep back to the embassy. Getting to the raid sites had gone at light-speed in comparison, but now navigating the narrow Pakistani roads during midday madness, it was a challenge to move forward even a few feet at a time. There were only a few other people on the bus with him, who by his estimations, were not carrying any concealed weapons, which would leave him to play sheriff if push came to shove. It wasn't a comforting feeling.

He was weary. His eyelids burned because they were constantly open, his throat was dry, and a headache hammered a steady beat at his temples, but he did not relent. He stayed painfully awake; remaining focused, alert and ready. He kept his mind sharp by playing out silent what-if scenarios and identifying the other passengers' strengths and weaknesses, their assets and liabilities laid before him. It wasn't a pretty picture. To distract himself he thought of his home in Washington State, his boat, and his girlfriend Sandy—but as soon as he did, his brain was jolted into devising yet another what-if scenario, as the bus became boxed in between other buses and vehicles. He tried to will his mind to stop contemplating all the angles, but he couldn't. His body, even in its exhausted state, was primed for action. He wanted to run down the aisle of the bus and rip the driver out of his seat; he wanted to get off the bus and march back to the embassy; he wanted to do something, anything. But he kept his impatience in check. He knew that all he could do in that moment was squirm in his seat and try to sweat it out.

The bus finally reached the manicured lawns of the embassy grounds, where it pulled into the circular drive and under the awning at the main entrance. When it stopped, Chris was apoplectic. He stood and was about to scream at the driver to move the bus away from the main entry when a Marine sprinted out of the embassy, pointed a shotgun at the operator and ordered him to keep driving. The Marine and Chris had the same thought: that buses or any other vehicle could carry explosive devices which could easily take down the front of the red-and-white-brick building. The driver, in his panic, missed a gear and started backing up, then shunted violently forward. Chris, tempted again to take over piloting the vehicle, held on to his ever-thinning composure. The Marine was still ordering the driver to move, and other passengers joined in the growing discord, but the bus finally gained some momentum and found its way to the compound's rear parking lot and to a safer spot to stop—one void of angry, shotgun-toting Marines.

Chris hurried down the aisle. He stopped to look at the driver, who was sweating buckets. Chris put a hand on his shoulder and smiled at the man, urging, "Breathe, take a deep breath, breathe . . . deeply. It's okay we are here, we are safe. Thank you, my friend." He tapped the man on the shoulder, then trotted off, swearing to himself, *Jesus Christ, that's the last bus ride I'm ever taking!*

Chris checked in and showed his ID to the Marine stationed at the embassy's fourth-floor conference room, known as the IGLOO. He'd been there on multiple occasions while in Pakistan, but today was different; it wasn't so quiet. The room, which was probably close to 500 square feet in area, at the moment resembled the chaotic floor of a stock exchange, or a racecourse with bookies running to and fro, with sheaves of papers, maps, cell phones, bottles of water and snack items. It was so cramped that there were some spaces where you couldn't even swing a dead cat without hitting half a dozen people. The room had been soundproofed, but it mattered not. As soon as the door opened the noise attacked the senses—even causing the Marine on guard to wish that he could wear earbuds. CIA analysts, NSA technicians, FBI profilers, even NYPD officers busied themselves in the chamber. There were cables strewn everywhere to keep the gathering's computers, phones, printers, and fax machines humming. Technicians strove to keep the chaos working—continually restringing power cords, replacing phones or updating computers.

Chris dove into the mosh pit and headed to the rear of the space, where he located the situation board. The loosely termed "board" was in fact three huge sections of whiteboards. One was framed red, one framed blue, and the last green. Chris started reading the board on the right, the red—or "action now"—board. There were several action items on a list that he scanned to see if SAD had any new immediate tasking that he could offer his services to. Operation Torque wasn't the only ongoing mission in Pakistan, but for SAD at this hour, there were no others. He moved over to the center blue "process" board, which was divided into two horizontal parts by a thick black line. The top half listed items being processed to move into the red action board; the lower half contained a list of items being processed down to the green board as completed actions and follow-up items. Again, though, Chris found nothing of interest for himself, he noted after a few minutes' observation that the red board was constantly being updated.

He looked up at the clocks above the boards, showing various international time zones. It had been over four hours since Zubaydah had left Pakistan airspace. An LED clock in the center showed the count-down timer for the next heads-of-department meeting. The timer showed forty-five minutes, meaning that an hour after that, someone would update the board. He moved on from the situation board and made his way to the mugs alley. There he found a large board affixed to a wall with numerous photos of suspects—some with red crosses marked on them, meaning deceased. Photos turned upside down meant those were in custody, and pictures without markings were those that were still being hunted. He took his time at the wall, memorizing the faces and names. He'd spent hours at this board before, and he was happy that there were more red-crossed photos than those without. But he knew that in an hour or two that could all change.

Chris found his way to the fridge, where he retrieved a large bottle of water. He mooched around a little longer, trying to find a space where he wouldn't be jostled out of the way or told to move to make room for others. He spotted a familiar face updating yet another status board—one that took over a complete wall; they called it the Web. Chris made his way over to say hello.

"Hey Rich, how's it going?" he offered.

Richard Meyer was the FBI's best terrorist profiler. He was tasked with creating a semblance of order out of the sometimes-overwhelming operational mayhem. Using large sheets of paper, he could map out entire terrorist networks from information gathered by people in the field. As the keeper of the Web, only Rich was allowed to update its complexities and link its data. He had two assistants who uploaded all his information electronically and then disseminated the completed work to the various agencies and departments that were engaged in counterterrorist operations. Everyone regarded Rich as a genius with a photographic memory, and the man was a machine. He never stopped working, only needing four or five hours sleep a night. He was staring at the board with a black pen in his hand about to write something on the Web when he heard the voice next to him; he glanced behind him.

"Hey Chris! I heard you want to be a bus driver when you grow up."

"Don't get me started." It disappointed Chris that Rich may have found out about his differing opinions with certain CIA officers; however, he kept a salty response to himself and played nice.

"The intel help you at all?"

"All intel helps Chris—good, bad or in between. It has to be looked at no matter what. The tough part is separating the wheat from the chaff. But to answer your question: it's still early, but yes, TIGER was up to snuff, and we have some promising leads."

"Zubaydah?"

Rich was still staring at the Web. "Nothing yet, as far as I know; he's not talking much. I heard they shot him up pretty bad."

"Yeah, it was touch and go there for a while."

"I'm surprised that you aren't holding his hand."

"Like I said, don't get me started." Chris wanted to change the subject. "Anything new you can share?"

Rich stopped looking at the board, then moved off to the side without saying a word. Chris followed close behind. The expert terrorist profiler stopped at the red action board, added an item to the existing list, and then plodded away to attack another task. Chris stared at the big, bold letters he'd left behind—**WHO IS MUKHTAR????**

Karachi, Pakistan

Mukhtar left the room still holding the long blade. His men wisely kept out of his way. Thick red blood ran down the knife as he placed it on a table in a makeshift kitchen. The fat man let the blood drip from his hands onto the floor, then ordered one of his men to get him the video of the execution he had just conducted. He stepped to a sink and ran water over his hands to wash away the mess, then removed his black headdress that doubled as a mask, hiding his face. With the camera hooked up to a TV, he watched the three-and-a-half-minute video in the dank light of the kitchen four times before finally nodding his approval. He smiled to his team; his enthusiasm was infectious.

"God is great my brothers, God is great."

The single comment became a chorus in an instant, with six men chanting the same as their leader. They knew they had dealt a glorious blow to their common enemy and were equally thirsty for more. Mukhtar calmed the group by raising his hands.

"We must cleanse ourselves from this infidel. There is no time to waste. Come, let us finish, you all know what we must do." His men scurried away and then he turned to the camera operator. He ejected the memory card from the camera and placed it in the young man's hand. "Wahid, go now and take someone with you. I want you to wait until midnight to send this out, but make copies. You understand that this cannot fall into the wrong hands, my friend. Do not disappoint me, do not let me down; your life is in your own hands." Wahid shuddered a little at the veiled threat. His eyes grew in fear and anticipation. He nodded, then took the cartridge as if it were the keys to the Islamic caliphate and left to carry out his leader's command.

One of Mukhtar's soldiers came into the kitchen and dumped other blood-soaked butcher knives into the sink. As the man proceeded with the business of cleaning the tools, Mukhtar looked on and reflected on his performance. Butchery was second nature to him, but performing before a camera was not. As a vaunted leader within al-Qaeda circles, and a confidant of the great sheik, he commanded respect and fear from his peers and subordinates alike. He could have easily ordered one of his men to carry out the killing, but he wanted to prove to his men, his followers, and his organization, that he was not just a planner, a manager, or a leader. He wanted to show that he too could get his hands dirty to further the cause; that he too could continue the fight with his men; that he too could take a life when it was necessary. However, the slaughter of the man in the next room was not one born out of bloodlust; it was designed to send a message. A message of fear.

Mulling over his actions, he watched his men doing his bidding. A pang of regret entered his mind for a brief second; not for the killing, but for conducting his own non-sanctioned operation without informing Osama bin Laden.

US Embassy, Islamabad, Pakistan

Chris milled around the conference room until he thought he was truly just getting in the way. He had hoped that someone would give him a task, a new mission, something to get his mind active again. After an hour he was getting bored. He wandered out of the IGLOO and down the corridor to the communications center—ICE CAVE. They denied him access, which he expected, but he hung around the hallway, hoping that he'd bump into someone who knew if something was brewing. It didn't take long for one of the senior SAD team members to appear.

"Hey Ben," he called out as the man approached.

"Chris, I was just coming to find you."

"What's up? Anything new cooking?"

"Negative, we're standing down for a while. Seems that everyone wants to process all the intelligence we've been getting before we get back out there."

"IGLOO is jumping off the wall," Chris mentioned off-handedly. "They got a ton of stuff to go through by the sound of things."

"Yeah, everyone's taking stock for the moment. I'm heading back to the safe house. You may as well come with me. There's nothing for us right now. Want to walk?"

Chris couldn't tell if that was a suggestion or an order. He contemplated the statement for a second. He still didn't know if he was on someone else's shit list besides Jon. A request to head back to the safe house with someone wasn't unusual. The SAD rented a house just a few miles from the embassy grounds. While most of the Americans, be they CIA, FBI, NSA or whoever, stayed in hotels like the Marriott, Hyatt, or Ramada, the SAD team chose to get away from centers of attraction, aiming to reduce their risk profile. However, they were under strict orders not to travel alone between the embassy and the house. If Ben wanted to yomp, then Chris had little choice but to agree; otherwise, it could be a long wait for transportation back to the abode. "Sure, I could do with a stretch of the legs, get a hot shower, inspect the insides of my eyelids, get some decent food."

"I hear ya. I haven't been out of this building for three days. I've been crashing on a cot in the corridor on the fifth floor."

Chris sympathized. The embassy had turned into a hotel, being overrun in the last month with temporary employees from a myriad of three-letter agencies. There were people sleeping under desks and in closets; they even installed a bed in the ambassador's office.

The duo left the embassy chancery after checking out with Marine Post 1, the main entry to the embassy. On exiting the building, Chris noticed that, likely after the debacle with his bus, a temporary barrier was now present, preventing traffic from getting too close to the building. Why it wasn't there before mystified him. Relieved, Chris shared the story with Ben, and both chuckled at the inanity of it, but as soon as they got outside the gate, their demeanor changed. They were all business.

Both men instinctively switched on their sweeping radars, scanning the surrounding area to spot surveillance or threats to their safety. With no prompt, Chris took responsibility for their right, and Ben the left. Mostly they marched in silence. A few inquisitive glances their way caused whispered exchanges between the pair, but each perceived no threat, and continued on. They hustled with a purpose, but didn't rush to cause more attention. Although the streets of the Diplomatic Enclave were quiet compared to downtown Islamabad, the lack of movement didn't allow the team members to relax completely. Everything was a target; every movement or non-movement was a threat; every car, bike or bus was an opportunity. It was tiring work to remain in a constant state of readiness, reacting to a split-second movement or shadow, or trying to sense a feeling from a stare, but it was necessary. It kept them alive.

Once they reached the Embassy of the Philippines, Chris dropped back a few steps and Ben strode on a step quicker. They passed a small, brushy hillside that could have easily cloaked a hundred men waiting to ambush them. It was along an open stretch of road with a few two-story apartments off to their left, but to their right, it was only green and the red-brownish dirt of camouflage. It was a good killing ground. Nothing stirred, except for the sweat running down Chris's back and forehead. It wasn't just due to the heat of the day and the nervousness of the environment, but his memories of patrols in Northern Ireland kept him vigilant, and perspiring. He'd seen death from ambushes, experienced the smell, the sights, the sounds of violent death, the aftermath of decaying bodies. He didn't want those senses repeated.

Without incident, they crossed the main road into a small hamlet that boasted a few decent homes. As the streets once again became constricted, the pair closed up, covering each other's arcs of responsibility. When they approached the street for the safe house, Ben spotted the truck first. "Dump truck straight ahead," he remarked almost casually.

There were three men sitting on the tailgate, looking directly at the two foreigners advancing towards them; none of the men were talking to each other. There was a big pile of dirt on the road behind the truck, with two shovels sticking out of the mound. It was Ben's first indication that something was up.

"There's no hole in the ground," Chris offered.

"They ain't loading it up either," noted Ben. "Call the house, let them know we may have guests, two minutes out."

Chris complied with the order, all the while scanning and searching for correlating actions to the potential threat before them. As soon as he hung up the phone, the three men got off the tailgate and two of them began shoveling dirt into the back of the truck. "Done with the smoke break I guess," he observed.

"Nobody flicking dead butts . . . no smokes," Ben added. "They're not dirty either, look how clean those clothes are."

Ben switched his passive sonar to active. His job was now to focus on the three men in front of them while Chris scanned the area for new threats, connecting movements, or sounds. Both men were in hyper-vigilant mode, waiting for an action that would prompt them to draw their concealed weapons and engage the enemy. As they drew parallel with the truck, nothing happened, but Chris noted a motorcycle parked nearby with the engine running. "Bike is running, not good," he whispered.

"Roger."

Chris wanted to call the house again. He hoped that there were enough of his team members with heavier weapons ready to assist if things went south. But he refrained from using the phone, needing his hands ready to draw, aim, and shoot.

The two men with shovels didn't make eye contact with the foreigners. But the third, possibly the supervisor, gave Chris a long stare, then turned away and headed to the cab of the truck. "Here we go, got a skinny heading to the cab."

"Need to see some metal in that guy's hands, Chris."

Chris maintained his composure; he'd been in this situation before . . . and not acted. He wanted Ben to know he was ready. "This sucks chunks. If it's going to go sideways, you get the cab guy; I take the other two."

"Roger that."

Chris had still not placed his hand on his weapon, but he was visualizing every movement he needed to make. He was waking up his muscle memory, telling his body to be ready to move into action.

The SAD duo glided past the truck without incident. Ben continued his forward observations, but Chris moved his surveillance from passive to active by turning around and walking backwards, observing the action back at the truck as he strode with Ben. He was now acting as rearguard, and he didn't care if the three men saw him do it. In fact, he wanted them to know that he had seen them, that he was not a soft target and that the element of surprise they thought they enjoyed had evaporated into thin air. Ideally, the SAD men would have carried on walking up the street as not to give away the location of a CIA safe house. However, nobody knew what traps lay further up the road. Their best course of action would be to get into the house and evacuate with the support of the rest of their team.

Ben reached the drab, olive-green safe house first, where the door opened from the inside as he approached. It was a small two-story home with a backyard leading to a trail that gave the SAD team an exit strategy. At the rear, two Toyota Land Cruisers were sitting in wait. Ben entered the house, followed closely by Chris.

"Everyone grab your shit, we're leaving!" he shouted to his team within. "We have three possible targets outside, stinks like shit. Let's get moving!"

Chris hurried towards the kitchen to pull out a kit bag of supplies from under the sink, but a strap caught on a pipe, causing him to kneel to inspect further. As he looked underneath, he heard someone in the house shout at the top of his voice.

"GRENADE!"

Chris almost looked up, but held on to his better judgment. He left the bag and made a dash for the corridor that led to the back of the house. As he scrambled for sufficient cover, he heard an explosion and the breaking of glass. Expecting another grenade, he held on for a few seconds before drawing his weapon. When nothing came, he got up and ran back to the front of the house. His ears were ringing, but he was otherwise uninjured.

He pointed his weapon at the now-missing front door, then cautiously stepped forward to the opening, expecting another grenade or other attack—but none came. Strewn with debris from the explosion, Ben was lying face down near the entryway, but conscious and trying to extricate himself from the mess. Propped up against a wall, another SAD officer was removing large wooden splinters from his bloody forearm.

Chris holstered his weapon and kneeled down to help Ben. As he did, one of the men they'd spotted at the dump truck ran into the house. He stopped dead in his tracks when he made eye contact with the men inside. He then spread his arms open wide. Chris spotted the wire leading to his right hand first; he saw the explosives vest second.

There was no time for Chris to draw and shoot the man; there were milliseconds left before the terrorist blew them all over the house and neighborhood. He stared directly in to the assailant's eyes. They exchanged no words. Precious life-giving seconds were passing by. Chris could tell the man was scared. He wanted to reach up slowly and diffuse the situation, but it was too late. The man pushed the plunger for the detonation. It never came. He looked at his hand in surprise; he pushed again, with the same result. He pushed and pushed, then inspected the cables attached to the explosives on his chest. The device did not explode.

He stared back at Chris in disbelief, then turned and sprinted out of the house.

Chris Morehouse had stared death in the eyes once more. His body quivered. This was the closest one yet, and by the law of averages, he should have been dead a long time ago. He assumed that someone was once again looking over him, even though he didn't believe in angels. "Holy Shit!" he spat as he drew his weapon. "You going to be all right Ben?"

"What the fuck just happened?"

"Suicide bomber . . . got to go!"

"Chris what the fuck are you doing?" Ben called, but it was too late. He watched as Chris ran out the broken door, weapon in hand, looking for the man who had come so close to ending their lives.

Chris sprinted into the blinding sun. He ran for cover and hid behind a low wall to see what was transpiring down the street. He put his left hand up to shield his eyes, and spotted the bomber jogging down the road, paying attention only to the vest around his chest. In the far distance, Chris spotted the motorcycle with a driver raring to go, while his partner stood nearby holding onto a camera, ready to film the destruction and carnage they'd hoped to witness. They did not expect to see their comrade retreat out of the house and running towards them, panicking to get the explosives off of himself.

Chris maintained his distance and watched for a few seconds more. He chided himself for being outside the safety of the house. The SAD team had preplanned actions for this exact scenario. He should have remained inside to help evacuate the team; by this point they'd likely already all be on the road to the safety of the embassy. But he wanted to secure the area, to make sure there wasn't an additional threat; he was uninjured and capable of mitigating fresh problems. In the few seconds before he moved into action, he'd rationalized that he needed to rebound from the mess at the airport with Zubaydah; he had to get a win for his team, for himself. He wanted redemption.

Their only escape plan was for the grenade guys, he surmised, *so the bike makes sense. The bomber wasn't meant to survive.* His mind quickly juggled his options. None of which were sound or clever. *Go after the bomber . . . stupid. Go after the bike . . . won't catch them. Can't shoot the bomber, he's too far away.*

To make matters worse, a small crowd was now gathering on the street, having heard the noise from the grenade attack. Chris ran over more factors. *Shit, there are innocents in his path. Get close enough for a head shot? His two buddies don't have weapons!* He broke cover and ran down the road towards the trio of terrorists. He was still trying to figure out what to do when the problem threw out another variable.

The motorcycle sped away without the cameraman. The bomber now stood in the middle of a four-way intersection, and the cameraman ran off to Chris's right and away from the bomber. Chris stopped in his tracks and aimed his pistol at the bomber, but he was still too far away for an accurate shot. He didn't want to get too much closer. *How much explosive is that? Am I safe standing here?* The bomber, who was still trying to defuse the device on his body, spun around, searching for his own escape. He spotted Chris with his weapon pointed at him. He furiously clawed at the wires, detonators and explosives, but he wasn't getting anywhere with his efforts. He moved to the left to get away from the approaching Westerner.

Chris lowered his weapon as he watched the bomber move further away from him. *That thing will go off any second. I don't need to be here when it does.* He looked to his right and caught sight of the camera-carrying terrorist sprinting up the street, he dropped his camera as he ran. The Brit didn't need any further prompting. He holstered his weapon and ran after the man, but he had some catching up to do.

Chris lost sight of his target but kept up a steady run, hoping that he was on the right track. The road ended, then transitioned to a creek with a weak stream running through. He saw his quarry running up a dusty hill on the other side. Just then his map memory kicked in. *Shit, he's going for the Muslim Colony.* He briefly considered giving up the chase; he knew he shouldn't go into bandit country. But his adrenalin was up, he was enjoying the pursuit, and he wanted to catch one of the bastards that almost killed him and his team. He continued on, splashing through a few pools of fetid water, all the while trying to keep his eye on his prey. The terrorist reached the edge of the colony, but Chris wasn't far behind. He heard a loud explosion behind him in the distance, which interrupted his attention. He turned around in time to see a large black cloud form above the village from where he came. *There's no point in turning back now*, he thought.

For all his perceived advantages, Chris's confidence stalled as he entered the rabbit warren of streets and alleys. If it wasn't for the yelling and disruption of everyday life in the enclave, he would have become disorientated, but the disturbances gave him all the compass points he needed. He imagined the terrorist panicking, like a deer surrounded by a pack of wolves, trying to evade his hunter by pushing and shoving his way through or past people out and about in the colony. Chris sprinted faster, fearing that the man was heading to safety, to his home, to his compatriots. He knew he shouldn't have been there, without support, without a plan, but he pushed on.

Just then his phone rang. "Chris, where the hell are you?" Ben screamed.

"Muslim Colony. I'm after one of the bombers. I see the prick. I'm in the south end."

"Abort, abort! Get back here now!"

The terrorist took a hard fall as he tried to jump over a street vendor's wares at a small market. Chris was almost within arm's reach; he didn't need the distraction of a phone—and an order to quit. He ended the call and stuffed the phone back in his jacket pocket. As he did, he too fell. But the man was up and running again. In a last-ditch attempt to catch him, Chris lunged forward and ankle-tapped the terrorist, causing the man to fall again and face-plant into the cobbled street. The SAD man recovered quickly. He jumped up and dropped a knee onto the man's back, knocking him breathless and into submission. Chris held him down with his own weight, giving him no option to wriggle his way out of the situation. He patted the man down quickly, expertly searching for weapons—and hoping not to find another suicide vest. On happily finding nothing, he wrangled the terrorist's left hand into a lock behind his back, but the man wasn't so submissive with his right; he didn't want to play nice, and flailed. Chris used his right-hand index finger, jabbing it behind the man's right ear, where he pushed hard. Putting pressure on the point worked its magic, taking away the fight long enough for Chris to wrench the man's right hand from the ground to his back.

Chris had caught his man, but he still had to get him out of the enclave and handed over to the authorities. He looked around quickly for a way to restrain the terrorist—a rope or wire, or something to make his task easier—but there was nothing except for the grumbling voices and beady eyes of the locals, who didn't like what they saw. Chris changed his position by pivoting his right knee from the man's back to the ground next to the man's head. He still held onto the man's hands, but knew that he had seconds before the terrorist would recover and attempt an escape. He released the man's left arm, then changed his grip on the right wrist to force the terrorist to get off the ground. "UP! UP! UP!" Chris ordered.

The pressure on the captive's right arm, now stuck in a lock, forced him to comply. When Chris got him to his tiptoes, he spun around and placed the man's arm into a gooseneck wrist lock. The detainee attempted to scream, but Chris preempted an outburst by applying more pressure, and marched off as quickly as he could with his prisoner.

Chris held the terrorist tightly to his body. The man danced and squirmed like an eel trying to escape a fishing line. But the more he struggled, the more pressure his captor exerted. Realizing there was no escape, the man called out for help. His pleas fell on deaf ears at first, but as his calls became more vocal, other people took notice. Before there were curious beady eyes and grumbles, but now interest was more concentrated, loud, and spreading. Chris couldn't understand any of the local dialect of what was being shouted, elevating his level of concern. Until this point, he'd been in charge, confident he could get the man out of the colony, but now with the gathering crowd and raised voices he worried that things were not going his way. He looked sternly at the men around him and bravely pushed his way forward. He'd seen the look before, men on edge that if provoked were ready to take action.

He'd first seen that look on the Falls Road in Belfast when arresting IRA suspects while on patrol with the Royal Green Jackets. First there was silence, staring eyes, and a disbelief that something profound was happening. Second was the vocal dissention from the unwilling participants or silence from more serious actors, who were each telepathically saying "Someone needs to do something." Third was a light push, shove or quick movement from someone in the crowd to instigate another act. Fourth was violence.

As words spewed loudly out of the terrorist's mouth, more attention was being created. A large man with arms folded across his chest barred Chris's way. He was a formidable character, with a small supporting cast standing close behind him. Chris didn't hesitate, kicking him in the balls and pushing past him and through the crowd, using the terrorist as a ram to clear a path. The shouts got louder. Chris caught the sight of a waving club and a few whip-like sticks. He picked up the pace, making the terrorist dance even more.

The first blow caught Chris on his right shoulder; excruciating pain numbed his entire arm. If he'd wanted to draw his weapon in that moment, he wouldn't have been able to. A hand grabbed at his collar, which fortunately did not take purchase, but a glancing blow to his head caused him to duck and loosen his grip on his prisoner. He kept in charge of the man, but the blows to his head and back were becoming incessant. It forced his head and eyesight down, putting him at a significant disadvantage; he felt like he was in a standing scrum, a rugby maul. He knew he had to push forward because if he fell, the mob would be upon him.

Tripped from behind, Chris didn't fall to the ground but fell forward enough that he sufficiently released his grip on his prisoner so grabbing hands could rescue the native. Staggering, Chris fell to his knees after a few steps. As he did, the riot pounced on him, kicking him and using the whip-sticks on his back. He dropped to the ground and curled up in a ball, accepting each fist, foot, or object being foisted on him. He closed his eyes tightly and tried to ignore the pain, forcing himself not to move or open up another vulnerable area of his body for attack. He despaired when he tasted blood in his mouth; he shut his eyes and willed the melee to stop.

To his surprise, the lashing abruptly ceased. The beating had played tricks with his senses, as differing blows sent differing messages to his brain. He could sense some things like blood, but his hearing had shut down. Thus, he didn't hear the car horn or the shouting of English-speaking voices; but he sensed the crowds parting and the violence stopping, then felt firm hands grabbing one of his arms.

"Chris, Chris, get the fuck up!"

Chris opened his eyes to see Ben crouched over him. He couldn't believe it for a second, and didn't move. Ben repeated the order. "Chris, get up, we've got to go. Get up!"

"Ben?"

"Chris, we ain't welcome here. Let's go!"

Chris moved groggily to his knees; his head was spinning. Ben raised him up and wrapped a supportive arm around his back. They staggered together towards one of the team's Land Cruisers. Three other members of the SAD team, with weapons drawn, were keeping the crowd back from the vehicle—and Ben and Chris. A stone hit the roof of the vehicle; a second hit the rear window, smashing it. More projectiles rained down as the SAD contingent were loaded up, but without a shot being fired the team hastily scampered out of the colony.

Lyari Town, Karachi, Pakistan

The two undercover officers first heard the argument at the Alishan Bakery and General Store. The two men, acting on a tip, scoured the most densely populated and dangerous areas of Karachi in search of a purported member of al-Qaeda. Their information was flimsy, but the senior of the two, always known for taking chances on vague, loose or sometimes casual leads, threw caution to the wind and dipped his hook into an infested sea. Not knowing where the tip would take them, they paused at the bakery to drink tea, and watch and wait to see if something would transpire. A shouted name, Wahid, piqued their interest immediately.

When they tuned their senses toward the cause of the raised voice, they both spotted an altercation in the throng of people that plied the street outside. It was an older man, holding a young man by the scruff of his neck as he tried clumsily to mount a bicycle. Jawad Halabi looked over at his junior comrade and moved casually toward the dispute. When he did, he surreptitiously brushed his right ear signaling for the activation of the recording device. Karim Basrawi complied by reaching into his right pocket to flick a switch.

The heated conversation on the street was hard to comprehend. Jawad, a senior intelligence officer with the Saudi General Intelligence Directorate (GID), understood the basics of the local Kutchi dialect, but the two men before him were drifting in and out of two languages; the first Kutchi, and the second, Balochi, a northwestern Iranian language. For his immediate purpose, the mix did not bode well. He strained his ears as he sauntered by, trying to decipher a smidgen, but he could not discern the words he heard as any common phrases he could translate. He only hoped that the listening device Karim carried could pick up enough of a clear recording for later translation. As Jawad passed by the arguing pair, he depressed the switch on his hidden camera, trying his best to get a facial composite from both parties. He was unsure if this was the Wahid they were looking for—a young man supposedly with some technical know-how, who bragged of posting something on behalf of al-Qaeda to a media outlet.

The shouting match continued between the two antagonists, with the older dragging the younger off his bike and striking him about the face a few times with an open hand. A second, young man joined in the fracas and attempted to pull Wahid's bike back towards the bakery. The clamor drew some attention from others in the street, and a large, muscular man interceded. Jawad was still at a loss with the words spoken or shouted. But he, like many others around, stood and watched the fight. The powerful man separated the three fighters, but the older man took offense to the interloper and lashed out at him, a silly move.

The strong man punched the older man to the ground. At the behest of the strong man, another two men pushed through the crowd and also set about the hapless figure and the young man in possession of the bike. Wahid eventually regained his composure and his bike, but instead of wheeling away, he watched as the three men continued to dish out a beating on the older man. The muscular man was the first to relent. It was as if by order. The other two also ceased.

Before Wahid stole away, he looked down at the battered and bleeding figure on the ground, and shouted words that this time Jawad could comprehend.

"Mukhtar will find you. He will kill you."

Landstuhl Regional Medical Center, Germany

The doctor stood at the foot of the bed with a clipboard and chart of Chris's condition. Gene Brooks, Chris's friend, mentor, and boss, sat in a high-back chair in a corner of the private room. With the morning's pleasantries completed, the doctor read out the list of ailments.

"Multiple contusions about the head, neck, back, arms and legs. The one on your right shoulder will take the longest to heal; the others should heal relatively quickly, seeing that you are quite a fit man. There's not much we can do to treat the bruises, and rest is the best medicine. The swelling should go down soon." The doctor paused for a second, not looking up from his notes, then continued. "You have one broken rib and a hairline fracture on your left elbow. Your liver and spleen are fine; however, I'm sure you've wondered why you have blood in your stool—that is from a blow to your kidneys."

"I've had issues with that in the past, Doc," Chris quipped. "Gene helped me through that one. He held my hand the whole time."

The doctor looked up from the chart and raised an eyebrow—first at Chris, then Gene, who was shaking his head. It wasn't his place to judge, and he carried on with the summary. "That's something we need to monitor. You were dehydrated, but that's only half the problem. There may be some underlying issues, so you may need to consult with your local doctor when you get back to . . . wherever. Anyway, you have quite a few scratches; the ones on your palms and knees will heal up in time. The swelling on your face will go down too. But your inner right elbow, is that an old injury?"

"Yes."

"We saw some metal fragments; care to elaborate?"

"No," Gene answered.

The doctor paused and looked at Gene, then back to his patient. He knew that there was some secrecy involved with these men, though it wasn't his place to ask.

"We patched it up in the field a long time ago, Doc," Chris explained. "I never got around to getting it done properly."

"Fair enough, we will take care of that. You also had a concussion, hence the reason why you are here. Any lasting symptoms? Confusion, memory loss, nausea, vomiting, tiredness?"

"No, I remember puking up in the back of a Toyota, but since then, been okay."

The doctor, satisfied with his patient's condition, tucked the chart and clipboard under an arm. "Good. I'm guessing you are in a lot of pain in a lot of places. I want to keep you here for a few days so you can get some rest, and to take care of that elbow, amongst other things."

"Make it three doctor," Gene ordered.

"Very well, three it is. We can run more tests, check on your blood levels, and take another MRI. I have a course of painkillers for you to get you over your initial pain, but let's see if we can manage that down over the next few days."

"Don't I get a say in this?" Chris complained. "I'm not lying here for three days!"

"Shut up, Chris," Gene interjected. "Thank you, doctor. Is there anything else?" Gene smiled, stood, and reached out his hand to the physician. The doctor shook Gene's hand and saw himself out of the room, closing the door behind him without adding anything to the summation.

Chris was pissed off. "What the hell Gene? I don't need to be here for three days, I'm fine!"

Gene plopped himself back down in his chair. "Chris, I'll decide what you need. When I say you need a rest, you need a rest. You want to do it here, or do you want to go back to your girlfriend and lie to her about why you look like death warmed over? What the hell were you thinking?"

Chris said nothing for a moment. Instead he played with the IV tube taped to his wrist. "This is horseshit," he finally said.

"Which you created!"

A gulf of silence separated the two. Gene got out of his chair and shuffled it around so he could face Chris. He stared intently at his charge. "Do you know how many people died in Pakistan by that suicide bomber?" Chris did not. Nobody had spoken to him directly after he was picked up by Ben. He'd been rushed to the embassy and treated by a Marine corpsman, but he was unaware of the situation he had left behind. Out of an abundance of caution, the Marine deemed that Chris's injuries were damaging enough that it had warranted a medivac to a military hospital in Germany.

Chris stared at Gene, waiting for the news. "Sixteen, Chris, sixteen," Gene reported somberly. Don't ask me how many others will die because of their injuries, but there were dozens of people hurt. Women, kids. The carnage was horrific."

Perplexed, Chris wasn't sure what Gene was trying to say. "Are you trying to blame me Gene?"

"Don't be an idiot. On paper, it doesn't look good. Right now, the headline reads: CIA officer sees suicide bomber, runs the other way, causing terrorist to blow himself up in a marketplace."

"Fucking hang on a minute," Chris protested. "They attacked *us*. They came knocking on our door with a hand grenade. We're lucky the bomber's vest didn't go off when it was supposed to. You and I wouldn't be talking right now if it did."

"But you didn't need to go chasing him, Chris. It's probably because of you that the guy panicked and ran off." Gene was incensed, his words direct and stern. "We'll never know if the bomb went off by itself or if he tried to dismantle it and failed. BUT HE PANICKED BECAUSE OF YOU!"

"So, I was supposed to do nothing?"

Gene stood quickly and pushed his chair back in frustration. "You were supposed to evacuate, just as Ben ordered you to."

"What if the asshole came running back into the safe house? What if the other two idiots came in, guns blaring? Someone had to go out there and secure the retreat."

Gene knew Chris was right, at least in part; it was the right thing to do, but Chris could have secured the situation without running through the streets of the Muslim Colony. He could have been watching from a position of cover; he could have communicated his actions with his team. He did not. "This is not a war game, you're not in the infantry anymore. What you did was reckless." Gene stood over the bed, hands on his hips. He shook his head slightly. "You put your team at risk by them having to come and get you. Ben has some glass splinters in his eyes, for Christ's sake. If it wasn't for that Marine corpsman, he could have easily lost his sight. You fucked up, Chris."

Chris, from his bed, stood his ground. "My job is to chase terrorists. Are you telling me I can't do that anymore?"

Gene was losing what little composure he had left. He leaned forward, spraying spittle, which almost hit Chris in the face. "YOU'RE SUPPOSED TO BE PART OF A TEAM, GODDAMMIT!"

Chris had to admit that Gene was correct on that one. Gene continued to berate the younger man. His tone and pitch was higher than it should have been; he didn't know who might be lurking outside the door, listening in. He should have dialed things back, but he continued. "I protected you last year when you absconded on your wild adventure to Karachi. You still don't know the shitstorm that created. The end result was laudable, but as usual with you, it wasn't sanctioned, supported or approved. I still don't understand what you were trying to prove, but you were lucky you had people from both MI6 and Saudi intelligence on your side, or you'd have been history."

Chris had nothing to say. He didn't have the chance, anyway, as Gene continued his rant. "You fucked up royally with Jon in Pakistan. It's lucky that Zubaydah is alive and talking. If he had died on the way to . . . well let's just say he got where he was supposed to go, but face-planting him into the tarmac was not a good move. Then to top it off, you go and piss off one of the shining stars in Operations. Jon has the Director's ear, but we're lucky that your news hasn't gotten up that far. He wants you gone because of Faisalabad, and after the mess you created in Islamabad, there are some people back home who are pretty pissed off and wondering about your future longevity with us."

"Like who, Gene?"

"None of your business. I don't want any attitude Chris. You should be listening and not talking. I don't want any of your snarky or witty comments." He let things settle in, then notched back the attack slightly. "You need to be quiet, OK? And that's why you're taking some R & R in that bed. You've put me in a bind. I need all the players I can get right now. After the success of Torque, we've been getting more requests for help, and with people injured who need not be . . . it makes my ass itch even more. I haven't figured out where I'm sending you next, but you're on a knife's edge, Chris. You need to put up and shut up, or you're on the way home—permanently."

"How did they know?"

"Know what? And who?"

"How did al-Qaeda find us at the safe house? We're the best at surveillance, Gene. We should have spotted them days or even weeks before. You know the score: target acquisition, operational planning, finance, and logistics. All that basic stuff for a terrorist attack. It doesn't happen overnight. None of us spotted surveillance; we would've shut it down before it got to the attack stage. Someone tipped them off that we were on the way; they were waiting for us."

Gene hadn't progressed that far in the attack's investigation. His focus was only on the public relations aspect of the chaos. He remained silent, ruminating. But his subordinate broke his train of thought.

"You might think Torque was a success Gene, but it could have easily gone sideways." He didn't give his boss time to interrupt; instead he explained the debacle with the bus ride to site TIGER.

Gene sighed. He could tell that Chris was trying to justify his actions, and control the direction of the conversation. He had to close him down before he bounced off on another tangent. "I hear you Chris, I do. There's still a lot to discuss with everyone involved. There are debriefings taking place right now . . ."

"I should be there!" Chris blurted.

"Shut up, Chris. Don't try to deflect your performance by bringing up something new. I heard that there were some logistical challenges, and believe me there will be a lessons learned sermon coming out of it."

"And al-Qaeda? They found us because . . .?"

"Chris . . . give me a break. Will you just shut up for once!"

"You need me back there. Give Alex a call, get him to put a team together, and we'll go hunting. Fuck the Pakistanis; they're the problem. Let slip the dogs of war and all that shit. Get us back in the game; let's find these goatfuckers!"

Gene dove into Chris's personal space and pointed a hard finger at his chest. Chris sucked in a chunk of air, surprised by his superior's quick movement.

"DON'T YOU UNDERSTAND?!" Gene bellowed. "There *is no* team. Nobody wants to work with you. People think you are a fucking liability, Chris!"

Chris at last shut down; the last words stung. He avoided Gene's menacing gaze; already beaten up physically, his mental strength now faced an attack. He felt a measure of vulnerability that he wasn't used to. His face turned as solemn as a gravedigger, his heart sank, and he tasted bile as he swallowed.

Holy shit, a liability, what . . . what? Are you shitting me, what the . . .? His mind danced with a mix of emotions; the shock hit him first. His unbelieving eyes blinked a dozen times as he looked at Gene's face. His lip quivered; his breathing became sharp single intakes of stifled air. Anger came next. He gritted his teeth, willing his hands to stop balling into fists, ordering his legs to stop being so restless. But then the embarrassment hit him like a cold chisel on a stone. He felt humiliated and worthless. He fought back a tear; his stomach turned cartwheels. He turned away from Gene in rejection.

CHAPTER THREE

Junejo Park, Karachi, Pakistan

JAWAD HALABI EXITED THE CAR and proceeded to the center of the green teardrop-shaped park. He surveyed the area cautiously as he watched Karim drive away, looking for signs of surveillance, or sudden untoward movements that would spell impending danger. He strode from there at a confident, unrushed pace. After navigating a few tight alleys, he found his way to a wide, dusty-brown expanse known to the locals as "the playground." There, as he expected, he saw groups of young boys playing cricket and arguing rules as if they were playing for their country at Lord's, against archrival England. To the south end of the grounds he saw a lone figure sitting on a set of concrete stairs that led to nowhere, a makeshift set of bleachers to watch the games that were underway.

Jawad sat next to the man, who seemed engrossed in each play. "Are you able to follow the game?"

"We are Saudi, Jawad," his handler, Hamid Deeb, replied without looking up at his visitor. "How are we expected to know of any sport, other than football?"

"Hamid, my friend, it would pay to have an understanding don't you think? One has to have the ability to blend in, adapt to the culture, understand what motivates a country."

"Quite so. There is wisdom in that. However, have you tried to understand this?" He gestured with his hands. "This soap opera is something only those playing can understand. It's unfathomable for the likes of us, Jawad."

"Opera you say? You must have some respect for the game."

"We are Saudi, Jawad; we don't understand opera." Hamid shook his head as one of the cricket players disagreed with a decision made by the opposing team, creating chaos in the dust. He quietly added, "May my next assignment be in a less-complicated, and more civilized country."

Neither Saudi had anything more to say for the moment. They watched in silence; however, each were looking beyond the boys in the brown dirt of the playground. Jawad wanted to get down to the reason he was there. "The tapes, Hamid. I hope they were of use."

"It was difficult to capture all the faces, Jawad, at least those of importance. The audio was acceptable, and we have translations. I can get you copies of the transcripts."

"They are of no use to me here. Tell me."

"One of the two men who were arguing is the one you know as Wahid; the second was his uncle. We don't have his name, but that is not important."

Jawad wanted to know more. "What were they arguing about?"

"The conversation was already underway when you started your recording. It is difficult to surmise the exact pretext, but the uncle was urging Wahid to not leave. He was trying to get him to go back to university, to stay away from 'bad men.' He had high hopes for him."

Jawad nodded while picturing the altercation he had witnessed. He had come to a similar conclusion. He let Hamid continue with the summary.

"There was something about an inheritance, and that the money was being wasted on men who were not his friends. The money was being put to no good use. There were some things at that point which were inaudible, then more discussions about him being sent away before he became penniless. Wahid countered with his religious beliefs and his want for joining a worthwhile cause. He wanted to go to Afghanistan. I'm paraphrasing, Jawad. You must listen for yourself if you want all the details."

"Go on. There was something about Mukhtar."

"Yes, Wahid stated that he would bring on him the wrath of Mukhtar; he would have his uncle killed if he tried to stop him."

"And that is when those men assaulted the uncle."

"That was all that you gave us."

"Does The Center have a synopsis, Hamid? Not that I care."

"Of course, Jawad, but it is my turn to urge you. Be mindful of your paymaster; you should take care. You do not have free rein over this operation. It is not for you to decide these outcomes. Riyadh will inform me of your next steps, and I in turn will give you your tasks."

"You are correct, Hamid, forgive me." He replied, hoping to placate his senior colleague. But as he said this he thought, *As if I would answer to you. Buffoon.*

"Jawad you would be wise not to pacify me with your hollow words. You may have succeeded in the past with the American undertaking, but your actions in Karachi with the British and American agents still irks many of our senior colleagues at The Center. You may think you are getting near to this 'Mukhtar' but there are those that believe you should not be party to this operation. You are too, how shall I put it . . . abrasive. You have lowered your standing, and the image of the agency, by wanton killing. We are not a nation of thugs, Jawad. We pay others to do our dirty work. You should not be here soiling yourself, picking through slums. It is beneath you; it is beneath us."

"Hamid, are you telling me to stop?"

"Not yet, my friend. But Riyadh—"

Riyadh, Riyadh, is this fool devoid of original thought? Why do I waste time with him? Jawad reflected. A bitter taste was forming in his mouth.

"—wants the Americans to take over," Hamid continued, hoping that Jawad was listening.

He was, and he was alarmed. "Why? We are so close; this Wahid is proof. There is something here, you understand that, don't you?" Jawad's mind was in a fluster, much like the arguing boys they watched playing in the distance. He pushed on with his train of thought, desperately wanting Hamid to urge their headquarters to reconsider their plan, "The Americans cannot penetrate this den; the CIA has no operatives, no agents or assets here. Nothing, Hamid. They have spent—"

"The Americans are closely aligned with the Pakistan ISI, Jawad. They should be the arbitrators of collusion and subterfuge, not us."

"The ISI is corrupt!" Jawad countered. "They are implicit in allowing al-Qaeda sanctuary. Why don't you understand that? I have talked at length to The Center about this, and yet you all question my veracity. I understand that the CIA has asked our agency for help, but they are not here. I am not hiding an American agent under my bed!"

Hamid remained quiet. He wasn't ready to pull the plug on Jawad's mission, and neither was the GID headquarters, at least in principle. Both men continued to watch the cricket match in silence as the words settled in.

"Do you know what the CIA calls assignments to places like this?" Jawad asked.

Hamid looked back at him blankly.

"They call it the 'diarrhea syndrome.' Few Americans in the CIA want an assignment in a place where enemies live in harsh environments. Uncomfortable places where they don't speak the languages or understand the culture. They don't want to go into the bowels of the third world, the shantytowns, the slums, the caves, or the mountains. They are the cold warriors of the Soviet era. They value their comfort, they want to be healthy and safe, and only come out when they have security sacrificed by others."

"They have closed down major operations and networks all across Pakistan, Jawad; they are succeeding."

Jawad reached over and grabbed his colleague by his wrist. He wanted desperately to make a point. He let go after a second, but the situation still annoyed him. "You are not listening to me, Hamid. The Americans have to rely on others to find their information for them. Yes, they have the technology, resources, and money, but they need people like us. If you spent more time with the Western intelligence agencies, you would know that they call it 'liaison intelligence.' Intelligence gathered from others who have loose or low standards of truthfulness. They waste many of their efforts because they cannot verify with their own eyes. Blind money cannot win against al-Qaeda."

"Jawad—"

Jawad was becoming exasperated; he had come to this meeting for information, not to give a lecture on intelligence relations. "Hamid, we are the only ones here. We can atone for the New York attacks. We can remove the shadow of shame that shrouds our country. The Westerners will never forgive us or trust us again because of what our countrymen did, but we have this opportunity to strike and play our part. We need to show the West we can help, we must . . . We are close Hamid; we cannot falter now, it is absurd to even think about it. This Mukhtar, he is the one that must pay—"

"But it will not be you, Jawad. If you find this man, you cannot kill him; it is for the Americans. They must have him and extract information. They are owed their pound of flesh."

"They are taking too long!" Jawad barked.

"Everyone is taking too long." Hamid answered as calmly as he could. "It is the nature of the business that we are in. We still don't know who this man is. You must show patience, Jawad. You still have time to identify him, and then you must withdraw. We will pass the information on to the Americans and they can take risks. Not us."

"Are we that soft, Hamid?" Jawad asked almost resignedly. "Must we agree with the world that we have no backbone, only oil? Is that what you want?"

"It is not for us to choose our destiny Jawad; what we want is irrelevant. We serve our kingdom and if our betters deem it so, then we shall obey without question or recourse. You and I, we swore an oath Jawad, we swore to follow orders for the sanctity and safety of our people, our country, our king. You talk of faltering; it is you that cannot flail in the wind. Obey your commands, or I will find someone to take your place."

Jawad held back, but wondered. *Perhaps it is you that needs to be replaced, idiot.*

Once more, only the sound of excited boys and the din of the nearby city of Karachi enveloped the pair. Neither looked at each other; neither wanted to send the next volley.

"We cannot meet here again, Hamid; against my objections, this is the second time. I will find a new place."

"You are paranoid, Jawad," Hamid countered with an air of derision. He was tiring of there being tension where it need not be. "We are safe. I was not followed, and I assume you took precautions."

Jawad brushed off the obvious. "I can look after myself as you have pointedly stated, however, you are the only one at the consulate who knows of my work. You cannot be the one to take risks, Hamid. I would prefer if you had someone nearby, for your safety."

"You insult me Jawad. I am no child; I do not have to justify what I do to you. Risks or not, you see things that are not there. Perhaps it is time for you to come in, drop this charade. Let the Americans take over."

Jawad was worried about his handler and looked at him with a sense of curiosity. The conversation had taken a different direction from what he had hoped. He knew his colleague was under strain since the Saudi government went public with their promise to help America bring to justice the perpetrators of 9/11. But he thought the offer from his government, while heartfelt, opened the door for al-Qaeda to look at the Saudi establishment in a different light. But Jawad sensed something else, a hesitancy in the man he sat next to.

Jawad had had enough. He stood to take his leave. He caught sight of Karim in the distance, waiting in the shadow of a tree on the edge of the playground. Before he moved off, he left his friend with a parting comment. "I will call you with a new meeting place, Hamid. We should not meet here again."

"Be prepared, Jawad. Our next meeting may not be so cordial. We may be recalled, you and I, and this endeavor of yours may be halted. You are right, I may not be alone next time, but if someone accompanies me, it will not be for my safety."

"Since when did you become such a loyalist boot-licker?" Jawad cursed in return. He stormed off the field in a huff, like one of the young cricketers on the playground bowled out for naught. He didn't look back.

The Royal Consulate of Saudi Arabia, Karachi, Pakistan

Hamid closed the door to his private office on the third floor of the consulate. The office was more like a sitting room, as per the norm for Middle Eastern diplomats in service for their countries around the world. Replete with comfortable couches, soft cushions, overstuffed chairs, and decorative coffee tables, all facing a large-screen TV attached to a wall. His plain desk, alien to the rest of the décor, was stuffed into a corner. It was kitted out with only the most functional basics: one computer screen and one phone.

He plucked a cigarette from an attractive silver box on the coffee table, then sauntered over to his phone, punched in a number and ordered tea from a servant who serviced the third-floor staff. He lit his cigarette and paced, contemplating his next actions.

The tea arrived in less than a minute. He didn't thank the man for the delivery, and paid him no attention when he entered and departed. He switched from staring out the window to gazing at the blank TV, to studying a traditional Arabian painting that hung on a wall. He stubbed out the cigarette, took out another, and played with it for a few seconds before he lit up again. After ten minutes of this, he locked his office door from the inside, turned on his PC, entered his password, and accessed the GID network. It took him a few minutes more to navigate his way through the secure software before he finally got into the case file he was looking for. There was no need for him to code the information or enter the date and time; it was an automatic process. The template he filled out was a typical intelligence memorandum. The first two paragraphs required a simple preamble about his activities; the where, the when, mitigating circumstances, challenges or attributes, language used, those present, those not, duration of conversations and other mundane snippets of information. Then in the table's main body, he entered:

> *Subject Sand Cat did not show for a prearranged meeting in Karachi. This is the second occurrence that Sand Cat has missed a meeting. His subordinate Subject Jerboa was not present for either meeting. It is assumed that*

both Sand Cat and Jerboa have been compromised and are in captivity or
are deceased.

This office will undertake all measures to locate both agents and ap-
proach local authorities only when all avenues have been exhausted.

He finished the memo with the usual salutations and praise to Allah
and the Kingdom of Saudi Arabia. Without hesitating or overthinking
his actions, he hit the send button on the transmission and closed the
terminal down.

While the PC began its shutting down process, Hamid retrieved a
set of keys from his pocket and unlocked a drawer in the desk. He
retrieved a laptop from within, and booted it up. Watching the screen
come to life, he tottered through the mental motions of how he would
write his next piece of correspondence. Satisfied he had a grasp of the
text, he found a blue network cable under the desk and plugged it in.
Opening his Hotmail account, he composed an e-mail to
gold_crack@yahoo.com.

To the untrained eye, the beginning of the e-mail looked innocent
enough. It was as if Hamid was talking about his adventures in a
foreign land to a friend or relative, Mohammed, with complaints about
the heat, the food, and the people. He wrote about the many sights he
had seen and his plans for future outings in the country. He also
reminisced about the past, his time in Riyadh where, as youngsters,
they chased sand cats and jerboas out of the kitchen with sticks and
stones. Hamid wrote further about their times together and how he
wished that they could see each other once again soon, and perhaps
find their favorite foods and desserts in the souk, the marketplace where
they used to steal from unsuspecting vendors.

He finished his e-mail by asking Mohammed to call him and left a
telephone number for him if he had the time. Praising Allah and
wishing Mohammed his good health, he signed off with just his initial.

Hamid waited a few seconds for the e-mail to go through, then
closed down the open browser and shut the machine down. Next, he
opened a combination wall safe hidden behind a bookshelf. Inside were
a stack of files, a pistol with spare rounds, many passports of Saudi and

other nationalities, and two memory cards. He quickly found the file he was looking for and immediately shredded the contents. Returning to his desk drawer, he fished out a cigar clipper; however, this was not a typical device for trimming tobacco. It was a specialty tool that he had manufactured for destroying memory cards or sticks. He inserted the first card into the clipper and hacked away at the stick until it disintegrated. He repeated the exercise again with the second stick, and wiped the shavings and micro pieces of memory into the shred bin.

Satisfied he had all the damaged pieces collected, he opened the window of his office, set the metal bin on the wide outside ledge and dropped his lit cigarette inside. The smoldering soon became an open flame, and the smoke billowed out into the Karachi air, only ceasing when everything had been incinerated. Content he had cleansed himself of Jawad Halabi and Karim Basrawi, he unlocked his door and again hit the tea boy's number on the phone.

The servant came rushing to his master, who offered the shred bin to the boy and ordered. "Wash."

Lyari Town, Karachi, Pakistan

Mukhtar read the body of the e-mail twice, then focused on the telephone number. He scratched the digits onto a piece of paper, then made the calculations to authenticate the message. He added and subtracted the sequence to arrive at the correct code, happy his agent was following procedures, concerned that he wanted a meeting.

He sat alone in the small, dirty, second-floor bedroom in a mouse-infested house. A home furnished by a sympathizer to the cause and a trusted distant relative. A single light dangled from the ceiling and strained to give off sufficient light. The juice for his laptop, strung out on yards of extension cables and cords, came from a junction box in the street serving twenty homes. His spotty Internet connection: stolen from a nearby post office.

The sparse room contained only a table for his work, a single bed for his sleep, and a mat for his prayers. Common to his upbringing, he was comfortable in his simple surroundings, however he was also adept at fitting into situations of comfort and opulence at some of the finest hotels and restaurants the world over. But it was here, in these most austere of environments, he felt most at peace.

The house was as many in the town, made of brick, mud, and corrugated rooftops, with power lines spliced, water faucets shared, and dirty communal toilets. But it was safe from prying eyes. The residence was a minuscule home in a sprawling town. A suburb of Karachi, a city of more than a million people, where outsiders, including the authorities, seldom ventured. Ruled by drug dealers, black-marketers, gangs, and tribal discipline, it was the veritable den of iniquity, with a maze of narrow mud-rutted roads and alleys that hindered the unaware but helped the familiar get around.

Known to but a few in the enclave, Mukhtar hid in plain sight. Aware that the authorities were hunting him, he feared no treason, no betrayal, and no need to lay awake each night. The Baluch community of Lyari was both his security blanket and his shield. If he could not trust his own, he could trust no one.

But tonight, the al-Qaeda operations manager was restless. It concerned him that his agent, who slept comfortably in a luxurious apartment roughly twenty miles from Mukhtar's haven; had reached out, and had done it so openly. As instructed, his agent had used the codes given him, but he risked exposure to the organization and himself by leaving an electronic trail. A knock at the bedroom door interrupted his thoughts. He looked up from his laptop as a giant of a man entered the room.

Mukhtar looked sternly at the man, but he didn't admonish him for the intrusion.

"Mukhtar, Americans, the ISI and the Rangers are mobilized. They are on the way here; we have one hour."

Mukhtar didn't expect an apology from his chief of security for entering the room, nor did he question the man's source.

"They will not find us," his man continued. "But we must leave at once."

The leader's reaction belied his soldier's concern. "Nabeel. I trust your counsel, my friend; however, we are in no danger here; this is my home. Our people will protect us." He raised his hand to stop the man from insistence. "It is time for us to leave, anyway. We shall go to Quetta, but there are still things to do. Wahid will travel with me, but I want you to stay here, dispose of his uncle."

Nabeel, though pensive, nodded his head, waiting for the next order.

"There are also two rats in Karachi. You must find them. They are Saudi and need not be in our community; they should be easy to identify. Hold them until my return."

"Yes Mukhtar, but I must insist that you leave now."

"As I have said Nabeel, you must trust me, we have nothing to fear. The ISI will not find us, my friend. You have a vehicle ready?"

"Yes."

"Good." Mukhtar got up from his desk and unplugged his laptop. Without turning it off, he turned the computer over and removed the hard drive. He gave the useless laptop to his man. "Destroy this Nabeel."

Mukhtar stuffed the hard drive and what meager belongings he had, including his mat, into a small carry-all and left the room. He hustled through the house at the behest of his security man, only pausing briefly to thank the home's proprietor for his hospitality.

Once outside, he mounted the rear of a motorbike and waited for Nabeel to issue orders to his men. Mukhtar spotted Wahid as a passenger on another bike behind him, and saw another scooter with two other men patiently waiting ahead. The small convoy kicked up only a little dust into the midnight air as they pulled away slowly from the small house. Within a few minutes, the convoy joined a stream of traffic heading to and from the city. With a shawl around his face, Mukhtar slunk off into the night, believing that the ISI were nowhere near capturing him.

Forty minutes after leaving the safety of the house in Lyari, Mukhtar and Wahid transferred their skimpy possessions into a waiting car. As they took to their task, a set of headlights burned through the night air and pointed its way in their direction. Mukhtar ordered his men to carry on packing his vehicle while he watched the car approach with interest. One of his men retrieved an AK-47 from the trunk of the car, but his leader waved him down and the man stashed the weapon away, while keeping the trunk open.

A silver Kia sedan drove up close to the small group, and parked facing the nearby deserted Naya Nazimabad football stadium. The driver doused the lights and killed the engine. He took a few more moments to exit the car, however Mukhtar, confident there was no threat, smoked a cigarette and squinted his eyes through the dust cloud the visitor created. He continued to watch as a tall, gangly man exited the Kia and made his way towards them. Mukhtar ambled casually away from his cohorts, expecting the tall man to do the same. The conversation they were about to have was not for the ears of his followers.

"I see you have travel plans," the tall man inquired, feigning a quizzical look. The casual comment was anything but. They continued to amble in the shadows of the sparse trees and bushes lining the football club's empty parking lot.

"My people are adept at keeping me safe, Rashid, but tonight, I fear that the Americans were close, too close my friend."

Rashid sensed he needed to defend his position. "I gave warning to your man; this was not of my doing."

"Yet here I am. We had no time to prepare for our departure."

"Yes, you are here, and not in captivity," Rashid continued. "You should be grateful to me for slowing the operation down. They were not looking for you. It was, as the Americans like to say, a fishing expedition."

Mukhtar stopped mid-stride; he gave Rashid a stern look. He stubbed his cigarette out on the ground and retrieved a set of prayer beads from his pocket. He toyed with them for a moment, then looked away as if in deep thought. He then asked the question that had been on his mind for days. "What of our brother?"

"He is being held by the Americans."

"Where?"

"He is no longer in Pakistan, Mukhtar."

"Where is he?"

Rashid answered reluctantly, with his head slightly bowed. "I fear we will never know. The Americans have transported him out of the country to what they call a 'black site.' It could be anywhere in the world."

"Our agreement was that you would protect us, Rashid. Your ISI was supposed to forewarn us of these raids," Mukhtar demanded.

"The government is bowing to international pressure, Mukhtar. The ISI still has influence, but there are some at the cabinet level who believe that it is time to curtail our powers. I feel that there is a sea change coming my brother; there may be a time when we cannot protect the organization."

"And the sheik? What message shall I pass to him? That the Pakistani ISI are now our enemy?" Mukhtar pressed.

Colonel Rashid Ghazini pulled on Mukhtar's wrist gently to get him to stop walking and to face him. "Mukhtar, please . . . do not offend me by questioning my loyalty to the cause, nor that of the ISI. We are all committed to the same goal. This will pass; you have my word. There are enough of us who feel the same way. The Americans will become tired. They cannot survive here very long; they have no stomach for a long campaign. As long as we can arrest some individuals from time to time, we can appease—"

"I have given you enough, Rashid! Abu was my friend, a friend of the sheik. He was not a simple offering of appeasement. You allowed him to be captured."

"He was careless, Mukhtar. We warned him to leave, you know that—but the Americans are becoming sophisticated in their methods. They may not last the course but they can be tenacious. You must listen to what I am saying, things are getting heated within the government. There are political and economic circumstances that are causing—"

Mukhtar scoffed at the last comment. "Economics, is that what the ISI is afraid of? Losing their funding because of American pressure?

What is it this time, a new contract for F-16s?" He asked this without expecting a direct answer, but he pushed his scorn a little further. "And for me to offer more of my brothers so you can adorn yourself in Western decadence and visit Florida with your Western whores? Your reasoning appalls me Rashid."

The tall man, embarrassed, covered his Rolex watch. He wasn't sure how Mukhtar had found out about his latest American vacation; he chided himself for being so careless around the man. He needed to be careful; the terrorist had spies everywhere. He didn't like the direction the conversation was going, so he tried another tack. "The execution of the journalist was a mistake Mukhtar; how did the sheik take the news?"

"So, it is now you who is on a fishing expedition, Rashid. What has transpired between the sheik and I is of no concern to you."

"But it is of concern." Rashid insisted. "The more, how shall I put this . . . the more ambitious your activities are, the more attention you draw to yourself and the more condemnation you will achieve. The Pakistani government met this very evening on the subject. You did not make any new friends in Islamabad tonight."

"What is done is done," Mukhtar replied, almost nonchalantly. "It should not be a surprise that we have to take this fight to the Western world. We must drive these unbelievers out of the holy lands, and they must pay in blood. The Jew journalist was a legitimate target, but I need not justify my actions to you. Your lack of protection and cooperation is why I am here. You must do more to slow the Americans down. This group, the SAD, they cannot continue their work."

"Mukhtar, we gave you information about that team. It was your men who failed."

"But it was the ISI who provided the explosives, so who may I ask is at fault now Rashid?"

Both men stood in silence. They gained nothing; they lost nothing. Blame was apportioned on both sides. Rashid looked Mukhtar in the eyes and thought deeply about the man in front of him before he spoke his next words. He knew that the man was a terrorist, but no simple assassin or bomb maker. He was smart, devious, cunning and danger-ous, the famed architect of 9/11. However, he wondered if Mukhtar's latest callous act of terrorism was borne out of rage rather than savviness.

"Exacting revenge with emotion will curtail logic and hamper suc-cess, Mukhtar. I understand your desire for making the Americans pay for Abu. Perhaps we were too hasty to feed that need, and our plan was possibly flawed before we set in motion."

Mukhtar's stony face gazed back at Rashid, his mind rushing with thoughts; he didn't appreciate the lecture on Sun Tzu's principles, however, there was some truth to what was just stated. Though sometimes brutish, he prided himself on his self-discipline and rational approach to problems. His fame within al-Qaeda, while unwanted, fed his ego and his thirst for more actions against his enemies. He repressed the fleeting thought of ridding himself of the man standing before him though, as he appreciated the mutuality; the "we" and "our" comments sat well with him.

Despite the setback of the foiled attack in Islamabad against the SAD, Mukhtar's execution of the journalist was, in his mind, a success. He did, though, learn a lesson from Rashid's sermon. While al-Qaeda needed the protection of the ISI, it also needed its money and intelli-gence, but from this point forward, he would not be so trusting. He contemplated the conversation a little longer but then reminded himself that he needed to be mobile; he had a journey to complete. The ISI officer broke his train of thought. "You may want to decrease your activities, Mukhtar," Rashid finally offered, then paused to gauge the mood. He drove his point on. "After this attack and the journalist, the Americans will send more agents—"

Mukhtar grinned ever so slightly and raised his eyebrows as he surmised, "More targets, Rashid."

Lufthansa Airlines, Frankfurt Airport, Germany

Chris struggled to lift his carry-on bag up into the overhead bin. It surprised him when the tall raven-haired woman behind him took the bag without saying a word and stuffed it in the compartment. At first, he thought it was some rude, impatient Brunhilda who was rushing to get to her seat, and he was in her way, but when she smiled at him, his thoughts changed. "Thank you," he offered.

Taken aback for a second, she appreciated the politeness, "You're welcome."

Chris turned around to look for his window seat, found what he was looking for, and gingerly sat himself down. He was in a lot of pain from his injuries, and with his arm still in a sling he was having difficulties getting basic things done—and therefore happy to have a sympathetic assist from a fellow traveler.

He looked around to see where she was seated, and found her placing a three-foot packaging tube above his row of seating. He noted the laptop case and matching purse hanging from her shoulder, then looked down and over the seats in front of him, and saw that boarding was almost complete. She was one of the few people still standing. After closing the bin, she placed her purse in the aisle seat in his row and placed her laptop on the floor; she then looked over at Chris, who glanced quickly out the window. She took off her suit jacket and placed it in the middle, unoccupied seat.

Within a few minutes, the captain announced the usual news about the flight and weather and the obligatory need for keeping seatbelts fastened. With the declarations made, the cabin doors were closed and the taxiing process began, with the somber Lufthansa stewardesses going through the motions of what to do in case of an emergency. On completion of the do or die messages, Chris closed his eyes. He woke just in time to ask for some water from the in-flight service.

Raven hair assisted once again in passing the plastic cup of water over to Chris.

"Thank you, my nurse has the day off," Chris quipped.

"You're welcome." She smiled.

Not American, not British; are those the only words she knows? Chris quickly calculated.

"You have a nurse?"

It was Chris's turn to grin. "No, I'm just joking." *French perhaps?*

She looked closely at his bruised face. "May I ask what happened, you look in pain."

He virtually kicked himself; he saw a can of worms opening up. *Why can't I keep my mouth shut?*

"Car accident." He answered, hoping to keep things brief.

"Nothing too serious, I hope." She questioned sincerely.

"No, no, but you should have seen the tree, there was no saving it, we tried our best." Chris replied, attempting to keep the light conversation going.

She giggled a little. Chris wasn't sure if he amused her or she was just pretending because she felt sorry for him. He knew better than to open up a conversation on a plane. She seemed nice; he was lonely and needed an outlet. He was sick of lying, but his job demanded it. Knowing that more innocent questions would come, he prepared himself with a new legend; saying he was in the CIA was not an option. *She's not a threat, chill out.*

"Did it happen in Frankfurt?" Her voice once again showing genuine concern.

"Just outside, Bad Homburg. I was with some business colleagues, we got hit by a drunk driver."

"No tree?"

"No tree, sorry, I'm just trying to be positive. It could have been worse." Chris smiled.

"I understand . . . what business are you in?" Raven hair quizzed.

She's harmless. Be nice. "Logistics, you?" He answered with a standard line from his legend.

"Architect."

"Are you from Paris?" Chris asked, trying to point the conversation away from her innocent but risky direction.

"Yes, I work in my family's company." Her English was excellent; so, he let her continue driving the dialog with polite smiles, yeses, and noes when needed. He remained cautious and probed her words for signs of deceit. He was happy that it seemed there was no need to worry.

They continued to chat for the rest of the flight. He talked about logistics and the challenges of shipping everything from toilet paper to talcum powder for his company; she talked about architecture, Paris and Europe.

The plane landed without incident at Charles de Gaulle Airport on the outskirts of Paris. It was one of Chris's least favorite airports in the world. He returned his gaze from out the window towards her, then held back a grin when he saw his travelling companion holding a business card. "If you would like to keep in touch?"

Momentarily taken in by her deep blue eyes, he took the card and read her name: *Gabrielle Caron.*

"I'm George, George Mitchell," Chris lied. He wasn't sure if she was expecting a business card in return. He had none to give.

"It's been a pleasure traveling with you, George."

"Likewise. I hope our paths cross again somewhere."

She smiled. Chris noted that she seemed to do that a lot, but neither offered much more.

The pair waited for the cabin to clear before they got up; she retrieved his bag first and handed it to him. He gave her his thanks and watched her get her things together and file off the plane.

Once they cleared the jetway, she turned to him. "Where are you staying? Are you going into the city?"

"Yes," he said as he dropped his bag to fish out his travel itinerary. "Le Meridien Etoile, 17th Arrondissement."

"You pronounced that quite well George, there is hope for you, my English friend. I am in the 8th district; we can go by taxi together if you wish?"

The ride took almost an hour; they could have easily taken a train and then the metro, but the taxi ride would be more comfortable in his condition. Chris was, however, still skeptical and cautious without showing it. He had been to Paris many times before and had the major routes, landmarks, and locations of the districts memorized. He wasn't in any shape to fight his way out of a situation, but he mentally prepped his body to run if they were heading to parts unknown. He kept telling himself that she was just trying to be nice; he was just trying to trust someone, even if for a few minutes.

A sense of relief welcomed him when they arrived at the hotel and she didn't exit the car when he got out. He tried to pay for the ride, but she insisted that he not.

"You can buy me dinner sometime George."

Chris blushed slightly; he wasn't used to being picked up. "Let me recover a little, and I may take you up on that, thanks for the ride, and the company, Gabrielle." He shut the taxi door and watched as it pulled away. She was looking over her shoulder; he gave her a faint wave. As he watched the car leave, he considered out of an abundance of caution not checking in and looking for another hotel to spend the night. He did a quick scan of the area and weighed his options. He chose to let his paranoia sleep a little longer.

During the hotel check-in, Chris read a note, left by Gene, to be ready for a pickup at 0830 the next morning, outside the main door on the right. Translated to SAD code, it meant he needed to be ready for a 0730 pickup anywhere on the left side of the street.

He found his room on the eighth floor, did a quick scan for anything unusual, then crashed onto the bed. He lay there for ten minutes with his eyes shut before deciding to get up and dive into the shower. It was another twenty minutes before he emerged.

Refreshed, but still in pain, he took two Percocets and donned the last set of clean clothes he had. He looked at the clock next to the bed and did a quick calculation; it wasn't too late. He made his way over to the window, then dialed his girlfriend's number. As he stared out at the innards of the Paris concrete jungle, he willed the ringing to stop and for a familiar and soft voice to answer. The ring tone continued in his ear. The call then switched to her voicemail box . . . it was full.

Chris found the TV remote and buzzed through the dozen channels on offer. The only one that he could comprehend was CNN. Everything else was in French, unless he wanted to pay for his pleasure, and he needed no language skills for that. A breaking news story was being reported by a field journalist in Tel Aviv, about the latest round of tit-for-tat attacks between the Israelis and Palestinians. The body count was mounting with no end in sight. He continued to watch the story as CNN doled out talking head after talking head, who espoused their thoughts and opinions of what was happening, and what should happen next. Some guests on the show were bona fide experts, but the majority were has-beens, wannabes, or just plain clueless. But the news network had to fill in the gaps and keep things in-your-face, so they were ready for when more details were released or they had their next "exclusive" story.

Chris found the mute button on the remote and dialed Sandy again. He paced around the room hoping she'd answer, but once again there was no reply. He ran through the same exercise three more times in the space of two hours, but it was all to no reward. He tried in vain to come up with a plausible reason why she didn't or couldn't answer, but realized that it was an exercise in futility. Besides, he wasn't being fair. It wasn't like he would answer her calls while he was on assignment; she didn't even have his cell phone number. He meandered over to the bedside table to place his phone down, but stopped short as he spotted Gabrielle's business card. He looked at the clock, picked up the card, and read the number.

He stared at the wall for a few seconds, then looked down at his phone. He entered the number, but didn't hit the call button. With his thumb poised, he asked himself if he was ready to cheat.

CHAPTER FOUR

Le Meridien Hotel, Paris, France

CHRIS SPENT A RESTLESS NIGHT, alone and full of self-doubt. He chastised himself for thinking he could lose himself with a night of potentially meaningless physical contact and the possibility of feeling guilty for the rest of his relationship with Sandy. She would never have known if he strayed, but he would never have been the same with her again. He'd had ample opportunity to get into bed with other women and he always stayed true, but his current state of mind regarding his job was clouding his judgment.

Were he not on pain medications, he would have wound up drunk in a bar looking for a fight; though lately, the penchant for that release was slowly waning, and he thought Sandy's positive influence likely had helped keep the urge in check. He knew deep down that she loved him, and he her; but as much as he tried, he still couldn't commit to her fully if he remained in this job. It was too demanding, too costly, too dangerous. And despite telling Gene that he was tired of it, in truth he was not. He loved what he did.

Kicking in doors, dragging shitheads out of hovels, asserting ultimate force, being part of the greater good—these were all things he fully enjoyed. He had killed men and almost been killed several times; he'd hurt others and been injured himself, yet he still turned up for work day in-day out, wherever and whenever they needed him.

The war on terror gave him his true calling. It was accurate that he had sadness in his life; he had seen people die in his arms, within arm's reach and from afar, but he told himself that he had to stand up and be counted. Terrorists had attacked his adopted country. As a capable and willing fighter, he thought he owed the over 3,000 victims of 9/11 to do

something about the scourge, the plague, the cancer of terrorism. He
didn't feel like a superhero, and he desired no fame; but to work in the
shadows to find those responsible was all that he wanted. "Seize,
interrogate, dispose" became his mantra, and he didn't care how he did
it.

He wasn't sure why he was in Paris. According to Gene, he was
persona non grata in Pakistan from his bust-up with bearded Jon. His
antics in Islamabad also put him on an uneven keel with his team, so it
was possible that Gene had found a hidey-hole in which to stash him
until the dust had settled. His worst fear, though, was that Gene might
stick him on the longest layover flight known to man: back to Washington State with a "services no longer required" stamp on his forehead.

It was 0445 when he got out of bed and sucked down half a bottle
of water to accompany more pain meds. He got dressed without his
arm sling, and left his room to head to the street. He had time to kill, he
couldn't sleep. His mind was being assaulted by one word—liability.

Plodding through the lobby, his brain played high-speed ping-pong
with that fateful word. The more it bounced around, the more he hated
it. It forced his eyes and his posture downward; he wasn't paying
attention to his surroundings, which for him was out of character. He
wasn't alert; he wasn't aware; he was in danger of becoming an average
Joe. As soon as he turned right out of the hotel, a female suddenly
sprang out of the shadows. Chris had his hands dug deep into his
pockets and his shoulders were almost touching his earlobes, his chin
was resting on his chest. He bounced back two feet and froze. Instead of
looking around for other movements or threats, he stared at the woman
in front of him, astonished that he didn't see her.

"Are you staying here at the hotel?" she asked in French.

Chris didn't understand completely and didn't reply. The woman
asked the same again in English. Chris only nodded; he was in a state of
confusion. He wasn't sure if it was the drugs, but he felt he was drifting
in a semi-fugue state. "Do you want a massage, or—"

Chris squinted at her. *What the hell does she want?*

"I can come to your room, if you want to fuck?" she added with a thin smile.

Well shit, really, a hooker, at this time of day? He caught movement behind the prostitute. It was another smiling face, ready for anything to suit a man's desire.

He smiled at the first girl. "No, thank you, no."

"You can have us both if you want?" she playfully replied.

His grin got broader, but he took a few steps to disengage and then offered a parting comment. "I'm sure that would be fun, but not today."

The girls offered no more; another unsuspecting male was moving towards them.

Chris moved on at a brisk military marching pace. He wanted to run; he needed to exercise, to get his body moving the right way and force his mind and senses to keep pace. But he felt as rusty as an old can of tuna, half empty and soured. Once again, he blamed the drugs. He knew he should rest, eat properly and follow a mundane, predictable schedule, but he wasn't like that. He never was. He lived for the hectic, the rush, the adrenalin punches, the fear, the elation of winning, the camaraderie—but today it was all missing. He moped along the Parisian streets like a jilted lover, alone with dark thoughts as tiny peeks of sunlight forced strings of reality to assault him. He finally found his way, without trying, to the Arc de Triomphe.

Chris found welcome relief as he watched traffic navigate one of the largest roundabouts in the world. He sat on a bench and marveled at the skills and sheer bravado of the Parisian drivers, fearless as they dove into the fray, five, six, seven abreast when entering the arena. Then there were those he imagined as akin to circus or rodeo clowns—riders on mopeds or motorbikes zipping in between the cars, vans and busses, defying the odds to cross the unmarked cobblestones and find the smallest of gaps to escape. He could have sat there for hours, looking at the faces of anger, fear, and bravery of those who crossed the field. The British SAS motto, "Who Dares Wins" came to mind, and he thought how apt it was for the scene.

He looked around to see if he was being watched, if there were figures lurking in the failing shadows, a car with darkened windows, a gun being drawn. He looked at the parked cars, the cyclists who stopped and moved off, the pedestrians, the newspaper vendors, ordinary people doing ordinary things. But then he came to a sudden conclusion. *Nobody is watching me; I'm not watching anyone. I have nothing to do, nobody knows where I am. I'm in limbo . . . and it feels good.*

At first, Chris thought he was entering a prison. They were patiently waiting for the solid twelve-foot white gate on the Boulevard Mortier to slide open. Chris, from the rear of the car that had picked him up from his hotel, took in the sights. He still didn't know where he was, and Gene, who was sitting in the front passenger seat, wasn't sharing. Chris noted the thick, white brick walls topped with well-maintained rolls of menacing razor wire. Every twenty to thirty feet he spotted a camera affixed to a wall or pole. In areas where the walls were lowest, motion detection sensors mounted to tall brackets sprouted up like string beans. Police officers patrolled the streets outside and motorcycle cops ensured that traffic kept moving.

Once through the main gate, yet another closed tall gate hindered their progress. They had to wait for the main gate to close behind them before the next could be opened. With a loud *clunk* behind them, they became trapped in a sally port. A police officer exited a booth and two others presented themselves, machine guns at the ready and focused on the car and its occupants. After a brief exchange with the driver, the officers stood down and allowed the vehicle to pass.

After a few more minutes of navigating a tightly packed compound of drab, low-rise buildings that left nothing to the imagination other than to show off a cheap governmental "bureauville," the car halted outside a much more formidable structure that looked like part of an old fortress, likely built in the eighteenth century. They exited the vehicle and Gene passed his thanks on to the driver, then headed for a closed solid door. As he approached, he turned to face a camera mounted on a wall. After a few seconds of recognition, the door clicked open and they entered a small space that once more doubled as a sally port. Chris noted the trend; and someone obviously took security seriously as another armed police officer appeared. He checked Gene's ID and passed Chris a lanyard with his picture affixed to a badge. Chris looked on and tried not to show surprise when he saw his own face. It was still a mystery to him why he was entering a secure facility in the middle of Paris with an access card, and it seemed too permanent for his liking.

Making their way steadily past the policeman, Gene strode off toward a staircase that led downward. The duo remained silent, and Chris tagged along like an obedient hound, trying to avoid gazing at the cameras peppered around the stairwell and other corridors. Three flights down, they found a closed steel door. Gene presented his badge to a card reader on the door, allowing him access. Now on the lowest level of the basement, they entered a room full of office cubicles.

The place was abuzz with activity. Gene hurried through the maze, and Chris tried to count the number of languages he was hearing. French, German, English for sure, but they were hustling as if Gene had no time to waste.

They finally entered a corner office. If it wasn't for the artificial light, it could have easily doubled as a dungeon. He imagined it might have been part of a castle's perimeter wall if it had been above ground. It looked and felt very cold. Gene threw his coat over a chair and walked around a desk to sit down. Chris stood. "This place makes the Bastille look like a play date, Gene."

"Be careful what you wish for Chris; this will be your home for a while. Shut the door, sit. How's the arm?"

"I could bitch all day, but I'm grateful that it's been taken care of, so no complaints."

"You'll be happy to know you're going to get a fat ass while you're here. Your off field ops for a while." Gene stated this casually, hoping his underling would take the hint that he would be under a microscope from here on out.

Chris wanted to protest, but he resolved to take it on the chin. At that moment he just wanted to keep his job, and if it meant working out of a hole in the ground for a while, then so be it. He nodded silently. Gene was expecting some witty comeback, but was happy there was none. He started his briefing. "Welcome to Alliance Base, Chris. We're in the headquarters of the General Directorate for External Security, the DGSE, if you haven't guessed yet."

Chris hadn't. It was a surprise to him and he thought it ironic that he rarely set foot in the CIA headquarters; he didn't even have an access badge. But here he was in the basement of the French version of the CIA, and it sounded like he would be here a while. *How things have changed.*

"All this is new." Gene spun his hands in a circle. "I'll give you the nickel tour soon. But here is where you will live and work. Things have a habit of changing, so I don't know exactly how long that means. There are apartments here in the compound, you can get whatever you need right here—food, sports, medical, all that happy camper crap. It doesn't mean you're confined to barracks, but you should take advantage of what's on offer. Let Sandy know you're here . . . ask her to come over for a while maybe, there's plenty of hotels around she can stay at." Gene raised his eyebrows suggestively and gave an awkward smirk.

"I'll give it some thought," Chris conceded.

Gene leaned toward his desk, picked up a notepad and pen, and scribbled. "Here's a list of your new team. All SAD. There are plenty of Americans here, the majority belong to the agency, as we're funding the entire enterprise."

"Alliance Base?" Chris asked.

"Yes, it's a joint task force hosted by the French, but commanded by the US; it's staffed with us, the Brits, Germans, French and Spaniards. Now and again, we'll have other NATO members pop in, but the core group is what I just mentioned." Gene looked at his watch, then back at Chris. "In case you're wondering," he added, "Alliance Base is a direct counter to al-Qaeda's base."

"Makes sense." Chris supposed. "So, what do I do?"

"Same as before, rendition. This time you're working as liaison. European theater only. I need a German speaker to work closely with the Bundesnachritendienst. Everyone around here speaks high-level English, but when things get heated, and they will, foreign nationals tend to fall back into their own language. That's where you come in, and the rest of our team. The people on that list speak the languages we need." Gene didn't pause. "Basically, when it comes to picking up a suspect through intelligence captured here at the base, either SWAT teams or Special Forces will be dispatched to apprehend. We'll rendition those subjects out of whatever country we pick them up in, and ship them over to our black sites. Details of which are to be determined by us and only us. We also have representatives from Special Forces here in the base, as all operations will be commanded and coordinated from down the hall. Again, you'll be knee deep in that. This is a fresh approach to catching these asshats, and there's still a matter of incomplete trust between governments. Shit, sometimes we can't even talk to each other in the US; how that differs here is beyond my pay grade to figure out. But someone thinks this open sharing with foreigners is an attractive proposition, so like it or not, we're the new guinea pigs. We've been up and running just over a month, more on that later, and we haven't been tested 100 percent yet, though the few nibbles we've had have shown a few weak spots, ergo, you sitting here."

"You have my interest, Gene."

"Excellent. I was hoping you'd say that." Gene leaned back in his chair. "If you think I'm hiding you down here and restricting your capacity to wander . . . you think right. You don't want to fuck this up, Chris. You are officially a desk jockey and the more assignments like this you get, the more popular you become. You need to put your friendly can-do, go-team, rah-rah, face on and then kiss some ass to get shit done. Follow the processes and procedures, embrace the move-ment, be one with the mission, cross your I's and dot your T's, that kind of shit. There will be a ton of administrative crap to sort through, lots of reports to file, all that happy office shit I've been dealing with for years.

If you want to continue your career, Chris, I want to help you, but you need to show some willingness and initiative, and it needs to be right here, and right now."

"Do I need to bend the knee—"

Gene raised his voice. "See! That right there!" He pointed a finger directly at Chris. The older man became flushed. "That is exactly what I'm talking about. You need to cut that crap! I know we have history, Chris, but you need to remember that there needs to be a line between us. You work for me. I am not your fucking friend, so cut the funny shit out, and I mean right now, or I will send you packing on the next steamer to fucking Bora Bora."

Chris drew a long breath. His face blushed with embarrassment. *Oops, he's serious.* Though it hurt him to hear that Gene was not his friend, he was right; he needed to maintain respect for his boss. "Ok Gene. Sorry."

Gene got out of his chair quickly. He wanted to throw out a few more fucks around, but he held back. "Let's walk before I question your sincerity anymore."

Chris was glad that Gene had given him the names of his direct teammates. Upon leaving the office, he shook a dozen pairs of hands and heard twenty different names in the space of a hundred feet. Gene pointed out who did what, who they worked for and where they were getting their information from, and on and on. He also gave him a list of do's and don'ts and noted the important meetings to attend, as well as the not-so-important. During the tour he showed Chris to his new desk, where he gave him a list of contacts of all the agencies, both American and foreign, who were at the base. Chris did a quick speed-read and found at least a dozen departments from the CIA, about five or six from the FBI, Department of Justice, Secret Service, MI5 MI6, BKA, BND, DGSE, DGSI, the Spanish National Intelligence Center, the Civil Guard. And then on the flip side of the document were all the Special Forces units from the various countries including Navy Seals, Delta Force, SAS, and GSG9. The list seemed endless.

His head pounded lightly, reminding him he needed to take his meds again. He was slightly overwhelmed, akin to being in a pitch-black room, then suddenly having a flashlight go on directly in your face. He knew there was so much more to absorb, and it would take him weeks to understand the operation and the full scope of his job, but for now he had a mouthful to chew on.

As they trudged around and chatted with various people, Chris realized how involved Gene really was. He waited for a break in a conversation with a Frenchman before he asked his question. "You've got your fingers in all the pies around here, Gene. How did you get roped into this one?"

"I'm not in charge here, Chris. There are many brighter minds than mine around here."

Chris wanted to float him a humorous jibe, but remembered Gene's earlier warning. He let him continue.

"I'm fortunate to be on the management team, but all of this, setting up a European base for active measures, has been floating around, way before 9/11, and was never on my radar. But because of our culture and the reticence of other nations to share, nothing materialized. The twin towers changed all that. The Brits were all over it; they were happy to set something up in London, but the French and Germans not so much. So, CIA Operations started planning to set up shop outside London, when someone drove a truck full of explosives into a synagogue in Tunisia. Fourteen Germans were killed, two French and three Tunisians; and over thirty injured. Basically, that was the catalyst to all of this. The French government eventually came to us with the offer; we answered that we'd only join if it was a coalition led by us. The Germans didn't hesitate; they wanted revenge for their losses, and here we are."

Chris nodded, taking in the information. "How is that going, anything pan out yet?"

"Speaking of catalysts," Gene responded. "Yes, al-Qaeda claimed responsibility for the attack on the synagogue, but we have our eyes on a German person of interest."

"That's why I am here." Chris once again supposed.

"You got it. There's also a Spanish connection, but it's early days. I'll lean on you to feed me what you can about the German end. I think they'll want to extradite whoever gets picked up. I can't always be here to prevent that; I've got other places to be. But what I don't want is for this to turn into a political football. Eyes and ears, Chris, eyes and ears."

"Roger that Gene, have a name?"

"Come with me, we'll get you what you need," Gene commanded.

The pair made their way through the last of the office spaces and down a long dark corridor. At the end were three doors, each secured by a card reader, camera and intercom system.

"Straight ahead, communications center. There's no need for you to go in there, period. Here on the left is the Special Operations Command Center. You can go in there by invite only. That's where all your gung-ho, shoot-em-up, bag-um-up boys conduct operations. We don't need to go in there right now. Here on the right is the base command center, where all the data is analyzed and distributed. Manned 24/7. You have access, but don't overstay your welcome." Gene carded himself in. "One at a time, anti-pass-back, whatever that means. Wait for the door to close, use your badge."

Chris mirrored Gene's actions. By the time he'd passed through the door, Gene had already gone down a flight of stairs. Just when Chris thought he'd reached the ends of the earth, the steep staircase led down another two floors. At the bottom, Gene tapped a six-digit pin into a keypad. "Use your last six digits of your employee number."

Chris waited for Gene to enter and followed his lead. They were in a huge, dark, quiet but populated auditorium. Gene motioned Chris to follow him up some steps to a glass-walled meeting room that over-looked the theater-like environment. "The French liked to build bunkers, what can I say."

"Cold War stuff." Chris added.

"Yes, part of the reason the French wanted us to come on board was, they had the right place for us. Just beyond these walls is a nuclear bunker and miles and miles of corridors that string through Paris."

Looking over the expanse of the command center, Chris couldn't help but notice the similarities with the setup he'd seen in the ICE CAVE in Islamabad. Color-coded situation boards on a giant screen that stretched from floor to ceiling, ten to fifteen feet high. This time, however, everything was electronic and much, much more professional. There were no people running around like mad-hatters; instead there were nodes of people, fifty or more with multiple computer screens each beavering away without causing a ruckus or drawing any attention. A quiet, studious place.

Gene followed Chris's gaze. "These are some smart people, Chris. Mostly our guys; not to say the Europeans are not smart, but we have a fair balance. All stakeholders are represented here. There's a lot of actionable information that gets produced, but like I said, it's still early days. We're still looking for that one lead to go grab some scumbags."

Chris was cradling his injured arm, but pointed at the screen, where he saw another item he remembered from ICE CAVE. "Who is Mukhtar, Gene?"

"You'll see that in most every situation room in intelligence circles right now," his boss answered. Chris turned to face him for more information. "Mukhtar, is Arabic. It can mean "the head," "the brain," or "the chosen one," something along those lines."

Chris was a little confused by the answer. "So why the intense focus? We don't have a name to go along with that? It's not bin Laden?"

"No, but bin Laden called him out," Gene responded, with the latest CIA conjecture on the matter. "Soon after 9/11 a video emerged of him praising his attack on the US. Bin Laden's face was the only one we saw on the tape. He blabbed on about giving thanks to Allah, the usual religious rhetoric, but he turned his focus away from the camera for a second or two and thanked Mukhtar for his leadership, expertise and devotion to the cause. So, someone in his inner circle was there during the taping of his sermon, a chosen one."

Chris nodded. "One of his minions doing his business."

"We think it's more than that. The Directorate of Intelligence believes that bin Laden is like a CEO," Gene continued. "He runs a corporation, a large company that has products and services just like any other multinational. It just so happens that his expertise is terrorism. But within his organization there are multiple layers, divisions, departments, etcetera. He may be the head, but he's no expert. We don't think he's that smart. He may have sanctioned and funded 9/11, but the idea never originated with him. He didn't design it. There was an architect, a designer, a planner. A Mukhtar. We hope that the guy you face-planted in Pakistan can shed some light . . . you understand the importance of his capture, right?"

Chris didn't to respond, as their conversation ended when they both noticed a flashing red border appear around the giant screen of the situation board. One corner of the video wall flipped to an image from CNN, marked in big, bold letters: BREAKING NEWS.

Gene turned back from the window and grabbed the TV remote from the conference room table. He turned on the large screen at the back of the room and found the news story, coming out of Atlanta. They joined the story midway through the dialogue.

"*. . . once again, a story first aired by Al Jazeera reporting that kidnapped journalist Daniel Pearl has been executed. It has also come to our attention that a video of the execution has also been released; however, CNN cannot confirm at this time how accurate that claim is. We have reached out to the White House for comments but have yet to receive a response.*" The news anchor shuffled some papers around his desk, looked at the camera and added solemnly, "*We'll be right back.*"

Orchard Towers Food Court, Singapore

Hamid swiped away the biggest cockroach he had ever seen with a large plastic-coated menu from the table. He had lost his appetite while walking down to the basement, as the smell of cigarettes, alcohol, cheap perfume and puke all assaulted his nasal cavities. When he sat down opposite Mukhtar, his stomach took another turn and all he wanted to do was to get out of there.

Mukhtar was scarfing down a hefty-sized plate of pad thai and giggled when he saw the flight of the cockroach after being sideswiped by his friend. "He is only in search of a morsel, Hamid. You should sympathize."

"Why do you bring me to this hole, Mukhtar?" Hamid asked, disgusted with his surroundings. "Even this is beyond you. This place is a whorehouse."

"The best in Singapore, my friend," Mukhtar replied between slurping his noodles.

"You make light of this situation, Mukhtar? You are a fool."

Mukhtar stopped what he was doing and wiped his lips with a cheap serviette. He wasn't angry, but he didn't appreciate the words. "You would be wise to hold your tongue, my friend. Be fortunate that I am in a good mood."

"Mukhtar, please accept my apologies, I mean no disrespect, but this place—" He touched the table and regretted it straightaway when his fingers found a sticky substance. He reached for a serviette. "—why could we have not met at my hotel, or one of the many fine restaurants in the city?"

Mukhtar continued to twiddle his chopsticks around his dish. "Look around you. Look at this place. There are a hundred faces here, nobody is looking at us. We are just two more businessmen having a meal before we travel up to the floors above to be seduced by a host of Asian beauties."

Hamid shook his head. He was trying to understand the newly anointed prince of the jihad. Osama bin Laden had blessed the man and thus he could do no wrong. But while their leader lived in squalor in the caves and mountains of Afghanistan, his top man was in the West, whoring and drinking. They were traits that the Muslim core abhorred, and behaviors unbecoming of a devout practitioner. He knew it was what many in al-Qaeda leadership feared. A man such as Mukhtar who had spent too much time living in America, in University, being perverted away from the mission of Islam, besmirched by decadence, tempted by flesh and immature pleasures such as alcohol and drugs. He questioned the depth of his corruption. He was concerned for the man who may one day rule over the organization in place of the great sheik.

Mukhtar could sense the conflict that Hamid dealt with, but devalued his opinion. He had heard and nullified the rumors of his extracurricular activities outside the shroud of Islam. Bin Laden mostly ignored his methods, while they were disliked by many in al-Qaeda. It was, as he explained, a method of subversion, a misdirection of his true beliefs. He argued that in order to understand his enemies, he had to blend in, play the part, gain confidences. His party act was exactly that, an act to the untrained, to the uninitiated in the game of subterfuge.

Mukhtar took a long swig from his bottle of beer. "You must join me, Hamid. Drink with me."

Hamid raised an eyebrow. He reeled back a little from the table. "I cannot brother, please, I beseech you, do not ask me again. Do not tempt me."

"Your pious self-righteousness is your concern, Hamid. But we are here in a public place. We must look as if we fit in. If you will not drink or eat with me, then state your business and be on your way."

Hamid looked at him, hard. His leader's words were measured, neither angry nor offensive. Hamid wasn't afraid of him, nor should he have been, but he knew that out of sight somewhere one of Mukhtar's men would be lurking in the shadows, waiting for the slightest of signals to act.

"I wanted to meet with you to tell you that the Americans are close, Mukhtar. They grow bolder each day, and the Pakistanis are conceding, they are allowing them to succeed."

"You don't think I already know this? Why are you wasting my time Hamid?"

"I've come to tell you that you are no longer safe. We cannot trust our friends in the Pakistan government anymore. I know one of your men was captured a few days ago. It is a question of time before they get him to talk."

"Once again, this is no news to me. Do not concern yourself with my men; they are disciplined. A traitor lives in Lyari and we have identified him, his actions will be accounted for. But what concerns me is that the organization has entrusted you in placating the ISI. You are the one to alert us to their activities; you should have given me more warning, Hamid."

"Karachi and Islamabad have become infested with foreign agents, brother. I tried to warn you about two Saudi agents close to tracking you down. They are still there, looking for you. But my informants tell me that the ISI are happy to give the Americans low-hanging fruit. They feel that they are legitimizing their promises to assist in the war against us by allowing them access to their resources. But I have been assured, not all is being shared, my friend. We still have allies, true believers in our cause. Men we can rely on for solid intelligence." Hamid concluded.

Mukhtar didn't stir. He took a small sip of beer. He looked around the food court, at first for his man in the background, then for potential adversaries. Hamid offered something that piqued his interest further.

"You were not the target of the raid in Karachi, my friend. It was the big man that you employ."

Mukhtar frowned but pretended nothing was wrong. *So, Wahid's uncle knew of Nabeel, he's hard to miss, easy to trace*, he considered. *But who else knew of him . . . the Americans? If so then they are truly close.* He needed to change the subject before his mood worsened. "I assume the last of the money has been transferred?"

Surprised by the change of tack, Hamid narrowed his eyes, his brow furrowed. "Yes, but why do you ask?" he whispered, not needing to as the din of the food court drowned out any single conversation.

"Our next operation is close at hand. I have completed the planning. We need to pay for our services before we can commit our warriors." Mukhtar responded quietly and shifted his eyes slightly as he scoured the room.

Hamid beamed; he could not hide his joy. He knew of an Asian operation; however, he was not aware of the details; though it promised to be another praiseworthy attack against the nonbelievers. He wanted so much to ask, but this was not his place. "Our Saudi brethren have been most giving," he offered. "Since our glorious—" He let the comment fade. There was no need to mention the attacks in the United States, but still he continued. "Our friends have been most generous. Our coffers are healthy."

Mukhtar should have perked up on hearing this news, but his demeanor showed the opposite. "That is reassuring, my friend. Our allies include a fully stocked account. But I am reminded of a troublesome issue, something you mentioned triggered a question that has been on my mind." Mukhtar held his gaze on Hamid. "My good friend Abu Zubaydah, I believe that he was in possession of some credit cards when he was captured?"

"I warned about this lack of security many times, Mukhtar. But it is my understanding that steps have been taken in our financial institutions to mitigate all risks. However, the Americans have the technology to trace such things. We can eradicate the surface level, but deep down, there is a history that we may not easily erase. I hope that you are not falling into the same trap?"

Mukhtar gave the man across the table from him a look of death. He didn't answer.

"Sorry, I mean no disrespect," Hamid said, flustered. "Please forget that I asked. Sorry."

Mukhtar gave no immediate response; he let his tense body language do the talking. He watched as Hamid squirmed and sweated before him; it took him almost thirty seconds of staring before he responded. "Hamid, you have become soft, you are worrying without need. Do not become a liability to me, to our cause. For I will not take it kindly if you are the one that is being careless because your nervous disposition is getting the better of you. Normally I would take offense when you deny my offer of food and drink. However, these are unusual times. We are at war and we must be mindful of our actions, perceptions and the environments that we operate in." There was a slight pause in the conversation as he looked around the room, spotting a signal from one of his men.

Jawad started the scooter and pushed it off its stand. He fixed the strap on his helmet and waited patiently for Hamid to get into a taxi. Karim wobbled on the sidewalk of Claymore Road, pretending to be drunk but noting the car that his target was getting into. As soon as the cab pulled away, Karim straightened up and pulled out an earpiece from under his collar, then relayed the information over radio to Jawad and the other agents on the surveillance mission.

Jawad pulled out from the bushes that separated Orchard Road and the Forum shopping mall, then headed southeast, keeping a safe distance from the taxi. Over his earpiece, he heard the report from two of his team who had been in the Orchard Towers food court and were now mobile and a short distance behind him on the same road. A second radio transmission confirmed that Karim had also left the nightclub and was heading to the rental car to join in the pursuit. The small team coordinated their movements by swapping positions on the road and finding alternate routes to the target's supposed destination; the Raffles Hotel.

The two girls from the food court arrived first at the circular drive-way and made a quick reconnaissance of the Raffles Hotel lobby, but quickly dashed back out before Hamid arrived. There was nothing to report, so they split up, each looking for a vantage point to observe the target arrive and to watch for other potential meeting partners arriving at the hotel. Jawad, satisfied that Hamid was about to settle in for the night, trailed quietly along behind the taxi as it pulled in, then he also sped off in search of a viewpoint. One of his girls left her perch and marched into the hotel. She spotted Hamid heading for the main staircase and ascending to the second floor; she assumed that he was bedding down for the night. She followed him up the same stairs and along the same open hallway to his room. When he produced an access card to his room, she stopped and began searching for something in her purse. She turned her face away from him, hoping he would not recognize her from the food court. He did not. As soon as the door closed behind him, the female surveillant turned back the way she came and made her way out of the hotel.

Five minutes later, the small team convened at the Tan Kim Seng Fountain. Jawad was last to arrive. He parked his scooter and turned it off. As he removed his helmet, he noted that Karim wasn't there. He should have been.

"Anything from Karim?" he asked his girls. Both shook their heads. There was no radio communication, so he assumed that something had caught his attention and therefore could not converse. "I will wait here for him, but give me your report."

Both girls, on loan from the Malaysian government, gave Jawad the verbal after-action report as precisely as possible describing all of their activities after entering Orchard Towers. Jawad listened carefully and kept an open mind regarding the other participant of the meeting that Hamid attended. It both surprised and impressed him the level of detail the girls gave, the body language, sudden or slow movements, voices raised or hushed. The girls looked the part, young, pretty and naïve, but they were far from it. He wished that he could have these types of operatives on his staff. While they were talking, he made a note to recommend them highly to his Malaysian counterparts. But that would come later. He had too many things on his mind, Karim for one.

"Mukhtar . . . are you listening, Jawad?" asked one girl, trying to get his attention.

"What did you say?" he replied, confused at what he'd heard—and also what he'd not heard.

"Hamid called him Mukhtar," the older of the two girls stated again.

Flustered on hearing the name, Jawad's pulse started racing. "Are you sure? Mukhtar? Are you positive?"

"Yes, I was sitting close enough, I heard it more than once," the older girl affirmed. The other girl nodded in agreement.

Jawad was silent. He stared at the two girls, deep in thought, lost for words. He paced; the two girls watched him, saying nothing. His mind bounced between several thoughts at once. *Where is Karim? We have to go back . . . need positive ID . . . need a picture . . . how?* "We need to go back; we need to find him," he finally responded.

"Karim?" The younger girl asked for clarification.

"Mukhtar." Jawad spoke confidently; he had a new mission in mind. "We must get a picture, perhaps Karim has found something. Yes, we have to go back."

"What about Hamid?" the older girl asked.

"He's here for the night. He's leaving in the morning for Islamabad. Tomorrow, we can make sure he gets on a plane. We need to return to Orchard Towers, now!"

Jawad parked his scooter near the same spot as he had earlier in the evening. There were crowds of people lining Orchard Road near the Towers, and dozens of blue, white and red flashing lights belonging to the emergency services now also competed with the bright lights of the city. Jawad looked around and saw his two team members coming towards him. "Circulate," he ordered, "see what you can find out; be back here in ten minutes."

The girls split up and mingled with the crowd of onlookers. Jawad remained at his post, watching the comings and goings, hearing mixtures of various languages—but it was the unmistakable Australian accent of three young drunks sitting outside a coffee shop that captured his attention. He took a few steps closer to listen in. At first, each bragged about the women they were dancing with and the promises of sex, but the conversation soon turned to a fight that had broken out on one of the upper levels. One of them said he thought it was a bunch of Arabs going at it, but he hadn't been paying full attention, as he was too interested in protecting his newfound girlfriend—who then mysteriously disappeared when the police showed up.

The two Malaysian agents showed up after ten minutes and confirmed what Jawad had heard. The police had evacuated the towers after a fight broke out, leaving one person dead. Jawad nodded, he was tempted to raise Karim again on the radio, but he held back. Despite his concern for his friend, his thoughts turned to Mukhtar, who he thought must be anywhere but here. No terrorist in their right mind would stick around for the police to question him over a bar fight. He peered across the street to find an answer; anything to create a plan for himself and his team to move toward—but nothing was coming. His mind was a blank. His mission was to follow Hamid, who he had long suspected of being an ally to al-Qaeda; however, he lacked proof.

Hamid's insistence of letting the Americans take over the search for Mukhtar spiked his worries. What concerned him more, however, and thus spurred him into action, was a message he'd received from an ally at his headquarters in Riyadh, stating that Hamid had sent information regarding his own demise. Therefore, Jawad hastily created a surveillance mission to explore what Hamid was getting himself into. But the challenge was that he could neither muster enough Saudi agents nor technological support in a short time frame in order to mount a large enough force to cover all his bases. Two men and two women were simply not enough for the task.

Contemplating his next move, he watched in silence as two medics carried a stretcher with a limp body out of the towers. Jawad was too far away to see whose body it might be, as the police cordon prevented the curious from getting too close. As they loaded the stretcher into a waiting ambulance, Jawad spotted a uniformed police officer handing over what looked like a radio to a plainclothes officer. Both were looking at it with great interest. Jawad, suspecting the inevitable, pressed the send button on his radio twice. He got the reaction he was dreading. On hearing the radio squelch, the plainclothes officer spoke into the microphone.

"Hello, hello, who is this?"

Jawad turned to his two agents. "We are too late. Karim is lost. I need to clear this up. Go back to the Raffles Hotel. We must not allow Hamid to leave. Watch him, and report to me if he makes a move. As soon as I can get some support from the authorities here, we will take him."

Raffles Hotel, Singapore

Jawad marched into the Raffles Hotel, followed by a gaggle of Singapore Police and intelligence officers. He found one of his two agents patiently waiting in the lobby; she was looking tired and a little bedraggled, in need of sustenance and rest. It was 0435. The night manger came running out of a back office, angry that so much activity was taking place, and mortified that the police wanted a suspect in "his" hotel. He only relented to a search of a particular room because a senior police officer, whom he knew, assured him they would make no damage to the antique building, nor allow any newspaper headlines to tarnish the establishment's image.

The police deployed their teams on various exit and entry points, and a small contingent of armed officers proceeded up the stairs, manager in tow, carrying the administrative access card.

Jawad tagged along at the back of the train, being the only person in the squad of men who could identify Hamid. The night manager timidly tapped on the door and spoke as softly as a mother nursing a baby. "Good morning sir, night manager here, can you please come to the door?"

Jawad rolled his eyes. He thought it preposterous to treat any kind of suspect with kid gloves. If he had his way, he would have rolled in a heavily armed SWAT team and kicked in the door. The Saudi government would have paid for the damages a hundred times over if that's what it took to capture a suspect. But he had to remind himself that he was not in his own country. He had no jurisdiction, and he was working with people he didn't know, based on a thin story that al-Qaeda terrorists had killed his comrade and another operative was at large. It took several calls between the Saudi and Singapore governments before any action took place. But he worried that his efforts would be for naught.

The night manager daintily tapped on the door again, and in his most forgiving tone asked for the door to be opened. For good measure, he added a thousand apologies for the disturbance.

Jawad almost threw up in his mouth. He brushed past the police officers and shoved the manager out of the way, simultaneously snatching the access card from him. He opened the door, then stepped back and allowed the police to enter. Jawad turned to the night manager, who looked as if he was about to cry. He gave him the card back and shoved him down the corridor. Standing in the hallway, he heard the police call out. "Clear!"

Jawad could hear the word echoed several times as they searched each room in the suite. He knew, however, from the lack of disturbance or the sound of protestations that Hamid was not there; they were too late. Jawad entered the room and found no trace of his target; it was as if the room hadn't even been occupied. His mind came to a quick conclusion. It was the same move that he would have made. Book two or three rooms in a foreign city, but only use one. Use different names and enter the hotel before bedtime, proceed to the room that would not be used, exit furtively after a quick stop, then head to the next hotel on the list. This washing of surveillance wasn't new, but it surprised him. Hamid was playing the game; he knew exactly what he was doing, and Jawad saw the reason. He was in league with al-Qaeda.

Jawad sat down on the edge of a couch, and the senior police officer showed up and stood before him.

"What now?" he asked.

Jawad stared at the carpet and scratched his brow. There wasn't much time left. There were hundreds of hotels in Singapore. Finding Hamid would be a huge undertaking; even if he used his real name, he could be registered in a dozen places. They would not find him. There was no arrest warrant for him so he could have already left the country, the easiest way being the Singapore/Malaysian causeway at Bandar Johor Bahru. "I saw some cameras around the hotel. We can at least establish what time he left."

"Very well." The police officer turned to one of his men and gave him the order to find the security office. "Perhaps you should apologize to the manager before we proceed," he added, looking back at Jawad.

Jawad shook his head in disbelief. "Of course, of course. I was rude. I will speak with him." He wanted to do nothing of the kind. He couldn't believe the juxtaposition of elements he had to deal with. On the one hand, there was a dead foreign intelligence officer found in a whorehouse, likely killed by an international terrorist organization who were roaming the streets of the city. On the other, a culture so fearful of losing its badge of hospitality and honor that it worried about scratching a door or paintwork in a luxurious hotel. He wondered where the Singaporean mindset was regarding terrorism. A bird with its head stuck in the sand came to mind. He resolved to submit a generous donation to the historic hotel's restoration fund on behalf of the Saudi government to appease the lap-dog manager.

Under objection, the night manager relented with the request to view the camera images, which took almost an hour to sift through to see whether they held something worthwhile. Jawad saw Hamid enter the hotel and proceed up the stairs to his room. He saw his surveillance agent going about her business and then leaving the hotel. Less than twenty minutes after she left, Hamid strode quickly out of his room, took the emergency staircase at the end of the second-floor hallway and proceeded down and eventually out of the back door. He was alone. The last image that Jawad could find was a partial view of Hamid hailing a cab, but the image was obscured by street signs and foliage. He'd found his dead end, at least in Singapore.

Jawad reluctantly conceded to the failure of his mission. He sought out his two Malaysian operatives and brought them up to speed on the situation. During the debrief, it was evident that the only silver lining from the disastrous episode was that although the Orchard Towers food court was a dark and busy place, they were certain they would recognize Mukhtar again, and were willing to continue with the task to find him. He found solace in the fact that the two ladies were keen to continue their work. The two Malaysian girls also recommended a relocation to Kuala Lumpur to extend the operation to search for Hamid and Mukhtar. Their argument was that their organization, the Royal Intelligence Corps, had experience and knowledge of the activities of terrorists in the region, and their cooperation and reach extended to many other like nations and establishments.

Although sold on the idea, Jawad still had to deal with the sadness of arranging for someone at the Saudi embassy to take care of Karim Basrawi. The investigation into his death would take time; however, his body had to be transported back to Saudi Arabia posthaste, for a timely burial according to Islamic custom. It wasn't a conversation he was looking forward to having with the ambassador of the mission.

⸙

Mukhtar looked over at the Raffles Hotel from his sixth-floor room in the JW Marriott Singapore South Beach Hotel. He stood a few feet away from the window and toyed with the set of binoculars in his hands. The flashing police lights had ceased long ago, but he was still interested in the activities below. From his vantage point, he witnessed the comings and goings of a host of people—but he was waiting just for one.

The curtains, drawn to a point that hid his image from the street below, were open just enough to allow him to watch the goings-on in the bustling downtown corridor. He drew satisfaction from the fact that things were de-escalating. The more police cars that disappeared, the less focus there was on the hotel. If the police had a lead, be it for himself or Hamid, then there would have been a flurry of activity below him. Of course, there would be an investigation into the stabbing death of the Saudi agent, but he and his team would already be plying their trade elsewhere before the authorities had a notion of what really happened.

The hours passed by, but still Mukhtar waited patiently for his quarry to appear. Finally, he spotted someone who carried himself differently. A man of confidence, awareness and arrogance.

"Hamid, come," he commanded over his shoulder.

Hamid got off the couch and took the binoculars from Mukhtar. He adjusted the device to the shape of his own boney features, then adjusted the lens. "Yes, that's him." He handed them back to Mukhtar, who made similar adjustments and zoomed in.

"Jawad Halabi, we meet at last," Mukhtar sneered. He followed his enemy with the binoculars as the man got into the back of a police car. Mukhtar had no idea of where he was going, but it didn't matter. He would not use this place as a killing ground today. He was content to let Jawad live, for now. "So, this is the man that is causing us all so many sleepless nights?"

"He is very accomplished, Mukhtar. Do not underestimate him."

Mukhtar cocked his head slightly at the comment. "Why would I?" He watched Jawad leave and then moved back from the window. He threw the binoculars on a desk and took a seat on a high-back chair.

Hamid remained standing. His knees trembled a little, but he had to go on the defensive. He knew how the situation looked for him. "He disrupted Operation Najd, Mukhtar. He killed our chemist; he has killed many martyrs." Hamid tried his best to control his emotions as he presented the information.

Mukhtar sighed; he didn't appreciate Hamid's negativity. "That is of no consequence to me. Operation Najd was not my design, not my idea. I objected to it, and I was right to do so. Your voice carried some weight with the sheik for that mission. But not I. I believed, and I still do, that chemical attacks on the United States were a despicable idea. I cared not for your friend the chemist; however, I care about how disruptive this man Jawad can be. If he has followed you here to Singapore, and he has searched for you in one of your hotels, it tells me that he has the blessing of your government, and has convinced the local authorities of our presence."

"Mukhtar, I—"

"You, my friend, are compromised. These two men are the rats you wanted eradicated in Karachi, are they not? The men you warned me against."

A bead of sweat ran down Hamid's temple. Even with the air conditioning working its magic, he sweated. "He knows nothing of your enterprise, Mukhtar. His focus is Pakistan . . ."

"Yet, they are here. You are here. You brought them to me. You put our operations in jeopardy. The sheik will not take this lightly,

Hamid."

"I do not understand how they suspect me. I have been careful."

"Not careful enough, I fear," Mukhtar cautioned.

Hamid dropped heavily onto the bed. He leaned forward and placed his sweaty palms over his knees. He was afraid of Mukhtar. The man's words, once again, appeared restrained and presented no threat, but beneath his dark eyes there was a plot afoot, a reckoning that Hamid feared might make him the next victim.

"You cannot go back to your work in Karachi. Your time as a servant of your kingdom is over," Mukhtar continued, his words this time offering a tone of finality. Hamid had no answer. He sheepishly looked at Mukhtar but did not engage in his stare. He then looked down at the ground. His head was falling into submission.

After a few seconds, the taciturn Arab forced the direction of the conversation. "There is much work for all of us. The enemy may be near, Hamid, and we need depth in our defense, but there is something you can do."

"Anything Mukhtar," he piped in excitedly.

"You need to bring him to me . . . not here, not now. Jawad is too high-profile with the local authorities for us to take action. But you need to lure him back to Pakistan, where we can control him."

"Mukhtar, I fear that this is not the best course of action, we should not—"

The terrorist finally lost his cool and rushed over to Hamid, then stood in front of him with clenched fists. He needed obedience, not discussions. "Find Jawad. Assume that he is with your government here," he hissed. "Give him a story that you have found me and I wish to surrender. Tell him you have been negotiating with me for some time. Then arrange a meeting for us, draw him back to Karachi. I will extract the information I need when I have him."

Hamid rocked back. "Mukhtar, he suspects me. I cannot—"

"You will, Hamid, you will. I have complete confidence in you. Nothing will come of nothing. For that is what you have now my friend. You are a smart man, and as you have explained he is a worthy adversary. You can work this out. You can and will succeed."

Both men engaged in the art of silence for a minute. Mukhtar ru-minating scenarios, Hamid debating options with his inner voice. The Saudi diplomat tried once more to squirm his way out of the task. "What if he leaves before I can persuade him? What if he enrolls with his allies—the British, the Americans?" he pleaded.

"Then you must hurry," Mukhtar commanded, then circled around the room, as if contemplating the possibility of Jawad's escape. "You have sources in other countries, you have a network of agents. Use them. Contain him. If we cannot get him back to Pakistan, then I will send someone to get the information I need. But, you Hamid, you need to make this happen."

There was a knock at the door; it broke the tension. Mukhtar made his way over to answer. He placed his hand over the peephole. He waited patiently for a tap at the base of the door. Satisfied that the visitor had presented the code, he removed his hand and spied two of his men in the corridor. He tapped the base of the door with his foot, acknowledging the all-clear sign. He opened the portal and let his men in. "It is time, Hamid. Forgive me if I feel a little insecure at the moment, but my men will escort you to the embassy. Here we must part. God willing, I shall see you in Pakistan, my friend."

Hamid was uneasy. He hadn't had enough time to process the plan. He hadn't been able to formulate his words, his tactics in approaching Jawad. He would have to make something up; he had to buy time. But before he could ask for more, Mukhtar was exiting the room. Hamid rose to join him but one of Mukhtar's men stood in his path. Hamid sat back down and watched as the door closed, his mind was spinning in different directions, contemplating his next move. Show true obedience to Mukhtar, Osama bin Laden, al-Qaeda, and the cause—or find flight and throw himself at the mercy of the Saudi government, confess all?

Contemplating his options and looking at the two foreboding men in the room with him, he chose the former.

CHAPTER FIVE

Alliance Base, Paris, France

ALMOST A WEEK HAD PASSED since Chris arrived at the Alliance Base. At first things were intense, hectic and intriguing. He had learned a lot in a short time; however, there was still so much for him to comprehend, devour, and soak in. One of his greatest challenges was being given only heavily redacted information to work with. His job was to get his rendition teams in place along with logistics and resources, in two places simultaneously. One, the pick-up site; and second, the drop-off location. To add to the complexity, and hence the chief reason for his working in a multi-agency environment, was establishing if a subject captured by an Alliance nation would be handed over to the CIA for rendition. Challenging these requests were the French and German governments, adamant in their stance that citizens of their countries would not face extradition or harsh interrogation methods; however, other foreign nationals were fair game. Chris was fortunate that Gene, who was engaged at the political level, gave the SAD team notification of actionable operations, thus negating him from the mud-slinging office bun fights.

Though Chris had settled into a routine at his new post, he was getting a little bored with the minutiae, lame tasks, and frequent false starts. He often complained to Gene about time, resource and monetary waste, but the argument for pursuing every lead and the "gloves-off" mentality of the CIA needed to prevail—not his penchant for impatience. The CIA checkbook was open, however, Gene told him, and as long as there was an audit trail, it would justify everything Chris might want to spend funds on. As the days droned on, the mystery of Mukhtar's true identity was the only blip on his otherwise sedentary radar.

There were some times at the base that Chris had little to do but watch and wait. During those periods, he formed bonds with new colleagues, both American and other nations. He was eating healthy food regularly, sleeping well, and slowly getting fit again. After being checked out by the on-site medical staff, he determined that his body was indeed healing. He wasn't able to run yet, but he'd made good use of the stationary bike and weights at the gym, as well as the swimming pool, and the indoor shooting range to bring his skills back up to par. When he left the confines of the DGSE headquarters, he never left alone and often spent time with the German intelligence team or other small groups with the French, Spanish, American and British contingents. For all his frustrations at being a desk jockey, he was actually feeling good about himself again. He'd began talking to Sandy, though he still had a hard time convincing her to visit him in Paris. She said she was open to a vacation—as long as he could commit to being there with her in both body and mind, but she was uncomfortable visiting a non-English speaking country, she claimed it was out of her comfort zone. He wasn't so sure if she was telling the truth, or if she was still mad at him from the cancelled yachting vacation, so he chose to retreat from the battle and pushed no more.

With his body healing, he fought a relentless clash with his mind. He tried his best not to focus on the boredom or negativity surrounding the base's lack of progress in finding Mukhtar, and searched out something to keep him focused.

Chris found one positive aspect of the activities conducted at the base: each of the investigators worked assiduously and carefully. Not being trained as a sleuth, he found it refreshing to understand the FBI's approach to the challenges of finding terrorist perpetrators. It was to let the evidence lead the way. But you had to work with what was in front of you, and then get more. It was only when there was no more information available that people needed to worry. To Chris, it mattered not that he was bored or underutilized; everyone else around him was as frantic as a dog digging a hole on a beach. However, as methodical and sound as this process was, Chris realized that there was a flaw in the law enforcement agency's idea: it was reactive. The FBI was expert at investigating crimes, finding suspects, accumulating evidence, and presenting findings to prosecutors—but what they couldn't do was to stop terrorism from happening. It was the bug bite that Chris had to ignore. He wanted to be back on the rendition teams, wanted to be the first through a door, first to slap PlastiCuffs on some piece of shit and drag him off for questioning. He wanted to stop the terror. But from the confines of a basement desk and a by-the-book boss, he, like the search for Mukhtar, was stuck in the mud.

———⦿⦿⦿———

Chris was quite pleased with himself. He took a chance on an early morning run around the track at the DGSE compound. He jogged for the first lap, just under a quarter of a mile, then walked for the second, then jogged the next two. His condition and stamina were fine, and his bones, although creaky, plagued him just a little. Confident that he could improve on his next outing, he took a break before a casual thirty-minute swim. He arrived at his desk at 0645. Ten minutes later, the dam broke.

Gene, with other SAD team members, stopped by his desk and dragged him into a conference room.

"All hands on deck," Gene commented to nobody in particular, as everyone took seats at the oval table. "There was a lot of activity overnight and we have a ton of work to do. Here's what we know so far. There were plots to attack the US Embassies in Paris, Yemen, and Albania. On top of this, though I haven't been able to confirm it, the Belgians are tracking something down near or at NATO headquarters—"

A CIA Operations officer butted in through the door; he held a piece of paper in his hand.

"—Turkey, armed suspects arrested near the American Research Institute in Istanbul."

Gene was about to say his thanks, but the man had already left. So he took a seat, then turned his focus back on his team. "Okay, looks like things are developing quickly, not just here, but there have been some other activities around the world. Local authorities in Singapore, Sydney, Pretoria and Jakarta have informed US Embassies that there are credible threats in those countries against US interests, which are now being investigated. The British and French are also being notified of similar situations at some of their locations. It seems like we've poked the right hornet's nest."

"Why now? what's changed?" Chris asked.

"Could be a few different things—the arrest of Zubaydah in Pakistan for one. Maybe al-Qaeda is flexing, or making a show of prowess to let us know they're still there and a threat. It's too early to say if these threats are realistic or past the planning stage, and if we have successfully interrupted the execution phase. We may find that out in the next few hours. There will be a lot of information to process before we can really know, but that's not our job. We have other stuff to worry about."

"Who can we get, Gene?" Ronnie Burch, a team member asked.

"Good question," responded Gene. He looked down on the floor a moment, contemplating his next words. He looked back up to answer the question. "I know who we can't get. If the French have anyone in custody, forget about them. They won't let us touch them."

"Not the Brussels cell either," Burch supposed.

"You're probably right, so let's not focus on that too much. But Ronnie, I need you to stay close to our sources here in case someone comes to their senses and lets us have a crack at them." He paused for a second as if in deep thought. He turned to the only female in the room. "Cassie, I need you to work with the FBI. The last thing I want is someone to get extradited to the US without our knowledge. I know what you're thinking, the FBI wouldn't do that, but our rendition strategy isn't flavor of the month with them, and they get pissed off when we abscond with someone they want to talk to. What goes around comes around, so stay close and let me know if they make deals with our foreign cousins."

"Roger that Gene," Cassie obediently replied.

"Yemen, Albania, Turkey, that's a go. If there are bad actors to be had, we want them. Chris, I want you to lead the charge on that." Gene saw his employee's face light up, but he put the brakes on straightaway by pointing to the desk. "From here."

Gene was right. But when he saw Chris slump his shoulders in defeat, he tried to pick him up a bit.

"All these happy faces with nothing to do are now assisting you, Chris." Gene noted. "Get the teams mobilized. I need to know your rostering for our air and ground assets, but keep in mind, kid gloves for individuals from Europe. I'm giving you Yemen as a bonus, not because I like you, but because our other rendition efforts in other parts could use a break. The Salt Pit and Bright Light are open for business, so let's start shoving people in that direction. Tier 2 suspects, Salt Pit; Tier 1 Bright Light."

Gene had given Chris the go-ahead to render actual terrorist suspects to CIA black sites. While he was happy being able to contribute at a high level, he still would rather have been out in the field, twisting body parts into compliance. "I know its early Gene, but how many are we talking about? Do you need some of us to go out there?" he fished.

Gene remained passive, though he had to chuckle a bit inwardly at yet another of Chris's incessant attempts to get his old job back. *I'm not biting that one, good try.* "You answered your own question, Chris. It's too early to know how many we have to deal with . . . and no. Let's meet back here in an hour. I may have more updates, but don't bet on it. If not, we'll meet here on the hour every hour until we have a handle on it—and that means everybody. Stock up on your sugar everyone, we are here for the duration."

Three hours into Chris's task, Gene showed up at his desk and looked over his shoulder. He didn't say a word, and just looked at the screen Chris was working on, then picked up a few sheets of paper from the nearby printer. "This the latest?" he asked.

Chris nodded and continued to beaver away at his computer.

"There's a lot of moving parts here," Gene noted. "You're doing a fine job, Chris."

"Be better on the teams," Chris fumed.

Gene picked up on the tone. He wanted his employee to remain focused, but not down in the dumps. "You are on a team, Chris. Don't fuck this up—you're making a difference here."

Chris wanted to say more on the subject; but he knew he'd planted the seed. It was up to Gene to let him loose, and he didn't seem inclined to do that anytime soon, but still Chris wanted to talk. He changed the subject. "I was talking to one of the Ops guys earlier, guess they have a live one," Chris offered.

"Was he asking for something?"

"No, I asked him what was going on in his world," Chris reported. "He said that the German guy that everyone was looking for is close to getting picked up."

Gene read one report in his hands and answered without looking at Chris. "Yeah, that's one of those political shitballs that we can't touch. The glamour boys at Ops want the glory, but it's going to be a combined effort with the French taking the lead, although he is a German national."

Chris was curious. "Because he's on French soil?"

"Going to be. The Spanish have him under surveillance in Madrid; expected to arrive in Charles de Gaulle Airport tonight. The Spanish have their eyeballs on five others, the German guy may be the cell leader, don't know yet."

"Nothing for us again, then?"

"No Chris, but I'm trying to get us a look in. We might get some leads out of him for some of this other stuff we're working on. I don't want us dropping in guys to locations where there isn't anyone to pick up. We don't know how deep this guy's knowledge is."

"I'm not stopping what I'm doing, right?" Chris wanted Gene to say no; he wanted another more important assignment—but knew the answer before Gene replied.

"Right. Leave the strategy to the amateurs, we professionals will work on logistics."

Gene continued to flip through the paperwork he'd picked up from the printer. "By the way, next time you're on a break, stop by the British desk. There's someone over there who'd like to chat."

The comment piqued Chris's interest. "Trimble?"

"Yeah, he's busy, but so is everyone around here; he was asking about you."

"He'll have to get in line for an autograph."

Gene dropped the papers he was reading, sighed, and shuffled away. "Always a smartass Chris, always a smartass."

Chris smiled and carried on writing a report. He was looking forward to meeting up with a friend, even if he was from MI6.

Engrossed in trying to decipher a CIA flight plan from Yemen to Afghanistan, Chris had lost track of time. He was used to seeing shadows come and go behind his back, and could ignore conversations, whispers or curses flying around the office cube jungle, until he heard someone clearing his throat directly behind him. He turned around to see his friend standing there.

"Hello Guy, nice to see you mate," he said genuinely.

Guy Trimble reached out his hand. "Chris, you look well. How are you keeping?"

"Me? Fit as a butcher's dog. How are you? What brings you down to the dungeon?"

"Bit of a flap going on all over the place, I'm afraid. Same as you and the French, lots of wogs giving us a hard eye, you know the drill. Everything has to be looked into and people need to be dragged over the coals . . . I'm surprised seeing you here though; what did you do to deserve the shackles?"

"Ugh, don't get me started Guy. It took me forever to wriggle out of our last adventure in Pakistan. If we get time, we'll go for a beer, shoot the shit, I'll tell you what I can. I'm just trying to organize our troops to make sure we get a few fish with all these pickups; the list of arrests is getting bigger, which means all the more paperwork I have to shovel . . . it's not all horrible though. Some of it gets pretty intriguing, complex."

Guy threw out an interesting tidbit to feed Chris's obvious interest. "They got that German guy."

Chris nodded and smiled; happy another idiot was in handcuffs. "What's the deal there, anyway?" he asked.

"German national with a Polish background. Christian Ganczarski," Guy answered, then continued to fill in the gaps. "Apparently, a bit of a holy warrior. A Muslim convert, spent some time in Bosnia and Chechnya, got a bit of a reputation while he was there. He led a few operations, got his hands dirtied. Anyway, the DGSE and your operations guys picked him up about an hour ago. They're looking at him for the Tunisian synagogue bombing. He could be the cell leader; nobody is quite sure yet. The Spanish took five of his chums in, but that almost went pear-shaped. Two of their guys got injured in a bit of a brouhaha."

"Where is he now?"

"Nice try Chris, but the CIA can't have him. He's locked up in Fresnes Prison, here in Paris. The froggies will have first crack at him, then the Germans."

"You know he's going to follow the standard procedure, Guy."

"What, keep silent for forty-eight hours so that his chaps have time to leg it and regroup?"

"Yup, but you know—"

"Your rendition teams—" Guy pondered the thought for a second without answering fully.

"Why not?" Chris carried on. "Don't look at me, but I heard some of our people have some persuasive ways of getting people to talk."

Guy knew Chris's statement was true. The CIA could easily break the prisoner of the habit of periodic silences. But he needed to slow his friend down. "Steady on, old bean, we shouldn't be having this conversation. The Frenchies have him, so let it be. They need to be showing a measure of success; this whole Alliance thing needs to be a win. Allowing Ganczarski to fall into one of your black holes would not go down too well. Although the operation to pick him up went relatively smoothly, it will only be a matter of time before his family starts banging on doors asking where he is. A CIA black site is not an answer anybody's government wants."

Chris raised his hands in submission. "I know, I know. I was just trying to . . . never mind." Chris admonished himself. He wasn't sure what he was trying to do, or prove, but he realized that he was over-stepping. He wanted to get things back on track. "Live video of the interrogation?"

"Yes, I believe so, Chris. Some of your chaps will be allowed to watch from here."

Chris nodded. He thought he could at least wrangle a seat at the table for that one. "You said he was German; how many languages does he speak?"

The question slightly confused Guy. "Don't really know, he must have some capability, something Middle Eastern possibly. Why do you ask?"

"Well, if the French start in on him in English, he will lie pretty easily. He'll waste even more time. I would say let the Germans in first. If German is his first language, then get him comfortable with that, and have a Polish speaker on hand as a backup." He could see that Guy was still a little perplexed. He explained himself further. "It's easy to lie in another language, especially if you're hooked up to a lie detector."

"You can't beat a lie detector that easily, Chris, surely?"

"No, that's not what I am saying. They're probably not going to hook him up, anyway. What I am trying to say is that your brain has an automatic delay when it comes to speaking other languages, it is like a computer, it still needs to process information and spit out a response. It may be milliseconds, but there is a bit of a lapse. If you are asked questions in your own language, you are likely to answer quicker and more truthful."

Guy pondered the statement in silence for a few seconds, arms folded across his chest, his head moving from side to side in deep thought. "I will have to take that one under advisement Chris. I'm not so sure. But you have me thinking. I'll run this past our boys and see what they think . . . but thanks for the tip, I'd never thought of that."

Gene surfaced from around a corner. "What are you two girls talking about?" he teased, though clearly, he was doing a bit of a check-up.

"Mukhtar," Chris answered quickly.

"Uh-huh, really. Any epiphanies, something illuminating?" Gene looked at him, then Guy.

"No . . . no, nothing new Gene." Chris offered.

Gene could smell the bullshit from a mile away. "You know, one of these days, the three of us are going to sit down and really talk about what happened in Pakistan last year." Gene referenced the time that Chris ducked out of his normal duties on an unsanctioned mission with the MI6 officer and a Saudi intelligence officer, resulting in the deaths of three al-Qaeda operatives and a substantial fire at a textile company in Karachi.

Chris could tell that Gene was ruminating on something. He jumped at the slight break in the conversation. "I heard that they have a guy in custody, Gene, the synagogue bombing?"

"You trying to change the subject again Chris?"

"Can we get a look in?"

"Get back in your box, Chris, that's seventy-five pay grades above you. Stick to your desk and the tasks I've given you." Gene exchanged glances between the two men standing in front of him. "I know you two are friends, and normally I would tell you to make out on your own time, but I prefer it if I could keep my eyeballs on at least one of you. That way I know that somebody isn't being hurt or dying on a street in some shithole that I have to clean up." He focused on Guy for a second. "Nice seeing you again. I can't tell you what to do, or where you should and shouldn't be, but do us all a favor and keep out of his business." Guy could feel the tension. Gene wasn't messing around. He looked at Chris, who gave nothing away with his body language.

Gene stood behind his employee and dismissed Guy without saying so. "We have a meeting in five. You ready, Chris?"

Gene strode off, Chris picked up his notepad and whispered to Guy. "Let's go for a pint as soon as we can."

His friend nodded, then quietly whispered, "I have some news about your brother."

<hr />

"Bojenga!" Gene repeated for Chris, as if he hadn't heard it the first time. Chris shrugged his shoulders.

"What does it mean?" Gene pushed.

"How should I know? It's not German, if that's what you are asking?"

Seated in a conference room, Gene, Chris, and five other members of the renditions team listened and watched a live feed from the interrogation of Christian Ganczarski. Chris smiled; it satisfied him to see that there were multiple interrogators on hand—French, German and Polish. True to form, the obligatory forty-eight hours had passed, and the captive was singing.

Chris was offering paraphrased translations for his team. There was no immediate need to, as the transcripts of all the conversations would be available from the prison in due course. But Gene wanted to have his team prepared on the off chance the prisoner let something important slip.

"I have something on a *Bojinka*, Gene," one of the team members claimed, as he hacked at a laptop. Gene's eyes lit up as if he remembered where he'd placed his lost car keys. He turned around to listen to the man, who continued, "—1995, Ramzi Yousef and Khalid Sheik Mohammed. Blah, blah, etcetera, etcetera, plotted a three-phase operation, code name: Bojinka. It involved a plan to assassinate the Pope, crash a plane into CIA headquarters, and blow up eleven airliners in Asia that were heading to the US. The entire enterprise was funded by bin Laden . . . Yousef captured in Pakistan . . . there's a ton of information here, Gene, I'm not even scratching the surface."

"But he's saying **Bojenga**, not **Bojinka**," Chris interrupted. "Wait—" Chris listened more to the questioning. "—He just said that Bojenga gave him the order for the synagogue bombing."

"Now who the hell is that?" Gene asked nobody in particular. The team continued to listen in to the interview, with Chris translating the important pieces.

It took another thirty minutes before the computer researcher piped up again. "Here's something interesting. When Yousef was in captivity, the FBI monitored his calls. Nothing new there, but he was speaking Baluch and was passing on coded messages to a Bojenga. Instructing him to torture and kill an informer. The FBI surmised that Yousef had found out who had betrayed him and wanted Bojenga to take care of them. But get this . . . Yousef also instructed Bojenga to attack the US embassy in Qatar or other similar soft targets as a retaliation for his and other terrorist arrests."

Gene sighed at the news. "Yeah, it's coming back to me, old history, but it seems relevant now. If this Bojenga was active in '95, and he instigated the synagogue bombing in Tunisia, then he's a player we need to get our hands on. There are two questions that come to mind: who is he, and what the hell else has he been involved in since 1995?" He scratched his ear, then rubbed his eyes. He sat in silence with his eyes closed. Chris ceased his narrative, though he still listened in to the interrogation.

After a minute, Gene got up. "I remember this shit. It took forever to unravel," he offered to his team. "The Pakistanis dragged their feet in getting us the translations. Neither the CIA nor the FBI had people or anyone else in the intelligence community who could speak this sheep-dip. They didn't even need to code their conversations; it was like the Navajo code talkers in World War II. Nobody could figure it out. Still to this day we struggle with some of those central Asian languages and it will be our undoing." He didn't need to explain to his team what he was doing. Everyone in the room could tell he was fed up and tiring. He made a move to leave, but Chris, getting up from his own chair, halted his boss's progress. He too wanted to run his thought process by anyone who would listen.

"I'm trying to wrap my head around this, so help me get this straight," Chris began. "Bojenga ordered the attack in Tunisia on the synagogue, for which al-Qaeda claimed responsibility. Bojenga has been around at least since 1995, so we know he's probably a big player. I realize that all roads lead to bin Laden and that is the priority focus. But we also have Mukhtar, who may be bin Laden's new best buddy, who may or may not have orchestrated 9/11. So, I guess my question is, do we have two top bin Laden lieutenants on the loose getting ready for the next spectacular? Are they just getting started?"

Everyone stared back at him blankly. Nobody spoke for almost a minute.

Gene took in a deep breath, then issued an order. "Someone get me a list of all terrorist attacks since 1993, focus on al-Qaeda. Look for all relations to Yousef, the first World Trade Center bombing, Bojinka . . . Bojenga, you all know what I mean." He looked at the confused faces around the table. "I know we have analysts to work this shit out down the hall and that's where I'm headed. But I want us to get a leg up. I need to know who Bojenga is. Chris, stay here. If that shithead mentions Mukhtar I need to know. I'm going to find someone who's smarter than me."

Royal Thai Air Force Base, Udon Thani, Thailand

Alex stood back from the hospital bed and watched as FBI Agent Ali Soufan softly rubbed a cube of ice to Abu Zubaydah's dry and chapped lips. The terror suspect was now medically stable; as such he was cuffed by both wrists to the bed frame, lest he try to leave his bed of his own accord. The terrorist thanked the man in Arabic for his kind gesture.

One of only a handful of FBI agents who was a native Arab speaker, Soufan had been on hand to accompany the CIA and their prisoner out of Pakistan. It was the first time to his knowledge that the CIA and FBI had collaborated on prisoner interviews, but it baffled him because his instructions were merely to accompany the CIA and observe the interrogation. Though he didn't complain, he hadn't expected to be holding hands with a terrorist or be the prime investigator.

Arriving in Thailand, six days ago, he realized that things were not as smooth as they seemed. The CIA interrogators hadn't arrived, and the dilapidated facility they were in, slated to be a CIA black site, was still under renovation. To compound the mess, the powers that be back in Washington were still at odds over who should take the lead in prisoner interrogations—hence further delays. One day the CIA were to lead; the next it was the FBI.

At a time when the men that mattered on the ground needed guidance, there was little on hand in the way of jurisdiction and authority; so, they made do as best they could. Alex was not an interrogator, per se; his job was strictly rendition, security, and team medic. It was out of his purview to get involved in any questioning, so he stood in silence, watching the FBI agent work, waiting for his next set of instructions.

Ali Soufan had rarely left Zubaydah's bedside the whole time they had been at the base. At first, he had not pushed the terrorist for information, not that he could anyway. The terrorist fought long bouts of pain and general discomfort from his wounds that made any structured questioning difficult. As such, he merely acted as a translator for his medical needs and basic humanitarian comfort, gaining his trust and confidence. Soufan's approach was to tread lightly and give him the assurance that he was there to aid in his recovery, but also to make him realize that he was in captivity and questions were going to be asked; that lying was futile.

Soufan laughed the first time Zubaydah denied who he was. The FBI agent countered this by giving the captive his own life story, which the terrorist rejected by stating that the profile he described could have been anyone—until Soufan called him a childhood name only his mother used.

Confident that they had correctly identified Zubaydah, the agent became frustrated when building his case profile as the terrorist blamed his cloudy memory on the medication he was prescribed, and would become drowsy and unresponsive, halting any progress. During these down times, Soufan swapped out babysitting duties with his colleague and chatted with the CIA at the base, noting that it was slowly coming together.

Alex liked Soufan and his approach with the prisoner. When Zubaydah was asleep, though, he offered him a word of caution outside of the room. "You may be running out of time."

Soufan looked at the tall CIA officer, whom he thought of as cordial and professional, not a threat. The comment intrigued him. "How so?"

"Look around you . . . all this stuff." He looked toward the hallways full of wooden crates and black equipment boxes, the types used by roadies at concerts.

"They're rushing to get things in place. As soon as it's done, you'll be out."

"I've hardly started!" Soufan replied, surprised and defensive. "I'm not going to be rushed, and definitely not by you. The FBI still has jurisdiction over this subject, not the CIA . . . I'm not going anywhere."

"I'm not the one you need to be worried about Ali. We're not having this conversation, by the way, and I'm not the enemy. I really don't care who's in charge of this, believe me. I don't care much for DC politics either. But like you, I want answers and I want to stop the next attack—and that's what the CIA's focus is right now, stopping the next 9/11."

Soufan and Alex stood face to face, arms crossed across their chests, both sets of eyes narrowed in focus. Soufan didn't reply.

"My gut tells me that you're going to be overruled and put on a plane, sooner rather than later," Alex stated quietly. "If you want your pound of flesh, your next lead, your crucial piece of evidence, you need to get moving and you need to make it fast."

Ali Soufan couldn't figure out if the conversation was an official warning or merely a concerned professional airing his opinion. He kept his own thoughts to himself, nodded his thanks and walked away, but he knew Alex was right. He saw the signs; he'd heard the hushed conversations in the corridors as new CIA officers appeared, then disappeared as soon as they saw him. Alex was the only constant face he trusted. Soufan wasn't familiar with what exactly a CIA black site entailed. His law enforcement personality told him he should know, but his soulful, caring persona told him it would be better not to.

Realizing that Zubaydah would be at rest for at least another few hours, Soufan retreated to his simple cot in a small room at the end of the corridor. He checked his pillow and thin blanket for bugs, spiders and snakes, then rested his head. The seemingly leaden weight of his eyelids forced him into a much-needed sleep.

After some time, Alex checked to see if the snoring that he heard from outside the room was real. Satisfied it was genuine, he strode outdoors and powered up his satellite phone. After the third ring, it was answered. He continued trekking away from the building as he spoke.

"Hi Gene."

"Hey Alex, what do you know?"

"I lit the fire. Zubaydah is out of it; his meds kicked in. But I think I got the message across to Soufan."

"Good. Good job, Alex."

"I don't like this back-door shit, boss. It's not our remit."

"I know Alex; you and I have had this conversation. I understand your point of view. I know how delicate Zubaydah is, and think we both agree that we need him to survive. But like I said, those contractors who are coming in, they have a way of doing things differently, and they like their privacy. As soon as they land, the FBI is out."

"Is that official?"

"Yes, it's all coming back into our house. The FBI will get the scraps we don't want."

"That's not right. You know it, I know it." Alex understood what lay ahead, with the new enhanced interrogation techniques now in place. "I'm worried about the legalities of it all."

"Alex, this is not the time and place for this discussion. I share your concerns, but you have a job to do and I know I can rely on you to do it, right?"

The former Delta Force operator answered dutifully. It was unlike him to show any form of dissent, and the bottom line was, he followed orders. "Yes Gene, absolutely."

"Good. Twelve hours and they'll be there. Understood?"

"Roger that." Alex hung up the phone. His voice had affirmed his commitment to his job, but his psyche was forcing guilt to question his motives. He headed back to the safety of the building to escape the swarm of mosquitos that had darkened over a still pond of water nearby. The last thing he needed was a dose of malaria.

Ali Soufan returned to Zubaydah's room, looking and feeling slightly more refreshed than when he left. He carried his Jornada PDA in his right hand. He looked over and nodded to Alex, who was leaning with his back up against the window. Soufan's FBI partner was dozing in the chair next to the bed, and Zubaydah was just coming out of his stupor.

Ali placed his PDA and a notepad on the bed, poured some water into a plastic cup and offered it to the patient by putting a straw in his mouth. The movement caused the other FBI agent to wake up. He never uttered a word, but watched as his colleague care for the injured man in the bed. He heard Ali ask Zubaydah if he was ready to look at some photos. The detainee nodded, wishing to comply.

Ali powered up his device and scrolled to a set of mug shots of terrorists from all over the world that he had uploaded from his laptop. Not all were al-Qaeda suspects. He asked Zubaydah to help identify two men involved in the 1998 US Embassy attacks in Kenya and Tanzania, hoping that amongst the faces he would point out the two the FBI were looking for.

Not long into the interview session, Soufan stopped the proceedings as Zubaydah tensed up and held his breath. To Ali's disappointment the photo that Zubaydah hesitated on was not the one he was hoping for. The picture was of the Kuwait-born Khalid Sheik Mohammed. "No, no," he started. "Don't waste our time Abu, after all that we have been through in the last few days. I thought I could trust you, and you me. Don't lie to me."

"Please, please I am not lying to you," Zubaydah insisted. "That is Mukhtar."

Alex bristled and stood up from his perch, inwardly thinking, *Holy shit!*

"I know all about him," Soufan bluffed, then continued. "He is not the one I am looking for; he is of no importance. I need you to identify the men in these pictures."

Alex couldn't tell if this was a ploy. He kept his mouth shut, but wondered, *What the hell is Soufan doing?*

The FBI agent continued to scroll through the pictures. He finally stopped on images of the men that the bureau had suspected of being linked to the embassy attacks. For the next fifteen minutes, they directed the interview session towards the two men, their motives, their locations, their actions, their connections, and the crux of the matter— their future intentions.

Soufan and his FBI colleague, content that they had finally made some progress, scrolled through more data on the PDA and were so engrossed in their hushed discussion, they did not hear Zubaydah's question. "How did you know about Mukhtar?"

"What?" Soufan asked with a quizzed look on his face, "What about him?"

"How do you know that he was the mastermind of September eleventh?"

Soufan played it cool. Deep down he felt like he was falling off a waterfall, his mind racing, trying to comprehend the rush of the new information. "I have told you many times, when I ask you questions, I already know the answers. But thank you for being honest, I really appreciate your help on this, Abu. Thank you." Soufan stood from his chair next to the bed. He collected his things and moved away from the prisoner. "I think we have done enough for now. You need some more rest; we shall leave you in peace, perhaps we can continue this later."

Ali and his colleague left the room, with Alex following close behind. The trio marched quickly down the corridor without saying a word to each other, Ali charging forward, looking for a quiet spot.

Once out of Zubaydah's earshot, Ali turned to the group and looked as if he could have kissed the Devil himself. Alex, too, was beaming. The other FBI agent was bouncing off the walls, smiling like he had just single-handedly won the Super Bowl.

"Can you believe that—" Soufan asked nobody in particular as he paced in a circle. "Can you fucking believe that?" he repeated, then turned his attention to Alex with both hands on his hips, his eyes looking left, right and everywhere else as he tried to compute the ramifications of the news. "Just a few days ago, the CIA didn't believe who he was, now . . . now, this guy gives us Mukhtar, the architect of 9/11. This is huge, guys, huge."

Alex wasn't catching the warm fuzzy feeling though. He was happy and still processing the enormity of the news, but he was a little more pragmatic; there was still an outstanding question to answer. "Ali, I hate to bust your bubble," he began, ". . . but where do we find Khalid Sheik Mohammed before he hits us again?"

Abu Dhabi, United Arab Emirates

Khalid Sheik Mohammed rode in the rear of the blacked-out G-Class Mercedes-Benz. Sitting to his left was one of his financial benefactors. Mukhtar, as he was known to the investor, listened to the land developer discuss the plans for a site in Abu Dhabi he called Yas Marina. His chauffeur drove cautiously along while a bodyguard, from the passenger seat, scanned all around for imaginary threats.

"Here will be the Ferrari World," the developer explained, "and directly behind it will be a shopping mall, restaurants, cinemas, and many entertainment venues."

Mukhtar wasn't particularly interested in seeing the development; however, it stirred his interest to hear that the Formula One Group had sanctioned plans to build a racetrack on the spot. He let his host carry on with the tour as he pointed out mounds of dirt and sand. "In the distance there we have plans for a harbor, a medical center, hotels, apartments. All very high-end, I assure you."

Mukhtar offered a dainty, polite response to the comment. "It is a huge undertaking, and I see that you have a daunting task ahead. But you have accomplished a great deal already, my friend."

"Indeed, but I am not alone in this endeavor. We have many investors, and of course the initial capital investment will be high, but the rewards will be substantial. I believe the deal for Ferrari's involvement is quite close. It is an exciting time in the emirate."

Mukhtar nodded and provided a wan smile for the tour guide. His mind was elsewhere. Something about this development triggered his operational mind. *Leverage, leverage; perhaps an interesting target one day?* "Tell me, my friend," he asked. "How many visitors do you expect when the racing begins?"

"We will have a capacity for 60,000 race enthusiasts, my brother. But that may fluctuate with other events leading up to and after the races. I am told there is a possibility of attracting some major music stars from all over the world."

"I assume from the Muslim world . . ." Mukhtar started.

"Of course, of course. But the Yas Marina will be an invitation to all; we want to open our country to everyone."

How liberal of you, you . . . pig. Westerners and whores, but a stone's throw from Mecca. How dare he promote this blasphemy, Mukhtar seethed silently. Then he complimented the man again. "I must congratulate you and your government in taking this step. It is wise to progress my friend, especially now that your country needs these investments for the future of the country and your people."

"Yes, God willing, we will be blessed with a fortuitous outcome, a spectacle worth being a part of—"

Mukhtar was tiring of the snake-oil salesman. He was only glad that he didn't have money to be shaken down by the camel trader. However, he needed the man. His investments to the cause were reason enough for Mukhtar to pay a visit occasionally, to stroke his ego and to request more. But Mukhtar didn't like the big picture of things. He feared that the idealist would shy away from al-Qaeda once his money became tied up with huge projects such as the vision under consideration. Mukhtar, however, saw an opportunity to dull the shining star of Yas Marina, if he didn't get his money. Just then his phone rang, interrupting his tour guide. "Please ask your man to stop the vehicle," Mukhtar said. "I must take this call in private. I'm sure you understand?"

"Of course, of course."

The driver stopped in the middle of a sand patch close to the water's edge. Mukhtar got out and paced fifty feet away from the vehicle. He was hot, but the call was more important than the momentary discomfort. He strolled closer to the water. "Wahid, tell me my friend."

"Everything is in place, Mukhtar."

"Excellent." He looked at his watch. "Tell them to proceed. When it is done, wait six hours and release the statement. You must not forget who's writing that is; it is important to remember, Wahid."

"Yes Mukhtar, I understand."

"God is Great, my friend. God is Great."

Mukhtar heard the young man repeat the words, then hung up the phone. He snapped the flip phone in two pieces and dropped them both into the water. He looked at his watch again, then turned to the south in deep thought. He ignored the heat and the beating sun as he pictured his attack team moving into action. He heard a call from the back of the Mercedes; it was the investor beckoning him to get out of the sun. Mukhtar nodded but did not reply. He trudged slowly back to the coolness of the vehicle, his mind still picturing the blue waters of the Arabian Sea.

Fresnes Prison, Paris, France

FBI agent Mary Wright studied Christian Ganczarski through the one-way mirror. She'd been at the Paris prison for almost three hours, but she wasn't yet ready to take part in the ongoing interrogation of the terror suspect. She watched and waited patiently, trying to identify his bluffs, his lies, partial lies, truths, or half-truths. It was doubly difficult with the delay in translations to her side of the interview room. The questions were asked in German, then translated in the observation room into English and French. It was a time-consuming affair which no one enjoyed; however, the suspect knew that the evidence against him was stacked high, so his willingness to talk was refreshing.

There was a welcome pause in the questioning when the suspect requested a lunch and bathroom break. Mary decided her chance to interact would have to come soon after the intermission, as Ganczarski was visibly tiring and the questions were becoming repetitive, irritating him.

After the interval and the resumption of the proceedings, she continued to observe—this time focusing more on the man's body language, his nervous twitches or movements, his posture, his smile, his eyes, his feigned yawns. Ideally, she would have liked to study the man over several days, but she didn't have that luxury, and she and her FBI colleagues supposed that a time would come soon where the suspect would begin shutting down on the advice of legal counsel. Not long after he was comfortable again, she requested access.

Mary sat opposite Ganczarski. He enjoyed the female distraction. The confrontations with his inquisitors to this point were all with hard-nosed intelligence men who weren't exactly warm or comforting. But he took note of the men that had interviewed him, and he had found preferences or strategies in his captors, seeing the different styles between the nations who were interested in him. The French were the most aggressive and wanted answers quickly. The Germans were softer, but possessed the most detail. The Americans wanted the bigger picture, were well prepared, and tread much more carefully. He wondered what type of agent the nameless female was, and what her purpose of being allowed into the interview room was.

"Mr. Ganczarski," she began, "I have some pictures that I would like to show you. I would like you to identify these men for me." She laid before him three images. Although her binder was full of photos, she didn't want to overwhelm him right away; she wanted him to take his time. She watched his face as he studied the faces on the first three pictures. Calmly, he identified two of the three. It was the two Tunisian synagogue bombers. The revelation didn't surprise her.

Putting away the first set of pictures, she drew out four more images and watched his face again. He gave no reaction. She continued the exercise a third and then a fourth time, scrutinizing his face closely. She thought he was being truthful when he stated that he didn't recognize any of the subjects. The next set she produced elicited a different reaction. Of the three pictures shown, he identified Abu Zubaydah in the first picture, glanced at the second one for a moment, and then focused on the third picture. She saw a classic tell: he was flustered and had identified someone, but was hesitant to speak.

Mary took the pictures from the desk and placed them back in her binder. She asked Ganczarski some random questions about the men in the pictures; he provided answers to the German interrogator. While he was talking directly to the officer, Mary shuffled some pictures around, then presented another three images.

In this set, he identified three Tier 3 suspects. She nodded, confirming what she and others suspected. So far, he was cooperating, but she didn't want him to burn out. She drew out another set, this time including the same picture where he'd hesitated earlier. He shook his head; she removed one picture; he said nothing; she removed a second picture; no response. He looked down at the last picture; again, he had nothing to say, but this time Mary could see his eyes had changed, his posture was stiffening. She left the picture on the table. Their eyes met across the table, they stared at one another in silence. Mary knew that he recognized the face. She had to be patient; she wanted him to say something, but it had to come from him. She wanted to be alone with him in the room; it worried her that the waiting game would push someone to speak out of turn and ruin the man's decision.

"Mukhtar."

Mary kept her composure. She knew who the man in the picture was. *Holy shit, at last,* she thought. *This is big.* With her face a mask, she collected her things and made to leave the room.

"You will not catch him," Ganczarski muttered in English behind her back.

She turned to face him; he was leaning back in his chair, hands linked behind his neck, and smiling.

"How do you know we don't already have him?"

CHAPTER SIX

Gulf of Aden, Yemen

ALFONSO, THE SHIP'S COOK, WAS meandering along the starboard
deck of the *MV Limburg* with a set of headphones on, listening to a CD
of The Three Tenors. He wasn't taking in his surroundings, as there
wasn't much to see except the vast expanse of the ocean and a few
other vessels in the distance. Each heading in different directions with
multitudes of cargoes. His ship, an oil tanker, had left the port of Aden
over two hours previously and his shift in the galley was still a few hours
away. As per his tradition on all his voyages, he took advantage of the
downtime to pace the decks and soak up the sun as much as he could.

About a quarter of the way down the deck, he stopped and looked
out over the side of the enormous ship. The massive 1,000-foot-long
tanker plowed through the waters with ease. He sensed no roll or pitch
that would throw him, and if a baby were aboard, it would be gently
rocked to sleep. He wondered if the rest of the journey would be so
smooth, as the vessel was headed to the Indian Ocean and on into
Malaysian waters—known for squalls and storms; which could delay or
hinder his ship's task. It mattered not to him, however. With the Three
Tenors for company and hungry bellies to fill, he was a content
crewmember.

At first Alfonso couldn't make out the dot on the water. He trained
his eye not to look directly at the object but to use his peripheral vision.
When he did, he saw movement in the water, but it was still some
distance away. He held onto the side of the ship and concentrated hard,
for there was nothing else to do. He looked up at the bridge, expecting
to see someone with a pair of binoculars also looking at the object, but
there was not. Being the ship's cook, it was not his place to venture up

there; he'd only had the onetime pleasure of being invited to the bridge by the captain. However, he had an immediate urge to get the officers' attention somehow. He didn't know exactly what was wrong, but deep down his gut was trying to tell him something.

He raised his hand to shield his eyes from the sun and stared at the object. It was getting larger and moving quickly towards the ship. He leaned forward and as he did his heart raced; he saw a boat—a dingy, with a high-powered engine—racing towards his vessel. The two men aboard the small boat had their heads down and were holding on tightly as the craft bounced hard on the waves. To Alfonso's horror he could tell that they were not trying to veer away; they were heading directly towards the side of the hull—directly to where he was standing. He stared in disbelief, then looked up to the bridge and back down to the dingy, trying desperately to comprehend what was happening. The speed of the event confused him, making his mind fuzzy. Then things slowed down. He knew that the dingy was about to collide with the ship. He leaned over the side. Then he saw the flash of bright orange-and-red flames.

Kuala Lumpur, Malaysia

Jawad was becoming increasingly frustrated. He'd been at the Royal Intelligence Headquarters, embedded within the Malaysian Ministry of Defence, for days. The promised collaboration between the two agents he'd borrowed from the organization was at first fruitful; however, with the identification of Khalid Sheik Mohammed as Mukhtar, the international manhunt had begun and his Malaysian counterparts were no longer enthusiastic about his undertaking, they had their own country to protect. Only one of the two agents he'd befriended was available for short periods of time, until she too became hamstrung by her managers to conduct her regular counterintelligence duties and thus ordered to leave the beleaguered Saudi to his own devices. He woefully retreated to the Saudi embassy in the city for some much-needed sympathy.

After a few hours of arranging a new flight plan and generally milling around the Saudi mission, he received a summons from the ambassador. He quickly made his way to the ambassador's office, where he was greeted by the emissary himself.

"Jawad, please my friend, sit, sit."

Jawad complied with the gentle offer. He made himself comfortable while the office tea boy poured him a cup of the hot beverage. When the servant left the office, the ambassador lit a cigarette and offered one to his guest, who declined. "I understand that your search has been less than successful these past few days," the envoy began.

"To some extent, your Excellency," Jawad reluctantly replied. "But I have been able to identify some suspects with the help of the Malaysian authorities. However, I must concede that yes, my search for Mukhtar has been less than successful."

The ambassador nodded his head slightly. He sympathized with the intelligence officer, but that didn't stop him from fishing a little. "What are your next steps, Jawad?" he pressed. "I understand that your organization has given you carte blanche to conduct your . . . activities, but this seems to be a dead end of sorts."

Jawad sat up a little straighter in his chair. He wanted to promote his cause with confidence. He needed allies, not someone who felt sorry for him. "One could look at it that way. I prefer to see the glass as half full. As I mentioned, there are some new suspects that will need a closer look, but I hope that I can pick up the trail of the terrorist soon. I have other avenues to pursue to forward my investigation."

The Saudi ambassador wanted to needle Jawad more, not that he needed to, but because he was curious. He studied Jawad through his smoke. He could tell the GID officer was tiring of the seemingly endless quest and was putting on a show for his benefit. "This scourge continues to haunt us, Jawad. It seems these terrorists know no bounds."

Jawad took a sip of tea, trying to read between the lines of the ambassador's statement, and surmised that he was talking about the latest al-Qaeda attack.

"I received this earlier today," the senior diplomat finally said. He held up a sheet of paper, offering it to Jawad. "Please."

Jawad took the note and read.

By exploding the oil tanker in Yemen, the holy warriors hit the umbilical cord and lifeline of the crusader community, reminding the enemy of the heavy cost of blood and the gravity of losses they will pay as a price for their continued aggression on our community and looting of our wealth.

Osama bin Laden

Jawad's shoulders shrunk upon reading the notice. He placed the sheet back on the ambassador's desk, freeing the weighty burden as though it was as heavy as the 90,000 barrels of crude oil lost at sea from the tanker attack.

"It troubles you, I see," the ambassador noted.

"Sir, you are correct." Jawad placed his teacup on the coffee table before him and leaned back into the comfort of the chair. "This latest attack is a direct warning to the kingdom. I am no economist, but I believe this incident will cause a short-term collapse of international shipping in the Gulf of Aden. I cannot fathom the actual financial losses, but Yemen will suffer. And if another attack happens in that region, then our products will suffer too. Confidence in oil exports will falter."

The ambassador remained silent, already knowing from conversations with other Saudi ambassadors that the same conclusions had already been made.

"If we are to use the Persian Gulf for all our exports, Iran may look at this as an opportunity to strike," Jawad surmised.

The ambassador, again confirming consensus from the Saudi diplomatic community, challenged the officer. "That's quite a harsh statement, Jawad. Surely Iran has no intentions. Unless I am mistaken and your intelligence is something . . . that perhaps I am not aware of?"

"Your Excellency, please accept my apologies," Jawad cautiously explained. "I do not intend to sow discord when I have no evidence to support my statement. I was merely trying to say that bin Laden is a strategist, and the Iranians are opportunists. My opinion is that never the two shall meet, however, if both parties can come to some . . . mutual understanding, then we will indeed need to be concerned."

"Bin Laden has no desire to ally with the Iranians, nor the Iraqis for that matter Jawad, surely?"

"I agree your Excellency, but he may need the support of silent partners—others who wish to further his cause who inwardly smile at the suffering. Bin Laden has woven an enormous spider's web of sympathizers to his organization. I do not expect more attacks like this in the short term, as many eyes are watching and waiting. It will increase security in the entire region, I am sure. But I believe he will strike again elsewhere, and at targets that we will not expect."

"You may be correct in your assessment, Jawad, however, I think these types of attacks have far-reaching implications, far outside the Middle East."

Jawad was unsure of the ambassador's message. He remained silent, waiting patiently for the follow-up.

"There are those here in Asia who are becoming nervous about bin Laden's atrocities," the ambassador continued. "They worry about the intentions of the man and the organization. I agree with you that we are unsure where and when the next strike will take place, and we must all be vigilant; however, my fear is that to further his aims, attacking Muslims—while somewhat incidental to date—will not deter him from his lofty goals."

Jawad nodded at the sentiment. He was quietly content in the presence of the elder statesman. The man was, in his opinion, one of the more intelligent and well connected of the Royal Saudi diplomatic corps. Thus the reason he wished to spend time at the embassy. "Which in turn will deter investors—" Jawad began in response.

"—Quite," the ambassador interceded, while stubbing out his cigarette. He stared at his task for a second, then leaned back in his chair, forming a pyramid with his fingers under his chin. "I had an interesting conversation recently with such an investor." He paused again, then continued, "I am sure I can spare the details with you Jawad, but I have a business relationship with Petronas and some of their executives."

It didn't surprise Jawad, and the ambassador was correct: he didn't need any details about the Malaysian oil and gas giant. But he leaned in, eager to hear the news.

"One of my contacts had just returned from a trip to Qatar where he met with several businessmen in the same field. While there, someone who was looking for investments in the new Formula 1 race venue in Bahrain approached him."

"Yes, I have heard of the development, it is a huge undertaking . . . oh, I am sorry Excellency, I interrupted you."

The ambassador smiled at his captive audience of one. "As you probably know, Petronas has substantial interests in the sport. However, what interested this man was news of the tanker incident in the Gulf of Aden." The ambassador paused for effect, inspecting the cleanliness of his fingernails. "This is third-hand information Jawad, and I do not relish in gossip, however this investor rejoiced at the sight of the burning ship."

Jawad stroked his beard out of habit when hearing the "gossip," and thought: *Interesting.*

The statesman continued with the account. "My business colleague wisely distanced himself from the man, and then reported the incident to his company—who later investigated the man, just to be careful you understand. Their due diligence warranted a company-wide warning to avoid any business with the investor." The ambassador could see that Jawad was on edge of his seat, in dire need of a punchline. "It seems that our racing fan has a colorful past with investments throughout the Middle East, including projects with the bin Laden family."

Jawad hated to bust the ambassador's bubble, but he needed to clarify the statement. "There are many such men in the region, your Excellency. Even our government has used the bin Laden family's services. We cannot paint every businessman with the same brush based on name association."

"That is true, my friend," the ambassador conceded. "However, I merely wish to convey what little information I can to your cause. I am unsure if this will help you, but it is what I have to offer."

"Excellency, I am grateful for your insights, and indeed this investor has garnered my interest. I will look into the matter."

"You understand that we have to be protective of our source, Jawad. Perhaps this man was overzealous, but I believe that these are trying times for our nation and we must help the international community where we can . . . you agree?"

"Yes, I agree, this certainly warrants further investigation. And please be assured your Excellency, I am quite the model of discretion."

The ambassador stood and smiled, showing the meeting was over. He rounded his desk to embrace Jawad, who politely asked, "A name sir? Do you have a name of this race enthusiast?"

"Yes, yes, how forgetful!" he said as he scuttled back to his desk and shuffled a few papers around. He shifted his glasses from the end of his nose to the bridge, held up a small piece of paper and read the name aloud. "Faizan al Shamsi."

Alliance Base, Paris, France

The CIA SAD team assigned to renditions at the Alliance Base filled the large conference room in the basement of the French DGSE headquarters. One of the team members was passing out brown internal mail envelopes to each of the attendees.

"Okay, okay, let's settle down, sit down, stand up, lounge around. I don't care, just everyone shut up," Gene ordered to quash the chitter-chatter.

"Those are not pay raises or bonuses being handed out," he continued. "They are your new assignments. As of today, SAD renditions are no longer active in Paris. With the disclosure of KSM—Khalid Sheik Mohammed, aka Mukhtar—as the architect of 9/11 by our trusted friends at the FBI, our focus has changed. For those who worked with the Feds recently: good work, congratulations. Two of their agents got separate confirmations on his identity, but the agency is taking some credit for getting the right people in the right places to make a lot of it happen. So glad-slapping all around, but we still have to find the bastard, so let's not lose sight of that."

"Fuckin' A!" came the comment from a former Special Forces soldier.

Gene raised his hands. "That being said . . . and to the gentleman with the potty mouth, the Alliance Base will continue on without us, and we will become an as-needs-service with only one liaison officer remaining on location. Everything from here on out will be coordinated from the US—but don't be surprised if you get called back into this theater of operations in the future." Some murmurs began floating around, and Gene raised his hands again before a gossip fest got under way. "I know that some of you have been frustrated by the lack of activity, and some of you have gotten bored but—"

Someone snored loudly in the background. There were a few giggles. Gene tried not to smirk, failed, but remained on task. "Pushups for the next person who falls asleep!" He remarked, garnering a few smiles from around the room. "I was going to say before I was rudely interrupted . . . the slumber party is over. Everybody now knows who our new target is. Alec Station is still the lead to track down bin Laden, but CTC is leading the charge to find KSM. You heard it here first; KSM is the new nomenclature for cable traffic, however, Mukhtar and other aliases will be investigated. The brain trust stateside—the FBI and all those other geniuses who are putting puzzles together—agree that KSM was the architect of 9/11, however, we will not be ignoring bin Laden and the other chickenshits, so we'll have our work cut out for us."

The whispering trees started again, their leaves rustling as feet shuffled and nods were shared. Gene kept his voice in control, his emotions in check. Many people in the room had stories of lost friends or loved ones from that fateful day.

"This is not a pep talk people . . ." Gene began. He knew that this was not time to shake the pom-poms. "Everyone here knows what that means to our country. We've identified the sonofabitch, and it's going to be our job to grab his sorry ass and drag him down a dark hole. We know *who* he is, but we don't know *where* he is. Since everyone and their donkey in law enforcement from Tulsa to Timbuktu now has a photo of our prime suspect on their desks, there's going to be Elvis sightings everywhere. Especially when CNN gets wind of this. Whatever the case, we will need to react, and react quickly . . . I shouldn't have to ask anyone here for their full commitment, nor will I."

His face was grave. He was borderline emotional, but held back from showing any chink in his armor. "As the Navy Seals would say, 'The easiest day was yesterday,'" he reminded them. "But our days will never be easy. We must find this man. Our country demands it, our country needs it." He paused as he looked at his staff, all staring silently back at him. He held up his hand. "I know, I know, I said this wasn't going to be a pep talk, but I think we all know what's at stake, we all have work to do. Anyway, you all have your assignments and some of you will be looking under the bellies of snakes for this asshole, but we need to find him before some other cowboy outfit does. I know we're on the same page, but if anyone wants to stand down, let me know now." He paused briefly, not expecting a comment. He already knew that the men and women in front of him were pleading for him to shut up so they could get to the real reason they'd joined the SAD: catching terrorists.

"Before I let you all go," Gene continued, "and just as an FYI, I didn't agree to putting us here in the first place. We all knew the Europeans wouldn't allow their nationals to be visitors at one of our guesthouses, but I will say it wasn't a complete waste of time. We've made some good inroads with some of our counterparts from different countries, and I think we've been able to understand everyone's capabilities and limitations. Namely, politics and public opinion. I think with the relationships we've built, we can expect other nations to come to us for help, and yes, that is a good thing; we need the work.

"In saying that, like it or not, management thinks—and I agree for what it's worth—the Alliance program is successful, but I don't see any real legs on it, just my humble opinion. We were in the right place at the wrong time, but it's time for us to move on. Most of you are going straight back out to the field, some of you will stay here to finish out what you are working on, and some of you have earned a vacation. I'll fall on the grenade and stay here for a while longer, but I'll be back in headquarters soon enough. Let's not make a carnival out of this. Leave as you came in, no fanfare, no parties. Shake hands on the day of departure. Got it?"

Although there were more nods around the room and a few sophomoric comments, Gene sensed that his team was happy for the reassignments. There were a few questions about ongoing operations and coordination with other teams, but most everyone in the room was clear about the briefing.

Chris hadn't opened his package yet. He wondered if he was being released back into the wild. He chatted with a few of his colleagues and noticed one or two others shaking hands already. Gene came over to him.

"I've given you some time off. I know your brother is having a tough time of it, Chris. Pay him a visit. Guy has vouched for you with the UK authorities, so there shouldn't be any misconceptions. I'll see you soon." Gene tapped Chris's shoulder as he walked away, distracted by another team player in need of some clarification.

Chris opened his envelope. It was a typical office memo with various buzzwords and acronyms. All he was interested in was where and when he was headed. He was immediately disappointed—Vacation/On Call/3rd Level support. He looked around the room but was feeling like a leper. Nobody was coming over to shake his hand. He slumped down into a nearby chair, gutted once again by the news that he was surplus. The only saving grace was that he had time off, and he had previously arranged for Sandy to meet him in the UK. But third-level support was akin to being the water boy on the football field, carrying the quarterback's helmet, carrying the team's towels, and picking up the shit that players left behind. He wasn't only upset, it offended him.

Winchester, England

Chris waited patiently in the visitor's center of Her Majesty's Prison Winchester. It was a single room with four round tables, cheap orange plastic chairs, a vending machine and a window barred from the inside. In his mind it did not have the attributes of a welcoming space. Although tidy, it was sterile, administrative, boring. It was his first time visiting his brother in prison, and he had hoped that he wouldn't have to see him in this place too often. But the news from Guy Trimble, who'd secured a visit for Chris outside normal hours, troubled him.

Ten minutes had passed when the door opened. A short, stocky man entered, followed by a prison officer. The short man, who was bald, had a patch over his right eye and was wearing gray sweats. "Hello Chris," he said.

Chris, who was standing with his back to the window, gasped. He involuntarily put his hand to his mouth and took a step back. He surprised himself by his reaction. He didn't even recognize his brother. Tears welled up in his eyes. He tried to blink them away, but he was fighting an emotion that he had never had before. He wasn't sure if it was sympathy, shock, or revulsion. He felt nervous, not because he was scared of being in a small room with a criminal; but because he was concerned and saddened to see what his sibling had become. "Terry, Jesus, you gave me a shock," he said. "It's been a while." Uncharacteristically, Chris made a move to hug his brother.

"No touching!" the officer barked. It stopped Chris in his tracks. He gave the official a two-second scowl, but realized the man was only doing his job. He backed away. Confused, he wasn't sure what to do next. He searched for words that didn't come. He looked at his brother's face, then looked away. He fumbled with his jacket, he was anxious, he was . . . ashamed.

"Sit down before you fall down, you idiot," Terry dictated as he pulled a chair away from the table. Chris nervously did the same and sat down.

The officer retreated slightly from the brothers and propped himself up against a wall.

Chris finally found something to say. "What the fuck Terry . . . what happened to you?"

"It's nice to see you as well, Chris. Good to see you looking fit and healthy."

Chris rubbed his forehead, trying to erase what he was witnessing. It was hard to see his younger brother in such a state. He leaned forward in the chair, rocking ever so slightly. He averted his eyes from Terry and looked down to the stained blue carpet.

"Look at me you dickhead. I'm not going to bite you," Terry snapped.

Chris brought his eyes up and looked on sadly. He still couldn't find the right words to say to his sibling. He studied the eye patch, multiple facial scars and missing teeth, the prison tattoo on his neck. It wasn't Terry; it wasn't the boy he grew up with.

"You should have seen the other guy," Terry joked. "Missing all of his teeth when they buried him."

"What happened Terry? The last time I heard you were in for assault. Now I'm told you have a murder charge?"

"I'm a lifer, mate," Terry almost proudly announced. "I pissed off the wrong people, and I got what I deserved. It would be nice to say nobody will fuck with me again, everyone knows I got nothing to lose anymore, but you can't trust anybody in here, not even the criminals. The only way I am coming out of here is in a pine box."

Chris's stomach twisted into a reef knot. He couldn't bear to hear the news. He wanted to get out of the room, the prison, the city, the country.

"I'm so sorry Terry—"

"Sorry? Sorry for what? You haven't done anything wrong. Don't feel sorry for me if that's what you are doing. I put myself here, and that's that."

"You've aged ten years Terry; you don't look well. What the hell happened to your face? Your eye?"

"It's kill or be killed in here, mate. Don't let the nice officer behind us make you think everything is peachy—it's not. It's a fucking ape colony." Terry smiled. He was happy to see his brother, but even happier that their mother was no longer living to see what he had become. He leaned forward to whisper to Chris, "I got jumped by two blokes a while back. One of them . . . well, let's just say I had my hands on his throat for a little too long and the screws laid into me. I was in the prison hospital for a while. Anyway, I get out and a few months later I get jumped again, and this happened." He pointed to his face. "I couldn't see out of that eye too well anyway, so no big loss." His show of bravado wasn't convincing Chris, who sensed there was more to come.

There was. "Trouble is," Terry continued, "I kind of put one of the screws out of action as well. I didn't kill him, but I fucked him up good. Now they all have it in for me. But between you and me, I'm not going down without a fight."

"Terry, what the fuck are you talking about?" Chris interjected, "Let it go, let it be! You don't need any more drama."

"It may not be up to me. It used to be easy to keep an eye out for trouble, but can't do that anymore," he joked.

"That's not funny, Terry."

"If the screws don't get me first, some other fucker will have a go. If he comes up on my blind side, then bingo! That's all she wrote."

"Can we get you out of here, transferred out to somewhere else, somewhere safer?" Chris inquired naively.

"Not going to happen. They want to see me suffer for messing up one of their own. It's only a matter of time, Chris."

Chris put an elbow on the table and placed his head in his left palm. He changed position to scratch his stubble, his nose and his eyes. He was deflecting the conversation, pretending not to believe what he was hearing, seeing or feeling. His emotions were catching up with him again; he could feel tears forming. He feared the dam could breach at any moment.

Terry interrupted a potential rupture. "Enough about my misery, tell me about you, Chris. Where have you been? What have you been doing?"

"You would know if I was here," Chris replied, reprimanding himself.

"Don't go down that road, Chris. We chose different paths; I don't blame you. I've missed my big brother, but you would have pissed me off if you stuck around."

"I should have been home. I should have stayed," Chris countered.

"You can't change that now you, idiot. What's done is done. Tell me, what do you do?"

Chris wanted to tell him everything, who he had become, what he was doing, how he was doing it. As much as he wanted to, he couldn't share any of it. But he too needed an outlet, someone to talk to, someone who he could fully trust. He thought it was ironic that he had killed more men than his brother, a badge of honor he was not proud of. Yet Terry, initially incarcerated for assault, had been forced to turn into an animal to defend himself, and now he was facing the rest of his life behind bars for murder.

They talked for another forty-five minutes mainly about his home in the United States, his girlfriend, his US citizenship, his 'consulting' job, and a few other minor things. It was unfortunately a dull one-way street. Terry was inside huge walls with few stories to tell. Chris, the world traveler and CIA officer, had a wealth of tales and experiences that he desperately wanted to share. But his occupation required him to keep things vague.

Before an hour was up, the prison guard abruptly cut off the visit. "Time. On your feet, Morehouse."

Chris stood up first.

"He's talking to me, Chris. You're not in the army now." Terry stretched out his hand to his brother. "Can you come back?"

"I'm going to try Terry; I'm going to try." He clasped his brother's hand and pulled him in. He hugged him as hard as he could.

The guard intervened. "Break it up, break it up. Back to your cell, let's go."

Terry left and Chris slumped down in one of the orange plastic chairs. He put his face in his hands and cried. He wasn't sure how long he had been there, but a voice finally drew him out of his grief.

"Time's up. Be on your way; you've got to pay to stay."

Chris was in no mood for quirky comments. He dried his tears on his sleeve and left the prison without looking at anyone. He made it back to the rental car he'd left in the parking lot, and tapped on the window. The first time garnered no response. He tapped harder and Sandy woke up from her slumber. She saw Chris and unlocked the door. He got in and started the engine, then pulled away, averting his eyes from both the prison walls and the semi-sleepy eyes of his girlfriend. "How did it go?" she asked.

Chris didn't answer; he was pretending to navigate a roundabout. She let things go for a minute before she asked again.

"Chris, is he okay? What happened?"

Chris couldn't look at her. Instead, he focused on traffic. "It's not something I want to talk about, okay?"

"Fine, whatever."

The mood in the car was frigid, like a mobile ice rink. Neither wanted to speak. Both looked in different directions. She was tired and cranky; and was in the middle of her monthly cycle. He was brooding and out of touch.

Chris's mood only changed as he entered the southeastern edge of central London. "Fucking muppet!" he shouted at a vehicle that cut him off. He smashed the horn with both his hands.

"Kermit can't hear you, Chris," Sandy jabbed mildly.

Chris looked over at her and a chunk fell off his icy façade. He even smiled a little. Sandy saw an opening. "You ever noticed in those action movies and there's a car chase?" she teased. He remained quiet but let her continue, unsure of where she was taking the conversation.

Sandy became animated as she told her story. "You get a guy in a car, and it's always men by the way, because women can't drive especially if they are being chased right? Anyway, every time they get into heavy traffic or get cut off, they shout and scream, 'GET OUT OF THE WAY, GET OUT OF THE WAY!' It's like who the hell can hear them? The guy in front is listening to 50 Cent and his car is bouncing all over the place, he can't hear his own farts."

Chris's grin broadened, but she hadn't finished. "On top of that, why should they just get out of the way?" Chris shook his head. "And,

and . . . if they have a car chase in Italy, or Thailand, or somewhere foreign, who the hell can understand an American who's shouting for them to get out of the way?"

Chris giggled; his smile was back. He appreciated what she was trying to do, and had done. She'd left him alone with his morose thoughts, but she also wanted to catch the downward spiral before he sank too deep. "Thank you," he said, "I needed that."

She reached over and touched his arm, then she looked over at him. "I understand you're going through stuff, Chris. But don't shut me out completely. I'll give you time and space, but don't treat me like an alien, okay?"

He took a deep breath, not just to get his composure back, but because another vehicle swerved in front of him.

"Fucking muppet!" Sandy blared.

Grasping his girlfriend's hand, Chris rushed into the Rifleman pub in Twickenham just in time before the heavens opened up. The promise of real fish and chips in an English pub revived both their moods, and Chris was eager to have Sandy meet his friend Guy Trimble. Chris decided to leave the rental car at the hotel so that he could enjoy a beer with his friend. On the train ride down from central London, they finally chatted about the visit to the prison, with Chris telling Sandy about how sorry he felt for his brother. The message that Sandy was getting, however, was how much deep-down grief Chris was carrying for not being there for his family.

He missed his mother, and had been mortified to hear about her death weeks after her passing because he'd been away, working in some foreign land he couldn't even remember. He also learned later about his brother's demise, being arrested for an assault on hospital staff because of the perceived lack of care for their ailing mother. He argued that if he had been there, he could have prevented Terry from acting out. Sandy consoled him as best she could, but her lack of proper sleep put her patience to the test. She'd been in the UK less than forty-eight hours, and her new experience with jet lag drained her resolve. She hoped that meeting one of his friends could divert his focus from his self-loathing, while also easing the physiological burden of having to be fully attentive.

Chris spotted Guy at a dark-stained oak table near an unused fireplace. He waved to Chris, who acknowledged him, however, by this time was already checking the place out from a threat perspective. The place wasn't busy, with three men at the bar, two of which were wearing desert wellies. *Squaddies,* he thought, using the slang for British soldiers. *No threat, unless they get drunk. Two blokes at the other end of the bar: locals, no threat. Female bartender: no threat. Quiet, cozy. Good, he's picked a nice spot, semi-secure.* He pulled Sandy over to Guy. As he did, he gazed down a corridor that led to another room. He couldn't see what was in there, but he assumed it was another lounge with an exit to an outdoor toilet. Typical British pub layout. He would make an excuse soon to check out his exit strategy.

"Hello mate, this is Sandy."

"Sandy, nice to meet you." Guy reached out his hand and shook hers warmly. "Please sit, sit. I understand this is your first visit to a pub."

"First of many things, I've never been to the UK, never been overseas," she replied with a smile. She took an instant liking to Guy, who seemed charming.

"Really, where are you from?"

"Parsippany, New Jersey, not far from New York."

"Well, what has your man got lined up for you while you are here? Tower of London, Buckingham Palace, that sort of thing?"

The conversation was only interrupted by Chris, who suggested they order their meal and drinks. As promised, the fish and chips were spot on and a hit with Sandy. She was happy to get a decent meal and a classic English pint, and was having a good time talking about London, the UK, and just everyday matters. She was also content with neither man talking about work. It was refreshing to see Chris relax for a change.

"Another round?" Chris asked. With nods to the affirmative, Chris made a move to the bar. He sidled up to the oak counter next to the three soldiers. As he did, the pub's door opened and three Arabs entered. He saw their reflection in the mirror and immediately upped his level of alertness. *What do we have here then?* he wondered.

He wanted to switch off and just enjoy his time with his girl and his mate, but he could not. It was an occupational hazard to see threats everywhere. He already knew which way he would exit and how he would with Sandy, if need be, but these three men piqued his interest. Not known for being connoisseurs of alcoholic beverages, he immediately questioned the scene. *Why are three Arabs walking into a pub? Sounds like a bad joke.*

He ordered his round and watched the men move towards Guy and Sandy. His senses elevated immediately. One of the three—a large man with a face only a mother could love—sat near the pub's front door. *Security?* One man sat at the same table as Sandy and Guy, and the other one took up a spot on the table next to them. They made themselves comfortable and leaned over to talk with Guy. By this time Chris had a plan.

"How's it going, lads?" he asked the off-duty soldiers.

"All right," came the cagey reply.

"You boys on leave, or just a night out?"

"Night out. Bit nosey, aren't you?" the tallest one asked.

"Guards?"

"Grenadiers, who's asking?"

"I'm Chris, ex-Royal Green Jackets. Can I buy you boys a pint?"

"Can't say no to that."

"Be rude not to," replied another.

Chris monitored Guy and Sandy. He could tell from her body language that she wasn't comfortable. She looked over in his direction a few times. He gave her a reassuring smile. Chris looked over at the ugly Arab sitting at the empty table near the door, minding his own business. Their eyes met for a second. *I see you shit for brains,* Chris transmitted nonverbally. As Chris waited for the drinks he ordered, he leaned in to the soldiers. "Listen, can you boys do me a favor?"

"Depends, what's in it for us?"

Chris fished out his wallet. He pulled five £20 notes and laid them on the bar.

"Here's a ton—see my mate over there?" They turned in unison, as he intended.

"He runs a modeling agency in Chelsea. Those twats who have just come in are from Jordan or some other fucked up sand dune. They've been chasing my mate for weeks, offering him all sorts of money."

"For what?" the tall soldier asked.

"Girls. They want to buy some of his models to take back to some rich sheik or camel jockey in the Middle East."

"You're having a laugh, mate."

"I'm not fucking around. How often do you see three Arabs in a pub and not order something, eh? Listen, I can take care of the faggot in the suit and his bum chum at the table. I just need you boys to make sure idiot stick over by the door stays in his box if things go pear-shaped. I don't want to go off on these pricks, but they need to be told to fuck off. I'm not going to give anyone a tuning, maybe some gentle persuasion, but I don't need this grief either. If the ugly twat gets up, sit him back down for me. You in?"

The soldiers looked at each other. The tall one took the cash on the bar. Chris was happy to have some backup. He picked up the three drinks he'd ordered and made his way back to the table, placing them gently down in front of Guy and Sandy. He looked at the two visitors. "Sorry chaps, wasn't sure what you were drinking? Scotch and soda, Guinness, Babycham, what can I get you? My treat."

The Arab closest to Guy thought Chris was one of the bar staff until he sat down. Chris sized the man up. *Nice suit, hair coiffured, neatly trimmed beard, manicured hands, good-looking, should be in an expensive watch advertisement. This guy is the brains. Chummy next to him; ruffled suit, nice hair, chubby, seems a little out of place, probably a used car salesman. He's probably half a threat, he's not going to win Mr. Universe anytime soon. He goes first. An interesting trio.*

"What are we chatting about? It all seems rather cozy," Chris queried.

"Seems like these chaps are looking for a friend of theirs, Jawad," Guy reported.

"Oh, well, isn't that interesting?" Chris replied. "And who might you be?" he asked the suit. Sandy found his hand under the table and clung to it. She was fearful of what may come, she recognized a change in his attitude.

"That is of no importance to you. I do not speak to lackeys," he answered without looking at Chris. The suit leaned forward and stared at Guy. "Mr. Trimble. It is of the utmost importance that I speak with Jawad. There are matters of state that require his immediate attention. I ask you again. Where is Jawad Halabi?"

"I have told you already. He and I are no longer in contact. I have not seen or heard from him in quite some time."

"And what of your service? Are they not aware where their agents are?"

"Sir, I don't want to keep wasting my breath. Jawad is not in our employ, and neither I nor my service know of his whereabouts. If he is in this country, then it would be a surprise to me."

"Am I to believe that the British government is denying his whereabouts? Are you holding him captive? He entered this country yesterday." The suit banged the table for affect. "Tell me where he is!" he demanded.

"Oy!" Chris interjected scornfully. "Are you taking the piss or what? I'm trying to drink my pint. Stop banging the table and open your fucking ears. The man said he didn't know where he was, and if he says he doesn't know, he doesn't know!"

The suit paid no attention to Chris. He kept looking at Guy. "As I have said, and it's better if you listen. I do not talk to errand boys. Mr. Trimble tell me where Jawad is, or—"

Chris bashed the table hard, spilling his beer deliberately towards the suit. Out of the corner of his eye, he saw the ugly Arab get up from his perch. He stared at the ugly man and pointed a stern finger. "Sit down Princess, Karaoke is tomorrow night!" he blasted. It was the cue that the three Grenadier Guards needed. They scurried over to the oaf and surrounded the table where he was sitting. When Chris focused his attention on the threats before him, the suit was cleaning the spilled beer from his clothes. His bum chum was reaching inside his jacket. Chris picked up an empty plate that once served fish and chips and smashed it across the man's face. The man reeled back in pain. Chris got out of his chair and picked up one of the fresh drinks on the table and threw it all over the suit. The man jumped out of his chair, giving Chris enough time for him to rush him and grapple him to the ground. He held him in place with his knee on his chest and a strong hand around his throat. Before his next action, he looked around to see the ugly Arab being persuaded not to get up by the soldiers. Chummy, with a new porcelain scar, was bleeding and dabbing his face with a napkin.

Chris was in control of the situation. He looked down on the suit, who was whimpering below him, arms raised in defense. "It's only spilled beer, it could be worse," Chris calmly stated. "Stop struggling." The man on the floor complied, as Chris expected he would. "You haven't been that nice to me, but I've been told that sometimes I need to be the bigger man. Someone said once that I'm a little aggressive, need some anger management or some shit like that, so I'll be nice for a change. I'm going to gently help you up and I don't want any pala- ver . . . that's bother to you foreigners. Later on, send the cleaning bill to my good friend here and we'll all be happy campers. We can put all this down to a misunderstanding Okay?" He squeezed the man, waiting for a response, and sensed the suit release tension in his body. Chris eased his grip slightly but didn't let go. "Smashing, I'm glad we have an understanding—you can pay attention to a lackey after all. Now you have to admit I have been on my best behavior, but now it's time to tell you to *fuck off*. Don't you ever come into this pub again. I don't want to see you, don't want to smell you, and I don't want to touch you."

Chris punched him hard in the face. "Oh shit, sorry mate. Forgot to tell you I was a lying bastard." He picked the man up off the floor and shoved him in the door's direction; then he reached over to chummy and did the same. The three soldiers followed suit and pushed the ugly Arab out the door.

"Bloody hell mate!" one soldier started. "Is that what the Royal Green Jackets call gentle persuasion?"

Hotel Novotel, London West, England

Chris was thanking Guy for the ride to his hotel when Sandy got out and slammed the car door. The force shook the car, and both Chris and Guy cringed as if a window was about to pop out of Guy's aging Jaguar. She hadn't waited to thank their host for the evening, nor say a goodbye. She was in a foul mood and left the two friends to chat at the curb while she made her way into the hotel and up to her and Chris's room.

Chris apologized profusely to Guy for Sandy's abruptness. He wanted to talk about the skirmish at the pub but Guy cut him off. "She's upset Chris, I get it. Nobody wants to get into a brawl at a pub, no need to apologize."

Chris wanted to explore the incident more but knew this wasn't the time or place. Guy could tell that Chris was hesitant and selected first gear in his Jag, presenting a nonverbal clue to his friend that the conversation was over. "Let's see if we can hash this out tomorrow. I think your girlfriend needs you right now. Thanks for stepping in by the way, I was getting the heebie-jeebies with those fellas."

"Guy—" Chris started, but it was too late. The MI6 officer tapped the accelerator, "See you tomorrow Chris."

By the time Chris made his way to the room, Sandy was in the shower with the bathroom door locked. He sat at the foot of the bed, turned on the TV and surfed around for a few minutes, eventually settling for a rerun of *Only Fools and Horses*. Twenty minutes later, Sandy appeared from the bathroom.

"You okay?" he asked, but it was clear she'd only come out to retrieve something from her bag. She was wearing one towel around her midriff, and another on her head. She didn't look in his direction when she answered. "I guess" she said curtly.

"Is there something—" Chris began, but she was back in the confines of shower steam before he could finish his question. He looked blankly at the TV, unable to catch the light mood of the canned laughter from the show. After a few minutes he ignored the jokes and pondered on his situation. As he was taking stock of what happened in the pub, he realized that he had stepped on a landmine. Sandy was pissed, and he gave her good reason to be. He had let her down . . . again. Sandy was hoping to have a good night out, some fun with one of his friends, instead she witnessed yet another one of his fights. *But this is the way I am, I can't change that, can I?*

His eyes wandered down to the TV remote that he toyed with. His mood was flattening, his adrenaline from the fight, long worn off, all he wanted to do was rest. Part way to closing his eyes he stopped himself, *why am I so selfish? This is not about me, there's two of us in this relationship, and one of us doesn't understand the other . . . do I need to tell her? Do I need to man up and start being honest with her?*

It took another fifteen minutes for her to appear again. He was still sitting on the edge of the bed. He wasn't sure what was going on, so he muted the TV and looked over at her. She was in her nighttime sweats and rubbing lotion into her hands. She pulled back the covers on the bed—not the one he was sitting on—and sat there looking at him, her face scrunched up, full of scorn and pent-up anger.

"Did I do something wrong?" he asked cautiously.

Her posture was ramrod straight, but she then slumped her shoulders slightly and shook her head. She didn't reply, and looked at him inquisitively.

He returned the look as if to say, *I know I've screwed up*. But what came out was: "So now we're not talking."

Her brow creased somewhat. It was a look that he'd seen on her before and he didn't like it. "Seriously?" she asked.

Chris tried a stall tactic, and push the start point of the conversation over to her. "You want to tell me what I've done, or am I going to beat myself up for the rest of the night not knowing how you feel? What I've done to piss you off?"

"What have you done . . . what have you done? Chris, oh my God." She stood up and paced. He tried to grab her hand gently as she passed him by. She recoiled from his touch.

"Sandy, you're scaring me. What's wrong?"

She stopped in her tracks. "Jesus Christ, Chris. You're not the one that needs to be afraid. I'm the one that's scared."

"Scared of what . . . if you're talking about those guys from the pub . . . there's nothing to worry about. We'll never see them again—"

"—It's not *them* I'm afraid of, Chris!" She shouted. "I'm afraid of *you*!"

Chris got off the bed and slipped into panic mode. "What? What? You can't be afraid of me Sandy. I would never, ever hurt you. You know that, Sandy. Please, I'm sorry." He reached out to touch her again, but she waved him away.

"Don't come near me, Chris. Don't touch me right now." He sat back down on the bed. She paced around more. He could tell that she was trying to figure out a course of action. He wanted to reassure her, but he also wanted her to talk, to get things off her chest so he could respond. She stopped in front of the TV and looked at him. "Do you remember the first time we met?"

"Why wouldn't I?"

"I took you to my home. Why?" She didn't give him an opportunity to answer. "Because I felt sorry for you. Why? Because you were in a bar fight . . . why? Because that is what you do."

"That wasn't my fault Sandy—"

"I'm sure it never is, but what worries me Chris is the way you do it. I saw dozens of fights in the bars I used to work in New Jersey, I hated it. But it's the way you handle yourself, that's the scary part."

Chris looked at her, feeling uneasy. He was stupid to think that she wouldn't have a reaction to what she was a part of in the pub. He had to know it would upset her, cause her to question his actions. But he was ignorant. He almost thought of her as one of his team, another operator who would do the same as he did in such a situation. Not a person dear to him with feelings and an abhorrence to violence.

There was a lot more to the fight at the Rifleman than met the eye, and it was something he needed to go over with Guy. But what bugged him was that he didn't have any answers as to why the fight happened in the first place. He relied on his instincts to resolve an issue, but the consequences of his actions seemed even more of an enigma. He wracked his brain trying to piece together a feasible story to give her without explaining who Guy and Jawad were, and how he knew them. He thought of concocting a lie perhaps to appease her, but he held back knowing that he had to tread carefully as his brain was sometimes two steps behind his mouth.

She paced again, wringing her hands as she did.

"I was watching you at the bar, talking to those other men. I saw the look in your eye the moment those Arabs showed up. I could tell you were making a plan, and I was right."

"I did what I had to do. I had to keep us safe."

"Safe? Safe? Safe from what? I wasn't feeling comfortable with them, and I didn't understand what was going on, and Guy was handling things, but you had to take things up a notch."

"I perceived a threat and dealt with it," he barked defensively. "One of them reached for something, I reacted."

"You're missing the point. The way you smashed that plate in the man's face—then you put that other one on the ground and talked to him so nicely, as if it was someone's grandmother. What's wrong with you?"

"I needed to make a point."

"Oh, you made a point all right. Everyone in that pub got that. As soon as you get some alcohol in your system Chris, you become a different person."

"It's not the alcohol, Sandy."

"Then what? What is it with you?" She stood in front of him, hands on hips, waiting for an answer. She pushed for an explanation. "Every time you come home you have another bump, bruise or scar. I never want to ask, but now—British government, Arabs, agents. . . what the hell does it all mean Chris?"

"You know I can't talk about my work."

"Honestly, I don't give a shit about what you do. Really! That's not what I'm asking."

"Then what, Sandy, what do you want from me?"

She paused, judo wrangling the words she'd had in her head for the last hour. Whatever she had prepared wouldn't come out right. "I will not visit you in prison. I don't want to see you disfigured; I don't want to see you suffer." Sandy was flustered. She loved him, but she was tired of his way of life. Her thoughts were a jumble of sympathy and dread, clouded by her need for him in her life. She knew deep-down he was a good man, who was capable of good things. Her time at the farm and on the boat with him would be memories that she would cherish, and she knew that he would too. He was relaxed. He had a constant, genuine smile, the one she fell in love with, but she also discovered a cool, goofy side of him that he had never shown before. It was a welcome relief, but that was then, it was different now. He looked different, he was acting different, she felt sad.

Still rattled, there was one more thing she wanted to get off her chest. "And I don't want to be around when whatever you 'do' goes bad."

Chris had no response but he knew he couldn't remain mute, it would only exacerbate matters. "What are you trying to tell me Sandy?"

She tilted her head to the ceiling, searching for words that were not up there. She looked around the room for something that would give her a clue, trying anything but looking into his eyes. She walked over to the desk and leaned back on it, then folded her arms across her chest and faced him. "We were supposed to be making a home in Washington State. The farm, the boat, all of that, but you . . . you. I'm not sure you want that." Her words were soft, reasonable. But the next were like a death knell. "I think you like to hurt people, Chris."

Chris took a sharp intake of air. He was gobsmacked for a moment, but then recovered. "Now hang on a sec—"

Her anger was back, and her next words came out quickly. "I saw the look in your eye. I saw how coolly you managed that whole fight. You're so capable, so quick, so smart with your hands—and your words—when you want to be." She shook her head; her eyes were welling up with tears, but she fought them back. She was still anxious, but there was more to say. "I don't know, some women may get turned on by that but me . . . I was disgusted, ashamed. I wanted to . . . I felt sick to my stomach Chris, so sick I wanted to throw up!"

He imagined he was being punched in the face by twenty men at the same time. *Ouch, fucking ouch,* he thought. *I've fucked up this time.* He searched for an excuse, anything that could calm her down and offer some sort of explanation. "Sandy, please, my job, my training—"

"You're not listening. I don't care about what you have to do for your work. I used to feel safe around you, Chris. But when we're out somewhere together, nobody wants to know us, nobody comes near us. You scare everyone with your looks, your stares, your moods . . . It's only now that I'm realizing it, tonight, that fight, that man with the blood on his face. People don't like you because they are afraid of you. I understand it now. I get it."

"Sandy, I'm sorry. I've been conditioned to trust nobody; it's something I can't easily break. I have to be careful. I want us to be safe."

"I think it's more than that, Chris."

It stumped Chris to hear that; he wasn't sure what she was getting at; then she kept venting.

"You told me about your father, a prison guard. He got in trouble for beating up prisoners, and he hurt you and your brother when you were young. Your brother, he's now in prison for violence, and he will die there."

She could see the confusion on his face, and pressed on. "How many fights have you been in Chris? How many men have you hurt; how many have you killed?" He didn't respond; he didn't like the line of questions. "How many more fights, Chris? You've always told me that one day you'll come across someone you can't beat. Will that be today? Tomorrow? Or are you just going to keep searching for that one man and say 'fuck the consequences'?"

"Sandy," he pleaded.

She held up her hand to stop him. "I think there's something wrong with you. Something deep down. I don't know if it's genetics or something that can be treated, but your appetite for violence . . . your choices, your way of life . . . I can't be around it anymore. I don't want it for us, for you. I think you need help, Chris."

They looked at each other in silence, neither wanting to shoot the next volley. Chris had nothing to counter with. He thought it wise not to say any more; she had spoken her mind. And deep down, he knew she was right. It was time to take a step back. He hadn't seen her side of things until now, but she had some valid words. He sat there like a lemon, not knowing what to do next, other than to keep quiet. He was proud of his abilities to take men on, but he was pathetic at dealing with feelings, or any conversation within an intimate relationship.

Sandy rubbed away a line of tears that were running down one side of her face, then again headed for the bathroom. She locked the door behind her, leaving Chris to decide for himself what he should do.

Ten seconds of feeling like shit was enough. He grabbed his jacket and left the room.

CHAPTER SEVEN

Hotel Novotel, London West, England

CHRIS LEFT THE HOTEL ROOM with no particular destination in mind. He wanted to give Sandy some space, but he also wanted to clear his head. The things she said resonated with him. She had pushed his buttons and his resolution was to run away, at least for the moment. He wasn't looking for a remedy, nor had he a plan to deal with her or the things on her mind. He only wanted to walk and be alone.

His thoughts became as muddled as a London street map. Like his mind, it was complex. There was no rhyme nor reason to his feelings, or the streets he traipsed. Sometimes straight and narrow, sometimes curved or ending abruptly. Sometimes there was a shortcut; sometimes there was only the long way around.

Getting lost on the streets wasn't easy for him, as his inner compass was as efficient as a Swiss watch. But the orientation of his feelings, which he followed now, was about reliable as an ashtray on a motorbike. He had never adventured into some inner-city streets, nor into the depths of his mind to explore what really made him who he was. He marched through dreary streets that matched his mood; then perked up when he saw bright lights and people. But he wasn't at all sure where he wanted to be. Searching for light? Or finding solace in the darkness of ignorance?

One thing became clear to him as he trolled the streets. People would momentarily stare at him, then glance away. He felt in those instances like the elephant man, like he had a disease, an affliction that people saw—and then prayed it wouldn't happen to them. But still he couldn't avoid the stares, he couldn't go anywhere with his head down, or off a swivel. His built-in self-defense mechanism was too strong; his will to be secure and aware was fierce and firm. His demeanor was stiff and unapproachable, just like Sandy claimed, but it was his nature, a trait that he couldn't or wouldn't relinquish. And therein lay the crux of the matter. Did he want to bend to be happy? Did he want to give up what he was, his independence, his reliability, his talent?

He stopped for a minute on the busy Kensington High Street. He watched as a crowd of young men were being ushered out of a pub. It was kicking-out time, and the streets were about to be inundated with hordes of young people, looking for taxis, fast food, a fight, or all of the above. A scuffle broke out on the street between two bouncers and some young lads. Chris stood in place, hands dug deep into his pockets. He had a fleeting thought of sprinting over there to waylay into the minor melee. He didn't know who he wanted to punch or kick, but the will brewed within him. He looked on as a few more men joined the fracas, obscenities abound echoing off the building walls around them, though these were more the pushers and chest pumpers, aiming to look brave for their women.

Chris evaluated who he would take care of first, what tools he would use, what direction he would approach, and who would be the next on the list for attention. It was a simple, quick analysis. When one man fell to the ground, a girl got in between the bouncer and her lover. Chris thought that was the point to move in, but he held back.

He shook his head, then dropped it in shame. He knew Sandy was right. It was in his bones—the violence, the call to action, the satisfaction of hard bone meeting soft flesh. The adrenalin rush, the speed of engagement, the superior feeling of control. He loved the smell, the taste, the sight. The only justification he could muster towards fulfilling these needs was that he could control it. Despite what she thought, alcohol didn't trigger his aggression. He could turn the fight on and off whenever he needed it.

The challenge would be to convince Sandy of that. It would mean a complete sea change in his behavior. If it were to be the transformation that she wanted, then it would mean that he would have to be a better person. It meant embarking on a different line of work, and that he would have to give up the CIA, or at least his current job in the agency. He wasn't sure if he wanted that. Or if there was there another way, another option? He plodded on and ignored the brawl outside the pub.

Chris turned away from the hustle and bustle of the High Street and began wandering through middle-class residential areas. The famed London fog descended on him like a silent murmuration of starlings. The stillness of the mist caused his pulse to thunder and his brain to gong like a grandfather clock. If only his thoughts weren't so mechanical, his actions not so methodical, he could have sought out his deeper feelings and brought them to the fore. Not have them hide in the hard-to-reach places of his very being.

He passed by parallel-parked cars on both sides of the streets, jammed nose to tail, with barely enough room for a cat's whisker to squeeze through. He looked on at the Georgian-style homes, with their neat railings and black outdoor plumbing pipes running three stories high. Where people existed and lived a perfectly predictable lifestyle and were going through the motions of wake-up early, commute on the Tube, reverse the process in time for dinner, and be in bed at 10:30 pm—only to repeat the same exercise the next day. He wondered if he could accept the monotony of such a life. Could he be another cow-chewing-cud, bored-faced commuter in a field full of ignorant 'follow-this,' 'follow-that' sheep? He didn't know.

He thought about the farm in Washington State. When he was there, he was happy, relaxed and content. But of late he was spending more and more time away from it. It didn't surprise him that Sandy had a vociferous opinion of his actions; she was a robust woman, always compassionate; sometimes mouthy. She hadn't seen all the good in him yet, but she had seen some of his sordid behavior, and she, up until this point at least, still wanted to be with him. Fortunately, she had not seen the deaths he had meted out on people. He hoped that she never would.

The overarching question was, did he want the comfort, the quiet-ness, the love and affection of a serious relationship. She was all he had. His mother and father had long since passed; his brother, waiting on death's door every day behind steel bars. There wasn't anyone else.

He couldn't find the answer he was looking for. *Give up this lifestyle for her? Or continue with death, destruction, misery. Can I make a difference? Bring shitheads to justice. Make them pay, do something worthwhile, leave a mark.* These were the words bashing into his tired brain like a wayward anchor bouncing off the hull of a ship in a storm. *So, what do I do . . . go live on a farm and raise chickens? Go to church every Sunday, play happy family, get a dog, a couple of kids . . . Jesus, me and kids? Is that what she really wants from me?*

He continued to traipse the lonely streets. His negative thoughts pushed his face downwards and off his robotic swivel sweep of his surroundings. He bucked up when he heard footsteps down the street. He evaluated the situation and determined that it was nothing, just a middle-aged man on his way home. He returned to his thoughts. *Is this who I am? I don't trust anyone . . . is everyone is a threat? How long can I keep this up? Is this even healthy?*

He thought of his brother and his horrible situation. He wondered if he could have helped him if he'd stayed home, or if he too would have fallen into the same trap of drink, drunk, disaster.

But even after all his musings, he knew, deep down, that there was still so much to do in his role with CIA. There was a war going on, men like him were needed, and terrorists like Mukhtar needed to be eradicated. He knew he could be good at what he did. He was physically fit, talented and willing to get things done when others played armchair quarterback. However, what plagued him was that he was on shaky ground with the CIA. If they one day said, "Thank you, but your services are no longer required"—what would he do? If he couldn't commit to Sandy and a stable family life, what could he do? Who would want a former soldier and CIA officer with a fondness for violence and insubordination?

The stench of an Indian curry house tipped his thoughts into a different direction. It was one of a few cuisines that he couldn't stand to see, smell, or taste. The aroma reminded him that he would soon be on the road again for his job, if he wanted it. He would end up in some third-world country eating shit food, getting sick, being dirty, and missing sleep, if he wanted it. He didn't relish the thought about going back to work right now, as Sandy's harsh words and his own depressing self-reflection were dragging him down.

He suddenly found himself at an intersection with four different streets to choose from. He looked around him, analyzing his situation and trying to decide which way to go. *I can't settle yet,* he told himself. *I can't switch this thing off, yet . . . but I will have to one day. But it's not today, I'm still in the game.*

With relief, he spotted the sign for the London Underground at Fulham Broadway and made a beeline towards it.

Chris felt his cell phone vibrating in his pocket. He pulled it out, looked at the number and rolled off the bed, still fully clothed.

"Hold," he answered.

He straightened his attire—the same from the night before—and made for the bathroom. He saw Sandy still wrapped up in the bed-clothes. He wasn't sure if she was truly sleeping, or awake and pretending to be asleep. He shut the bathroom door behind him.

"I'm here," Chris said, "what's up?"

"I don't want to cut into your time off, but we have something for you. Can you make it to the embassy?" Gene asked.

"Sure, how long?"

"You've got a few hours yet. I'm still in that place where we last saw each other."

"Okay."

"You know the drill. Speak to you soon."

It was a recurring event. Gene would call him up at all hours of the day. It didn't matter if he was in the capital cities of Tajikistan or Tibet. "Getting to the embassy" meant that he needed to be on a secure phone for a mission briefing. All he had to do was present himself as "George Mitchell" to one of the Marine guards, and he would be ushered to the CIA station within the building. He hung up the phone and placed it on the bathroom countertop.

He looked at the mirror and didn't like what he saw. The bags under his eyes almost reached down to touch his kneecaps. His eyes looked like road maps crisscrossed with red lines.

After he had a long shit, and an even longer shower, he looked and felt slightly better off. Though his beard, much to Sandy's disappointment, he left untouched. The bloodshot eyes would take some more effort, but the drunken look had begun to disappear. He wrapped a towel around his waist and made for the bedroom to find a fresh set of clothes. As he passed the dresser, he noted the time; it was 09:45 and Sandy was still motionless on the bed. He stood for a second looking at her. She must have noticed his presence, she stirred. She looked over at him; they exchanged a glance. Her eyes too looked like a geographical survey map. He surmised that she had spent a long night of crying. From her expression, he wasn't sure if he wanted to poke another stick in the hornet's nest.

"I want to tell you about what I do," he began, nervous and unsure of how she would react. She didn't reply, but straightened herself up, anxious of what he was about to say.

"I want to tell you everything but . . . I can't—"

"—So, the CIA is more important to you than I am?" she quickly remonstrated.

Chris raised his hands to head off a potential fight. He kept his voice low. "That's not what I am saying Sandy. What I mean to say is I can't tell you yet."

"Horseshit!"

"There's so much at play here, Sandy. I can't go into everything; it will take too long—"

"—then make time Chris."

"Sandy, I can't . . . really, I want to, but not now." He sat down on the bed next to her and gingerly reached out to hold her hand. She recoiled from his touch. "I know I haven't been there for you, not been honest with you, but last night in the pub . . . I . . . I don't want you exposed to that kind of thing—"

"Because that is what you do Chris, isn't it? Are we just going to rehash our fight from last night, or do you have something new to say? Because if you don't, I don't want to hear about it."

Chris looked away; he couldn't look her in the eye. His immaturity in managing relationships was again coming to the fore, like it always did. He sat in silence, not knowing what to say or do, but he could tell that she wasn't budging—and she was right. He'd offered something, but naively couldn't deliver. He felt like an ass.

He cowardly retreated from a deeper confrontation. "I have to go out for a while. I will be back as soon as I can . . . can we talk then?"

She didn't reply, and sat motionless on the bed. He got up and got dressed. By the time he was ready to go, she had pulled the blankets over her head. He wanted to say something more, but couldn't. He left and gently closed the door behind him, leaving the Do Not Disturb sign on the door handle. He peered down the corridor in both directions, looking for a threat. He was back in mission mode.

US Embassy, London, England

"Moldova?" Chris answered, surprised he was going to a country that he had never been to before. "I thought I was support staff."

"We have a German that you need to get," Gene said. "It's still low-key stuff Chris; don't get your hopes up for guns and glory."

Chris was happy for the consideration. But he was still wary, unsure of the mission. "What about the Germans, Gene? Don't they want their boy?"

"No; they deny that this guy is a threat—they don't have him on the hook for anything he's done in their realm. The authorities in Chisinau handed him over to us yesterday, and we've been trying to figure out why. Perhaps by the time you get there it'll be a nonissue. He's been holed up in one of our safe houses, but the station there doesn't have the capabilities to hold him too long. We need to move him as soon as possible."

"How soon, Gene?"

"I need you to be there in the next 24 or sooner. There'll be a rendition kit waiting for you. I can't spare anyone else to support you. The local station will have to pitch in. Can you make that happen?"

Chris knew he was in a bind. Yes, he wanted to go back to work and get into the thick of things. But then no—he needed to work things out with Sandy first. Before he answered, Chris tried to deflect to see if what he was about to say would influence the request and jeopardize his participation in future missions. "Gene, I need to tell you about last night."

"What have you done Chris?"

"Guy and I were out at a pub last night—"

Gene interrupted him. "—Jesus Christ, Chris. I really hope for your sake I don't have to cover your ass again. Tell me, what did you do this time?"

Chris decided not to beat around the bush. There was no point in telling him it wasn't his fault, or he was just in the wrong place at the wrong time. He explained the story, leaving nothing out. He finished by letting him know that Sandy was with him the whole time, and that he wasn't about to go looking for trouble and put her in danger.

"Fair enough, Chris. I still don't like it. Does Guy know where Jawad is?"

"If he did, he didn't tell me. I'd like to see him, though, before I go anywhere. I need to know if I need to watch my back, or if there's something else at play here."

"And Sandy?"

Chris held his breath. He wasn't sure what to say; he didn't know where her frame of mind was.

"Chris, if you need to deal with her, fine, go do that. I can find someone else for Moldova."

The offer tempted Chris; he knew deep down that he should stay and work this out with his girlfriend if he wanted the relationship to succeed. He also knew that she was also right; he had to confront his inner demons and his penchant towards violence. He knew he needed to settle down, lest he be the one with a hand around his throat on the floor of a bar—fighting with a man he can't beat.

Gene was holding his tongue while Chris considered, but he needed an answer.

"I'll let you know as soon as I can, Gene."

"Don't be a stranger, Chris. Let me know one way or the other."

"Roger that—I'll be in touch."

An hour later, Chris sat in a coffee shop at the Victoria train station in the center of London. He spotted Guy checking out the large overhead digital train schedule. Chris sipped on a bottle of water and scanned the area around Guy, who was deliberately paying no clear attention to his environment. After a minute, Guy causally tapped his right thigh with a newspaper he was carrying, then turned around to leave the station. Chris watched his maneuver but still concentrated on the surrounding area. After thirty more seconds, he left his spot and followed in Guy's direction. He kept Guy's shape in his line of sight, but he wasn't watching his friend too closely. Chris was watching everything else but him.

Guy left the station and dashed into the Sainsbury's supermarket off Wilton Road. He perused the aisles for a few minutes, then exited the rear of the shop onto Guildhouse Street. Without hesitation, he took a left turn towards Warwick Way, and eventually entered the Queens Arms pub.

Chris casually dawdled into the pub ten minutes later.

"All good?" Guy asked. He was leaning up against the bar, back to the front door, eyes on the mirror behind the barman. Chris joined him there.

"As far as I can tell," Chris replied, having conducted his surveillance detection duties.

"What would you like?"

"Half a shandy wouldn't go amiss."

"Bit dainty, don't you think?" Guy teased.

"Job on, mate. I could kill a pint right now but I need to be on my best behavior."

"Gene giving you a hard time? Sorry, shouldn't ask, not my business."

"He's all right. I understand where he's coming from, he's got a job to do."

The drinks arrived, and Guy and Chris found a small table in a corner, where they began speaking in a whisper. Chris had already explained to Guy over the phone that he'd have to travel soon, but they needed a debrief from the previous night's activities before he could leave.

"I needed some background on those chaps from last night, so I reached out to the boys at 5," Guy began. Chris knew that he was referring to MI5, the British equivalent of the FBI.

"Anything there?"

"The gent that you so politely put on the ground was a Saudi national. Same for the chap with half a plate of chips on his face. They have some standing with the Saudi community here, but to our investigation, not in an official sense. The third guy is a mystery, but the consensus was that they hired him for the muscle aspect, and therefore, he's of no consequence. Our thoughts are that he was there to take care of me if I decided to not be so cordial. They weren't expecting you."

Chris told Guy the story he'd given to the three soldiers he temporarily hired. They both laughed a little and sipped their drinks.

"So, Jawad?" Chris asked.

"I really don't know where he is. He called me from Kuala Lumpur the other day, told me he was on the way here and that he wanted to meet. I've heard little since. If he really is here in the UK like those chaps think, then it really is news to me."

Chris was curious. "Did he say what he wanted to meet you for?"

"He had a lead that he was exploring."

"Well, that's clear as mud."

Guy raised his eyebrows slightly and sipped at his beverage. "Yes . . . I detected some concern in our conversation. He wanted to meet face to face. I agreed, but I honestly don't know how I am going to help."

"Any special reason why he was in Asia?"

"He's hell-bent on bringing down al-Qaeda, Chris, you know that.

Nothing has changed. From what I can fathom, he apparently became suspicious of one of his countrymen and followed him to Singapore. I don't know how he ended up in Malaysia, but one of his men was killed during a surveillance op, prompting Jawad to believe his instincts. And now the guy he was watching has gone missing, adding to the mystery."

"So, I'm guessing you're not handling him anymore?" Chris quizzed.

"No, we had to cut our ties with him after our Karachi enterprise. I think he's becoming a lone wolf of sorts. He's desperately looking for allies, hence the reason for his visit to the UK. His cousin is the ambassador here; perhaps Jawad was meeting him to further his investigation. I don't know, I'm just guessing."

Chris mulled over the last comment. His impression and experience with Jawad confirmed what Guy was saying. The initial brief that the CIA gave stated as much.

"Jawad and I have a long history," Guy said, "you know that, and I trust him. He's a smart and capable guy, Chris, and he has admirable intentions. But he has been shouting from the rooftops to our service and to Whitehall, and for that matter, to anyone who will listen. He thinks there are still powerful elements within the Saudi establishment at the highest of levels, who were implicit in the attacks on September 11. Recently he has been telling us that the Saudi government are more closely aligned with al-Qaeda than he first thought."

"Is someone trying to shut him up?"

"It seems so," Guy confirmed. "I don't know where he is, what he is doing or anything."

"Didn't he finger a bunch of Saudis already?"

"He did, and they dealt a few of them swift justice. I believe that from that success, and his killing of the Karachi chemist, he's taken on a whole new direction with his quest to find more scorpions in the Saudi Kingdom—and has won some enemies, by the sound of things."

"He could be a little too close to the truth; someone wants him shut down," Chris inferred.

Guy nodded in agreement while sipping on his beer. "I'm afraid so," he finally offered.

"You seriously don't think those fairies from the pub are a genuine threat, do you?" Chris asked.

Guy laughed at the suggestion. "Somehow, I don't think so—but you never know how desperate they may be. And another thing: we don't know how far their reach extends."

"You need to be careful too—your personal security sucks. They followed you to your local pub. That's not a good thing. They may come knocking again," Chris suggested. He worried for his friend's safety.

"I know, the boys at 5 had the same opinion. I'm in temporary lodgings until this all blows over. Meanwhile, 5 have some people looking for these guys. When we find them, we'll keep them under surveillance in case they get up to any more shenanigans."

"Since I'm off to other parts, and you don't know where Jawad is, how are we going to warn him?"

"I don't think we can, Chris."

By the time Chris had shadowed Guy, as far as MI6 headquarters in Vauxhall, he'd been away from the hotel for over five hours. He finally made it back up to the room, prepared for another confrontation with Sandy. Although he'd told Guy that he was leaving, which was partially true, he didn't tell him exactly when he was going, nor had he fully committed to Gene's request. He had set up a range of flights to get to Chisinau, Moldova, and he had passed the itineraries on to his boss, but he still wanted to discuss the situation with Sandy before his next undertaking. And he had resolved to cancel his flights and let the Moldovan mission go to someone else so he could stay and focus on his relationship—if she still wanted to. She still had four days left before her return flight home. Perhaps that was enough time to turn things around. He knew he wasn't being fair; after he cancelled their sailing trip together, it taken a lot of coaxing and convincing for her to drop everything again to visit him in the UK. He just hoped there was still room for him in her heart, her life.

He didn't call out for her when he entered the room, but it was cold inside. The bed was partially made; the TV was off; the place was empty. She was gone. He didn't know why he bothered, but he made for the bathroom, only to find writing in lipstick on the mirror.

"YOUR ACTIONS—YOUR RESULTS!!!!"

West Middlesex University Hospital, England

The emergency care nurse stood back as she watched the doctor use his stethoscope on the patient one last time. Withdrawing the device from his ears, he took out his penlight and raised an eyelid and shone it directly into the patient's eye. He turned the device off and placed the pen back into his chest pocket. He looked at his watch while removing his protective gloves.

"Time of death, 4:32 pm. Cardiac arrest." He reached over and turned off the switch to the ventilator. "Is there a next of kin?"

"No, doctor," the nurse replied, handing him a clipboard with a form attached for him to sign.

"Is that police officer still here?"

"Yes, I think so; he was in the break room. Shall I fetch him?"

"No, I'll take care of it." He looked around at the solemn faces of the crash team. "Thank you, everyone." He wanted to say more, but he had no words. His staff removed the equipment from the deceased man, preparing to move on; they had other patients in need of attention. The doctor grabbed a plastic bag of the patient's belongings from a nearby table and headed out of the accident and emergency room. Before he did, he turned to the senior nurse again.

"Can you inform the morgue that we have a deceased Muslim?"

"Yes, doctor."

"Straightaway if you can. Thank you."

The ER doctor found the uniformed police sergeant sitting in a comfy chair reading a newspaper. He stood up as he saw the white coat approach.

"He's passed," the doctor said. "I understand there's no next of kin. These are the last of his effects."

"I'm sorry to hear that, doctor. His body, you know he was an Arab . . ."

"Yes, we are well aware; our morgue is prepared for that kind of thing."

As they were chatting, three men approached the doctor and the police officer. The sergeant straightened his posture as he recognized a senior member of Scotland Yard in plainclothes. "Sergeant Abbot, I presume," he began, then nodded at the white coat, "Doctor . . ." He extended his hand to one man, then the other, saying "Chief Inspector McNeill, Scotland Yard. These gentlemen with me are with the security service. How is our patient?"

"I'm sorry to inform you," the doctor began, "but as I was just explaining to the sergeant, the patient has expired. Cardiac arrest." The doctor noticed one security service man take a sharp breath and a short step back. His head also drooped at the news. The doctor continued. "We did all we could, but the damage was quite substantial. The long-term prognosis would not be in his favor, as there were other serious injuries that would not have sustained a good quality of life. This happened just minutes ago."

"Thank you, Doctor. Please thank your staff for their efforts. I assume these are his belongings?"

The doctor dutifully handed over the clear plastic bag to the Chief Inspector, who passed it on to one of the two men behind him. "And the taxi driver?"

"He's currently in surgery. His prognosis is slightly better, but he'll be in our care for some time. He paused, then asked, ". . . if there's nothing else?"

"No, no please doctor, thank you very much. We'll take things from here." The doctor turned and walked away. His mind was elsewhere; he didn't need to concern himself with matters of the police.

The Chief Inspector turned to the policeman. "Sergeant Abbot, how is the investigation going? What have you learned?"

"As first reported sir, a traffic accident. We have no other evidence to suggest otherwise. The lorry driver was arrested and taken into custody, drunk, well over the legal limit. He was carrying a load of scrap steel with insufficient safety or security measures. While navigating a roundabout at high speed, the load shifted and broke away from the bed, crushing the taxi as it was passing on the outside."

McNeill nodded and looked over at the two men from the security service, one of which was going through the plastic bag. The Chief Inspector led the sergeant away to whisper in his ear. He put his hand on the man's shoulder. "I need you to stay here. Someone from the embassy will be here soon to retrieve the body. I need to know who that is, you understand?"

Abbot looked over at the two quiet men busily inspecting the contents of the bag. "Yes, sir," he replied.

"Alright, now the taxi driver, tell me about him—"

While the two policemen were chatting, Guy opened up Jawad's diplomatic passport, and a note fell out onto the floor. He picked it up and read a name on the small piece of paper: Faizan al Shamsi.

Karachi, Pakistan

Alex Faber sat in the rear of a jeep, hanging on to the support structure of the canvas roof. He was muttering to himself that the large convoy he was traveling in was too obtrusive, too bold, too much. Before the mission to raid a suspected terrorist safe house in Lyari got underway, he'd objected to his leadership about the size of the raid team. He recommended splitting the operation into smaller parts and pursuing different routes to the target. He had been in the city occasionally and identified multiple avenues of approach for the task; however, his objections were overruled by the Pakistani forces who were leading the charge—they wanted to maintain control of the entire team into potentially tight quarters. As the convoy lumbered on, Alex's instinct told him this was one of those raids that would not result in much new intelligence nor suspected terrorists. But being the good soldier, he followed orders, sucked it up and went along with the team.

Also sucking it up on the seat opposite him was a female FBI agent on her first raid into Pakistan. She coughed and gasped, though she didn't complain, as the dust and fumes assaulted the less-immune newbie Westerners like her, welcoming them to the daily grind of the polluted city of Karachi. Alex's eyes were burning, and he too coughed a few times, hoping that the immediate effects wouldn't hang around long-term. The haze of smog and the taste of diesel gave him a headache. He wondered how his latest FBI partner, Mary Wright, would endure the ride, the stench, the untimely bowel movements, and the disrespect from the locals. He didn't envy her. A female in a world of testosterone-charged Americans mixed with culturally disrespectful Muslim men: it wouldn't be a simple mission. With nothing better to do, he looked at her and questioned what got her to this place. Was she just following orders, or pursuing a cause? Or was she playing the desktop wannabe on a thrill seek? He wasn't sure, and he was even less sure how long she would last. He guessed her to weigh around 150 pounds, and stood probably five-feet-seven in height. She wore her mud-blonde hair in a tight bun, hidden from view by a scarf, following the cultural norm.

What struck him most, however, was the missing smile, and her dead-eyed stare. She'd been easygoing until this point, a plus in Alex's book; meaning that she was absorbing and learning before opining. But he couldn't figure out if her steely façade was one of strength, or frailty.

The convoy came to a halt in a quiet neighborhood. The streets were dimly lit, narrow, dirty and devoid of many movements. Natives of the enclave who were present stood and stared at the spectacle, leaving the raid team precious few minutes to act out their tasks before the grapevine started a hum of trouble in paradise.

Alex and Mary, in one of the rear vehicles of the convoy, got out and followed the briefing instructions to wait within the Pakistani police cordon. Only when the targeted building was secure could they join the investigation. Mary, eager for something to do, moved toward the Pakistan Ranger raid team.

"Slow down, we have to wait," Alex ordered.

"How do we know that this is the right spot, the right building? They all look the same to me," she said.

Alex knew she was right, but he was trusting the CIA to trust the Pakistanis. He found a wall at the end of a tight alleyway to lean against. "This is my third this week," he said. "We've dragged out a few nobodies, in-the-wrong-place-at-the-wrong-time lookalikes, and nothing has transpired. This is no different. Just chill for a while, let them kick doors; we'll get a look in soon."

Mary nodded in disappointment but paced around, bobbing her head up and down like a whack-a-mole at the slightest disturbance near the target house. Alex looked like Cool Hand Luke, minus the Stetson, with his back to the wall and his right leg propped up for support. He kept the alleyway to his front right as he looked on at the action up the street. He might have looked relaxed, but he was expertly taking in his surroundings, watching for threats from the dilapidated two-story houses and small businesses around him. Further behind him were two Pakistani police officers manning a temporary barricade, preventing the looky-loos from entering the target zone.

The unmistakable sound of two shotgun blasts killed the quiet and froze Mary in place. She stared up the street, imagining the actions of the men in uniform—going through the motions of blasting a door off its hinges and then rushing into the unknown as a perfect team, clearing room-to-room, engaging threats as they appear. Her adrenalin was up, she was eager for action. She looked over at Alex, who remained laid-back and noncommittal. It then got quiet, and for a while Mary couldn't figure out if she was happy or disappointed that there were no more shots coming from the target house. Happy there was less potential for loss of life, sad that there were apparently no combatants, or at least no active terrorists, in the house. She thought of Alex's earlier words, "third time this week." She looked over at him still leaning on the wall, as casual as if waiting for a bus. Then she heard the shouts and screams of people being dragged out of the house. She bobbed and weaved around a vehicle to get a better view.

"Not yet," Alex coolly stated. He shifted his weight from one foot to another. As he got comfortable, he heard something sliding in the alleyway nearby. He cocked his head to peer into the darkness and heard a loud thud as something or someone landed in the path. His senses told him something was wrong, and he moved a few feet into the alleyway just as a large man came barreling down on him.

Caught by surprise, Alex was thrust backwards as the man fell into him. The assailant's outstretched arms and bloody hands aimed for Alex's throat and found purchase, and they both fell to the dirt. Alex tried his best to wriggle free but the confines of the two walls of the alleyway surrounding them stalled his efforts. However, he kicked and squirmed his way out a few feet from the alley entrance and into the road. The large man's powerful hands were still working on choking the life out of the man who'd blocked his way. Alex tried to punch and kick back to no avail; his vision was clouding; his strength was weakening; he was getting to the point of no return.

The large man sensed his opponent weakening. He was having the better of him, but with his eyes bulging and mouth frothing in rage and sheer madness, he paid no attention to his immediate surroundings. He never heard someone approach in back of him, though he felt a set of fingers dig deep into both his eyes from behind. He released the throat of the man he'd attacked for a brief second as his head was pulled backwards by the piercing fingers. The pain was excruciating, forcing him to yield his grip on the man altogether. He writhed rearwards in pain, only to feel a kick to the balls from the man on the ground. With more kicks to his genitals and stomach, he reeled backwards to escape the pain. As he did, the fingers relented, but a forearm now wrapped around his throat, and a set of legs were desperately trying to wrap themselves around his torso. He fell backwards to the ground with his assailant firmly attached to him.

Mary, now on her back, took the full weight of the large man. She was struggling to hold on. A nearby police officer assigned to the mission saw the struggle and ran to assist, using his rifle as a battering ram against the big man's upper body. Alex extracted himself from the mess, crawling away on all fours, gasping for breath. Weak and disorientated, he had little strength left to keep moving, but then he heard Mary cry out.

"Alex, Alex! Backpack, jeep, taser . . . taser, Alex . . . now!"

Alex, still out of sorts, spotted another police officer arriving to assist, but the big man was thrashing around on the ground and nobody but Mary was in control—though she was barely hanging on.

"ALEX! MOVE, GET MY TASER!" she shouted.

Alex thought he would throw up. His head was spinning, but he got to his feet. He staggered to the back of the jeep that they'd used to get to the site and found Mary's bag. With his vision blurred, he fumbled around for what felt like an eternity, but he finally found what he was looking for. Moving like a drunk, he loped over to the fracas and pushed the two police officers out of the way. He depressed the taser trigger and let loose.

The large man sat up against the wall with his hands securely hand-cuffed behind him. The two Pakistani police officers who aided in subduing the mystery attacker, stood on either side of him, rifles at the ready, prepared to lash out a beating if the man moved more than an eyelid. Alex stood at the rear of a vehicle, using water from a bottle to wash his face and neck of the blood that the assailant had gotten all over him.

"You're going to have some bruising, you feel okay?" Mary asked as she looked on.

"Yeah sure, my throat is a dry as hell. I'll live." He looked up at the FBI agent. "How about you?"

"Won't lie, I have a bit of a headache. I may have a few scratches, and my right elbow is hurting like a sonofabitch. My arms and legs feel like noodles too."

"Adrenalin is wearing off. Next hour or so, your elbow will be on fire, and all the other scratches will be feeling like someone is stabbing you with needles." He reached into his backpack, fished out his first-aid kit and handed her a pack of Extra-Strength Tylenol and a fresh bottle of water. "Here take this. Let me look at your elbow." She complied with his request.

"What do you think?" Mary asked, nodding toward the captive.

"Has to have something to do with the raid, but he wasn't on the list of suspects supposedly here," Alex said.

"I checked the alleyway; it's a dead end. My guess is he came down off the rooftop, saw you and panicked," Mary stated, trying to comprehend what had just happened. "Ouch!"

"Sorry, my hands are a little wobbly." Alex apologized for carelessly digging at her wound. "If he came out of that house, he's fair game. They're fucking with us . . . again. They ID him?"

"Don't think so, you done yet?"

He finished wrapping a bandage on her elbow and then gave her a fresh bandage and a pack of gauze. He then produced more Tylenol and a few Band-Aids. As he was putting his kit away, he noticed a young man in handcuffs being led away by one of the ISI officers. "Exactly what I was talking about," Alex nodded towards the scene.

Mary followed his gaze and saw the pair get into a car with a driver at the wheel. "They taking someone in?" she asked. "What the hell now! They're supposed to be running everyone through us."

"This is the horseshit we've been dealing with for months," Alex added. "They get to pick and choose who we get. And whoever that is, it's unlikely that we will ever get to see him again. I've complained about this type of action, but nobody wants to rock the diplomatic boat. It grips my shit to no end."

Mary shook her head and stashed her items into her backpack. She thought she couldn't do much about what was unfolding, but she figured she could at least try to do something with the captive sitting in front of them. Digging into her backpack once again, she pulled out a large folder. She jumped up onto the tailgate of the jeep. Alex leaned back to see what she had. "Flashlight?" she asked.

Alex drew out a Maglite from his trouser pocket and illuminated the pages as she flipped through them. The CIA man was astonished to see the number of mug shots of suspects she had in the pages. They weren't sketchy black and white images either, but full-on color, close-up passport-style photos, and some partial shots. The folder must have contained a hundred images.

"Holy shit, where did you get that from?" Alex exclaimed, surprised at the level of detail in the folder.

"It's my personal stash," Mary bragged with the tiniest of smirks. "I've been working on this since the first World Trade Center bombing in '93. I graduated from the academy the same year. The director of the FBI sent me out here with this as we're trying an alternative approach. I know that this is not news to you, but we know that the ISI has been suspiciously slow in identifying some of these guys, and a lot of them are falling through the cracks before we can process them. It was my job in DC to figure this crap out, but I wasn't getting anywhere; I had to be on site to witness what was going on. The Director agreed, and here we are. Most of the time, a raid like this nets five, six, maybe seven guys. The ISI tells us they can't ID all of them and lets some of them go. The ones that are worthwhile get turned over to you, and the FBI are back to square one not knowing who the ISI or the CIA has in custody. No offense, but I'm here hoping to break that cycle."

"Why am I only seeing this now?"

"Because it's a one-way street Alex, sorry. The FBI is willing to share information, but you guys are not. All you want to do is get information out of anyone you can get to, then either turn them or set them loose so you can focus on bigger fish. The FBI has to have evidence so we can prosecute. If this guy—" She motioned her head towards the big man again. "—If he's in this folder, then we have something on him already. Something he's already linked to that is evidence based, and enough to bring him to trial. I know there's a focus on stopping the next terror attack Alex, but we still have to have accountability. If this guy falls into one of your black sites and you don't tell us, then how the hell are we supposed to build a case?" She ignored his inquisitive look and leafed through the pages of her folder.

Alex couldn't argue with her. He knew she was right, but he too had a job to do. If this guy was someone worthwhile, he had to extract him out of this environment. There had to be an interrogation. The man needed prodding for information, no matter how difficult or how long it would take. Alex wasn't ready to relinquish a high-value asset, if that's what he was, to some greasy-haired liberal lawyer who argued for due process in the eyes of the court in another country that the terrorists wanted to destroy. It made zero sense to him, when there were still plenty of bullets available in the world.

"Bingo!" Mary exclaimed. She pulled a photograph out of a plastic sheath and flipped it over. "Nabeel, no last name, aka Mohammed Al Bishi." She read the case file number to herself, then found what she was looking for. "Shit, he's an al-Qaeda enforcer, Tier 2 suspect."

Alex hurriedly grabbed a black cloth hood out of his backpack and dashed toward the captive. Nabeel was now his. He would not let him out of his sight.

⸜⸝

Colonel Rashid Ghazini told his driver to pull into the Karachi Zoo parking lot and find somewhere suitable to stop the vehicle. The parking area, closed to visitors for the night, was a brown dirt waste-land, empty of human activity but filled with the nearby sounds of captive wildlife. Rashid got out of the car and opened the back door. "Lean forward," he urged the captive.

The man complied and relaxed himself as his cuffs were released. Once unshackled, Wahid rubbed his wrists, trying to massage away the discomfort he'd been subjected to. Rashid moved away from the car and beckoned him to follow. He headed to a single high-canopy Indian almond tree almost in the center of the parking lot. By the time Wahid had caught up to him, Rashid had lit a cigarette and stood with one hand in his pocket, the other holding the burning ember. "You were lucky this evening, Wahid. You were warned about the raid; why were you still there?"

"I only answer to Mukhtar; it is his orders I follow," Wahid responded defiantly.

Stupid boy, he should show some gratitude, Rashid thought, frustrated by Wahid's naiveté. "Your loyalty is to be respected my young friend, but I suggest that you concern yourself with the immediate situation. The Americans watched as I took you away. They will have questions for me . . . what am I to say?"

The young man stood mute and shuffled uneasily on his feet. He peered to his left and then his right, searching for a quick avenue of escape. Rashid caught his nervousness; he took a long drag on the cancer stick, masking the smile in his eyes. "Wahid, you may leave whenever you want, I do not wish you any harm. But you have to know I am your ally, you do not need to run from me." The young, skinny IT expert dove deep into his brain, trying to come up with something smart to say, but he had nothing. He preferred keyboard games, not games of the mind. "Why were you there, why did you wait for the raid, tell me?" Rashid asked.

"Nabeel," the boy finally answered.

Rashid's interest nosed up a notch. He wasn't sure what answer he was going to get. He had warned Nabeel about the impending raid, and it bothered him that the enforcer was now in the direct captivity of the Americans, but that was out of his control. "What about him, Wahid?"

Wahid shuffled in place again. He was getting antsy. Rashid was also getting impatient, but held on to his cool. He needed the young man to offer information. "Wahid, what of Nabeel? Tell me."

"He killed my uncle!"

Rashid tried to hide his smile, but his eyebrows lifted at the thought of this speck of a youngster who wanted to take on a giant of a man. "And you went there to confront him, is that it?" Rashid asked. Wahid didn't answer. He dropped his head in shame, but then when he looked up, anger was in his eyes.

Rashid looked at him with a little sympathy, but he needed to stop Wahid's fury in its tracks. He really didn't want him to run off with vengeance on his mind—it was the easiest way to make a mistake. "My young friend," he began, "if that is true then do you think that it was his decision?"

The indirect question escaped Wahid; still with much pent-up emotion, he answered too quickly. "The man is an animal, that is what he does. He kills men, women, children."

"And you think you can prevent him from carrying out his duties?"

"He killed my uncle; he had done nothing wrong!"

The young man disappointed Rashid, as he was still not getting his subtlety. He discarded his cigarette and let out a long plume of smoke into the night air. "I think we both know that the man is a ruthless killer, but he is an assassin. He is paid to kill, Wahid. He kills on the orders of Mukhtar. You must know this, surely?"

Wahid took two steps back. His eyes narrowed as he tried to comprehend what was just said. Rashid recognized the look of confusion in the young man. It took a few more seconds for the light bulb to go on. Then his face changed. Rashid, seeing the transformation, drew close to him. His voice was almost a whisper. "Correct me if I am wrong. But did you not say to your uncle that Mukhtar would find him and kill him?"

Wahid felt like he had just received a hit to his head with a tire iron. His eyes sprang wide, his mouth fell open. The ISI man insinuated that he himself was responsible for his uncle's death. His first thought was denial, but in the short few seconds he took to rationalize the possibility, the more he realized that he was right. "What have I done?" he said, almost crying.

Rashid saw the opening he was hoping for: guilt. He pushed the envelope. "Wahid, how would you like me to tell Mukhtar about the capture of Nabeel?"

"What? What do you mean?" Wahid whined.

"I will have to tell him that I warned you to stay away, both of you. But you were there. You escaped, and they captured Nabeel. He will ask why. What would you like me to tell him?"

"This is not my fault . . . this was not of my doing; he will understand that. He knows I am loyal, I would not betray him, or the organization."

"I know your loyalty and your intentions are sound, my friend. But will he see it so? Nabeel was one of his favorites, a powerful man that will be missed." Rashid paused, trying to gauge Wahid's new disposition. "And let us not forget what Nabeel may say to the Americans. How much does he know? Does he know where Mukhtar is, his intentions, his operations?" Wahid turned around like a startled rabbit, looking for an exit, somewhere to run to. Rashid caught him by the arm before he took flight.

"Wahid wait, wait." The younger man struggled, but Rashid held on tight. "Where are you going to go? You have nothing. You cannot run, he will find you. He has more than one soldier, Wahid. There will be others that can kill."

"What am I supposed to do, what . . . let go of me." The younger man tried to wrestle himself away, but it was useless. The taller, older man had him in a vice grip. "Wahid, I can help you . . . We can help each other. I can keep you safe."

Wahid almost wanted to scream. He tried once more to wrangle himself away. He backpedaled, but as he did, he bumped into Rashid's driver, who blocked his way from behind.

"Wahid, I need you to calm down," Rashid said. "I need you to listen to what I have to say. I will keep you alive, you will be safe, but you need to listen to me."

CHAPTER EIGHT

Pakistan Air Force Base Masroor, Karachi, Pakistan

ALEX WALKED BRISKLY INTO THE pilots briefing room. There, faced with six men from the Pakistan ISI, he laid out his plans to move the prisoner. He'd already given Nabeel a medical once-over and was satisfied that despite some bruising around his face, the man was fit to fly. He placed his tote bag on a table and drew out his trauma kit, then a hypodermic needle. He looked at the men in front of him.

"First, he needs to be uncuffed and stripped of all his clothes. Cuff him again with his hands behind his back. You will need to restrain him while I give him a sedative." He held up the needle for show. "I will inject this into his right shoulder. He can remain seated. It will take a few minutes to work." He paused for questions, but none came.

"Second," he said, pulling out a rubber hot water bottle with a tube attached. "I need someone to fill this with warm water, not hot, then bring it to me. Once we have it, we need to stand him up, turn his face to the wall, bend him over and spread his legs. I will insert this tube up his rectum and flush the warm water into him." The last comment made everyone in the room cringe and shift awkwardly in their seats. "Once that's done, we'll need to move him to a bathroom quickly. Uncuff him again at this point. Sit him on the toilet and leave him there for ten minutes. At this point he'll be feeling weak from the sedation and the flushing of his bowels. I will stay with him to watch over him."

He paused once more, expecting a comment or two, but the process either horrified or intrigued them. He plowed on. "Third. He will need a shower with these." He produced plastic bottles of surgical soap and shampoo. "Fourth, he will need a towel. I will assist him in getting dried off, then I may need help to put this on him." Alex produced a

MAG—a maximum absorbency garment, an adult diaper used by NASA astronauts.

"Fifth." He produced an orange jumpsuit, a set of blacked-out ski goggles, ear protection, shackles, cuffs, and rubber slip-on shoes. "I will need help in dressing him and putting the shackles on. The ear protection will only be put on when he is about to board the plane. We will instruct him through the entire process. We need him to comply with all of our orders. The last thing I want is to sedate him again and carry him onto the plane. He needs to walk but he will be weak so we will have to support him."

He looked at the faces before him; he wasn't feeling very warm and fuzzy with his newfound friends, but he had no choice. He was on his own as four Tier 3 terror suspects were in a barricade situation with hostages in a suburb south of the city, tying up the other members of his team. The decision to move Nabeel had priority over the ongoing situation, however, as the window for the rendition flight was closing. The Gulfstream IV sat on the tarmac, awaiting its passengers and clearance from the authorities.

"Once we have air traffic control clear us for takeoff, we have thirty minutes to complete these tasks. Should I repeat the process?" A few of the men looked at each other, and it sounded like they were debating who would do what, how and when. Alex took a deep breath. "One, he will need to be uncuffed—"

Quetta, Pakistan

Mukhtar held court in a fully functioning fruit warehouse in the southern suburbs of Pakistan's tenth largest city. Known as the fruit garden of Pakistan, Quetta was one of the architect's preferred cities, with its favorable climates and its proximity to the Afghan border. Never one to call somewhere an office, Mukhtar nonetheless felt safest here to conduct his business reviews with his cohorts, agents, couriers, benefactors—and when needed, officers of the ISI. The veil of a nearby wedding party enhanced his surreptitious gathering and the frequent comings and goings of his guests. He stood at the head of a large table that was normally used to box and ship produce. Once he sat, the general meeting got underway.

At the outset, he announced to his leadership team that as his identity was now publicized by Western intelligence agencies, this would be the last time they would meet in such a large group. They would hold any future meetings face to face with individual managers at his behest, and at locations of his choosing.

With the first item on the agenda dictated and agreed to, Mukhtar moved on to the subject of security. "Four soldiers captured by the Americans, *four* . . . and why?"

"Let us not forget I also lost a man in the operation, Mukhtar." The comment came from the manager of logistics.

"I am aware of the loss. That, too, is unacceptable." He turned to his security professional. "What do you have to say? What happened?"

"A local man betrayed us, a neighbor near the house. It was not our fault, Mukhtar," the security man proffered.

"That is not true," the logistician argued. "We were betrayed because those men who were caught insisted on smoking outside at all hours. They made a spectacle of themselves, they showed no caution, no respect for the neighborhood. They were sloppy, noisy, careless."

Mukhtar raised his hand; he didn't want to allow any more strife. Losing the men, while disturbing, did not affect any ongoing operations. His risk and immediate concern were the exposure of support staff: the group's Karachi realtor and his employees who ran a network of safe locations throughout the massive city. He glumly supposed that it was likely that network was now compromised.

His thoughts also shifted to his friend, Nabeel. That was a huge personal loss, but in the scope of things, the loss of his IT consultant would have been much more devastating. The only saving grace from the latest American raid was that the highly valued Wahid had escaped. Mukhtar had his ISI agent to thank for that.

"We must move on," Mukhtar said. "There is no point in squabbling amongst ourselves. The Americans are using these raids to divide us." His voice was neither raised nor hushed, but controlled and firm.

"Let us focus on our mission, my brothers. We all know we must overcome these obstacles; we must not let these minor setbacks discourage us." There were nods around the table, though some inwardly grimaced, frowned or contained their thoughts, lest they encourage the wrath of the sheik's chosen one. "There is still much to do," he continued, "the sheik has blessed us with this jihad. We cannot falter, we cannot fail. But we must maintain our composure, and we must improve our security—"

"We are doing our best Mukhtar," the security manager offered.

Mukhtar paused. He wanted to rip into the man for interrupting his train of thought, but calmer heads needed to prevail. "Winston Churchill once said," he remarked, looking at the group, "it is no use saying we are doing our best. You have got to succeed in doing what is necessary."

"—You choose the words of an elitist, an imperialist warmonger? You have become soft, Khalid; you have spent too much time in the West," spat the manager, a little too loudly.

Mukhtar smiled. He appreciated constructive criticism, but this man who raised his voice, who used his actual name in an open meeting, was being disrespectful. He stared directly at the man, while his peripheral vision tried to check the looks on other faces around the table. "Dissention is a sure way to failure," he finally said, "and I will not accept that." He stared deeply into the eyes of the unruly man, holding his gaze for a few seconds, expecting more. But his look sunk the man's attack.

"The sheik will not accept that; none of us should accept that." Mukhtar continued, determined to bring a measure of decorum to his meeting. But his temper was simmering, close to boiling. "I choose such words hoping that we are mature and experienced enough to take such messages to embolden our cause." His voice rose as he spoke, his face was becoming flushed as he failed to keep his ire in check. "Words that will encourage our men to move forward into battle, to do what is necessary, to do more than our best!" He slammed his fist down on the table and leaned forward. He wondered how committed this man was;

if he was loyal to the cause. He needed the man to perform, but he questioned if he was irreplaceable.

He pointed a steely finger at the man. "You need to do more! I will not hear of another failure. If you need more resources, tell me! If you cannot manage your task . . . tell me, and I will have you replaced." He needed to get things back on track. He would think more about the lack of respect later. Mukhtar could tell that the man was about to utter a response, but he cut him off with a dismissive wave of his hand.

"We will distract the enemy; we will divert their attention from us. We will shore up our defenses, but we will strike, and when we do, we will strike hard. Everyone must do what is necessary NOW! We cannot afford any lapses in security or in our methods. There are many operations to consider and time is against us. The Americans grow bolder each day." He looked down at his teacup for a moment then sipped the warm beverage. He ignored the faces in the room for a few seconds more. He was drained and weary, but he needed to focus his group, he straightened up. "Let us move on . . . Kuwait and Mombasa, we are in the last stages of these operations—what is left to be done?"

The general meeting rolled on throughout the rest of the day with brief breaks for lunch and refreshments. During those down times, Khalid Sheik Mohammed spoke with each individual member of his executive team and encouraged them once again to not use cell phones and rely on trusted messengers, or coded email. He could have easily issued a direct order to the group at large to stop using the devices for security's sake, but he wanted to have personal conversations with each of his team to discern if they were following his wishes, or were reluctant to comply. It was his way of finding out who would follow his orders, and who would not.

By early evening, the senior members of the al-Qaeda team had dispersed and made their way either back to Afghanistan, other parts of Quetta or the surrounding areas. All that remained in the expansive warehouse were his personal security team and his accountant. Mukhtar was busy, engrossed in the finer details of the account book, and failed to see a new visitor standing before him. He only looked up when he heard a faint cough from the man he recognized instantly. "Peace be upon you, Hamid. Sit, sit, please my friend. It's so good to see you. How was your journey?"

"And upon you peace, Mukhtar."

Mukhtar poured some tea for his guest, but as he was doing so, he looked at the leather case being held firmly in Hamid's hands, and across his chest. Hamid's silence surprised him. He was normally more engaged. He surmised that something was wrong.

"I don't appreciate being a courier for you, Mukhtar," Hamid stated.

Mukhtar smiled as he lit a cigarette and leaned back in his chair. He sipped some of his tea, letting the Saudi stew in his consternation a second or two longer. "You do not wish to serve, Hamid?"

"That is not what I am saying. I think that there are others that are more suited for this type of work."

Mukhtar scoffed. *Typical of a high-born Saudi—they never want to get their hands dirty*, he thought. Yet his words differed, "Then please accept my apologies." But Mukhtar had lied; it was neither heartfelt nor meaningful. He didn't need to apologize to the Saudi, however he needed to placate him for a few minutes more.

"The money you have brought is important to me," he continued. "Thank you for your service Hamid." He held out his hands for the bag, which Hamid gladly handed over to Mukhtar, who then passed it over to his accountant, who emptied the contents.

As the accountant began his task, Mukhtar turned back to his visitor. "So, tell me of your adventures. Why did you come all this way to see me?"

"Faizan told me you needed cash. I met him in Abu Dhabi, and I told him I needed to see you."

"While you were searching for Jawad?"

"Yes. My sources informed me that Jawad went to London to meet with the British authorities, but he was killed in an automobile accident. He is no longer a threat to us, Mukhtar."

Mukhtar already knew of the Saudi intelligence officer's demise.

He'd wanted confirmation from someone other than Hamid. "And you trust your informers? This account is accurate?"

"Yes, Mukhtar. I still have some people loyal to us in England and at the embassy there. Jawad is no longer with us."

"It saddens me to hear the news. I was hoping to be the one to . . . discuss with him his . . . thoughts about his activities against us. It is God's will."

"Indeed, it is, Mukhtar."

Mukhtar looked across to the accountant, who nodded in confirmation that the amount received was the amount requested. The accountant took the bag, got up from the table and left the meeting.

Mukhtar held a smoking cigarette in his right hand, which rested on the large table. With his other hand he toyed with his bushy moustache, contemplating what Hamid expected were fantasies of torturing and butchering his former Saudi compatriot.

But Hamid's thoughts were only about his own subsequent moves. He wanted to know what was in store for him. He had delivered the message and the cash. He had no job; he had no country; he was now at the mercy of the fat man with the far-away look sitting in front of him. He sweated nervously.

The man had read his thoughts. "So, what is next for you now Hamid?" he asked.

"I am at your service, Mukhtar, God willing I am at your mercy, for I have nothing."

Mukhtar conceded that his last statement was true. Hamid was indeed a lost soul. Although Mukhtar disliked Faizan, his silent Middle Eastern investor, the man was shrewd enough and committed enough to the cause to recognize Hamid's vulnerability and lack of direction. It was his initiative that led Hamid to Quetta with the supply of cash. Faizan knew Hamid was weak, and if not redirected, would become a risk to the organization.

As Mukhtar was contemplating what other duties he could assign to the Saudi, his accountant entered the warehouse with a younger man in tow. The accountant presented a note to his leader and stepped back.

Mukhtar read the message and turned the note upside down on the table in front of him. He turned to the young man, then stood up to greet him and hug him. The show of intimacy confused Hamid. It was a trait he had neither ever seen, nor heard that his leader was capable of. He was more of a standoffish, no-contact type of man.

"Majid, how are you my American friend?" Mukhtar asked.

The Arab American addressed him with the customary Arabic greeting and smiled at his host. Hamid noted that Mukhtar seemed genuinely pleased to see the visitor and he listened intently as they briefly chatted about various things that were not of a military or operational nature. Hamid was jealous of the familiarity that he too once enjoyed with his leader.

"Please sit, please sit, my brother," Mukhtar told the young man. "No, not there, next to my friend," he suggested as he pointed at the chair next to Hamid. "Hamid, please say hello to Majid from Baltimore. Majid, may I introduce to you my friend from Riyadh, Hamid."

The men acknowledged each other and then looked at Mukhtar across the table, both apprehensive, waiting for the fat man to talk.

Finally, he addressed the new visitor. "Majid, I have a mission for you."

"Yes, Mukhtar, I am ready."

"Hamid, who did you say your sources were in London?"

"I have a variety of sources there," Hamid replied, "what is it you wish to know?"

Thus, Mukhtar began a three-way tennis game with the two men before him. "Majid, I need you to go to Jakarta."

"Of course, as you wish."

"Do your sources in London include the authorities there, Hamid?"

"Mukhtar, I . . . have—" Hamid stumbled but couldn't finish his sentence.

Mukhtar ignored the pathetic plea, but spoke to the Arab American again, "I want you to meet Hambali, Majid."

"Answer me Hamid—were you in contact with the British MI6?"

"While you are there, Majid, you are to pass on a message from the sheik."

Majid wisely kept his mouth shut. He let his leader play the mind game with the man sitting next to him. He was startled by the interactions, as he wasn't sure what this man had done to expect this treatment, but he was not the reason why. He calmly kept his hands clenched on his lap and dared not look over to his fidgety partner.

"A member of MI6 has become interested in Faizan," Mukhtar stated to Hamid.

Hamid panicked; his heart bounced quicker than usual. "What, what are you saying . . . what are you inferring?"

Mukhtar bounced back to Majid. "I have some cash that you need to deliver to him."

"Who have you been speaking to Hamid, what have you said?"

Then back to the new visitor. "As we are experiencing some security issues, I need you to follow my directions closely, I know I can trust you to follow orders Majid." The Arab American nodded and remained quiet.

"Answer me, Hamid! What have you done?"

Hamid's heart fluttered again. He was trying to maintain control of his faculties, and not to show any weakness toward the infamous butcher. *What does he know?* he wondered.

"On your journey I want you to be escorted," Mukhtar noted to the younger man. "These are hard times for us all and we must take precautions; you understand?"

"Of course," Majid answered.

Mukhtar was now leaning on the table with both his elbows, leaning forward, changing his emotions and tone depending on who he was talking to. "Before you left Singapore, after you left the Saudi embassy you went to the British Hamid, why?"

"Mukhtar, I have sources everywhere—"

"When you leave here, Majid, I will have someone take you to Karachi, where you will board a plane to Oman, from there to Sri Lanka, and then on to Jakarta."

"Hamid, talk to me, what have you done?"

"Mukhtar, Jawad was a spy for the British, I merely tried to establish his location, that is what you wanted of me."

"Majid, this journey of yours will last a few weeks my friend. You will meet with many of our brothers, and I am sure that you can be discreet with your mission."

"It is an honor to serve, Mukhtar; I will not break your faith."

Mukhtar smiled. He often received appreciation for his actions, but knew that this was a heartfelt one. His grin dissipated as he again turned to Hamid. "Yet you went to Faizan, you have exposed him."

"I was transiting to London, Mukhtar, he and I met to discuss—"

"You must pass on our gratitude to Hambali for his help in the jihad, Majid. The sheik holds him in high regard and sees more cooperation between our two organizations in the future."

"You met to discuss what, Hamid? What did you need to talk to him about? How to clear out your secret bank accounts?"

The tennis match continued between the three men; Mukhtar was relishing the contest. Majid was an active and willing participant, but Hamid was suffering, badly.

Mukhtar continued, "The sheik and I have also approved of his operation in Bali. It is important that you stress that point, Majid. We approve of this action and his upcoming projects in Jakarta."

"Mukhtar, I have done nothing of the sort," Hamid pleaded.

Mukhtar rocked back at the denial. "Do not insult my intelligence Hamid. You are one step from running away. You are a coward. You were turning to the British in London for safety; you met with Faizan for help with your investments."

"Mukhtar, that is not true—"

"The cash that I am giving you, Majid, is more than what we agreed upon. It is a symbol not just of our generosity, nor our affluence, but one of reward for what he is about to do. You must relay that message for the sheik."

"I completely understand Mukhtar." Majid kept his responses brief; he sensed that more volleys would fly towards the unwilling Arab participant.

"Your only saving grace in this regretful episode, Hamid, is that you did not get to London. I believe that you did not tell them much in Singapore because you knew you would not be safe there from me."

"You and I must have dinner tonight, Majid. We must discuss your plans for attacks in the United States; I am very intrigued with your ideas."

"Mukhtar, please, I beg you, I have no intentions of running away," Hamid interjected, desperate to turn the conversation away from the clearly impending danger.

"Yet you chose to empty your accounts, for what?"

Majid wanted to ask a few questions of his own. He assumed there would be more time for him later to do just that. He sat in silence, watching his leader in action. The man's tactics were impressive. Some watching might have thought he was bipolar, crazed, or had some other personality disorder. Majid didn't know, but he watched, waited and learned.

"For safety, Mukhtar," Hamid pleaded. "I don't know how much Jawad knew of my association with you."

"He knew enough for you to lead him to me, idiot!" With that, there was a momentary break in the play. Mukhtar stood, but placed both hands on the table and leaned forward, toward Hamid. "You have exposed Faizan. How do you know the British did not follow you?"

"They did not follow me . . . it is true that I wanted to clear my investments—"

"Don't worry about your money Hamid. The sheik and I thank you for your contributions."

Majid smiled. He often thought about where the money for operations came from, and now he was witnessing a shakedown; he wondered if the timid Arab had more to offer.

Hamid's shoulders slumped; the news of losing his hard-earned money destroyed him. "You cannot do that Mukhtar! Why are you doing this to me? I do not deserve this—I have been a loyal soldier, I have done nothing wrong." He pleaded, staring at his tormentor, his hands balled into fists, his eyes watering, sweat drenching his body.

Mukhtar studied Hamid closely, frustrated with himself for trusting him to find Jawad when he knew it would be a futile task. His gut had told him to take care of Hamid in Singapore, and therefore avoid this confrontation. However, if he did, then he would not have added more money to the al-Qaeda war chest. In the big picture, it wasn't much, but it was exactly what he needed to appease the leader of the Indonesian terrorist organization, Jemaah Islamiyah.

Mukhtar backed away from the table. "Majid, my brother, come let us eat, we have more to discuss." Before he walked off, he looked at one of his men, who unbeknownst to Hamid, was standing a few feet behind him with a garrote in his hands, waiting for the signal to kill Mukhtar's traitor.

Mukhtar nodded and slithered away.

Chisinau, Moldova

Chris tapped gently on the door of the CIA safe house. It didn't take long for a woman, who he guessed to be in her early sixties, to open the door. She didn't speak but urged him to enter, shutting the door quickly behind him while pointing to a corridor that led to the back of a typical residential house on a typical residential street.

Chris set his bag down on the kitchen floor and did a quick reconnaissance of his surroundings. As he was doing so, a tall, young, fit-looking man appeared from another room holding a shotgun. They both nodded at each other; two professionals who needed no words.

The woman appeared again after a few seconds. "Front door, if you please," she told the shotgun soldier. He obeyed without hesitation. "There's one more upstairs with our guest," she commented for Chris's benefit.

"Marines?" he asked.

"Yes, that's all I could get. I have one of my staff out getting some food. He should be here shortly."

Chris stuck out his hand, addressing the woman. "Chris Morehouse, nice to meet you."

"Kathleen Hayes, Chief of Station."

"I heard you were a bit shorthanded," Chris said. "I don't know how long I'll be here, but I'll try to get this thing moving as quick as I can. Did Gene update you on a flight?"

"There isn't one," Kathleen responded flatly.

Miffed, Chris tried not to show his annoyance. He knew it meant that there was something amiss in the planning. He had been working flight schedules for the rendition teams while he was still in Paris. He wondered what the delay was, and if he was there taking care of business, would there even be a problem? "I'm sure that's not what you wanted to hear," Chris responded blankly. "I'm sure he's trying to get things sorted; I know how complicated it can be."

"Gene and I go way back, Chris. He's sympathetic to the situation here, but I guess you boys have been busy lately, and this guy is way down on the prioritization list. He says we may have to sit tight for up to thirty-six hours."

"It's not as if I've never babysat before. Where is he anyway?" Chris nonchalantly replied, trying to keep the mood light.

"Upstairs bedroom. We've secured him as best we could. Your package is also upstairs in the adjoining room."

"What's your read on him Kathleen, threat or no threat?"

"No threat, Chris. Seems pretty meek, a little frail if you ask me. He's a bit beaten up though; the local border police roughed him up trying to drag information out of him. They didn't get very far with him and handed him over to us because of a false passport and a US Visa that hasn't been used. He pled innocence, but we ran him through Langley and he is a person of interest."

Chris wasn't there to second-guess the CTC's rationale; neither was Kathleen. It seems they were both shoved into a low-key affair, and all they had to do was follow orders. Agreements or disagreements would not enter their minds.

"Language? I hear he's German."

"He has some English, but I don't think he's comfortable with it, but then again, he could be playing us." Chris didn't need to ask if she had done any interrogation, or at least quizzed him on the basics. He wouldn't be there if she hadn't. He thought that she must have vetted the detainee somehow, hence the rendition request. "Mind if I take a look?"

"Sure, come on up."

When the pair got to the top of the stairs, they encountered the second Marine, who was cradling an M4 carbine across his chest. He never opened his mouth, nor did he acknowledge the visitors. But he made his way to a bedroom door, looked through a peephole, retrieved a set of keys and opened it, allowing the two CIA officers to enter. Kathleen entered first, with Chris behind. The Marine stood in the doorway, weapon at the ready.

As described, they had shackled the man loosely by one of his feet to one end of the metal bed. He sat up when Chris and Kathleen entered. He remained quiet, as did Chris, who could tell from the man's eyes that they scared him. Kathleen described him as meek, which wasn't too far off the mark. Chris would have said the captive was timid, even shy. His graying, close-cropped hair was well maintained, his teeth were white, his fingernails clean. He was skinny, almost sickly, and was the type of guy who would need to run around in the shower to get wet.

Chris was expecting a more belligerent captive, someone more taut or hyper, but this man was different. Chris imagined that if he raised his hand to swat a fly, the man on the bed might wince and cower, like a dog scared of his master's beating.

One of the prisoner's eyes was blackened and his lower lip was swollen, from the police beating that he had received. Chris wondered what other bodily damage there was, and reminded himself to ask Kathleen for a doctor to pay him a visit before the rendition got underway. He needed to establish the man's fitness before he gave him the sedative for the journey ahead.

Chris studied the man further and noted that he was still quiet. Once again, Chris thought it strange. He saw his shoes, neatly tucked under the bed. He was wearing a white, blood-speckled shirt, tucked into black trousers. *He looks like a fricking waiter that's been up all night*, Chris thought. *Is this the right guy? What's wrong with this picture? He's not the definition of a threat.*

After only being in the room for a minute, Chris turned around and left, followed shortly by Kathleen. The couple retreated to the kitchen once again.

"Want something? Coffee, water?" she offered.

"Water will be fine, thanks."

Kathleen opened up the fridge and passed Chris a cold bottle. He opened it up and guzzled half of it down.

"I know what you're thinking. He's not the one, right?"

Chris wanted to be on his best behavior. Kathleen had stated earlier that she and Gene were friends. He needed to toe the party line. "I appreciate you trying to confide in me," he said, "but I'm here to follow orders. My opinion doesn't matter."

"Gene tells me different." She smiled.

I'm not biting, he told himself. He was going to be all business. Then he remembered that he wanted to ask Kathleen something. "Is there any chance we can get a doctor to see him? His face is bruised up, but who knows if he is nursing something more."

"Yes, I think I can arrange that . . . seeing that we'll be here for a while. Anything else?"

"I can feed him, help if he needs a bio break, all that stuff. The Marines here for the duration?"

"They're yours to use as you deem fit. Here . . . let me give you my number. I'll stick around a while longer, but if you need something, anytime, call me, I'm about ten minutes away."

"Thanks, but I want to keep things quiet around here. Don't need nosey neighbors and we don't need a ton of traffic going in and out. I'll split shifts with the Marines, keep them here. It would be great if you can make sure there are enough edibles for a while."

"Sure. Do you want to call Gene, or should I?"

"I can do that. I have a bit of a background in our logistics; perhaps we can figure something out to speed up this process. I don't want to be a drain on your manpower here, and I don't want to disrupt whatever . . . other activities you may have going on."

Kathleen's phone rang, and she wandered away to take the call. She came back after a few seconds.

"Food's here, there're some plates and things in the cupboards . . . if you don't mind?"

Chris was comfortable with Kathleen. Just because she was stationed in some faraway forgotten outlier posting, it didn't mean she was a dud. It would be quite the opposite, as the region she was responsible for extended way past the borders of the small eastern European country. She was probably an ally that he could depend on.

For once he was strangely at ease. He wanted to desperately to get back into the swing of things after his injuries from the beating in Islamabad, and the unfortunate fight with Sandy. But now, sitting at the top of the stairs with a shotgun in his hands and two Marines eating in the kitchen, he felt relaxed. He didn't feel threatened; he didn't expect the door to explode, or masked intruders land on the roof. But he sensed the danger of boredom creeping in.

After both Marines ate, he prepared a meal for his captive and took it to him. He never spoke when he entered the bedroom, but passed over a hefty plate of goulash soup, bread, and a bottle of water. He wasn't sure what reception he would get—if the meal would be thrown back at him, not eaten at all, or devoured in seconds.

"Thank you," came the simple reply in English. Chris still didn't say a word. He made his way over to the window, kept his distance from the glass, and stared off into the night sky. A trailing thought of a sniper shot flitted through his mind quicker than the attention span of a goldfish. He was out on the edge, in a backwater with nothing to do but wonder what this man did, or was about to do, that gave the CIA so much interest.

He turned back to the man on the bed, hands in his pockets, mind in neutral, brain checked into dullness. He watched the man eat his meal slowly, relishing each morsel as if it were his last. He didn't rush, didn't ponder, he just seemed grateful for the meal.

Chris spotted a TV stashed in the room's corner and made a move to drag it out. He couldn't find a remote, and he had to plug it in. He found the function keys on the front of the screen and hit the power button. He wasn't sure what he was going to find, so he hit the up and down arrows until he found a football game. He paused and turned around to see if the man had an interest. "Bayern Munich, Eintracht Frankfurt," the captive reported.

Chris, sensing that there was a curiosity, turned up the volume, found a chair and sat to watch the game. It didn't matter that neither of the men in the room understood what was being said by the commentators on the TV. The commonality of the world's biggest sport joined the two in a temporary cessation of psychological hostilities.

It took Chris only a few minutes to figure out that the captive was a Munich fan from the few harmless curse words that he quietly used whenever Frankfurt had an advantage. It took him a few minutes more to figure out the man was probably a resident of Bavaria, as his use of certain phrases piqued Chris's own memories of his time there.

The man was loosening up and sitting up on the bed as the game continued to swing both ways. When the first goal was scored, the captive tried to jump off the bed. Chris didn't see the move in full view, but his peripheral vision caught it, and made him jump out of his chair and stand over the man.

"Take it easy, sit down," he ordered forcefully. The captive shied away from Chris, avoiding eye contact, and then tried to see around his captor to watch the replay of the score. Chris backed away and sat down. He looked over at the man again. *What the fuck am I doing here? Either this guy has been taking acting lessons from Laurence Olivier, or some Muppet has got this wrong.*

They continued to watch the game, however the man became more subdued as the game crept on without little action or fanfare. It ended with a single score, and the captive lying back on the bed, left to stare at the ceiling. Chris tried his best to find something different on the channels, but found nothing of interest. He turned the TV off and paced the room. He'd been contemplating talking with the man, but his rulebook told him not to. It was not his remit to interrogate, or even open up a conversation about something as benign as butterflies and fairy dust—but he couldn't scratch the irritation that he was feeling. This man didn't belong here, and he wanted to know why.

"Why are you here?" he finally asked.

The man sat up straight. He smiled. "You speak German."

"Why are you here?" Chris repeated himself.

"I don't know," he answered sheepishly, shoulders slumped in defeat, dread, and finality.

Chris paused. His experience told him that the men in captivity picked up by the rendition teams were more or less the same. Unusually quiet and in denial, and accepting of their fate; or loud-mouthed, combative and physically a handful to maneuver. This man was neither.

"Why did the police beat you?"

"Money."

Jesus, what now? Chris tried to mask his disgust.

"That can't be the real reason. Do you know where you are?"

"No."

"Do you know who we are?"

"American, British . . . I don't know."

Chris paced around again; his hands were dug deep into his pockets as if searching for answers. On the one hand he knew he should shut up, as it was not his business to get into; but on the other, he felt as if he had to.

"The police stopped you for a reason. Why?"

"I was driving . . . they wanted to see . . . my passport." He stammered; his eyes were filling up. "They said . . . I was driving too fast . . . they wanted money."

Kathleen hadn't told him about this side of the story; not that she needed to, but he now questioned if her earlier fishing expedition for his opinion was a game that she and Gene had concocted. He put the thought out of his mind, for now.

"You are German?"

"Yes."

"Where are you from?"

"Ulm."

Chris was correct in his assumption that he was from the German state of Bavaria. "How did you get here?"

"I drove . . . with my car."

The answer caused Chris's eyebrows to lift. "You drove all the way from Germany to here?"

"Yes."

"What type of car?"

"Mercedes . . . the Police, they took it."

Oh, for fuck's sake. They pull him over for speeding, beat the shit out of him for his money, take his car, and hand him over to us for a fake passport. The bloke has been taken for a ride. Chris sighed heavily. Showing emotion in front of a prisoner was another no-no, but so was asking questions. He was out of his swim lane. But he believed he was right to do so, now that he had heard the man's story. He knew he should have given up thinking about it right there and then, but the unfairness and unjustness of the situation demanded that he find out more. He continued his question-and-answer session, not allowing his captive to ask anything; only for him to reply to what was being asked.

After a short time, Chris, seated opposite the captive on the bed, sympathized with the lackluster German. It was too late to call Gene, and he trusted no one else at CTC to discuss his findings, so he stored away those thoughts until the next morning. But he plowed on with his questions. Thirty more minutes into the quiz, Chris got to the bottom of the man's epic driving journey. "Where were you going?"

"Odessa, Ukraine."

Shit, the poor bastard almost made it; another three or four hours he would have gotten there. "What's there?"

"My daughter."

"You just wanted to visit you daughter? That's a long way to go. Why didn't you fly?"

"I wanted to bring her back with me, her things . . . she doesn't belong there. She needs to come home with me, away from her boyfriend." The captive was welling up again.

Family drama, really? This just gets better and better. Chris let a pause drag out a few minutes. He could tell that the man was close to his daughter, but he needed to be objective. There had to be more to this man. He couldn't ignore the fact that someone in the CIA had flagged him for a reason, which warranted a rendition to a black site. He didn't envy his captive; someone was going to run him through the mill and extract some kind of information out of him. Chris became interested in the carpet's pattern before him. He reminded himself that he was there to do one job, but the situation hounded him. "What's wrong with the boyfriend? Why should she come home?" he asked, genuinely concerned.

"He is a rich man, too rich. He is a gambler . . . a nasty man. He has abused her . . . she was pregnant but—"

Chris looked up; the man was crying. He let him carry on.

"She lost the baby; he beat her one night."

Chris felt sadness and anger at the same time. *Mutherfucker.*

"He cheats on her," he continued. "He has whores, other women . . . he buys them gifts, drugs, he gives them money . . . he is no good." There was another long pause as the two men reflected on the evil that men do. "He sheds humiliation on the Muslim faith."

Chris shot up bolt straight. "What?"

"He is not a devout Muslim. He brings shame to Allah, praise be his name."

That's a twist I didn't see coming. WTF? "What does this man do in Odessa? Where does he get his money from?" Chris asked, now with a sparkle in his eye.

"He is an investor, a businessman; he owns a hotel in Odessa, he has a yacht there. But he has many homes across the Middle East. My daughter tells me he has investments in Abu Dhabi, and he spends most of his time there. That is why I needed to go now, to get her, to take her home . . . before he takes her further away from me."

Chris looked at his watch. It was late. *Goddammit, I'm going to have to get this checked out before this goes too far.* "What's his name—the investor— what is his name?"

"Faizan . . . Faizan al Shamsi."

CHAPTER NINE

Chisinau, Moldova

CHRIS NEEDED TO TALK TO someone. Cooped up in the safe house for almost twenty hours, his patience was wearing thin. It didn't help that the two Marines were very professional about doing their job, by not talking to him or intruding on the operation—they were obediently following orders without a complaint or murmur of frustration. Chris tried calling Gene multiple times, but only received a voice mail for his efforts.

On two occasions Kathleen reached out to him as a standard check-in procedure, but on both occasions, she confirmed that she had heard nothing new about a flight for the captive. Tempted to share with her what he'd found out about the man, he held back his minor investigation, not knowing if he could fully trust the Chief of Station. He loped back to see the prisoner, to pick apart his story.

"I have been thinking about you," the man remarked as Chris entered.

"There's no need to think about me. You need to consider yourself."

"I have only told you the truth. I don't know who you are or what your name is."

Chris didn't know the man's name either. He shouldn't have even started a conversation with him, but his instincts told him he needed to. Then he had another dilemma moment. His job told him to shut up and treat the man like any other terrorist combatant, but his compassionate side, his humane side, one that rarely reared its head, told him to push on.

"Tell me about Ulm, tell me about what you do."

"You are British, you do not have an American accent."

"My business, not yours," Chris answered curtly. He didn't want to go down that road with the man. He was sympathetic, but he wasn't his friend.

"Your German is good."

"So is yours," Chris deflected. "Tell me your story again, from the beginning."

"But I want to hear your story."

Chris knew he should have gotten up and walked away, but he was feeling obstinate. He wanted to be sure that the information he'd gleaned the night before was still fresh in his mind before he talked things out with Gene. He also wanted to pick the story apart, spot an inaccuracy, a mistake, a new tidbit. He stood in front of the bed, arms folded across his chest, waiting for the man to speak.

The man was not forthcoming. Chris thought the prisoner might have had the chance to reassess the situation after he doled out his spiel the night before, and was now playing for time. The captive didn't realize that he was being held by the CIA and soon to be whisked away to a dirty dungeon in some faraway hole to face torture, beatings and humiliation.

Chris pulled up a chair and sat across from him, arms still folded across his chest. "Tell me about Ulm, tell me about what you do," he repeated.

"Why, why should I? I told you all that I know."

Chris noticed that he seemed a little more chipper than the previous evening. The man was feeling comfortable and was adjusting to his surroundings. He may have even thought, by explaining himself to his captor, that all would be well and they would release him. He didn't know that the tough-looking jailer was not his savior; he didn't know how much peril he was in.

Chris again reflected that he had overstepped his mark. He had provided his captive with a false sense of security, and he was now feeling at ease and less likely to cooperate fully. It wouldn't take long for the man to demand something, instead of asking. He preferred the man he met when he first entered the bedroom with Kathleen Hayes: wide-eyed, pathetic, sad and lost. An easy mark for a seasoned interrogator, something that Chris was not. He got out of his chair and started for the door.

"My name is Mahmud al Mouhammed," the man blurted, trying to stop Chris from leaving. He achieved his goal, as his captor stopped mid-stride and turned to face him.

"I was born in Lebanon, but I am a German national . . . I have a small carpet business in Ulm. I don't know why I am here; I don't know who you are, I don't know what you want from me." The puppy dog eyes were back.

"Tell me about your journey, tell me why you are here," Chris ordered.

"I am on the way to find my daughter—"

An hour after he started the Q&A, Chris left the room to relieve himself. As he was doing so, his cell phone rang. He cradled the device between his right cheek and his shoulder.

"Hang on Gene, just shaking hands with the unemployed."

"What? Chris . . . what the hell are you talking about."

Chris flushed the toilet, zipped up and washed his hands. "All good Gene. What's going on? Do you have some news for me?"

"Yes, be at the airport at 0300."

"Where to?"

"Salt Pit."

Shit, Afghanistan . . . this is bad. "Gene, we may have a problem."

"Chris, I don't want problems and don't give me that shit about providing your manager with a solution either; save that for some dippy corporate job. I don't want to hear about it. The next time I want to hear from you is when you're wheels up and out of country."

"I don't think this is our guy, we should—"

"—Tell me you haven't been talking to him." Gene almost shouted into his end of the phone.

Chris thought there was no way to sugarcoat his way around the issue. "I have—"

"—You fucking idiot! Not only is it not your job, but you may have compromised any investigation that we were about to conduct. What the fuck Chris? What the fuck . . . Goddammit!"

Chris had to hold the phone away from his ear for a few seconds. He too was getting flustered, and tramped out of the back of the house, through a small garden and into a shed at the end of a path. He needed to keep the conversation away from the Marines, and even further away from the prisoner. "Have you heard why he was picked up?" he asked Gene.

"I don't give a flying fuck why, where, or when, what he has done or not. Our job . . . *your* job is to transport him—and that's it. What the hell is wrong with you? I gave you a simple task, and now you are fucking it up. Jesus Christ, Chris, I thought I could trust you."

"Gene you've got to hear me out . . . give me a second here. Let me—"

Gene was still going off the deep end. The expletives were being shot at Chris thick and fast. He'd had had some searing verbal abuse thrown in his direction over the years in the British Army, but this was getting above and beyond what he was used to. He raised his eyebrows a few times; he rolled his eyes; he let out long deep breaths, and he willed his composure to level out. Gene was more than pissed off at him, he was apoplectic.

"Gene," he repeated, "hear me out!" His plea was falling on deaf ears. He had to shout just to get a word in edgeways. "Gene, for fuck's sake, listen for a minute!" Chris's words finally stopped the tirade, and Gene replied in a more somber tone.

"You are so close to being put on a plane home, Chris. Okay, speak to me."

"The guy is Lebanese-German. He doesn't know who I am or what he is doing here. I spoke German to him the entire time." Chris conveniently left out the part of being suspected as a Brit. "He doesn't have my name, and my conversations with him were all one-way. He talked, I asked, period."

"Chris, my patience is running thin; get to the point."

Chris relayed the two conversations he had with the prisoner. Gene cut in a few times to clarify a few things, but Chris was getting frustrated as Gene was preventing him from getting to the end of the story.

"Listen, I don't know what this means, but this girl's boyfriend . . . the investor, his name is Faizan al Shamsi—"

Gene, finally lost for words, stuck on the name he heard. He didn't listen to the rest of Chris's dialog.

"Say that again," he finally uttered, breaking into Chris's speech.

"What?"

"The name Chris, the name."

"Faizan, Faizan al Shamsi . . ." He looked down at the phone, thinking he had lost the connection. "Gene, are you still there?"

"Give me a minute, Chris, stay on the line." He put Chris on hold. *That means something at least; maybe it wasn't a dickhead move after all.* Gene came back on the line after a few minutes.

"Okay, I've kicked that up the line. Anything else?"

"Why was he picked up Gene? The cops beat the crap out of him, took his money and car."

"His name pinged a database, there were passport issues, that was enough."

Chris pondered the statement for a few seconds. He wasn't buying it. "His name, really? How many 'al Mouhammad's' are on our databases, Gene?"

"Not your problem, not my problem, don't want to hear about it, don't give a shit. We have a job to do. Anything else?" Gene answered abruptly.

"No." Chris realized that he was on thin ice, and didn't offer to interrogate the prisoner further. "What's next?"

"Next?" Gene asked, almost sarcastically. "Next, you have a flight at 0300, that's what's next Chris."

"After what I just told you, and you still want to ship this guy off?"

"I've kicked it upwards Chris. Someone else will catch it and run with it, that's all there is. So, don't piss me off anymore because I don't give a shit if you've been swapping spit with him in a hot steamy shower and you've fallen in love. Get him on that plane. I don't want to hear another fucking thing from you until it's done."

This is not our guy, this is the wrong man, this is wrong! Chris wanted to scream, but he held back. He knew now that fresh information had surfaced, someone at the CIA would want to know the source. Formal CIA or FBI interrogations were enough to establish good workable intelligence, but a name from an overzealous SAD renditions team member—one who had a reputation for working outside his remit—may not be considered a reliable source.

"Tell me you understand your orders, Chris."

"Yes Gene, understood."

Gene tamped down his tone to pass on one last piece of information. "Just one more thing before I let you go. Jawad Halabi was killed in a car accident in the UK a few days ago."

Chris closed his eyes. His eyelids burned; he bowed his head in silence, wishing the news wasn't true. A few seconds later, his eyes sprang open in confusion, "Wait . . . you're telling me this now? What the hell, Gene?"

"This is the first opportunity—"

Chris shook his head and stood up. He needed some air. "Car accident? Really?"

"What can I tell you, Chris. That's all the information I have."

"How convenient for you, Gene . . . one less person to muddy the waters in your precious game."

Gene was tiring of the constant bickering, "Now hang on a minute, buddy—"

Chris didn't respond; he hung up the phone.

Chris placed his tote bag on the kitchen table and drew out a trauma kit, then a hypodermic needle. He looked at the two Marines in front of him.

"First, he needs to be unshackled and stripped of all his clothes. Then cuff him with his hands behind his back. You will need to restrain him while I give him a sedative." He held up the needle for show. "I will inject this into his right shoulder. He can remain seated. It will take a few minutes to work." He paused for questions, but none came.

"Second." He pulled out a rubber hot water bottle with a tube attached. The two Marines looked at each other as if to say, *What the fuck?*

CIA Annex, Bagram Air Base, Afghanistan

Chris sat in the back of the briefing room, studying the white linoleum floor in significant detail while contemplating his current situation. He was happy to be part of the upcoming briefing session, but only because Gene wasn't there to chew the other side of his ass off. He was back to being miserable, lonely and confused. Torn after having completed his mission to deliver the German captive to the black site, his conscience was weighing him down. After loading the poor man aboard the CIA Boeing 737-700 all discussions and worries had to be put aside; the prisoner was now in the CIA system and being processed for interrogation. Chris didn't envy the carpet salesman from Ulm.

"You look like you've had better days."

Chris looked up to see his friend standing in front of him. "Hey beanstalk, how's it going?" he asked.

Alex pulled up a chair next to him. "Better than you; what's up?"

"You seen Gene?"

"Yeah, he's in the office."

"Fuck."

"What have you done to piss him off this time, Chris?"

"Long story. I've probably screwed the pooch a good one this time." Alex shook his head. He hadn't heard of Chris's latest misadventure and he didn't think Gene was on the warpath, so he wasn't sure what was amiss.

"Looks like we're running late. Talk to me."

It relieved Chris to get things off his chest. He didn't want a depression session, but he needed to air his thoughts. "I just got in from Moldova, picked up a guy there, dropped him off at the Pit."

Alex didn't see the problem. "So?"

"He's not a combatant Alex. We've got the wrong guy."

"Chris, we've all been there, shit I've been there. All you did was your job, you got him here, it's now up to the mind fuckers to sort it out. What are you worried about? It's out of your hands."

Chris looked at Alex for a few seconds before answering. He swallowed hard; he tried to look away, but soon faced his friend again. "I interviewed him."

Alex rocked back in his chair. "Oh, Jesus fuck Chris, what the hell?" His voice almost too loud. At least Chris said "interview," not "interrogation," that was a plus. "What the hell do you mean *interview*, what . . . what the fuck possessed you to do that?"

"I got a vibe, a feeling that it wasn't right."

"You know you could have compromised this whole fucking thing right? It's no wonder you're worried about Gene. Shit, you need to be worried about . . ."

Alex couldn't finish his thought as Gene swaggered into the briefing room behind two senior CIA SAD officers, and another CIA case officer he'd seen elsewhere but forgotten his name. The room was quiet. Chris looked down at the floor, trying to decide how difficult it would be for him to dig a hole to hide in. He didn't hear the beginning of the discussion, but he was feeling someone's X-ray eyes beam down on him. He was right. When he eventually looked up, Gene was staring at him—and him alone. There was a picture of a man on the screen, with his name printed below. Chris's eyes widened. Faizan al Shamsi.

"Our target is Faizan al Shamsi," one of the briefers began. "Suspected al-Qaeda financier. A citizen of the United Arab Emirates, he owns FII Holdings and Investments out of Abu Dhabi. We believe that he also has ties, or had ties with the al Makasseb General Trading Company in New York. The FBI is still digging into this guy, but they also believe that he may have provided some scholarship money to the University of Hamburg School for Applied Science." The CIA officer let the news sink in for a minute. "I'm sure we can all connect the dots here, even if it's high level. However, new intelligence has come to light and we have a green light to go get him." The last statement garnered a few nods from around the SAD team. "Our challenge is finding him. We're working with the FBI closely on this one, along with other allies in the region: Mossad, Saudi intelligence, the Pakistan ISI—"

"We'll never get him then," came a comment from one of the team, followed by a few giggles.

"Alright class of '82, settle down. CTC are following several leads, there are lots of digital trails to follow, stuff you need to be aware of. Abu Zubaydah, who we all know, was picked up in Pakistan with a cell phone and some credit cards on him, which are now in the possession of the FBI. Turns out that Zubaydah was texting someone at FII Holdings asking for the credit card limits to be increased. Since this is recent information, we haven't been able to follow through with him to find out who he was texting or asking for money. Our inclination is that Faizan or one of the minions at his company is involved. Good news for us, as we were able to find a few more individuals linked this way. The cards have now been turned off, however, if you come across any down the road, grab them—we need them."

Chris noted the briefer didn't say "grab them before the FBI or any other law enforcement agency did"—he didn't need to, everyone knew the hidden reference.

The briefer continued. "If you see a phone, we would like to see some numbers." The veiled meaning was once again surreptitiously dropped into the discussion. The CIA didn't want good workable intelligence ending up in the evidence rooms of the FBI, never to see the light of day again.

"Chris?" The briefer called out.

Chris almost jumped out of his seat hearing his name. "One of your buddies gave us a lead that's worth mentioning. Jawad Halabi, of Saudi Intelligence, who recently died in a traffic accident, passed on Faizan's name to MI6, who then shared it with us. We don't really know what he was investigating, but he had suspicions that someone in his own organization was involved with al-Qaeda." The briefer looked down on his notes for a name. "One Hamid Deeb, Saudi Intelligence . . . seems that he has disappeared, but his name popped up recently in some electronic and cash transfers out of FII. We also tracked him flying into Abu Dhabi, but that's the last anyone has seen him. If anyone comes across Mr. Deeb, we have space in our guesthouse for him."

"Anything on KSM; is there a link?" a team member asked.

"Possibly, but nothing is firm as yet. We're working on Faizan's phones, looking at his banking connections, his money, his business connections, the works. This guy is rich, and I don't mean, lottery rich, this guy has it all—yachts, planes, super cars by the dozen; he owns multiple properties, a hotel or two. It's all stuff we are looking at, but we want him to give us the keys. We need to figure out if he has a direct connection with KSM and bin Laden. We need to get this prick, and it needs to be done quickly . . . and, yes, I know, there's always a but . . . but we don't know where he is."

A grumble party began at the front of the group. The briefer raised his hands. "I know, I know, if it were easy everyone would be doing it, right?" Chris looked at Alex, who remained quiet but shrugged his shoulders.

"We have the Viewpoint surveillance team already out and about doing their thing. You lucky ladies will join them, but I'm splitting you up into two-man teams. We'll focus on likely haunts, but we will also reach out to our allies to play along in other potential places he could be." The briefer looked down at his notes.

"Assignments. Timms, Lassiter; Dubai. Parshall, Erickson; Abu Dhabi. Roberts, Cahoon; Marseilles, France. Kane, Wilder; Qatar. Faber, Morehouse; Odessa, Ukraine. Your travel packages are up front for you when you leave."

Chris couldn't believe his ears. *Well, fuck me sideways.* Gene was still staring at him. Their eyes met over the crowded briefing room. His boss was not giving anything away with his body language. Chris refocused his attention on the briefer.

"Our first objective is to locate him and keep eyeballs on him. Second objective is to see who he sees, hear what he hears; and that as you know all takes time. Third, is to get as much information out of him as possible, and our professionals will take care of that." The briefer gave a sly look at Chris, but carried on. "But . . . if he is about to leave a country, then we grab him by the nuts. He has one permanent bodyguard. But under the current set of circumstances, with KSM's name now out in the open, and if he is linked like we think he is, he could have gone underground and hired a full security team for protection. For all we know he could be in a bunker in the Swiss Alps, but right now we're focusing on the key areas I just mentioned. I hope that more evidence linking this guy to al-Qaeda comes to light in the next few days, but I don't need the FBI getting involved in this one—yet. In saying that, if things get hairy out there, then we'll need the support of local law enforcement, and you guessed it, we'll have to bring in the Feds. I can't emphasize this enough guys—but we have to communicate. We have got to be aware of where everyone is, and where the target is. If he jumps on a yacht, or a private plane, we had better be surfing a wing, or being dragged along by a frickin' anchor. We all need to know where he's going. Weapons are a go—just don't get careless. Questions?"

University of Karachi, Pakistan

Colonel Rashid Ghazini sat on a bench in the shade of a tree, calmly reading a newspaper while waiting for his appointment to show up. He sat with one leg across his knee, his hands holding the paper open and up in front of him. He leaned back into the bench, his designer sunglasses hiding his cunning eyes. He read one paragraph of a story, looked around for Wahid to show, but did not look at his watch. He read the rest of the story, looked around for another, then read again.

It took Wahid another twenty minutes to arrive for the meeting. While he was irritated by the lateness, Rashid showed no outward frustration. He carefully folded his paper, uncrossed his legs and beckoned the youthful man to sit.

Rashid spotted the first of his two security men, who gave him an all-clear sign. Without speaking to Wahid, he searched for his second man, whom he found in the distance offering the same clear-of-surveillance message. Satisfied that Wahid was alone, he began cordially. "My friend, I trust you are well?"

"Mukhtar will miss me," Wahid said. "I must get back soon." He placed the laptop bag that he was carrying across his knees.

"My friend, please. We both know that he is not in the city. Do not insult my intelligence." His words, still soft, didn't betray offense, but deep down it disappointed him that Wahid was not fully behind his plan. Rashid still appeared relaxed. He didn't want a confrontation, he didn't want to spook the boy, or force his hand so he would run—run back to Mukhtar . . . not yet. He changed the immediate direction of the conversation. "I understand you were a student here for some time. You studied in this very building." Rashid waved behind him to the Institute of Business Administration.

Wahid, taken slightly aback nervously spluttered, "How did you know . . . how?"

"Your instructors spoke highly of you. Your grades were exceptional."

Wahid nodded at the compliments; he had wonderful memories of his time at the university. But he wasn't sure what games the ISI officer was playing. He wanted to leave, but was trapped, beholden to the older, wiser man.

"Many of your instructors have missed you. They all talked of you fondly. You made quite an impression, and they often wondered what you did after your studies."

Wahid still had nothing to offer. His eyes narrowed slightly. He sweated in the midday sun.

"Shall we take a stroll to see them? We can catch up and tell them what you have being doing all this time. Wouldn't you like to do that?"

Wahid shook his head, sensing this was not a benign suggestion. He tried to calculate a way out of the mess he had gotten himself into. One

stupid mistake is all that it had taken to spin his life into a new direction, and it was taking him somewhere that he couldn't see.

Rashid was still speaking in a matter-of-fact, nonthreatening, non-
combative manner. "I'm sure they would like to hear that during your
spare time outside of the university how you helped others with their
technology and business matters—your family, your friends, your
neighbors." He continued, driving his knife point deeper. "I'm sure we
can leave out the part where you hacked into the university records to
change your results. I'm sure that is best left unsaid, don't you think?"

Wahid's head spun. He had to summon all his self-discipline not to
flap. *How? How does he know this?*

"But your secret is safe with me," Rashid said, tapping him reassur-
ingly on his shoulder. "However . . ." He then paused, breaking into a
wide smile, showing off his bright white teeth. He wasn't feeling as
benevolent as that smile looked. "I wonder what they would they would
think of your activities with al-Qaeda? The networks you have built for
them, your actions with all those hacker groups that you are affiliated
with. What is it now, eight . . . nine? I don't know; it is not important.
But your activities with Mukhtar, now that is something special, don't
you think? That is something we can share, for that is important."

Wahid tried his best not to run, but his eyes searched in vain for an
escape. His mind was working overtime, taking in as much information
as his brain could compute. He thought Mukhtar would protect him.
He resolved to tell him the truth about Nabeel. He would understand
that it was not his fault the security man was captured and he himself
had escaped. So Wahid pressed himself to stay. But first, he needed to
get his story straight; he needed to find out what the ISI man wanted.

"What do you want from me?" he finally asked.

Rashid was happy to get some energy from the inexperienced man.
He was defensive with his tone, but at least he wasn't whimpering and
unresponsive in a corner, waiting to get beaten. Rashid reached into his
pocket and pulled out a small USB device. Wahid recognized it
instantly.

"What do you want me to do with that?"

"Download the software onto your laptop."

Wahid grasped his precious laptop as if it were his last drop of blood. The device was never more than a few feet away from him, day or night. "And?"

"That's all."

There must be more to it than that. A program that I can get into, perhaps? Wahid mused.

"Do it now," Rashid ordered.

"Why? Why should I?"

"You need to do exactly what I say, Wahid. I am here to help you, and you are here to help me. Download the software now."

"And if I don't?"

"Wahid, please don't aggravate me. I am trying to help you." He placed a firm hand on the young man's shoulder and squeezed slightly, the threat of pain just seconds away. "You have choices, my friend. Indeed, you do. You may wish to ignore me. You may wish to talk to Mukhtar, and ultimately your choices will lead you in a direction that you may or may not regret." Rashid squeezed harder, making the younger man wince. "I have the ear of Mukhtar, you know that. He has questioned me about Nabeel's capture and so far, I have been able to appease him. Your name was not mentioned. However, that could change. He may believe you, but do you think he will trust you again if I mentioned that you were there, that you escaped? He has more than one Nabeel, my friend."

"He *will* trust me; I can explain to him it was a mistake . . . I should not have—" Wahid was stumbling over his thoughts, causing his words to not come out right.

"I know, I know," Rashid retorted. "You have made a mistake, but that is what you do, isn't it? You made another mistake when you created a name for yourself in this institution. One word to these fine fellows in these halls behinds us and your reputation, your name would be echoed in shame. This university is one of the oldest in the country and your name, your behavior would tarnish the elevated status and validity of our education system. It would devastate them to hear one of their best and brightest has brought it down. They will demand justice of you. You will pay the price. You will go to prison; and you will never come out, my friend."

Rashid let the news sink in for a few seconds more. Then he let another shoe drop. "Of course, the ISI, who have suspected you for some time, could interview you in a more formal setting—" He raised his hand as he anticipated a comment from the IT geek. "—and do not think you can bring my name into this; you would not see the light of day again. I will make it my personal mission in my life to extend your miserable existence as long as you have limbs left for me to remove."

Stuck with no way forward, and no way back, Wahid sobbed.

"There is one more option, Wahid," Rashid said, releasing his grip. "I could hand you over to the Americans. I understand their methods have improved. They will extract information from you in the most indecent of ways. Unless . . . you download the software as I ask."

Tears running down his face and sniffing his nose, Wahid choked out, "If I do, what happens then?"

"All you have to do is have it near you and turned on when you are with Mukhtar. Nothing else."

Wahid's internal bits and bytes were whirring away. *I can get out of this. This program can only be a GPS system. It would be easy to reprogram it, perhaps through the registry.*

Rashid saw a glimmer of hope in the young man's eyes. He still needed to corral him, however. "Do not attempt to circumvent this program, Wahid," he warned. "I have been assured that it will not be simple, and any tampering with it will send off an alarm. And when it does, look over your shoulder because I will be there."

While Wahid downloaded the software, he ran through dozens of lines of code in his head and scanned through a dozen more permutations of ways to hack the system that he was installing.

Rashid likewise engaged his brain, and had his mind directed in equally complex solutions. He had been searching for an umbrella policy for some time, even before Khalid Sheik Mohammed was outed as Mukhtar. He'd watched Wahid from a distance for a while, and yet it only dawned on him in recent weeks that the young IT expert carried his laptop everywhere, and had every time he was near Mukhtar. He often pondered if the laptop would be the key to tracking Wahid's location vis-à-vis Mukhtar. Discussing options with his own IT experts, a solution was developed and presented to Rashid for that purpose.

Rashid's challenge, however, was that he worked for an extreme hardline faction within the ISI—the SS Directorate—that specialized in covert action. The world of information technology was about as foreign to him as speaking to a penguin. To protect himself from the impending pressure from both the American and Pakistani governments, to find and arrest the architect of the 9/11 attacks, he knew he had to be proactive. He knew that the Americans would increase their presence in Pakistan to find the terrorist, and he knew that the president of Pakistan promised to hold nothing back by offering maximum support from the ISI and the Pakistan security apparatus. As the dragnet to find the man would close, so too would the scrutiny of the ISI. He knew it would only be a matter of time before the Americans and their vast array of technology and endless budgets would capture the architect of the Big Wedding, the attacks on 9/11.

Recruiting Wahid was neither planned nor well thought out, but Rashid did it for his own safety. He saw an opportunity to pounce on a weakness, a chink in the underbelly of Mukhtar's armor. If he could constantly pinpoint Mukhtar's location, and hold on to that secret until he had to play his last hand, he would avoid suspicion and conversely rise in stature within the ISI. His dilemma, however, was how long he could maintain control of the immature Wahid before Mukhtar suspected him, or before the terrorist's capture. The latter being the most danger to himself, as it would expose his name, and his agency, to the world as an aider and abettor of al-Qaeda.

CIA Annex, Bagram Air Base, Afghanistan

The briefing at the annex moved on to a more detailed affair. CIA analysts briefed the two-man teams, and each was pouring over maps, pictures, documents, schedules, and printouts of this, that and the

other. It took the teams a few more hours of brainstorming to determine who would do what, where and when. It was all contingent on
who would spot Faizan first, and who could rush to the intended
destination the quickest if the man were to board transportation, or
hunker down in one of his homes. Because Faizan had several properties and business interests in a number of countries, the SAD couldn't
possibly be in every place all the time. To compound these concerns,
the overarching challenge would be to coordinate efforts if the target
headed to a destination where the SAD team did not have personnel.
Everyone in the group knew that if that were to happen, they would all
have to start over again from scratch—and the further Faizan got away
from his favored haunts, the likelihood of catching him would diminish
by the day. Speed was key.

As the session carried on and the theories became wilder, each
person in the room became cognizant of the fact that the target could
run if something spooked him into action. The investigation into Faizan
brought to light that he didn't call any one place home base; that he
travelled extensively. He seemed to like Abu Dhabi as much as he liked
Monaco, or the Turkish Riviera, or the Gold Coast of Australia. The
what-ifs and doubts amongst the group were growing by the minute,
and yet at some point, the briefers knew they'd have to call it a day. If
the SAD didn't deploy soon, then the mission would become
overthought and shelved.

Gene re-entered the briefing room, paperwork in hand, and hands
raised. "Okay, listen up, listen up!" he barked. The decibel level in the
room died and everyone turned to their boss, hungry for information.
"For all you naysayers out there, we have some new intelligence on our
target. Our best friends from Mossad have happily shared some
information that will help in our justification for nabbing this rat bag."
He shook his sheaf of papers to emphasize his point. "Beirut: Hezbollah; Prague: Chechen separatists; Budapest: Chechen separatists;
Yemen: Houthi rebels; Buenos Aires: Hezbollah . . . the list goes on, but
you get the drift. This ass bandit Faizan has been meeting some of the
world's worst, and that's only the tip of the iceberg. The Israelis have

had their eyeballs on him for some time, but nothing has been sticking. The leads we've generated because of those credit cards have opened up a flood of fresh information." Then Gene held up a separate sheet of notepaper. "This here is a list of . . . I count nine aliases that he uses, so that may well be a reason this guy wasn't under anybody's microscope. The Brits and the French have also dialed in with some details of shady business ventures with the guy's fingerprints all over them."

Gene once again shuffled the paperwork in his hands, as Chris's eyes popped wider. *Fuck-a-doodle-do,* he thought, inwardly whistling. He was semi-proud of himself for his impromptu interview of the carpet salesman from Ulm. Gene piped up again before Chris's head swelled any bigger. "Here's another list of subsidiaries that his company operated under in . . . the Isle of Man—where the hell is that?" He looked up but nobody answered, so he kept going. "Zurich, Cayman Islands . . . Christ, Finland—who the hell does business in Finland?" He quizzed nobody in particular. He caught his breath, still looking through his papers. "We might have stumbled onto something major here. This guy may be one of the most important players in terror finance."

He stopped what he was doing and looked at those seated before him. "Does anybody want to ask any more what-ifs?" Gene received nothing but hard stares in return. The stakes had just been raised, and everyone knew it. "Didn't think so," he said, looking at his watch. It was getting late, but not too late to get some planes in the air with his operators on board.

"I need everyone to wrap this shit up. Deal with your wants, needs and wishes on the road. I need eyes on this dipshit ASAP. I'll try to get more bodies ushered around for support, but it's all up to you lucky bastards for now."

"What about KSM, boss?" someone in the crowd asked.

"Thanks for bringing that up. That butt-muncher is still the number one focus. That being said, Faizan may be the lead we're looking for to point us in the right direction to find him." Gene looked around the room, filled with apprehensive faces. He read the crowd. "Yes, I know, you all want to grab that shitwad, but seeing that we have no concrete way of finding him, we have to lean on these other clowns to lead us down a path first. Some of your colleagues are running other things down in other parts of the world and our "guesthouses" are getting steady business. The information that we're getting from those efforts is solid, and is coming in quickly. I know you don't want to hear buzzwords, but . . . it's a fluid situation. We have to remain flexible. The brain trust stateside is grinding away to come up with probabilities, and you can guarantee that someone with more than a community college degree will come up with some fantastical matrix or spreadsheet or data analysis projection or some other cowshit to tell us where to go next. No offense to our esteemed analysts in the room." Some of his team giggled at the comments, and Gene smirked. He wasn't trying to be funny, but he knew his crew. He knew that these people were eager to kick in doors and get hands on necks—but he needed them prepared, primed and ready for the right reason.

"Seriously, though," he began again, controlling the mood in the room. "We are getting closer. Our capture of Abu Zubaydah was a good day for us. Not just us, the SAD, or the CIA, but the country needed a win. Let's focus on Mr. Moneybags today. Let's get him in our control and let's see where it leads us." A few indistinct murmurs of agreement bounced around the room. But Gene hadn't finished speaking. "I have planes waiting. Everyone pack up, get to work people," he finally announced. He then looked towards the back of the room and his eyes zoomed in on Chris. "My office," he directed, then strutted off.

Chris got up to leave, and Alex wasn't sure if Gene wanted to see both of them, so he tagged along behind his partner. Chris presented himself at Gene's office door to find his boss throwing his paperwork down and reaching for a cup of coffee. Gene looked around to see Alex waiting behind Chris.

"Alex, do me a favor and tell me how many rocks there are in the parking lot," he said. "Thanks."

Alex took the hint and made himself scarce.

Chris picked up on the subtle "not-for-your-ears" request to his partner, then entered the office and closed the door behind him. Gene sat down heavily in a rickety old leather desk chair. Chris pulled over an uncomfortable metal chair and plonked himself down. He looked at Gene, waiting for his boss to open the proceedings.

Gene placed his coffee on the desk, then leaned back in his chair. "What am I supposed to do with you?" The question was presented gently, quietly; he wasn't expecting an answer. Although fed up and tired of berating his employee, he still needed him.

Chris didn't answer, knowing that this was the time to keep his mouth shut. He summoned what discipline he had not to throw in a snarky or witty comment and simply let Gene air things out. He prepared himself for a tongue-lashing.

"You can be an insubordinate son of a bitch sometimes, Chris, but what's frustrating is that you still get results," Gene started, an air of passiveness about him. "You piss people off, you say the wrong things, you go off in your own direction . . . you don't follow the rules. But you get lucky."

Chris still didn't respond. It relieved him that Gene was still talking quietly; he remembered the shouting match they had recently in the hospital in Landstuhl. He was expecting more of the same.

"I know this agency, and the SAD, need people with your skill set Chris, but it's becoming more untenable to manage you. I tried to put you in the right box with the right people, tried to protect you from the agency bureaucracy, but it didn't work." Gene paused, took a sip of his coffee, and held onto the cup a little longer for warmth. He was slow in formulating his next words, deep in thought. He tried not to look at the paperwork on his desk.

"Like I said, you're lucky," he continued guardedly. "I can't spare you, so you'll go on this next mission. I need everyone to be on board, but . . . after we get KSM, I think your time with this group will be over."

Chris had expected something like this. He could have easily lost his temper, or tried to defend his recent actions, but he knew that Gene, as well as his late mentor Richard Nash, had gone out on a limb for him once too often. It sounded like the last part of his burning bridge was falling into the water. He took the news on the chin. But on reflection, his own decisions were now becoming clearer. He wanted out; he wanted to do something else with his life. Perhaps this was the push he was looking for. He finally nodded his head to Gene's comment.

Gene, for his part saddened by the news he had just given, was taken a little aback by the lack of vociferous response from the Brit.

Meekly, Chris finally spoke up. "I understand where you're coming from Gene, and thanks for letting me go on this mission—"

"—Don't get that wrong, I'm not doing it for your benefit," Gene interrupted quickly.

Chris nodded again. He wanted to remonstrate, but instead continued softly. "To be honest, it's something that's been on my mind for a while . . . to do something else. This might be the right time to go."

"Don't go soft on me, Chris. I need your head in the game. It may take a while to get KSM—weeks, months, who the hell really knows. A lot can happen."

Chris didn't want his morale to be subject to a tennis match. The back and forth didn't suit him. He preferred black or white. He wanted Gene to be blunt with him; not wishy-washy.

"I get it. You have my attention. I have my orders, let me get going. Alex can't count past ten without taking his shoes and socks off."

Gene smiled. *Always the smart-arse; I'm going to miss him.* "This conversation is on hold Chris, but I think we both know where we stand . . . am I right?"

"Sure, Gene," Chris answered with resignation. "Let's get KSM, and then I'll go look for another job."

CHAPTER TEN

Quetta, Pakistan

WAHID FIDDLED AWAY AT HIS laptop as Mukhtar sat nearby, issuing orders to two of his men. His leader, once again held court. However, this time it was a much quieter affair. They were in a two-story nondescript house in the western part of the city. The new lodgings, located behind the Syed Abad Mosque, provided the terrorist leader the opportunity to pray, as well as offer his associates a legitimate reason to visit the area. The house, once owned by Mukhtar's father, a lay preacher, offered a secret passage between the mosque and the dwelling, thus misdirecting prying eyes into his whereabouts and the surreptitious activities of his colleagues. Born less than three miles from the house, Khalid Sheik Mohammed felt comfortable in these surroundings. He was at ease speaking his native Balochi tongue, practicing his religion near his birthplace, following his jihad, and waging war on the West.

Except for a pulsating red dot on a computer screen in the basement of the regional ISI office, Mukhtar was as safe as he could be.

Colonel Rashid Ghazini stood in silence and looked over a seated man's shoulder. He was watching the glow of the immobile dot, studying the location closely. After a minute he asked, "How long has it been stable?"

The officer looked down to the corner of the screen, where there was a timer. "Thirty-two hours and thirty-eight minutes, sir," he reported.

"The device works properly?"

"Yes sir, we run a diagnostic program every hour."

"I want you to run a test every thirty minutes," Rashid ordered without looking up from the screen.

"Yes, sir."

"You have exact coordinates?"

"Yes sir, would you like a printout?"

Rashid contemplated the question for a few seconds. He knew now was not the time. "No. You have my number, call me if he moves."

The junior computer analyst gazed at the screen. He was not there to question motives; his job was the same as any bored security guard: observe and report. "Yes sir," he responded to an empty spot where the colonel had stood but a moment ago.

Mukhtar joined Wahid at the kitchen table with a large bowl of grapes. He placed it between them and offered some to his young friend. As the leader picked the grapes off the stems, he stuffed his mouth with two or three at a time. Between repulsive loud chews, he asked Wahid about the satellite on the top of the house.

"Tell me, Wahid, can we get CNN, the American news channel, on the TV?"

"Yes, yes, we have Al Jazeera, we have—"

"CNN, please my friend."

Disappointed, Wahid would have preferred an Arabic channel, as his English, while possible was not at the same level as the American-educated terrorist leader. While Wahid toyed with the TV remote, Mukhtar spat grape seeds into his hand, while at the same time grabbing more of the green globes with the other. An image of CNN's Wolf Blitzer popped up on the screen. Behind him were the attention-getting words, SITUATION ROOM – BREAKING NEWS. There was no sound.

"Yes, Yes Wahid, that's it!"

Wahid concentrated on the remote again, and found the volume. They missed Blitzer's preamble, but listened in as he continued the report.

"An attack on US Marines on a training mission in Kuwait has resulted in an unknown number of American casualties and two or more terrorists dead," he said. *"Live in Kuwait City, we go now to our correspondent there, Matthew Chance for an update. Matthew, I understand that this attack has all the hallmarks of an al-Qaeda attack?"*

"That's right, Wolf. My sources in the region now say that al-Qaeda has claimed responsibility for the attack, which has unfortunately left one US Marine dead, and another wounded."

Mukhtar leapt from the table. "Yes, yes, yes!" he gleefully hissed.

Matthew Chance continued his report.

"The incident occurred on Faylaka Island off the coast of Kuwait, where the Marine Expeditionary Force were conducting joint amphibious assault training with their Kuwaiti counterparts. The US and Royal Air Force have since deployed aircraft to the island, where there are unconfirmed reports of continued gunfire. Details are still scant; however, it is believed that two terrorists armed with automatic weapons were killed during a firefight with the Marines. Back to you, Wolf."

Mukhtar slapped Wahid on the back forcefully, causing him to drop the remote. It was a playful action, as the terrorist leader was on a high. "You see, you see my friend? The American pigs struggle to contain us. Two martyrs is all it took to bring them to their knees. Two men, two men . . . hah! Even a mouse can scare an elephant! They are frightened, so frightened they need their warplanes, and for what? There is nobody else. They are fools, shooting at shadows."

He laughed and rolled his head back, then paced around the kitchen. He was once again proud of himself for his planning and leadership. It was, he thought, as the Americans like to say, an "on the fly" project. An opportunity presented itself and he could not pass it up. It was cheap, requiring minimum resources, and two willing participants already in place. He laughed again at the picture in his mind of the US military's finest, bravest and proudest, cowering in their armored vehicles, scared of what terror he could bring to them. It mattered not that only one Marine was killed. It was enough to merely bring a shiver to the Americans. It would cause the families of servicemen to pressure their precious children not to join, not to go overseas, not to engage in conflicts in places where they didn't belong.

"Find me Al Jazeera, Wahid. Let us hear what our brethren have to say," Mukhtar ordered his young friend.

Wahid surfed with the remote and found what he was looking for. Both men looked on as an Arab reporter dissected the same news story. Mukhtar continued his merry dance while still eating grapes. One of his men appeared in the kitchen at the sound of his leader, who was enjoying himself. The mood was contagious and after a few minutes another terrorist appeared and before too long; they were all praising Allah.

Odessa, Ukraine

Chris stared out the starboard-side window of the Gulfstream IV as it descended over the Black Sea on its final approach into Odessa. Alex was doing the same on the port side, but when Chris looked over to him, all he could see was his friend's outline blocking out the sunset, which was trying to filter its way into the cabin. Yellow and white lights in the city below were coming on, disturbing the shapes and outlines of the buildings, making it hard for Chris to determine landmarks or prominent features from high above. It was an exercise he tried to conduct every time he visited an unknown city, or a town he had never been to. Even if it was only to spot a tall building, a monument, the ocean, the mountains, anything that stood out, he just needed a reference point to allay his fear of being disorientated. Fortunately, the city below wasn't that large geographically, with most of its real estate along the northwestern shore of the Black Sea. It was, however, an old, densely populated city, with over a million people; meaning he would have to work in tight confines.

It would take Chris three or four days to get comfortable with his new surroundings, but not knowing how long they would be there, he didn't have the luxury of being able to take in the sights before his mission started. He knew that as soon as his boots hit the ground, he'd be off and running, checking out a lead or surveilling a location, hoping to find the al-Qaeda financier Faizan al Shamsi. He pondered the possibility of the Arab being in the city, if his lead would pan out—and if they could find him and render him to a CIA black site. He wondered how he himself would react, how he would approach the operation, how others around him would help or hinder the undertaking. He wasn't sure if he would or should take the lead, or instead rely on Alex to forge ahead. His thoughts were many, but his answers were few. The only conclusion he could come to was that he needed to chill out, do his job, and keep his mouth shut, but he had told himself on many an occasion to do just that, and it never worked.

His time for reflection was over as the undercarriage of the aircraft was quickly reaching for the ground. During the flight from Afghanistan, through the Middle East and Turkey, he talked with Alex about his predicament. He detailed the conversation he'd had with Gene at the CIA annex, and also filled his friend in with the contentious issues at hand. Namely, his unsanctioned interview with the carpet salesman from Bavaria; his argument with Jon in Pakistan over the transport of Abu Zubaydah; his reckless chase of terrorists in Islamabad; and his altercation in a London pub. To round things out, Chris also gave Alex the meat and bones of the action he undertook in Karachi the previous year with Guy Trimble and Jawad Halabi.

Alex knew the rumors, but was not privy to the details of how Chris had played a part in the death of three al-Qaeda suspects, and the burning of a textile plant. Now he knew. While Chris spoke, Alex listened. He offered no opinion, did not interject, nor judge. He wanted Chris to vent, to get things off his chest because he wanted him fully functional as soon as they landed. They had a task to complete, and Chris needed to be fully on board with the enterprise. For the most part, Alex nodded when he should have, shook his head when needed, and stayed silent to allow Chris to continue the flow of his story.

Though Chris wasn't looking for a pity party, Alex sympathized with his friend. But he could also see where the CIA were coming from, in two ways. They needed talented, dedicated, and smart foot soldiers to kick in doors and drag shitheads out of their beds to answer for their misdeeds. Especially now. But to do that, they needed men and women who were dependable, followed orders and played by the rules. In Alex's mind, Chris was wholly capable to run terrorists down and do what was necessary to bring them in. But his penchant for quick action, for snap violence and the constant opening of his big mouth at inopportune times was, and would continue to be his downfall. Alex liked Chris, and he enjoyed working with him. Out of all the team members of the SAD group, he could count just a handful he would take into battle with him; Chris was one of those. But he worried about the Brit too. He worried that his friend was on a slippery slope that Chris himself had created, and unless he was thrown a life line, he would be gone. The overarching question, however, was: would Chris be thrown a rope by the CIA, or shoved back down by a barge pole? To compound those scenarios, Alex worried that his friend would leave the agency of his own accord and simply let himself slip into oblivion.

After touching down, the CIA plane, led by a pilot vehicle, taxied away from the main terminal and over to the eastern side of the small airport. There the Gulfstream pilot, out of view of the civilian terminus, parked the plane near some archaic Soviet transport planes, and shut its engines down. By the time the steps were lowered, dusk had settled, and Chris exited the plane under cover of relative darkness.

While Alex busied himself with the pilot's logistics, Chris wandered around the outside of the plane, trying to get a bearing. There wasn't much to see around them, except the decrepit transport planes dotted around his immediate area. He noted the main complex of the airport and surmised that they landed from the south, facing north. It was all he had to go on for the moment. As he did another slow 360, he spotted a figure heading towards him, carrying a book. As the man got closer, he saw that he was wearing a drab uniform, including a peaked cap with a shiny gold badge.

"Alex, we've got company," Chris called out.

Alex pulled himself out of the conversation with the flight crew and headed down the steps. He did a quick analysis. "Looks official." By the time he made it down the steps, the man had halted in front of Chris.

The official touched the peak of his cap and smiled. "Passport please."

Chris fished his out, while Alex called the pilots to exit the plane for a customs check. All four presented their credentials. The customs officer took the passports, and without looking at them, opened his book. He stood there for a moment and just smiled. Open book in one hand, four passports in the other. Alex and Chris exchanged glances as if to say, *WTF?* Everyone stood around in silence, looking at each other. One of the pilots finally broke the impasse. He retreated to the cockpit and returned after a moment, with a black pouch. He opened it and retrieved five, one hundred-dollar bills. He placed the "entry fee" in the open book. The customs officer smiled, closed the book, and handed the passports back. "Have nice day," he happily offered, then sauntered off in the direction from where he came.

Chris wanted to be on his best behavior, so he kept his thoughts to himself. *Welcome to Ukraine, I guess.*

As soon as the customs man disappeared from view, a white Ford transit van approached. "Looks like our transport is here," Alex announced, though everyone else had also spotted the vehicle. The two pilots moved back into the cocoon of the cockpit. "Just me and you, Chris," Alex noted. "The pilots will stick around for fuel and wait for new orders, but my guess is they'll crash on the plane tonight and be airborne in the morning—"

"—You know they don't like that term," Chris quipped with a smirk.

"—Huh? Oh yeah, 'hunker down' on the plane tonight," Alex responded, trying to fight back a chuckle. "There's no guarantee that we'll have a passenger for them, anyway."

Chris nodded but thought back to the Zubaydah stretcher incident. The Gulfstream IV would have the same problem if they had to transport an injured man out of the country. Again, he kept his worries to himself. *Alex can chase that one down. I need to follow his lead for a change.*

Once on board the transit van Chris was happy to see a familiar face behind the wheel. "Lester, how are ya, buddy?"

"I'm tip-top, Chris. Long time, no see."

"It's been a while for sure. This is Alex, he's good people."

Lester, the Viewpoint surveillance team leader, nodded, then point-ed the van in the direction of the city. They chatted briefly about the everyday life of Odessa and the pitfalls and advantages of working targets in Ukraine. It was a light conversation that allowed Lester to concentrate on the route he was taking, and for him to spot a tail that he may have picked up on the way to the airport. They eventually got to a point in the discussion where Lester was comfortable enough to give the SAD players his briefing. The news surprised them. "Faizan landed about three hours ago. He used an alias, so he wasn't picked up straightaway, but we got lucky. His bodyguard, one of four with Faizan, used his actual name for a charter flight from Athens."

"Rookie mistake," Alex noted.

"It was," Lester agreed. "Especially since Faizan used a passport from St. Kitts."

"I wonder how much he paid for that—" Chris interrupted. "Sorry Lester."

"Nobody from your team or ours saw him depart the Middle East, not that it matters, but we haven't laid eyes on him yet. We have his waterfront penthouse suite staked out, but we have little intelligence other than that."

Both Chris and Alex knew that it would take a little time to estab-lish the target's true whereabouts, and then even longer to establish a routine. Patience would be key, as neither operator knew at this stage how soon they could feasibly apprehend their target. Other than the man's girlfriend, nobody in the CIA really knew why he was in Odessa.

"What about the girlfriend?" Chris asked.

"We've tracked her, but considering we've been here less than forty-eight hours, we haven't been able to make a positive ID. The driver's license photo we're working from is old, and the girl we have eyes on is probably a thirty percent match."

"You have eyeballs on her now?" Chris continued, hoping that they could help the situation.

"Yes, you remember Lucy?" Lester was referring to one of the

Viewpoint team members. A plump, bespectacled fifty-eight-year-old lady who looked like a happy botanist or quaint librarian.

Chris's eyes lit up. Another Viewpoint team member he enjoyed working with. "She's on the job?"

"Yup, the Bristol Hotel lobby, she's there right now. Last I heard, she was within fifty feet of the girl."

Nobody spoke for a few moments after the comment. Each ruminated, trying to concoct a new plan or idea to move forward. It was Chris who threw out the suggestion to Alex. "You want to go straight to work?"

Alex squinted his eyes at Chris, then asked Lester a question. "What's the backup situation Lester? How many people do you have on the ground?"

Lester was still navigating his way through traffic, and cursed a few times before answering. "I have one at the safe house managing communications; Lucy is inside the Bristol; and I have another two cruising the perimeter. Which reminds me, I need to check in. Before I left to pick you up, I got a call that an FBI liaison officer would join us from Kiev. He could already be here, he's supposed to drum up some local law enforcement support."

Although Alex was looking out the window, his mind was thinking of what Chris had asked. He was glad that Chris seemed focused on the mission. "How far to the Bristol?" Alex asked.

"Ten minutes from here, Alex, then another ten minutes to the safe house from the hotel." The Ford got stuck at a traffic light. Alex wanted to know what was on Chris's mind. "I'm guessing you have an idea?"

"She's German," he began. "I could start a conversation, see where it leads, but it's up to you. We can wait for backup if you want?" Chris stated almost nonchalantly. He was trying not to be too pushy; he wanted this to be a team effort.

"Lester, pull over when you get a chance," Alex ordered.

In a few seconds, Lester saw a parking spot on the side of the street. It was nearing the end of rush hour and the Ukrainian driving population wasn't too sympathetic about vehicles taking their own sweet time in maneuvering into tight parking spots. Greeted by honks and hollers, Lester ignored the complaints, parked the van and turned around to face Alex. Both Chris and Alex were scanning their surroundings, looking for people looking at them. Once deemed safe, Alex threw out the first command. "Call your girl . . . who was it, Lucy?" Lester nodded. "Call Lucy, get her to confirm that the girl is still there. Once you've done that, call the safe house, find out where the FBI is, and if they've coordinated with the local cops. Do you have a comm package for us?"

"Yes, behind your seat," Lester confirmed.

"I just need a cell phone for now Alex," Chris stated. "But I'll take the comm bag with me. I'll turn on the radio if I need it."

Alex nodded, though he was anxious. "Let's not jump the gun, Chris. Let Lester make his calls, then we'll hash something out." Alex retrieved the bag from the rear of the vehicle, opened it up and starting passing out the contents to his partner. Chris was studying the photo of Faizan's girlfriend and a map from the bag when Lester finally hung up his phone.

"The girl is drinking a coffee in the lobby; Lucy still has a visual. The FBI and the local cops have met up and are now heading to the Bristol. I told them to stage a few minutes down the street from the hotel. Everyone's waiting on you guys."

Chris was silently chomping at the bit to get going. It was his lead that had gotten them to this point, and after having received confirmation that Faizan was in town, it wouldn't be long before boyfriend and girlfriend met up. If he could ID the girl in the lobby, then they'd be halfway to eyeballing the Arab. He knew that this was an excellent opportunity, but he didn't want to make the call. He looked at Alex, apprehensively. Alex paused and stared back at Chris. He took a slug of water from a bottle that Lester had provided. They needed a decision, go, or no go.

"Lester," Alex began, "drop Chris half a block away from the Bristol; you drop me halfway down on the other side. You and I will stay in contact and coordinate the support team and the rest of the Viewpoint team. Let Lucy know that Chris is inbound." He looked at Chris, desperately wanting to tell him not to fuck this up, but he held back. Instead, he simply asked, "What do you need, Chris?"

"Lester, I'm taking this bag with me," Chris said. "I'm going to play a businessman. Call Lucy and tell her that when I approach the girl, I'll walk past her a few feet. I'll be speaking German on my cell phone to Alex. You keep an open line with her. I need you to tell Alex what Lucy sees. What kind of reaction the girl has to a comment I'm going to make. I'll have my back to her, so I need to know what she does: if she looks up, ignores me or whatever. I'll figure out the next move based on her reaction, but I'm not going to stick around too long. Then we'll regroup and think out our next move. You good with that, Alex?"

Alex didn't have a problem with the plan. It was quick, simple and low risk. "This is just an ID, Chris," he reminded his partner. "If you spot any muscle, you get out, and we'll let Viewpoint take over. Understood?"

Chris knew where he was coming from. Alex was being cautious. He didn't want to spook the girl, and he didn't want any trouble this early in the mission. If things looked shaky, Chris was to abort and let the surveillance team take over and painstakingly build a target package around the girl, hoping that she would lead them to Faizan.

Chris confirmed his compliance. "Understood."

Alex was in full mission mode, devoid of emotion, intent on success. He let Lester know to communicate the plan to the team and have them on standby in case he and Chris needed a speedy pickup. Before they pulled away from the curb, Lester gave Chris a rundown on the basic layout of the hotel, and where Lucy and the girl were. Once satisfied, the trio once again joined the flow of traffic and headed toward the Bristol.

Within thirty feet of the main entry, Chris pulled his cell phone out of his pocket and dialed his friend. He then rambled on in German about the difference between a German Koelsch and Alt Beer to a bewildered and uncomprehending Alex. As he zipped through the red double doors of the hotel, he kept his head down and turned immediately to his right, ignoring the reception staff on his left. His footsteps were loud on the ornate marble flooring, and he wished it were carpeting to mask his approach. The corridor he took was long and narrow, and decorated stylishly with high-back blue-and-gold-laced chairs, attractive coffee tables, sophisticated wall decorations, fresh flowers and well-maintained plants—all typical of a high-end hotel. He scanned the area as he moved through, still acting out his dialogue to Alex. Looking down, he swore he could have eaten off the white marble floor; it was that clean. He finally spotted Lucy, conjuring a set of knitting needles which were feverishly weaving their way into a new hat or scarf. She did not look at Chris, but she stared at someone directly across from her, just for a moment. The target.

Chris saw Lucy's nonverbal cue and increased the volume of his one-way German conversation. As he got closer, he could see the head of a woman sitting alone at a coffee table, reading a newspaper. He was three steps away when he did a quick review of his surroundings, checking for signs of a watcher, a minder or some sort of threat that would make him retreat. He didn't need to fret, as Lucy was conducting the same exercise and on an open channel with Lester, ready to warn of danger. Chris placed his bag on the table where the girl sat. "Verdammte Scheisse Nico, ich habe fertig," he bellowed into the phone. He didn't turn around for the reaction. He hoped Lucy had seen something, and he paused, waiting for the message to relay through Alex.

"She stopped reading the newspaper and dropped it down, she's covering her mouth, she's giggling," Alex reported, unaware of what magic Chris had just made up. He had no way of knowing that Chris had deliberately misused German grammar to mimic a character straight out of German pop culture.

Chris hung up the phone and turned around. The target was still giggling in front of him. The paper was making its way back up to her face; the *Sueddeutsche Zeitung*, Chris noted. *Okay, German newspaper, this is promising*, he thought.

"Oh, excuse me, I didn't mean to interrupt," he offered politely. He laid on a tint of an Irish accent when he spoke German to her.

When she smiled, he noticed the similarity of features with her father; however, the girl was beautiful. He felt a pang of guilt knowing where her father was now, but he had to wash the feeling away. He couldn't break his train of thought now. He was close to identifying Faizan's girlfriend. "It's fine, don't worry," she said, "I haven't heard anyone speak like Trapattoni in a very long time."

Chris laughed to prolong the scene; the act was playing itself out well. "He was a good coach; but his German was terrible." He was referring to Giovanni Trapattoni, former coach of the legendary Bayern Munich football club.

"Yes, it was frightful, but the press conferences were always fun to watch—you never knew what to expect." There was a moment of silence, but the newspaper was now resting on the table in front of her. She sized up Chris a bit. "But you are not German; how do you know about Trapattoni?"

"Ah, you have me there. I'm from Cork, Ireland. But I have been living in Germany for many years, Berlin mainly . . . and you?"

"Ulm," she politely replied.

Bingo. Chris smiled broad enough to make a Cheshire cat jealous. "We are both a long way from home." He reached out his hand. "Patrick Mahoney."

She graciously accepted the gesture. "Johara al Mouhammed, a pleasure to meet you, Patrick."

Just before Chris asked if he could join her at an empty chair, a tall, dark handsome man bore down on the friendly conversation. Chris didn't think the man was a threat, not yet, but he raised his left hand to his ear and scratched his left earlobe. Lucy saw the sign and relayed the message to Lester. As the man reached the table, he gave Chris a curious stare; he placed his hand on Johara's shoulder to show he was there. She looked up at him and smiled. He gazed to her, then back to the stranger, still wondering what was going on. He left his hand on her shoulder; she reached up to touch him.

Chris ran through what he was seeing. *That's not Faizan, he doesn't match the photo, he's too young. He's dark enough to be Arab, but not necessarily. Nice watch; Rolex? Cufflinks, nice. Grey suit, expensive, no tie, white shirt, probably one of fifty-three he has hung nicely in a closet just above his twenty-six pairs of Italian shoes. He thinks I'm trying to pick her up, jealous lover perhaps . . . interesting combination. He's pretty, wish I could have his hair . . . bastard!* He reached up to rub both eyes. *They look good together, they're definitely close.* Lucy relayed to Lester that they needed eyeballs on two targets. She watched Chris make a silent snapping motion with his fingers behind his back, showing he wanted photos. He looked at the cute couple before him and something profound came to him. *If he's the boyfriend du jour, then she doesn't know that Faizan is in town. That's a twist.* Just a second before an awkward silence trapped the three, Chris's phone rang.

"Hello ma," Chris responded, reverting to English mode. "Just hang on a second will you . . . yes ma, yes, I'm fine. I've been eating . . . yes, I've been sleeping well," Chris shook his head simultaneously as Alex did on the other end of the line. The second act was once again for Johara's benefit. "Ma, just wait a minute . . . yes, yes, stay on the line, I just have to say goodbye to someone . . . no, no, it's not a girl. Ma . . . ma. Just wait a minute." Chris pulled the phone away from his ear and placed it over his chest. He picked up his bag and looked back down to the target. He kept it brief. "It was nice meeting you, Johara Trapattoni, hope to see you again sometime." He turned and moved along before she could say anything, placing his phone to his ear again. "Yes ma, I'm here."

By the time Chris reached the Ford transit van, Lucy communicated that both Johara and her gentleman friend had left the coffee table and headed to the elevator, which took them to the fourth floor.

"This is a complication we don't need," Chris started. "If Faizan is in town and his girlfriend is playing around, how is he going to react? Does he know? Is he looking for her? Does he give a shit?"

"We assume that he's in town to meet her Chris, but . . . might there be something else here that interests him?" Alex replied. "There are a dozen scenarios that could play out here and I don't want to waste too much time going through all the potentials. If he's here, we have to make our move before he slips out of the country. He's probably spooked. Otherwise he wouldn't have traveled with four men and burn through his St. Kitts passport." Alex paused, hoping to have one of his two colleagues in the van respond with something brilliant to work with. He looked at Chris. "You think they were boyfriend-girlfriend?"

"The vibe I got tells me yes; I doubt if they are related. The carpet salesman would have mentioned if there was another relative here. He may not have come all the way from Germany to rescue her if there was a cousin, or other family member in the area. So, the more I think about it, yeah, they're fuck-buddies."

"Leverage?" Lester offered.

"You want to squeeze her because she's cheating on Faizan?" Alex asked. He was a little cross at the idea.

"It's not a shabby idea, Alex." Chris supported Lester's proposition. "If Faizan is here, and he hasn't come to see her straightaway, then he has other business in town. What that is, is anyone's guess. But he's not at the penthouse, and he's not with her. So who would he be meeting?" Chris let the question dangle for a moment longer. "Would she know who his business contacts are here are in the city? Does she have connections she's nursing on his behalf? Is the guy she's meeting in the Bristol part of the equation? Is she or Faizan setting the guy up for something we're not aware of?"

The tangents were mounting; Alex wanted to rein them in. "Like I said Chris, the permutations can go on and on, we can suppose all day and night."

Chris looked to Alex for a plan. "What do you want to do?"

"Let's suppose for a minute that Faizan is in the hotel—"

"We would have seen him enter," Lester countered defensively.

Alex held up his hand. "Not necessarily. You said yourself that you haven't had that much time to set up. He could have easily entered another way. He knows the town better than we do; he has contacts here."

Chris was on edge, still waiting for the next idea to materialize. He was back to enjoying himself again, on a mission, in focus. He wanted to say to Alex, *Let's go in, let's pay her a visit, she what she knows.* But his friend beat him to it.

"I think we should get to know her game a little better. Let's go in, pay her a visit, find out what she knows. We'll round up the FBI guy and his local cop contact and go and knock on her hotel room door. We might get lucky and have Faizan answer the door."

Chris smiled, he liked the plan. *We should be so lucky, Alex,* he thought, but he kept it in check. Instead he added a word of caution. "That's not our remit Alex . . . you know how Gene is about us interviewing people."

"That's what the FBI contact can do for us. We'll let him lead and we will play dumb . . . we can be . . . observers."

"I'm game, let's redeploy Viewpoint while we're at it. We may get a rat running out of here while we're getting all our ducks lined up."

"Good idea. Lester—" Alex began.

"—Already on it," the Viewpoint man replied.

Twenty valuable minutes had passed since Chris left the "impromptu" meeting with Johara. All three men in the transit van expressed their concern that they were rushing into things, but Chris's suggestion that Faizan may only be in town to conduct business and not visit with Johara sped up their plan. Nobody wanted to hear the news that Faizan was back at the airport boarding another plane. Due to the need for expediency, six men marched into the lobby of the Bristol Hotel: Chris, Alex, the FBI agent, two uniformed police officers, and Gregor Melnik, commissar of the Odessa police force. The latter approached the hotel staff first. After showing his credentials and having a brief conversation with the receptionist, he turned to the team.

"There are reports of a woman's screams from the fourth floor, room 415. They were just about to call us."

The group of six marched over to the bank of elevators, but Chris lost his patience while waiting and headed for the hotel's grand staircase, which accessed all floors. He ran up the steps two at a time, but as he was rushing, he reminded himself to remain in control. He knew he was fit enough now, after healing from his injuries sustained in the Islamabad debacle, but he wanted to make sure that he would be ready to take on an opponent at the top of the stairs, if need be. It wasn't a steep climb, but he was wary of someone rushing down to meet him and catch him unawares. He slowed his pace slightly.

When he got to the top of the stairs, he followed the signs for the rooms numbered 400-420. By the time he rounded a corner, the elevator doors opened and the group he'd left downstairs joined him on his march. Chris was the first to find room 415. He walked by the room, determined not to be the one kicking in the door, letting someone else take the lead. He paused on the far side of the door, checking the other rooms for potential wrong-place-wrong-time innocents. As he was making his check, he heard the unmistakable sound of an emergency stairway door close further down the hallway. He looked at Alex, who noted the same. The team formed up around the door, silently waiting for the "Go" order.

Gregor put his ear to the door of room 415. As he was doing so, a loud female scream shattered the silence. The commissar nodded to one of the uniformed police officers, who inserted a card into the lock, then, weapon drawn, quickly entered the room, followed by his partner and his boss. The sound of the woman's screams was now filtering out of the room. Chris, Alex and the FBI agent held station in the corridor. This was a police matter now and all they could do was wait for an invitation into the scene. The woman's screams eventually ceased as orders issued by police stopped whatever was happening in the room from continuing.

Gregor called the FBI agent into the room, and Chris tagged along, but Alex remained on post in the corridor. Watching Chris's back, he held his hand to his ear to listen to his radio earpiece.

The sights and sounds took Chris by surprise when he entered the large room. The two uniformed police officers were struggling to put cuffs on a naked man on the floor. Another man, also naked, stood sweating profusely with his hands behind his neck in submission. Gregor held his gun on the second man as the officers restrained the suspect on the floor. Gregor glanced over to the bed, then back at the man standing before him. He holstered his pistol, then kicked the man as hard as he could straight into his balls. The sweating man doubled over in pain. Gregor turned to the woman on the bed and he calmly placed a bed sheet over her naked body. She clutched it close to hide her shame. Her face was bruised, her lips were bleeding, her hair a mess, her makeup a disaster. In a chair near the balcony door, the pretty boy's limp body had blood flowing from his beaten face, which dripped down to the floor. His wrists and legs were bound to the chair, a makeshift garrote was lying in his lap. There was no sign of life.

"Chris!" Alex shouted into the room.

"Stand by Alex," he said. He needed to close a loop for the cops. "That's Johara, that's her boyfriend, don't know his name."

Gregor nodded. The two uniformed officers had turned the naked man on the floor over and onto his back. "Do you know this one, or that one?" Gregor pointed and asked.

"No."

"Chris, need you now," Alex shouted again. Chris promptly exited the room. "What's going on in there?" Alex quizzed.

"Looks like she was being raped. Pretty boy is dead. Two rapists in custody; don't know who they are. What's up with you?"

"Three men seen leaving the emergency stairwell; could be Faizan, nothing positive. Viewpoint trying to get a visual."

"We going?" Chris piped up enthusiastically. Alex didn't answer, but he turned away from room 415 and jogged to the emergency stairs. Chris tagged along close behind, stuffing his radio earpiece into his ear just in time to hear a transmission from a member of the Viewpoint team.

"Black Mercedes, license plate Hotel, Hotel, 9625, Charlie Echo. Three male occupants heading eastbound Bunina Street. Approaching construction zone on bridge. Designate Tango one mobile."

Neither Alex nor Chris needed to reply, nor had time to. They were both bounding down the steps, trying to get to the street before the suspects' car got too far away. Each of them was using both hands to hold on to the stair railings as they leaped downward, both wary of falling and compromising the mission. Chris was following close behind Alex, happy to be in chase mode but cautious about what was transpiring. Alex was a planner, a plotter, not a panster like Chris who was usually the one to conjure up a fly-by-the-seat-of-your-pants plan. Chris wanted to know what he had in mind; what Alex wanted to do when they hit the street. He wasn't sure how far his partner wanted to go to find Faizan and take him down. Chris wanted to calculate the what-ifs, but his legs were pummeling down the steps like a jack hammer digging up a road, averting the need to think hard about what was really going on.

Alex busted out of the door quicker than a horse out of the starting gate at the Kentucky Derby. He sprinted onto the pavement and headed east when another transmission crackled over the radio.

"Tango one mobile stuck in traffic. Traffic incident with bus and other vehicles. Tango one mobile boxed in."

The message pushed Alex along even quicker. Chris thought of himself as a fit and powerful runner. But Alex, the long-legged former Delta Force soldier, was pulling so far ahead that Chris lagged. He wanted to talk to Alex; he wanted to know what he was doing. He couldn't afford to drop himself in the shit anymore with Gene than he already had, but he knew he had to follow Alex's lead. His partner had something in mind and he had to support him; he had to keep going.

As both SAD operators neared the traffic snarl, the radio transmissions kept the duo up to date. Tango one mobile was still boxed in. "Alex, Alex what the fuck are we doing?" Chris screamed.

Alex, still running with a full head of steam answered in between breaths. "We're going to ID the fucker and drag his ass out of the car."

Chris almost skidded to a halt, but then continued running, trying to keep up. He wanted to shout back at Alex, *That's the plan? Jesus Christ, and I thought I was the one to take risks!* But he kept his mouth shut. He needed all the breath he could get. They spotted the Mercedes, still stuck in the traffic jam on a small bridge under construction. Only one lane was open to traffic, and it was controlled by a temporary traffic light, but a bus and a taxi had their own ideas about who should have priority to cross first, and neither wanted to back down. It was the only advantage that Alex and Chris had.

Alex finally slowed down to a jog, then a quick march as he neared the rear of Tango one mobile. He was trying to see into the car, but it was too dark. The car behind the Mercedes had its headlights bearing into the rear of the car, but the passengers were all staring forward, so none of their faces were illuminated.

Chris caught up to Alex and was about to ask what's next, but his partner took action before they spoke. Alex picked up a piece of pipe from some construction scaffolding that was being used on the bridge, and swung it hard at the rear of the Mercedes, smashing a taillight. It was the reaction that he was expecting. Faizan al Shamsi turned and looked in horror to see a tall man wielding a piece of steel pipe. He didn't know what to make of it.

Alex, still holding the pipe, strode quickly to the driver's-side door and smashed the window, raining shards of glass onto the driver. He was about to reach in to yank the door open when the front passenger door opened and Faizan's bodyguard got out with a weapon in his hands.

"GUN!" Chris screamed.

Alex pulled back and crouched down by the left side of the car, waiting for the inevitable shots to fly, but none came. Chris ducked to a crouch, too, tempted to engage the bodyguard with his own pistol, but he didn't have a clear shot. He instead picked up a similar-looking pipe to the one Alex was still carrying, and tossed it in the general direction of the bodyguard. The pipe bounced off the roof of the car, causing the bodyguard to crunch down into a ball. During the commotion, Alex reached up for the driver's-side door and yanked it open, only to face the barrel of a gun pointing straight at him. Before the driver could shoot, Chris tossed another pipe at the car, this time smashing the driver's-side mirror and scaring the driver from emptying a magazine into the defenseless Alex.

Alex, still not deterred from getting to Faizan, reached for the rear passenger door. Chris in the meantime kept lobbing steel pipes at the bodyguard, who was struggling to find a target to shoot at between ducking for his own safety. Alex gripped the door handle, but before he could pull it open, the driver, who had finally found some composure, moved the Mercedes forward. Alex sensed the movement and gave up on his task of trying to open the door. Instead he pulled out his Kershaw tactical folding knife and dug it hard into the rear tire. He drew it out, then stabbed the tire two more times before the driver gained some momentum and got the car moving with the knife still embedded in the rubber. Chris threw the last piece of pipe he could lay his hands on into the rear window, smashing it as the vehicle moved off. He stood there for a second longer, catching his breath, but then he too saw the wrong end of the barrel of a gun pointing at him. This time, however, shots were fired.

Chris dropped to the road quicker than a Marine recruit being shouted at by a drill sergeant. He looked over at Alex, who was also kissing dirt, neither of them daring to look up as shots continued to ring out from the rear of the beaten-up Mercedes. But the car was struggling too. The argument between the bus and the taxi was still ongoing, so there wasn't much room for the fugitive car to maneuver. But the Mercedes squeaked by the stationary vehicles, rubbing up against and scratching its way along those and any others in its way. When the other drivers got out to protest, Faizan's bodyguard pulled his weapon out of the window and shot several rounds into the air, causing many onlookers to run for their lives. *At least he's still trying to move; I'd do the same*, Chris thought. He caught Alex's eye and pointed to a pallet of decorative stones that could serve as protection. Alex nodded, and both men got off the ground and ran for cover.

"Thanks for sharing your plan, dickhead," Chris derided his friend.

"I took a page out of your handbook, asshole," Alex replied, almost smiling. "You good?"

"Wonderful. You wanna keep going?"

"I slashed one tire, may not be long till it shreds; we might catch them, if you're up for it. Unless you want to pussy out and wait for backup."

"Well, since I forgot to bring the picnic hamper and a bottle of bubbly, I guess there's no point in hanging around here; the view's lousy anyway," Chris responded, his dry sense of humor intact. "Just don't run off like a fucking gazelle again—my short stubby pins can't keep up with that shit."

Alex enjoyed Chris' sharp banter, but didn't wait to continue the conversation. They had a job to do. He got up from behind the stones and ran off in the direction of the traffic mayhem. Chris, once again, was two steps behind his galloping friend. *Oh, for fuck's sake!* he sighed to himself as he tried to fire up his legs into action.

Alex was once more way ahead of Chris as they both ran up Bunina Street. He stopped when they reached the intersection with Kanatna Street. "Follow the rubber!" Chris shouted as he tried to catch his breath.

"What?"

"His tire is failing; he's driving too fast. Follow the trail!"

Alex didn't need more of a prompt, he looked around the ground, seeing that his friend was right, there were pieces of tire carcass in the street—and his tactical knife. He ran to pick up the weapon, then looked left and sprinted off, following the rubber breadcrumbs. Up ahead in the distance there were long blasts of car horns overriding the din of other vehicles on the street. Two shots killed the sounds, confirming to the two SAD operators that they were on the right track. They both ran towards the action. It didn't take them long to find the Mercedes they'd been chasing, abandoned.

Steam was still rising from the front end of the car, now in a permanent kiss with a tree. A silver Audi, with its front end also smashed in, had somehow come into contact with the Mercedes and its driver was now sitting on the sidewalk, nursing a bloody wound from his shoulder. *That explains the shots we heard. He's alive, where the fuck are they now?* Another long car horn sounded, answering Chris's question.

Alex was still bounding ahead when he spotted the fugitive trio running diagonally across a side street, toward some steps that led down into what looked like a seedy pub or dive cafe. "Restaurant!" he shouted for Chris's benefit, then sprinted as fast as he could to catch them before they entered the safety of the premises. Alex's speed paid off, and he grabbed one bodyguard by the collar just as the man was approaching the door. He yanked him far enough back to toss him to one side, leaving him for Chris to take care of. He then attempted to move into the premises—but the barrel of a gun prohibited his progress. The second bodyguard, however, had made the mistake of leading with his weapon, giving Alex the advantage of disarming him quickly by using his left hand to knock the man's wrist up and simultaneously knock the pistol down and out of the man's hand. Once the gun hit the ground, Alex punched the man in the throat, then dragged the stunned bodyguard out onto the street by tying up the man's wrist into a gooseneck lock. Once he had control, he spotted Chris, who was still going to town on the first bodyguard. He heard sirens in the distance.

When Alex passed the first bodyguard over to him, Chris had immediately taken the man to the ground by rushing at him hard. He shoved his right hand into his opponent's throat while grabbing the man's left wrist. The pair crashed to the ground together, and to avoid any self-injury, Chris landed on top of the man. He then jumped to his feet quickly, but he was still in control of the bodyguard's wrist. Chris tried to flip him over, but the man was having none of it and punched Chris in the ribs. His injuries from Islamabad came back to haunt him, and he winced in pain, letting go of his captive for just a second.

The bodyguard took advantage of the moment and scrambled to his feet but was wobbly from the blows he just received. He ran into a wall he didn't know was there. His face collided with the hard stone, but he bounced away, turning around in time to receive two right hooks into his right ribcage, then a third and fourth on the left side. Winded and disorientated, he doubled over, but as he leaned his head down he felt interlocking fingers around the back of his neck, pulling him down, then a knee drive into his solar plexus. He was done. He fell straight to the ground and onto all fours.

Chris stood back and watched the man throw up from the damage he'd just inflicted, but gave no quarter. He moved behind the bodyguard and kicked him between his legs, forcing him face down into the pavement and into his own juices. Chris quickly searched the prone man and retrieved a Glock pistol from a holster, as well as two spare magazines from the man's belt. Chris dropped the magazine of the pistol and pulled the slide back to eject a round and lock the mechanism in place. He tossed the magazines and stuffed the gun in his waistband. Satisfied that the man before him was not a threat, he drew his own Makarov pistol and held it over his prisoner as well as the second bodyguard that Alex had unceremoniously dumped next to his partner.

"You got this? I'm going to find Faizan," Alex announced. Chris shook his head to convince him otherwise. Alex may not have noticed it, but they had an audience.

Chris motioned behind Alex. "We've got a fan club."

Alex turned around to see four beefy men standing causally outside the entrance to the restaurant; they were staring at the two Americans. Alex was feeling brave and still had his hackles up. He needed to find Faizan, and he wanted to do it *now*. He took three steps forward, but he quickly calculated that the mass that stood before him must have weighed over half a ton. He thought these men were likely a serious threat, and he was right, for as he approached, they tensed and stood up straight. All he could see was short haircuts, tight T-shirts, bulging biceps and no necks. Alex, not one to back down from a fight easily, knew that these men had never auditioned for the Vienna Boys' Choir, nor were they current Nobel Peace Prize contenders. They were the real deal, a genuine threat, silent men willing to hurt—and enjoy themselves while they were doing it.

Their wall of human brawn created a barrier that would not relent. Alex tried to plan a few moves, but he quickly realized there was no way forward. He didn't look around for help or options, knowing that Chris was taking care of the bodyguards, but he wasn't sure what kind of threat was standing before him. He was slightly happy that they hadn't yet moved forward to engage with him, or defend Faizan's bodyguards. He pondered the situation as a staring contest began. The only saving grace was that he knew exactly where Faizan was. How he would get to him was the actual challenge.

Chris looked over at the scene. He might have had his gun trained on the enemy in front of him, but he too recognized the problem standing in front of Alex. His stomach twisted slightly, and his eyes widened. *Holy shit, this is bad.* He counted off the opponents. *I've got two, he's got four. Don't see a gun from the beef squad . . . yet. But where is the first gun? This could go sideways quickly . . . for both of us if we're not careful.* He waited for Alex to make a move. He knew that his friend was armed, but hadn't shown his weapon yet. Alex was playing it cool.

Chris held his weapon on his prisoners, hoping he would have the skill, speed and balls to help his partner if someone made a move on him. He tried to think of a quick exit strategy, but was at a loss. This wasn't his city. He had no resources and no real clue where he was; he didn't know what to do. Sandy's haunting words suddenly filtered through from the back of his brain to the front: *"How many more fights, Chris? You've always told me that one day you'll come across someone you can't beat. Will that be today? Tomorrow?"*

CHAPTER ELEVEN

Odessa, Ukraine

COMMISSAR GREGOR MELNIK JUMPED OUT of the police car and rushed over to form a barrier between the beef squad and Alex. He didn't raise his arms or make any sudden movement that could cause an unintended escalation at the front of the restaurant. Soon two other police cars arrived, skidding to a halt, lights forming a kaleidoscope of colors bouncing off nearby walls and faces. Chris held his weapon on his prisoners, but as soon as the first officer appeared with cuffs, he holstered and stood down.

Alex was still tense. He'd got into a staring contest with one of the heavies he'd deemed to be the leader of the crew. With no words exchanged, the common mistrust of law enforcement and criminal was enough to keep the antagonists apart. The commissar broke some of the tension by politely asking Alex to back up slightly, so everyone was out of arm's reach of each other. He then turned to the steroid junkies to ask them to relax inside the restaurant while he took statements of who did what, where and when. It was simple crowd control, and as the commissar predicted, the professional killer and the professional criminals assented to his request.

As the group of adversaries stood down, more police cars arrived on scene. The commissar directed his men to create a perimeter around the site while he conducted his investigation. While the police deployed, Chris spotted Lester parking the Ford transit van nearby, allowing the FBI liaison officer to exit the vehicle and join the small group at the front entrance of the eatery.

"Faizan is in there," Alex started.

The police commissar nodded. "Are you sure?"

"Do you really think we would be standing around with our thumbs up our asses if he wasn't? If it wasn't for those grunts, we'd have him out on the street right now."

The commissar didn't reply. His hands were dug down deep into his coat pockets. He had the look of a man who bore the weight of all four brawny men on his shoulders. He shuffled from one foot to the other for a minute, then shouted at one of his officers to move a vehicle. It was as if he didn't hear Alex's words. He was looking for an excuse to do something else other than respond to the statement. Alex, puzzled, looked over to Chris, who had the same quizzical look on his face.

"What?" Chris asked. "What are we missing? Let's drag that prick out of there! Then we all go home. Job done."

"It's not as simple as that," the commissar replied, his face an artist's impression of despair.

The four men stood in a loose circle—the three foreigners looking hard at the cop for an answer, confused by the hesitation. The commissar was about to say something when a voice from behind interrupted him.

"Commissar Melnik," were the only words the three outsiders understood as the voice continued in Ukrainian, but they all turned to see who had started the conversation. A short, bald-headed man with stylish, grey, thin-framed eyeglasses approached the group. Chris guessed him to be in his early fifties. He was dressed all in all black—a black leather jacket, black polo-neck sweater, and black trousers and shoes. He looked neither slimy, nor skittish, but rather he bore an air of superiority, akin to an academic with street smarts.

Chris gave him a hard stare and noticed that the short man didn't back down from his look. He was completely unintimidated. He must have dealt with the commissar in the past, as they both lit up cigarettes and began a sort of puff diplomacy. The three American representatives remained mute while the two Ukrainians talked, but neither Alex nor Chris were idle. Both men were still on the hunt, and assessing how they could get to their prey. To an outside observer, it may have looked like the pair were casually taking in their surroundings—but to a trained professional, one could tell they were looking for ways in and out of the restaurant, if force were to become necessary to resolve the situation. Baldy saw what they were doing, however, and suddenly broke into English.

"You are Americans, yes?"

Alex answered with a mere nod of the head. He wondered what this man was about to offer. His adrenalin, pumped up during the chase, had simmered down, but his brain activity was still in hyper mode. He didn't show it, but he was planning to rip the short man's head off if he got in his way.

"I was just explaining to my friend the commissar here, this man you seek . . . he is of no interest to you. He is not who you think," Baldy continued.

But he interests you, no doubt, Chris thought, confused why this man was protecting Faizan.

Alex was still trying to figure out what was going on before responding. During the standoff at the restaurant's entry, his mind had been flipping scenarios around, wondering why *this* restaurant, why those men were barring the way, and what else was there to see. The short man had thrown a surprising element into the unsolved calculation. "What is your interest in him?" Alex finally asked.

"He is a guest of mine. He only wishes to dine at my establishment. Nothing more."

Chris couldn't hold back at hearing the blatant lie. "Fuck off Shorty—nobody's believing that horseshit for a minute. The man's a piece of shit. You need to hand him over, and make it snappy before I get pissed off."

Alex rolled his eyes, hoping that Chris wouldn't push it too much further.

The short man bristled at the comment. He didn't appreciate being called a liar. He took a cautious but deliberate step towards Chris. "Brave move for a dwarf," Chris he sneered, not budging an inch.

"Chris!" Alex hissed, trying to get his partner to shut up.

Chris's and the short man's eyes interlocked. Both men saw the threat in each other. Commissar Melnik once again played peacemaker, interjecting himself into the fray. "Okay, enough, okay," he said, pushing Chris back a step. But he did not touch the short man. Alex picked up on the move. *Afraid of Shorty; won't put his hands on him. Interesting.*

Shorty flicked his cigarette down the street. He fished out a pack from his pocket and lit another. Allowing the smoke to cover his face, he tried to again assert control of the situation. "You are CIA, FBI?" he asked. Nobody answered him. He knew the answer. "I appreciate your conviction, your dedication to your work. I really do."

As he spoke, Chris realized Shorty's English was getting better. "I like men like you," he continued, this time speaking in a more relaxed tone, as if they were chatting over a beer. "You have balls. I will give you that. You come here to my home and accuse me of lying. Few men would do such a thing and live to talk about it. Your insults . . . blah! Nothing. I have heard worse. But calling me a liar . . ." He waved a finger at Chris before continuing. The silent pause was deafening. Alex thought Chris had stepped too far; he may have crossed the wrong person this time, and the situation was spiraling the wrong way.

"There is something you must understand, my friends," Shorty lectured on. "When I say to you this man you want is a friend in my country, it means he is more than a friend. He is family. When a stranger comes to me and speaks ill of him, then I am offended, for you are talking of me. Do you understand? Perhaps something is lost in translation, as you would say. In Ukrainian it sounds better. No matter . . . my friend has joined me for dinner. If he is in trouble, I must offer my help."

"Do you really know who he is, this man you call your friend, or is he a business associate?" Alex prodded.

"That my friend is my business, not yours. Do not push your luck with me. I am tiring of this conversation. This man is my family, and he is my guest for the evening." Alex wondered how much firepower the local police department had, and if they could force the rat out of the hole. He had a nasty feeling about the short man, and didn't want to have to rely on force to get Faizan. He didn't know if the beef squad were already tooling up and ready to go loud in order to protect their boss.

"You know of his woman, Johara?" Chris asked.

"Yes, yes, she is a beautiful girl, beautiful."

"Not any longer. If we hadn't arrived at the Bristol Hotel this evening when we did, she may not have lived." Chris omitted pretty boy's demise. He wasn't sure if there was a connection with him and Shorty, and he didn't want to muddy the waters. "Faizan's men raped and beat her."

It was the short man who took a step backwards this time. He showed genuine shock at the news. He regained his composure after a moment. "That is not the reason why you want him I fear, though, as reprehensible as that is." It was Chris's turn to be stunned. *What the fuck is it with this guy? Now his English is excellent; who the hell is he?*

"He's also a terrorist," Chris announced, going out on a limb. "He is a financier of al-Qaeda terrorist operations."

"What?" Shorty gasped.

"He has links to Osama bin Laden," Chris lied. He couldn't prove the statement, but he thought from the body language he was reading, Shorty was on the ropes.

Shorty grabbed his chest. He dropped his cigarette; it looked like he was in pain. He cringed slightly and staggered back a few steps. Nobody in the small gathering knew if the reaction was due to a delayed realization of the act performed on Johara, or the reality that his guest may be a terrorist. Shorty stammered his next words. "Pppp lease . . . excu . . . excuse mmme." He scuttled away back to his restaurant, still holding his chest.

"What the hell is going on?" Chris asked nobody in particular. He turned to the commissar, asking, "Gregor, who is this guy?"

Gregor swallowed hard; also shocked by Shorty's reaction. "Maks Chornovil. They call him the Black Ox. He is the most powerful man on the Black Sea. From here, all the way around to Moldova, Bulgaria, Turkey, Georgia, to the Crimea. He controls it all: drugs, prostitution, weapons, machinery, cars, ships, everything; he has it all."

"Fuck!" Alex responded. "This is opening another huge can of worms. Where did he learn his English?"

"KGB," Gregor replied stoically.

Chris snorted, declaring, "This gets better by the minute."

Chris looked at his watch for the tenth time in less than twenty minutes. He was pacing up and down next to the Ford transit van where they'd set up an ad hoc command post for the two SAD operatives, the police, and the Viewpoint surveillance team. Lester was monitoring the radio traffic between his people who had deployed or were deploying to several vantage points, hoping to spot Faizan if he somehow slipped out a back door. Chris thought it was a waste of time but kept his opinions to himself. He thought it likely that Shorty was at this very moment quizzing Faizan about the allegations brought by the American agents outside his door.

Forty minutes had passed, and the standoff continued with no resolution. Commissar Melnik made a flurry of calls that both Chris and Alex assumed were to his superiors or other persons of authority. Chris was frustrated, he finally spoke up. "I've just realized something. Shorty hasn't called for any backup." He paused, letting the news settle in for a minute. Everyone looked at Chris, expecting more, which he offered. "I know we don't know how many of his men are in there right now. But nobody is getting in from the rear, and nobody has shown up here on the street."

"Meaning what Chris?" Alex asked.

"Meaning, he doesn't want a confrontation. He wants things to end peacefully. If he really has an empire, he can call in his army to help him . . . Gregor, am I right?"

"Yes, you are correct. There are several men he can call on, some nearby."

"So why hasn't he called them?" Chris continued. "My guess is that we told him something he wasn't aware of. And by the look on his face when we told him of al-Qaeda, he took it personally. I don't think he's a happy camper right now." He let the statement hang. Looking around at the glum faces, he was not expecting any retorts. He stared at the entrance to the restaurant and ruminated on the possibilities further. He wanted to do something before it was too late, before they lost Faizan to the Black Ox, but he had no plan.

A few more minutes passed, then the door to the restaurant opened and one of the beef squad appeared. He marched across the street, his muscular frame making it look like he was carrying two watermelons under each arm, large and in charge. He approached the law enforcement group and pointed at Chris and Alex. "Come," was the only word he uttered, then he turned to walk away.

Chris and Alex looked curiously at each other and bustled quickly after the man. They didn't need a second invitation; they knew it would be the only one they'd get. They entered the restaurant down the steps where their initial altercation took place with Faizan's bodyguards. As soon as they were inside, three of Shorty's men, who looked grim, menacing and ready for action, greeted them with daggers in their eyes. Chris spotted a shotgun hanging loosely by one man's side; he also spotted an AK-47 held by another, then slow hand movements towards waistbands. Chris's initial thought was that this was an ambush, but he didn't have time to dwell on it as one of the men moved a black curtain to one side, an invitation to move further into the establishment. Alex moved first, with Chris close behind. They were both armed, but not searched. He wondered why Shorty was trusting them. It was a good sign.

As they entered the restaurant proper, their minds changed quickly. The room was full of Shorty's men, all tooled up. Weapons were strewn everywhere, with boxes of ammunition on tables instead of romantic candles and wine glasses. Chris's supposition that Shorty had called for backup wasn't entirely wrong. He just didn't know that the restaurant was closed to paying customers, as a private party was about to get underway for his men. Shorty didn't need to call for backup; they were already there.

Chris and Alex gingerly navigated their way through the throng of gangsters, keeping an eye out for any sharp movement, scrape of a chair or cocking of a weapon. They both knew, deep down, that whatever action they would take to defend themselves would be an exercise in futility. They dutifully followed their chaperone through the large dining room, back into the kitchen, down another set of stairs and into a cellar where even more of Shorty's men were ferreting around, getting provisions ready for a fight.

Their escort led them through a labyrinth of corridors, and finally to a rusty steel door guarded by one of the beef squad. The man at the door motioned for the two visitors to raise their arms to their sides for a pat-down. Chris and Alex reluctantly handed over their weapons, knowing that to refuse would lead to a solid beating. The creaking door opened and the escorts ushered both visitors in. The door slammed behind them and Alex and Chris entered a spacious, but dirty and musty room, dimly lit by a few scattered light bulbs. In the center of the room, they saw Faizan, lying face down with a rope securing his wrists behind his back. The rope reached up to the rafters, and was held by one of the beef squad. Faizan was naked, bleeding and unresponsive. Chris noted that there were pools and spackles of blood in front of him, some of it new; a lot of it old. They had just entered Shorty's torture chamber.

Shorty, sitting in an old wooden chair, surveyed the activity around him. Though the light in the room was nearly worthless, Chris could tell that Shorty had changed. At first, he thought he saw a sadness; the man's confidence and arrogance seemed to have disappeared. But Chris wasn't so sure. He stared at Shorty a moment longer and noticed he was holding something. It looked like a picture frame. Chris looked at Faizan. He thought they were too late; it was likely he was dead, or at least close to it. He wondered why Shorty had treated him this way. All he had had to do was hand the terrorist over to the CIA, or the police. There was no need for all of this—or so he thought.

"Who is Mukhtar?" Shorty growled to his visitors.

Chris took a few steps forward. One of the beef squad moved to intercede. Shorty raised his hand, acknowledging that there was no threat. Chris took another step forward. He wanted to see what Shorty was holding. Shorty looked up at Chris, waiting for an answer.

"Khalid Sheik Mohammed," Chris responded. As he did, there was a brief movement from Faizan, recognizing the name.

Chris was amazed. *Fuck, he's still alive! We might have a chance of salvaging this.*

"What is he to this man? All he told me was that he feared Mukhtar . . . Mukhtar . . . Mukhtar, that is all he wanted to say."

"Khalid Sheik Mohammed is the man responsible for the attacks on the United States on September 11. He was the architect, the master planner. We need this man to help us capture him, we need—"

Shorty raised his hand to stop Chris from continuing. He shook his head, almost in disbelief. He never said a word, contemplating his next words, staring at Faizan, his gaze fixed in a trance. "And this man . . . he is responsible for finance, for providing the money to these terrorists?" he finally asked.

"Yes, we need to talk to him ourselves—" Chris began, but was interrupted by another wave of Shorty's hand.

Shorty again looked down to the picture frame he held in his right hand. He gripped it tightly. His hand shook. Chris tried to lean in slightly to see what was so precious to him. He inched forward.

"Maks," Chris whispered, addressing Shorty by his real name. "Let us have him. We are close to finding Mukhtar. But we need this man to put all the pieces together. We need to follow the money; we need to stop them from doing this again."

"Again? Again?" Shorty spat as he stood up. "Why didn't the fucking CIA stop this from happening the first time? It is your fault, you—" He pointed an angry finger at Chris, then to Alex. "Your fucking CIA is so incompetent, and to think we were really worried about you . . . what a mistake, what a colossal mistake. You are amateurs, you must have seen this coming . . . why, why didn't you?"

Chris could see that Shorty was livid. He didn't really know why, but he needed him to calm down. "Maks, please, we need him, we need him alive, he is of no use to us dead, we may never have enough intelligence—"

"—Death, you talk to me of death . . . you know nothing. This is death!" Shorty shouted, holding up the picture frame for Chris to see. It was a picture of a boyish man with features similar to Shorty, standing in front of the New York Stock Exchange, dressed smartly in a suit, smiling as if he had just won $100 million in the lottery.

A tear ran down Shorty's hard façade. "My Vitaly, my brother, dead because of the incompetence of the CIA!" he screamed. Chris wisely kept his mouth shut as he watched Shorty implode. He didn't know what to expect. Would he and Alex be next, hanging by a rope in this hole? He didn't panic, but his butt itched to no end. *This is going fucking pear-shaped; we are fucked. We're not going to get out of this, he's blaming us for his brother's death.*

Shorty paced around, not saying anything. He was fuming. Chris didn't want him in this state. He rationalized that Shorty was not a man to be congenial when he was mad at something. He needed him on his side.

"You fucking Americans think you know everything!" he spat on the ground in front of Chris, then paced around again. Chris looked at Alex, who shook his head slightly. It was the first time that he saw his friend with a worried look on his face. Shorty came back to the duo. This time his face was a little more reserved. "Where is this Mukhtar?"

"We don't really know, not yet," Alex answered.

"And you think this man knows?" Shorty quizzed.

"It's possible, we need him with us, we will interrogate him, we have a lot to. . ."

Shorty used one of his hand commands to again call for silence. He turned to the man holding the rope and nodded. The man, assisted by another, pulled Faizan up towards the rafters, arms still bound behind his back. He let out a blood-curdling scream, hanging in agony. Shorty turned to Chris.

"You must know a place, a country where this Mukhtar is. Tell me."

Chris hesitated, this wasn't the way he wanted to get information, but he thought of the enhanced interrogation methods that were used at the CIA black sites. This wasn't too far off the mark. "Afghanistan or Pakistan," he suggested.

The torture began.

An hour had passed since Chris had suggested the two countries he thought may have been al-Qaeda safe havens for Khalid Sheikh Mohammed. Faizan either didn't know, or was so disciplined, he could take the pain and not give up the location. Chris wondered how much more the Arab could take, but the Black Ox was good at what he did. He knew exactly when to question, and when to inflict physical discomfort. He knew what tools to use and what areas on the body were the most sensitive; he knew a man's limit, and he knew when to give up. The KGB had trained him well.

"This man does not know," he offered to the two onlookers. "We could take more time, take a more creative approach, but I am weary of such things. This is not something that I . . . what's the word . . . ah, yes, relish. This is the work for younger men." He nodded to his men, who loosened their grip on the rope and let Faizan fall to the ground with a thump. Maks then turned to other matters. "I have a business proposition for you," he said to the pair.

Shocked, Chris almost let his jaw drop. He didn't know if this was one of those join-me-or-die situations, or if the man really wanted to work with them. He stayed silent, waiting for the curious offer.

"If you leave me alone, my activities . . . you know what I mean. Then I will assist you in whatever way I can to catch these terrorists. I have contacts in many places—information that may be of use to you one day."

Alex didn't want to dance with the Devil. He knew it would be a slippery slope. He questioned the reasoning behind the offer. "Why should we do that? We're not interested in what you do; we don't care. As far as I am concerned, you have done nothing wrong."

"But you need my help in capturing these pigs, yes?"

Alex didn't give him a positive verbal response, but he nodded his head.

It was enough of a reaction for Shorty. He spun around and grabbed a pistol from his waistband with his right hand. He hustled over to Faizan and shot him in the head.

"Fuck!" Chris shouted uncontrollably.

Shorty spat on Faizan's limp body. "For Vitaly," he said coldly. He then returned to his two guests. He looked as if someone had lifted a mountain off his shoulders. He was back to being composed, rationale and amiable. "Now gentlemen, one last thing, and please accept my apologies, it was not you who I blame for the tragedy in New York. But my brother, you must understand what I have been through these past months. It has been torture for me, for my family. He was in the North Tower, the only Ukrainian to die that day. He was our shining star." Chris noted that Shorty had a far-off look in his eyes, tinged with sadness. A lengthy pause enveloped the players in the room. Neither Alex nor Chris knew what to say or do.

"I digress," the former KGB man eventually added. His eyes lit up when he looked at the two CIA officers. A thought came to light, even if outlandish considering the circumstances. "If you two gentlemen are in need of employment one day, I could use men with your skills." Shorty smiled at the proposition. He could do with a few more Americans on the payroll. "Just think about it, okay? You know where you can find me. You are always welcome to dine here. Now come, let's drink; let's put this episode behind us. I am celebrating. I have dealt with enough vengeance for one day, but . . . my friends." He closed in on the two CIA officers and raised his right index finger. In a whisper, he announced in a grim tone, "I am not finished, not by a long way. If you don't find Mukhtar, I will."

Chris tried to mask his surprise at the turn of events. *This guy is seriously fucked up.*

Quetta, Pakistan

The two Pakistani SA 330 Puma helicopters held station in darkness above the hills southwest of the city of Quetta, waiting patiently for the go order. The choppers, each loaded up with six commandos of Zarrar Company, Pakistan Special Forces, bounced lightly in the upwind from the hills below. The noise of their machines was masked by the cover of the hills and valleys, camouflaging their intent.

Loaded on a mixture of pickup trucks and jeeps, forty-eight more commandos from the same company rolled silently into the Gulistan Town neighborhood of Quetta, to wait for an order to execute their plan.

Closer to the targets' location, dozens of city policemen marched in silence to form a large perimeter to contain and quarantine the streets leading to and from the mosque, ensuring unhindered passage in and out of the area for the raid teams.

At the Musa College parking lot, two miles west of the mosque, the command-and-control element of Operation Breaker was studiously monitoring the deployment's progress, expecting the worst, but hoping for the best. The command center, on loan from the Pakistan Army, was comprised of three large trailers joined to form a T shape. It included members of the CIA, the FBI, NSA, and the US National Reconnaissance Office (NRO), as well as the Pakistan ISI, Pakistan Special Forces, Pakistan Army, and state and local law enforcement agencies. Needless to say, the fight for real estate in the cramped confines was contentious. However, everyone involved knew that the discomfort was only for a brief time, and the goal to capture Khalid Sheik Mohammed far outweighed the need for creature comforts.

Once notification came in that all units were in place, the final deployment of CIA, FBI and ISI officers was underway. The last checks from agents close to the Syed Abad Mosque confirmed that the location was quiet, with no activity detected. All eyes turned to the officer from the NRO for final clarification. The American officer looked at his secure laptop screen, and at the feed from the Key Hole (KH-11) digital imaging satellite orbiting the earth, making its second pass of the day.

The satellite, the size of a school bus, passed directly 225 miles overhead Quetta and delivered high-resolution images of the mosque and its surrounding areas, despite the low light. The NRO officer confirmed there was no activity of concern in the mosque itself, nor from the five sleeping subjects in the adjacent house.

When the CIA officer in charge of the operation acknowledged the last teams were in place, he bounced around the room for a last go/no-go confirmation. All agencies reported in the affirmative. The mission was a go.

Karachi, Pakistan

In contrast to the millions of dollars spent on secret satellites, high-tech communications gear, the deployment of hundreds of men and machines, and the countless hours spent to investigate the possibility of catching one man in Quetta, the bare-bones Project Tamandar was about to get underway in Karachi.

Designed on even less than a shoestring budget, Project Tamandar included eight men in four separate locations in the city's south end. They each drank tea and ate a simple breakfast before getting under-way. There was no need for the terrorist cell to coordinate or have a go/no-go meeting. Each man knew his assigned task and was given a time and date to be at a certain location, where the mission would begin. Nothing about Tamandar was high-tech or complex; nor was the target in doubt. It would be a simple, low-risk drive-by with a high probability of success.

In the predawn hours, four pairs of men left their homes and mounted four motorcycles, headed north towards the target. It mattered not that they were not in contact with another. If one pair did not show, the smaller team could still continue. They didn't need a full complement to complete the mission.

———————∞∞∞———————

The alarm tone sounded and the flashing Master Caution light pleaded for attention in the cockpit of Alpha Four Alpha. It was one of the two Puma helicopters hovering in place, waiting for the order to proceed into the city of Quetta. The pilot, using his night vision goggles, focused on reference points needed to maintain a steady hover, while his copilot looked down at the console and mentally processed the condition before him. The first indication of a problem was a transmission chip light, followed by secondary indications of a drop in transmission oil pressure, and a rise in transmission oil temperature. None of the tones or lights were good.

The copilot keyed the intra-cockpit communication system and hurriedly summarized to the pilot the situation they were facing: a catastrophic transmission failure. They needed to immediately land the helicopter at the first safe site they could find—and it was definitely not going to be in the peaks and valleys that shrouded their mission. The pilot toggled his radio switch and notified command and control that they were seeking a safe location to land the aircraft due to imminent mechanical failure. Alpha Three Alpha picked up on the transmission and relayed the news back to the soldiers in the cabin. The unwelcome news caused a stir with both the men in the air and the commanders on the ground.

A decision needed to be made: should the air component of Operation Breaker continue? Nobody knew if the problem the struggling chopper was experiencing was common to both craft.

As H-Hour approached, the time for twiddling thumbs was over. The commanders on the ground deemed that it was worth the risk to keep Alpha Three Alpha on mission, and proceed with dropping in troops on one of the targets two rooftops. The challenge now was just which rooftop to secure. The mosque, dedicated to Alpha Three Alpha, or the house, which had been tasked to Alpha Four Alpha. With only six soldiers now available to the task, and seconds to decide, the commanders reluctantly adjusted the mission for the remaining air element to deploy to the target area to watch and wait. If the suspected terrorists attempted an escape by the rooftops, the single remaining Puma would give chase and act as an aerial command post, controlling the ground troops efforts.

The four motorcycles arrived at the Karachi General Railway Store on Framrose Road at staggered intervals, each within thirty minutes of one another. It was still dark, and the dust clouds the party created rose to meet the thin veil of permanent smog that plagued Pakistan's largest city. The small terrorist cell blended in well with their environment; to the untrained eye, their attire, bearing, and mannerisms gave nothing away. But to the security professional, eight men on four motorcycles, traveling in unison, all unusually wearing helmets, each carrying backpacks, should be enough to warrant a second glance, and even a third, more serious look.

The small cell banked on surprise. Their target was still a few miles away, and up to this point in the attack plan, there was no need for hesitation. The group drove north for half a mile, joined the M.T. Khan Road at Harding Bridge, and headed west. Traffic was relatively light, with other motorcycles, cars, vans and trucks traveling at a steady speed down the well-worn highway. As the team joined the traffic, the last pair of terrorists were held up by a bus trying to navigate its way through the intersection to the highway. While waiting for the vehicles to clear, the two terrorists looked in the distance and spotted a courthouse. However, this was no ordinary court of law, it was the federal antiterrorism court. The two riders looked on, bewildered for a moment, wondering if they would soon be visitors to the facility; or if today's exercise were to be successful, it might become a new target of opportunity for the Tamandar team.

In a strange twist of fate, the two men were so focused on the building in front of them, they did not see a large colorful jingle truck bear down on them. Suddenly tires were squealing, brake dust was puffing, and there was the smell of burning rubber on tarmac. The impact knocked the bike and its passengers over. The weight of the truck, the failing brakes, the wild-eyed driver, unbelieving at the sight of an obstacle, accepted the inevitable and threw up his hands. The truck ran over the top of the two men—crushing them, and their dreams of a glorious jihad.

The terrorist team leader, who had pulled his following over for the men to catch up, saw the accident, and for a moment was tempted to turn around and help his brethren. In the time it took for him to contemplate an immediate action, a swarm of people poured out of the cracks of the neighborhood, and rushed to see the spectacle. It had only been a few minutes since he had been through the intersection, and then there were but few people in the area. Now it was like a sea of ants, carting away bits and pieces of the wreckage. There was nothing he could do for his men. He looked at the remaining members of the team. He had to decide: go or no-go?

Khalid Sheik Mohammed thought he was still in a dream when he heard the unmistakable sound of a helicopter approaching. His eyes remained closed; he was in a deep slumber, feeling warm, comfortable and secure in his bed. But the sound, like no other, was incessant. He finally opened his eyes, realizing it wasn't a dream. He felt the room vibrate. A helicopter was invading his space. He heard others in the house stir. He heard voices of panic.

The Zarrar Company assault team sped out of the gates at a ferocious speed, streaming through the tight streets and alleyways on foot like rivulets of mercury breaking through a dam, permeating every crevice, every nook and every cranny.

Police officers on motorcycles whizzed into the area, securing each junction and pathway, and urged nosy civilians to remain in their homes. The citizens of the suburb, curious at the early hour commotion, became mesmerized as masked soldiers crisscrossed their way past their doors and walkways.

As one team of Special Forces men lined up ready at the door to the Syed Abad Mosque, two pickup trucks manned by a squad of their colleagues squeezed their way down the narrow street, coming to a halt at the Mosque's balcony. Once in place, the soldiers jumped from the rear of the pickup, onto the cab, and climbed up and over the balcony wall. The ground floor assault team breached the main door to the mosque, and entered at the same time as the upper floor team on the balcony.

Team Charlie, responsible for securing the house to the rear of the mosque, entered the two-story structure three seconds after the teams entered the mosque. They were unfortunate not to have a balcony to access the property, and also were without the aid of a team on the roof; they would have to manage the operation from the bottom up. On breaching the door, a swarm of black-clad soldiers rushed into the house like a shoal of piranhas feeding on fresh prey.

During the commotion, Alpha Three Alpha communicated that a subject had made its way to the roof. The pilot reported that he was carrying a weapon. A sniper team, one of three positioned in and around the area, took a single shot from a quarter of a mile away. The sniper, through his scope, could see the man's head explode. There was no need for discussion, no need for jubilation—just concentration and anticipation that another target would appear.

Colonel Rashid Ghazini cringed involuntarily when he heard the shot. Escorting the American-led contingent to the raid, he wondered who it was that had fallen. He held his ground behind a line of police vehicles waiting for the all-clear signal from the raid teams. His emotions were mixed, as there were no more shots, no explosions, and little radio chatter. His American guests were chomping at the bit, worse than greyhounds in racing traps, eager to chase and devour their quarry. He held his radio tightly to his ear. He held his breath. He waited nervously.

The leader of the small terrorist team spotted the Stars and Stripes fluttering gently in the wind above the US Consulate. The flag, easily discernable from the M.T. Kahn Road, had just been raised by some US Marines, signaling that sunrise had finally arrived. Within a few hours, the diplomatic mission would soon be open for business and a horde of visa applicants would descend on the complex, ready to wait patiently for hours, for a chance to obtain a coveted pass to visit the United States.

The terrorist cell, however, had planned their attack for when they knew few or no Pakistani civilians would be present, and the Pakistan Rangers who guarded the American facility were at their lowest point of vigilance from a long, drawn out night of no sleep.

As the team exited the main road, they rounded the American complex from the north and headed down a one-way street towards the visitor interview gate. When the team was in sight of a contingent of Rangers, they slowed their momentum and readied their weapons. The Rangers took scant notice of the three motorcycles approaching, however, one of the uniformed men raised his Kalashnikov slightly, more out of habit than a feeling of impending danger. He turned his back to the approaching traffic to converse with one of his team. There were four Rangers in total patiently milling around, watching the clock creep slowly along, wishing their night shift would end soon. Two of the men leaned up against the compound's high wall, trying their best to stay awake; one sat in an open-top jeep. The approaching motorcycles were the first vehicles they had seen in what had been a very long, uneventful night. They should have paid attention; they should have seen the uniformity of the spectacle. They should have seen the machine guns pointing at them. They should have seen the pistol being drawn.

As the first shots rained down on the officers, a civilian on a bicycle, not initially seen by the terror cell, impeded a defender from returning fire, to his demise. When the officer fell to a bullet in the throat, a terrorist got off a motorcycle, picked up the Ranger's submachine gun and emptied the magazine into his already limp body. The terrorist continued to shoot at anything that moved, spraying the consulate walls with bullets. The Ranger jeep caught on fire, but the terrorists continued to shoot, injuring the three other Rangers. The terror attack only ceased when shots came from within the walls of the consulate. Two police officers, assigned to consulate security of the inner perimeter, bravely engaged the terrorist cell through a steel gate that secured the compound.

Although outnumbered, the two policemen used a shotgun and a pistol to repel the attack. One terrorist was shot in the calf during the skirmish, hobbled away, and almost reached the safety of a motorcycle when he was hit again in his upper thigh, taking him to the ground. One member of the team rushed to help his comrade, while another provided covering fire, pumping more automatic rounds into the consulate gate. The shots had the desired effect, as the police officers fired no more in return from within the American compound. The injured terrorist, finally placed on a motorcycle, held on as best he could as the team leader led the cell away towards the safety and anonymity of the Mai Kolachi Bypass. Just as they were about to merge into traffic, however, the injured passenger passed out and fell off the bike. The rider who'd lost his charge stopped the bike and looked back at the hapless figure on the ground. By the time he looked forward again, the remnants of his team were nowhere in sight. He gunned his engine and joined the traffic. The man he'd left behind was not a friend, or relative, he was merely a soldier. It mattered not that he would be captured; what mattered more was that Project Tamandar had achieved its aim.

Colonel Rashid Ghazini followed a Pakistan Special Forces soldier who hustled through the Syed Abad Mosque. Following behind were four members of the CIA SAD, an FBI officer, and two more ISI officers. They exchanged no words, as the rush to find out if the man killed on the rooftop of the house was the man that they were hunting. Rashid had his heart in his mouth as he traversed down through the basement passageway and then into the house at the rear of the mosque. While the entourage passed through the home's tight corridors, he stopped at a large room to find four men squatting on the floor, hands in shackles behind them, guarded by heavily armed black-clad men. He gave the prisoners a cursory glance. He was thankful that he did not recognize any of them. Once more, nobody spoke and the flood of people, all looking for answers without asking for anything, headed up the stairs to the rooftop.

There they found another soldier, guarding a body whose head was missing its facial features. Rashid looked hard at the lifeless man. He squatted down next to him, hoping to find some distinctive attribute that the .50 caliber round had missed. He kept his thoughts to himself and let the others standing around him make the heated suppositions. One of the Americans took out an electronic scanner and attempted to take an impression of the dead man's fingers. It was then that Rashid took his first real breath. The man was missing two fingers on his right hand. They were old wounds.

Khalid Sheik Mohammed opened the bedroom shutters of his room at the Choki Guesthouse. He was greeted with a vista that overlooked the Pakistan Military Academy in Abbottabad. From his third-floor vantage point he saw a Russian-made Mi-17 helicopter hovering in place above the academy, making him wonder what type of exercise was taking place there at this early hour. A second, then third helicopter took off from the base and joined the first aircraft. As soon as the three choppers assumed a formation, they headed north and away from the city.

He watched the helicopters float off into the distance. The shouts from elsewhere in the guesthouse that he'd heard earlier dissipated. He didn't know what the commotion was about, but he supposed that some of his men, nervous about being in such close proximity to the Pakistan military, had jumped at the sound of the activity, sensing a raid and thus raising a false alarm. He looked at his watch. He thought about

Project Tamandar and wondered about its progress.

It was another minor operation, but a necessary one. His men needed the boost of a victory, no matter how small, and he was eager to appease—and eager to mete out a measure of revenge against the Rangers for his friend Abu Zubaydah. He expected another success, and thought it wouldn't take long for news of the attack to reach the airwaves. In an hour, Pakistan would know that al-Qaeda had struck again. But by the end of the day, he knew he would have to answer to his Pakistan military allies for the rationale behind the attack. The backdrop of the US Consulate would be his ace, and the collateral damage to the Rangers, he would lie, would be regretful.

He leaned forward at the window's ledge to take in the fresh morning air. He marveled at the view of the Orash Valley and its lush hills surrounding the high-altitude city of a meager 200,000. His mind wondered as he contemplated the possibilities of creating powerful alliances with the dozens of hardline retired military officers who lived in the city before him. The "old guard" who often complained of their government's lack of willingness to support the Taliban, or desired the ousting of Western influence in the country; who worried about the Indian problem, the struggles of Kashmir, and the country's nuclear ambitions—all this held his attention. He was interested in talks of coups, proxy wars, Islamic militancy, war chests, weapon supplies, training and other minutiae of the day-to-day running of a terrorist organization. But he had to remind himself that his task, in this moment, was purely operational. The strategic alliances he pondered were out of his purview, at least for now. It was bin Laden's task to create and manage such agreements. But his reason for being in the military city was to show that he was a man who could represent al-Qaeda until such a time as it was safe for his leader to do so himself. He also wanted to show that he, the Baluchi of Quetta, the principal architect of 9/11, was a trusted partner—and the de facto leader of al-Qaeda in Pakistan.

He checked his watch once more. He had two more hours before he was to visit a site in the city's east. A location that could have potential as a new residence for a special guest one day.

CHAPTER TWELVE

Quetta, Pakistan

COLONEL RASHID GHAZINI WAS BESIDE himself. He paced around the rooftop of the house that once was the short-term residence of Khalid Sheik Mohammed. He made a few calls on his cell phone, each one curt, brief and sometimes rude to those on the other end of the line. Frustrated in more ways than one, his first concern was that Mukhtar escaped, which still worried him. He thought if they had caught the terrorist, it would only be to his and the ISI's advantage that he died during capture.

Seeing that the only casualty of the raid was a man missing his face, he assumed that Mukhtar was nowhere near the raid's vicinity, it meant the terrorist leader was still alive. Adding to Rashid's consternation however, was that he had no idea how close or far the American-led operation had been to capturing him. Despite his efforts at tracking Mukhtar's movements through Wahid's laptop, it seemed there was a technical malfunction preventing him from warning the terrorist of the impending raid, or Wahid had somehow circumvented the program. To make matters worse, Mukhtar was not answering his cell phone. For once, Rashid had no idea where the terrorist leader was. He was also in the dark about where his little rat Wahid could be. He didn't know if he was with Mukhtar, or operating on his own.

Standing still for a minute, he looked across the rooftops of the city and wondered if he had underestimated the young IT geek. If he did, it would be to his detriment. He made yet another call.

"Tell me. What went wrong?" Rashid ordered a technician at the ISI Quetta Field Office.

"Sir, it is a mystery—"

"—I don't want mysteries, idiot. Tell me the facts!"

The technician was glad that the colonel could not see the large eye-roll he had just made to nobody in particular. "Sir, the device was working until 1600 hours yesterday," he began. "Then it stopped. I have no explanation. Our diagnostics and tracing software are working correctly, and we have tried various devices to get into the program. All I can tell you is that the computer was at that location, but it is no longer there."

Rashid wanted to scream a hundred obscenities at the man and send him to some remote outpost to guard a snow-clad mountain, but he bit his tongue. He also thought about asking more questions, but realized it was fruitless. So he hung up the phone, leaving the technician to shrug his shoulders and conjure up his own offensive language for the arrogant senior officer. Rashid stormed off the roof and down into the dwelling below, just in time for someone to shout for his attention.

As he descended the stairs to the ground floor, he bumped into one of the FBI agents. The agent inadvertently caught Rashid on his shins with a clear plastic evidence bag that he'd swung accidentally. Rashid grabbed his leg and held back a curse. While doing so, he looked at the bag the man was carrying and saw a laptop. The FBI man apologized and scurried away, not knowing why the ISI man had looked so horrified at the simple bump. Rashid stared at the man's back as his mind panicked. He didn't have long to dwell, as a call for him to follow another ISI man came from down the hall.

Rashid followed his colleague, who led him into the kitchen where a large fridge dislodged from its permanent location revealed a hole in the wall. Without questioning its purpose, he followed his associate and climbed through it. The space behind the fridge led to a hole in the ground, complete with a ladder leading to a tunnel. As much as Rashid didn't want to rummage around in the bowels of the city, the probable escape route of the terrorist, he trudged on, playing the curious investigator all the while partitioning his mind in multiple directions.

Wahid had betrayed him, but he didn't know to what extent. He didn't know where either Wahid or Mukhtar were. Entrenched in another mosque in the city? Or happily traveling on the road to Kandahar? It was anyone's guess. To add to his worries, he didn't know if the laptop that the FBI man had secured was Wahid's, and if it had the ISI GPS tracking device still programmed on to it. He didn't know how long ago Mukhtar had escaped. He didn't know if he was safe. His list of unknowns was mounting, and so was his dread as he realized the darkness of the tunnel was as bleak as his future.

Islamabad, Pakistan

Surprised to be back in Pakistan, Chris was riding in the rear of a Toyota Land Cruiser. He had his head set to his on a swivel, carefully checking out his area of safety and only adding to the silence of the short transportation mission. Alex sat in the front, observing his own arc of responsibility. Another SAD officer was at the wheel. The quiet trio were concentrating on the surrounding traffic, the beady eyes of pedestrians on the street, the vehicles they passed, or others who just stared too long for comfort's sake.

Chris and Alex both held their weapons out of sight but in the ready position, expecting something untoward that would necessitate a swift reaction from the team. The small group wasn't on edge, but were vigilant, and primed to do whatever it took to get themselves to their location: a safe house on Rawal Lake, a reservoir within the city limits of Islamabad.

An hour after leaving the Islamabad International Airport, the SAD team reached a villa on the Jinnah Road in the Chak Shahzad district of the city. Although still daylight when they arrived, Chris and Alex had little time to check out their new surroundings before the sun went down. As they scoped out the place, a familiar figure greeted them.

"This way guys," a voice called behind Chris's back. He turned around in time to see bearded Jon walk back into the house. "Fuck," he whispered.

"Don't get your panties in a bunch, Chris," Alex countered.

"I thought he didn't like me," Chris complained.

"What the fuck do I know? I don't like you either, I'm just following orders."

"Wanker!"

Alex smiled, and with his tote in his hand, he strolled into the residence, with Chris following a few steps behind. Once inside, the Brit and the former Delta Force operator were met by bearded Jon and two other CIA Directorate of Operations officers with whom they'd had brief encounters on other missions. Standing with his bag in his hand, Chris, out of professional habit, began his robot-like scan of the room. There was a large opening to his front, with folded French doors that led to a veranda. From his limited position, he could just make out a green lawn that led down to the lake. The room had an open floor plan with a kitchen off to his left, an adjacent dining room, and a corridor to his right that led to what he assumed were bathrooms and bedrooms. A staircase led to an upper level, which made him guess it had a similar layout as the ground floor. The residence was in pristine condition, with new furniture, fittings, and decorations. He nodded his head in approval.

"Sit down guys, drop your bags there. You want a water, Coke, Sprite? Fridge over there, help yourself," Jon offered.

Chris placed his bag on a chair up against a wall and headed for the fridge. He retrieved a Sprite for himself and a Coke for his friend. He found a pillar to lean up against, still unsure of why he was there. Alex took a seat on the couch opposite the operations folks, and pondered what was to come next.

"I think we all know each other," Jon started. "At least well enough not to have to go through all that—'Hi, my name's Jon' horseshit.'" Lighting up a cigar, he continued with an interesting question. "How was your trip to Odessa?" he asked.

Chris shrugged his shoulders and Alex stared straight ahead, neither saying anything. This wasn't a debriefing; they didn't need to share what they were doing on a mission; it really wasn't any of their business. Chris smiled inwardly. *Only on a need to know basis, motherfucker.*

The tension in the room was tangible. The three operations officers looked cross, agitated and uneasy. They were expecting the meeting to go a little softer than the direction it was taking. Jon sensed the stress. "Look, guys, let's not dick around. We have ourselves an opportunity here, and in the scope of things it's huge." He looked at Chris first. "I think we both know that we don't care for each other, and that's fine, so fuck you."

Chris smiled at the honesty. He eased his death stare back a little. Jon capitalized on the leverage. "I didn't want you on this operation Chris, but we have a mutual friend that trusts you. And we need *him,* so by default, I need you." Jon let the statement hang. Confused, Chris didn't understand who Jon was talking about.

"So, I guess it's my turn to suck it up and put this personality conflict bullshit to bed. You good with that?"

"Yeah, you're right Jon," Chris replied. "I don't like you either, so fuck you too." He grinned before he sipped on his drink. After a long hard swallow, he asked the group, "What do you have in mind, and how can we help?"

Jon sat back in the comfort of the plush, white sectional he was sitting on. He blew a long plume of smoke up into the air. He held Chris's gaze for a moment, then laid out the situation. "There was a raid yesterday in Quetta to capture Khalid Sheik Mohammed. We got a tip, and we escalated with enough force to start a small war . . . I exaggerate. But obviously we came up empty, as we're still here and not popping champagne corks at the White House."

What does this have to do with me? Chris asked himself. He waited patiently for Jon to continue, and toyed with his empty Sprite can.

"We're still going through the intel from the site," Jon remarked between dragging on his cigar and studying the burning embers. "We picked up some interesting characters who are now on their way to some of our guesthouses, but I don't think we'll get much out of the expedition. I won't say it was a waste of time, but it causes us to look in another direction." He paused once again. Chris was getting impatient. *Hurry up already, I need a shit.*

"I know how much you SAD guys are frustrated in almost getting these assholes, and coming up short; so are we. We know where the problems lie, and yes, we're aware of the limited help that we're getting from the ISI. But time is passing us by and tangible results are getting few and far between. To add salt to the wound, there was an al-Qaeda attack in Karachi conducted at the same time the Quetta operation was going down. They hit the US consulate; however, we believe that the US was not the target . . . two Pakistan Rangers were killed, and another injured. The consensus is that it was a revenge attack based on our friend Abu Zubaydah's capture. But we need not rehash that brief adventure."

Chris cocked his head slightly at the thinly veiled sarcasm. He kept his mouth shut, but knew that although they were playing nice, Jon still harbored some resentment toward him.

"I digress, sorry, but the bottom line is that KSM is still out there, and al-Qaeda is getting bolder. However, we may have an opportunity to get some serious traction. And Chris, this is where you come in."

"I'm all ears Jon," Chris responded.

"We have an agent we're calling Asset X. He is sitting on a bench at the end of the lawn." He pointed with his cigar. He had a look of smugness about him. "He's probably enjoying the view of the lake as we speak . . . but he is a friend of Khalid Sheik Mohammed." Jon let the news sink in. Alex moved forward to the edge of his seat, and Chris stood up straight. This was big.

"We've been talking . . . or should I say, I've been talking to him for quite some time, even before 9/11, but we lost contact with him for a while. Fortunately for us, he just resurfaced. Our challenge has been, and it is common, that some agents we recruit are only comfortable with one handler. Asset X is no exception. I have traveled far and wide to meet with him, and often dropped everything when this guy calls. He is that important to us, especially now." Jon looked at Chris again. "Sit down Chris, relax, I'm not going to bite your head off."

Chris complied and sat next to Alex. Jon had their undivided attention.

"Before you meet him, we need to get on the same page, Chris. We have to handle this guy with kid gloves. He's fragile, unsure, and apprehensive. None of those traits bode well with what I am going to ask him to do."

Give me the punchline ass-wipe! Chris inwardly begged.

"You and I need to boost his confidence. Get him to commit fully. Assure him we have his best interests at heart and we will look after him no matter what happens." As Jon said this he could tell that Chris was waiting for the big reveal. "I need to put him in the same room as Khalid Sheik Mohammed. Once he can confirm that he is with him, we will do the rest."

"Does he know where he is?" Alex asked.

"No."

"Who is this guy, what's his connection with me?" Chris wanted to know.

"He is from the Balochistan Province, Quetta to be exact. He fancies himself as a bit of an entrepreneur, buying, selling, exporting, importing, that kind of thing. Some of it legal, some of it not. He's had a few run-ins with the law, but there's no outstanding criminal case against him right now, at least not that we know of. He left the country ten years ago, but has been in contact with many of his friends and family, and still continues his business dealings in both Afghanistan and Pakistan. This is why he came to our attention, and hence the recruitment. He has proven to be a reliable source for identifying black market routes in and out of the border regions. But, when I bumped into him recently, and mentioned Mukhtar, he offered to help . . . for a substantial monetary contribution, of course."

Chris rolled his eyes; money was one of the chief motivators of CIA assets. "How much?"

"$25 million."

"Jesus Christ!"

Jon played with his cigar, picking pieces of tobacco from his lips with his fingers; he didn't care about the money. It was a drop in the ocean compared with the PR value of capturing the architect of 9/11. He'd already captured one high-profile terrorist; capturing a second would send him into the stratosphere of CIA senior management. His career path could not look more promising. But he was not there yet. He still needed to put his hands on the terror mastermind—and sadly for him he needed the obnoxious Brit to help him out.

"You want to go meet him?" Jon asked.

Chris stood up and looked down at the lawn. He was still in the dark. He wracked his brain to find a connection to someone in his past who could be a link to the terrorist, but his internal database was empty. He needed to find out who this was; he needed to close the loop. He began marching off in search of an answer. He called out over his shoulder to Jon, "Let's go."

Jon and Chris moseyed side by side down the well-manicured lawn to the edge of the water. Neither man spoke, but Chris was going back into super-vigilant mode—expecting a trap, an attack, an event to send him to cover. Jon sensed the mood.

"Relax Chris, we're in a safe environment. Nobody knows we're here; nobody knows he's here. We're secure."

Chris nodded but kept his spidey senses high, no matter the assuring words from his new best buddy. The agent was sitting with his back to the house, focused on the lake before him. Asset X heard the two men approach and rose to meet them. He turned to face Jon and Chris. He reached out his hand to greet the Brit—whom he had indeed met before, and shared a meal with; they had even watched a soccer game together.

"Guten Abend, Chris," he said.

Chris felt like a lumberjack had just felled him. He stared at Mahmud al Mouhammed in disbelief, in amazement. He had no words. He wanted desperately to sit down. He was suddenly both physically and mentally exhausted. He blamed his giddiness on the lack of proper sleep and poor eating habits, not the shock of seeing a man that he thought he had sent to a dark hole. All at once he needed a break in a different place where he didn't have to carry a weapon, keep his eyes open for the smallest of threats, and where he could talk to other more sensible human beings who were not in 'The Game.'

However, he held his ground and followed Jon's request for presenting a confident front to the carpet salesman from Ulm. Chris had a hundred questions for both men, and held back to let Jon take the lead, but the senior CIA officer didn't have a chance.

"You saw my daughter, how is she?" Mahmud asked Chris in English.

Chris was taken aback for a second. He knew the man spoke a little English when he first met him, but didn't really know how much of his language skills he was hiding. *Another façade?* he wondered as he focused on the question; he didn't want to lie, establishing a relationship with an asset required elements of truth. He saw no point in obfuscating matters to win Mahmud's confidence now, he'd obviously won some points with the man; why else would he be there? But he now felt ambushed. Jon had clearly told the asset something of Chris's recent activities. He wondered if the senior officer had stepped over a boundary by revealing to a source the goings-on of other CIA operatives. He didn't like it one bit. He would have to take that tidbit to Gene when this part of 'The Game' was over. First, he had to maintain his cool.

"She has been through some things . . . but she's in good hands now."

Mahmud moved closer to Chris, his face in a panic; it wasn't the answer he was expecting. "What does that mean, Chris. Tell me?"

"I will not lie to you Mahmud, she is well now, but she was raped. It was Faizan's men."

Jon jumped in. "What Chris does not mention is that if he didn't take the initiative to establish contact with her, she may have been killed. We saved her life, Mahmoud."

Mahmoud fell heavily back down onto the bench. He stared down at the ground and tried his best to hold back tears. His hands were shaking. He looked up, glassy eyed. "Where is she now?"

"In a safe location in Odessa," Chris replied.

"What does that mean . . . what does that mean? Faizan, what of Faizan? He is still a threat?"

"No, he is no longer a threat. He has been dealt with, as have the men who attacked Johara. She is safe now; there is no need to worry about her. She is safe."

"Who is watching her, who is there to care for her? I must go to her!"

"She is being guarded by Maks Chornovil, Mahmoud."

Mahmoud looked perplexed. "The little Black Ox of the Black Sea?"

"I wouldn't call him that to his face, but yes, she is under his protection."

Jon bit his tongue; this was news to him. He knew of the attack on Johara, but didn't know the end result. He wondered how much leeway Chris had in the Ukrainian operation, but he was more concerned with a name he had never heard before. He wanted to ask his colleague, though he needed to do that away from the asset.

"I need to go there. I need to be with her. I need to take her home."

"Once this is over Mahmoud, you can be with her, you can go anywhere you want," Jon interjected. Mahmoud stood up and paced. The two CIA officers left him alone in his grief. There wasn't much to say. The only option now was to wait.

Chris was feeling uncomfortable. He looked around, playing what-if games as the light of day faded. His bowels growled, reminding him that he needed to shit, or at least let out a long fart. He looked down at his watch for no apparent reason. Jon stuffed his hands in his pockets and kicked around a few loose stones on the ground, deep in thought. After ten minutes of silence, Jon announced that they should head back into the house, as dinner would be served soon.

The comment flashed a giant question mark for Chris. *WTF? Dinner will be served?* He didn't ask aloud; he didn't want to show dissent in front of the asset. He kept his mouth shut and hoped Jon meant that someone from the team was cooking dinner—and not any hired help.

Much to his dismay, Chris was right. Hired help. Three men, dressed in smart white shirts and waistcoats, black bow ties, and black trousers were preparing the dining room for a feast. Chris ushered Mahmud down a corridor and out of sight. He shoved him into a bedroom and told him to sit tight and relax awhile as dinner was still a few minutes away. With the door shut firmly behind him, he stormed off to find Jon. He noted that Alex was missing from his position on the couch. He found Jon, who was back out on the veranda talking into his cell phone. Chris strode right into his comfort zone, requiring Jon to take a step back and apologize to the phone call recipient, saying he had to go.

"What the hell is wrong with you?" Jon asked a little too loudly.

Chris wanted to shout but leveled his voice so that only Jon could hear the question. "You haven't fucking changed, have you?"

"What's your problem?"

"Hired help, what the fuck Jon? This guy is about to give us KSM and you want a five-star meal? Who the hell are these guys . . .?"

"The embassy recommended them . . ."

"And you vetted them?"

"What?"

"You vetted them, right? You personally can vouch for them? Not one of them is connected to al-Qaeda or the ISI? Is that what you are saying?"

"Get off your high horse, Chris!"

"Don't be so fucking naïve Jon . . . if you don't get rid of them now, I will take him out of here and that will set your dream operation back by days." Though exasperated, Chris still maintained control of his voice. He needed to take charge of the situation. He gave Jon the order again. Jon blinked in denial that the upstart was once again undermining him. "Don't just stand there," Chris demanded. "Catch a grip, for fuck's sake! Get rid of them, tell them to leave the food and come back tomorrow. But tonight, we need to find somewhere else to go; we are not staying here. Got it?"

Jon was embarrassed; he knew Chris was right. It was an obvious oversight on his part. He shouldn't have made a big deal of providing his asset with creature comforts; he should have stuck to the basics of lying low. He headed off to the kitchen to dismiss the service.

Chris watched him leave, he shook his head in disappointment.

What the fuck is it with these Ops guys? Half of them want to kill all the terrorists in the world with a spoon and a piece of welding wire, the other half, like this prick, want to go to war in a Cadillac and sign autographs afterwards. What an arsehole.

Alex appeared from the front door. "Transportation is clean." He looked around to see Jon talking to the catering staff. "Is he getting rid of them?"

Chris nodded; he was happy that his friend was thinking along the same lines. "Fucking dickhead, he's got his head up his own ass with visions of grandeur. We need to move the asset."

"Care to explain?" Chris knew Alex wasn't asking why they needed to move the asset, so he brought him up to speed on who the man was. When he finished, he asked Alex to call Gene for a new safe house. While Alex carried out the request, Chris headed for the kitchen, made up two plates of food and headed to the bedroom to share another meal with the man from Ulm.

"We won't be here long, so eat up. I'm not sure how much time we have."

"Are you mad at me, Chris?"

"Eat," Chris ordered.

Mahmoud grudgingly obeyed the command, but watched his watcher as he ate. Both men dove into the hastily prepared dishes in silence. Chris coughed and sniffed a few times between bites, then drank some water to cool the spicy meal. "You owe me an explanation," Chris stated bluntly, still pissed about Jon's cavalier approach to security, and the surprise revelation of Mahmoud being an asset of the CIA.

"What would you like to know?"

"Why didn't you tell me who you were in Moldova?"

"I was going to my daughter. I told you this."

"But they stopped you at the border with a false passport; you must have known you would get caught?"

"No, I did not. The Black Ox, he is a friend of mine. He gave me the passport; I had no idea it would cause a problem. It was my way out. I wanted nothing more to do with the CIA; Jon knew this. I had no intention of returning to Germany. I was trying to disappear Chris."

This guy has friends everywhere, the Ox, KSM . . . who else does he know?
"But you gave me Faizan—why?"

"The Black Ox refused to do what I asked. He and Faizan had business dealings. I was going there to explain who Faizan was, I wanted to persuade the Black Ox . . . to kill him for me."

"But you used me, instead?"

"He needed to die, no matter how. If I was in a jail in Moldova, then how could I convince the Ox to do it?"

Chris finished his plate and drank some more water. He stared at the man with multiple names and multiple characters. He was not Lebanese as he initially claimed; he was from Pakistan. Chris had to admit, he'd been had by an apprentice of Laurence Olivier. It was a fine performance. "Yet you let yourself be taken to one of our detention centers . . . that takes some balls." Chris didn't know what had happened to Mahmoud at the Salt Pit, but he looked physically fine. He had no idea what, if any, mental torture he endured.

Mahmoud answered as if on cue. "As soon as you left, they placed me in a box. I will admit it was hard. But as soon as they took me for questions, I mentioned Jon's name and they placed me in a cell. He came for me and, well . . . here we are."

Chris mulled over the information for a moment. He shook his head a few times, then bounced from one side of the room to the other. He knew he shouldn't be pacing, as it gave the impression to the asset that he was conflicted. It was a sign of weakness, not confidence. He stopped mid-stride. He looked down to Mahmoud, but still didn't say what was on his mind. He let his thoughts wonder to Alex, and if he was having any success in finding a new safer location. He tried not to think of Jon. "And now you're committed to finding Mukhtar?" He didn't give Mahmoud a chance to answer. "Or is that, too, an act?"

Mahmoud remained quiet and looked at Chris with sad eyes. A staring contest began, with neither man relenting. Chris stood at the foot of the bed, arms crossed before his chest, feet wide apart, expecting an answer. He involuntarily let out a long fart. They both laughed, and

Chris made for the window. A gust of warm Pakistan air filled the room, diluting the foul odor that had emanated from the Brit's gut. Chris appreciated the momentary humor, but he wanted to get back on track. "You didn't answer me."

"I have known Khalid Sheik Mohammed for many years. Before he attended university in the United States, we were in business together. However, when he joined the Muslim Brotherhood, our religious beliefs were not aligned, but our mutual interests in commerce were. I don't know if you are aware of this, but he was a butcher before he became interested in engineering. I used to buy the livestock for his business so that he could sell the meat to gain enough funds for his studies. Over the years, after his return from America, he and I traded other things—textiles, manufactured products, food, spices, electronics." He paused, staring into space as if some ancient memory triggered an event. Chris could tell that the memories, both good and bad, ran deep.

"So, what happened, what happened that you now wish to—" He wanted to say betray but thought it too harsh. "—help us capture him?"

"It was when he asked me about weapons . . . guns, ammunition, explosives, that I had to step back. I had a vast network of trade routes, some of it was legitimate, but both he and I knew how to get around the authorities . . . he wanted to take advantage of me, Chris. He knew I could smuggle everything anyone ever needed across different borders, but I wanted no part in weapons of war. For a while, he let me be and our relationship flourished. I still continued to provide him things that helped his cause and I made a lot of money, but he continued to pressure me for war materials. I am not sure what happened to him during those years, but he traveled a lot, and I saw less and less of him."

Mahmoud paused and took a deep breath. He was hunched over, and looked pitiful. "Then, my daughter met Faizan in Abu Dhabi. I thought it innocent, but I was wrong. It was there I met Khalid again, and it was as if nothing had changed for him. He wanted me to help him again, but this time he said it was for materials outside of Pakistan—Afghanistan, Asia and other places. I refused. Faizan offered me more money than I could wish for, but I was adamant that I would not get involved. Soon after that, the abuse of my daughter began. I tried to get her to leave him, I talked, pleaded with Faizan to stop but I was talking to a wall. I met with Khalid again and asked him to intervene. He said if I could ship weapons for him, he would talk to Faizan, he would convince him to let her go. Then . . . the attacks in New York happened, and everything changed."

"It's not your fault Mahmoud, he got what he wanted from other people," Chris rationalized.

"That may be true, but I feel partially responsible . . . it may be my fault I enabled him over the years. I provided him with what he needed to build his reputation, his standing in this terrorist organization. The deaths of all of those people in America . . . it is a tragedy that need not have happened. If I didn't give him those things over the years, then perhaps . . . perhaps this wouldn't have happened."

Chris, though wary of a second act, sympathized slightly with the man sitting before him. At least now he knew, or thought he knew, the reasons the man wanted to betray Khalid. He wanted to stop him from doing it again. He wanted to punish him for not intervening with his daughter. However, there was still the question of a $25 million payout. He wondered for a second, who was taking advantage of who in this murky cesspool of deceit and counter-deceit? Was Mahmoud remorseful, or was he just a businessman trying to line his pockets?

Four of the six catering staff, riding in a catering van, left the villa on the lake in a huff. After all their efforts to put on a lavish dinner for their American guests, they weren't sure that they would even get paid for the evening. Each of the four had opinions and arguments about what had happened and why, and each tried to blame one another for not performing, or saying something untoward to get them fired from the job. They would have to do a lot of explaining to their boss why they were let go early, and why they left the villa without all the catering equipment used for the event. Somebody would get blamed, and someone would probably lose his job.

Two of the men, who were not in the same vehicle as the other four, were also wondering what had happened. They need not have worried about losing a contract or being asked to leave early, as their jobs were secure. The catering job was not their primary means of income. However, what they needed to worry about, and explain to their bosses, was if they'd gathered any intelligence at all during the short stint at the house.

The senior of the two men had taken a few photographs of the villa from the outside and inside, but he was unsure of how many faces he'd captured as he bumbled around promoting his act of being a simple waiter. The pair rode in silence back toward the city. Within thirty minutes they would be at their desks, comparing notes and download- ing their camera images onto the ISI database. Within an hour they would have their brief reports written and submitted via their comput- ers, and where needed, distributed to the applicable departments and division heads for further review.

The senior ISI man, unbeknownst to his colleague, would also send a separate email to Colonel Rashid Ghazini for his immediate atten- tion, and a send a text message informing him to review his correspondence. He'd hadn't seen the colonel for days, but he was on strict orders from him to report all activity related to American safe houses and the goings-on that took place therein. It mattered not to him that the evening was a bust; it mattered only that he followed his instructions and was happy that he was getting the rest of the evening off. He didn't care who was in the house; it was somebody else's problem now.

It was close to 2100 hours when Rashid powered up his cell phone as he sped through the arrival hall of the Islamabad International Airport. It took a few minutes to find a decent signal and when it did, his phone showed that he had missed several calls. There were a few voicemails and dozens of text messages. He hit the voicemail list first. Some of it was nonsensical and would require a follow-up once he read his email. Other messages, which were unimportant, he subsequently deleted. He attacked his text messages next. Once again, there wasn't much worthwhile to read, and he quickly deleted the garbage that he didn't need. But there was one message that stopped him in his tracks. He read it carefully and then read it again. He looked at his watch. He was tired and in need of rest. He wanted to go home to shower and sleep, recoup after his Quetta expedition. But something told him he needed to get to his office; he needed to see the latest intelligence on a CIA safe house.

Rashid booted up his computer at his desk at precisely 2205 hours. There were a few other people going about their tasks on his floor at the late hour, but he ignored them and shut himself in his office, where he waited for the device to run through its startup processes. During the time it took, he flitted through the snail mail neatly stacked on his desk by his assistant. Most of the mail he tossed to the side, there were only a few things of interest, but his mind was elsewhere. He lit a cigarette and stood at his desk. He picked up his phone and ordered tea from the houseboy.

By the time the boy appeared, his computer was ready to go to work. He sat down in his chair, sipped the hot tea, and found the email that he needed to review. He read and re-read the report on the CIA safe house on Jinnah Road, and thought discharging the catering staff before they served the meal was unusual. Unfortunately, there were no photos attached to the email, however a corresponding report noted that the team had delivered hard copy photos to his desk. He once again dug through his stack of letters and found a large brown internal mail envelope with his name written in the address line. He undid the clasp and pulled out a dozen black and white photographs. Most of them were useless images of the building itself, but then he saw the faces of the Westerners. One he thought he recognized, a tall, fit looking man, but he wasn't sure. The other two were complete strangers. As he flipped through to the last photo in the pile, he stopped and frowned. He stared at the image for a minute. It was of three men. He recognized the CIA officer they called bearded Jon, then a younger

CIA officer, who looked concerned, and wore a permanent scowl, but when he focused on the third man who was entering the house from the veranda, he stared at the image with both curiosity and concern. He couldn't make out the face, as the lighting in the house did him no favors. He grabbed his desk lamp and held the image directly underneath it. Still, the visage of the man was obscure. He retrieved a set of reading glasses from his desk and held the picture close to his face. His face lit up. He recognized Mahmud al Muhammed. He slumped down into his chair. *What is he doing with the Americans?*

Rashid leaned forward at his desk, still holding the image in his hand, sometimes glancing at it to confirm his belief. He ran through a list of potential possibilities. It had been many years since he had seen the smuggler, and even longer since he had him in his crosshairs for recruitment into the ranks of the ISI as a trader of illicit materials that could be used to the intelligence agency's advantage. But Mahmoud was a stubborn man, who traded in goods that only he was comfortable with. A criminal yes, but conversely, a man with a conscience. A rare breed in this part of the world. *Why now?* Rashid wondered. *Why is he here in Islamabad; what is his connection to the Americans?*

He stared at the photo again and reviewed the others in the pile on his desk. His mind switched to another gear. *Why did the CIA throw the catering out? Are they trying to hide Mahmoud?* He looked at the written report for the third time. His men stated that all the occupants of the house had their photograph taken. He pondered the statement. *If these were the only men in the house, then Mahmoud must be the one they are protecting.* He read on. He stopped at an interesting line. *One of the CIA officers ushered the non-American down the corridor to a bedroom. Interesting, they were trying to hide him, but why?*

He leaned back in his chair, he closed his eyes, partially from being worn down, but mainly because he needed to concentrate. He knew that Mahmoud had many business partners in Central Asia and the Middle East, but he tried to figure out what their interest was in him now, and why Islamabad. His mind drifted to the ongoing battles between the US military and the Taliban in Afghanistan. The war there was fully engaged and it would not be a stretch for the CIA to leverage contacts who had access to friends and allies in their attempts to pacify the combatants, or gain strategic advantages. But the more he thought about it, he deemed it less likely. The intelligence dossier on Mahmoud painted him as a pacifist, an entrepreneur, driven by greed. Not a warmonger, not like the traditionalist hard-nosed Balochis from Quetta.

The thought made his eyes spring open. It was as if Big Ben's chimes were going off right next to his head. He quickly searched his computer for an email that he'd ignored earlier. A few clicks later he found what he was looking for. The email told him that the United States reward to capture the mastermind of 9/11 was now $25 million. He involuntarily spoke aloud as he realized, "They were friends . . . he is betraying Mukhtar to the Americans."

CHAPTER THIRTEEN

Islamabad, Pakistan

CHRIS LOOKED IN THE REARVIEW mirror a third time. He checked his right-side driver's mirror, then the mirror on the left. He shook his head as if in denial, but kept his mouth shut. The drive from the villa by the lake was supposed to be uneventful. It was unplanned and low-key. However, Chris, now behind the wheel of the SAD Toyota Land Cruiser was feeling uneasy. It didn't take long for him to spot the tail. At first he thought it was it was nothing out of the ordinary, but he knew from his years of experience as a surveillance expert, one correlating action from one person could mean a whole host of actors were circling in the theater's backstage, waiting for their cue.

He confirmed his suspicions when he spotted a trade-off at an intersection. The tail from the villa was a motorbike with two passengers, the car that took up station four cars behind his Toyota also had two passengers. When the car pulled in behind Chris's line of traffic, the driver, with an open window, took his right hand off the steering wheel and dropped it down and outside the open window. It looked like a casual action, as if the driver was discarding something. But Chris spotted the wave-off to the trailing motorcycle, which pulled over to the side of the road and just sat there watching the Toyota's taillights disappear. If anyone could have read Chris's mind, they would have said that he was paranoid, especially at this late hour, especially in such a dense area of the city, especially with thousands of moving parts and pieces presented before him. He quickly calculated the risks and thought of the backup plan that he, Alex and Jon agreed upon before trying to transport their valuable asset to a new place. Compounding his rationale, he thought about his recent ambush in the city that had left him in a German hospital. His ribcage still gave him a twinge now and again to remind him he wasn't Captain Indestructible. Alex and Jon were in a vehicle two cars ahead of the mini-convoy. Mahmoud sat next to Chris, oblivious to the goings-on outside the vehicle, but he glanced at Chris, who had picked up his radio.

"Alex—baseline, baseline. Copy?"

There was a pause before an answer came. It wasn't the one he expected. "Negative, negative, push on as planned."

Chris cringed at the sound of Jon's voice. *Fucking imbecile!* he thought as he repeated the command. "Alex, Alex, baseline. Copy?"

Jon's voice once again crackled over the radio. "That's a negative, repeat negative, stay the course."

Chris swore under his breath, pissed off by Jon's lack of operational field experience and sound judgment. He didn't need this bullshit; he didn't need an action hero wannabee run the show; he weighed his options, but he knew that he was pissing in the wind when he talked to Jon. He had to decide. Go with his gut and head for the embassy as the backup plan discussed. Or follow the asshole in front and have God knows who, watching their every move to the soon-to-be-unsafe house. He didn't know who his followers were, or if there were other people out there watching. If his gut was right, he needed to know who he was up against. He wasn't sure if it was the ISI or al-Qaeda, but he knew sitting behind the wheel of the Toyota was not the place to have an internal debate about whose eyeballs were on him. He needed to make a move.

"Chris do you copy?" Jon radioed.

Chris had his eyes everywhere. He was trying to concentrate on the road, the people, the cars, anything that moved. He heard the radio but was so focused on a white car that had pulled in front of Alex that he pushed the radio transmission out of his head. He was seeing a pattern develop. His instincts told him they were being boxed in. It may not have been a vehicle ambush in progress, but whoever it was, they knew what they were doing, sort of. "Alex, abort, baseline now," he announced over the radio.

Jon's voice screamed over the radio, but Chris ignored it. He mashed the gas and took a sharp right turn away from the main thoroughfare and down a side street. He knew he was leaving Alex a little in the lurch. But he was driving with the asset; that was his priority. Alex could look after himself.

Chris dove deep into his memory banks for a map of Islamabad. The major roads and points of interest were fresh in his mind, but the secondary roads, not so much. His internal compass told him where his north/south bearings lay, but under the darkness of the night, every-thing looked different. His only saving grace was that the roads of the Pakistan capital city were broad, well maintained and relatively easy to follow. If he could get himself back onto some speed-giving streets, he could find his way to the safety of the Diplomatic Enclave.

Rashid Ghazini listened in to the surveillance operation from the command center in the basement of the ISI headquarters. He was not a cheerful man. On realizing that things were spinning out of his control with his self-revelation of Mahmoud's intent to work with the Ameri-cans, he hurriedly took action in the only practicable way he knew how. He grabbed as many junior officers within his short grasp and cajoled them into action. It mattered not to him at the time that they were untrained for the job, or assigned other tasks, or were simply inept. He needed bodies on the ground immediately, no matter if they were bean counters, policy analysts, or science geeks. It was their fault they were in the building at the late hour, and his to command as he deemed fit. As he found men, women, young and old, he tried his best to marshal his younger, less-experienced men with more seasoned veterans, but it wasn't easy at 11p.m. to find either.

It was past midnight when he sent out a force of twenty-five ISI agents. His orders were to watch the villa on Jinnah Road, and if the Americans moved, find out how many there were, and where they were going. He stressed the importance of remaining surreptitious, and with him in control from headquarters, he would lead and direct the effort.

Soon after the two CIA vehicles left the safety of the villa, he knew he was in trouble. The radio chatter was loud and ill-disciplined. He received a report that one vehicle was still at the residence so he tried in vain to marshal his men to cover each eventuality but his agents in the field were not listening to his directives. His ad hoc mission was falling apart before his eyes. He ordered his team to follow his commands, but the ramshackle amateur gang had other ideas. When he heard over the radio that the two SUV's they were following split up, he threw down his headphones in despair. It took him a few moments, but regaining a modicum of self-control, he divided what was left of his force and directed his agents to follow both vehicles. As the reports from the streets were coming in, he felt a wave of dread. The first vehicle was heading to the US embassy, while the second, on a parallel course, was doing the same.

Rashid angrily let the scene play out. He knew that if the CIA made it to the safety of the US facility, his game to reach Mahmoud was in jeopardy. He had a fleeting thought of intercepting the Americans and absconding with their charge, but not only did he not have the capable manpower to do so, he neither had the authority. The last radio transmission came only thirty minutes after his rushed operation began. One of the team announced that both vehicles that had left the villa were now at the gates of the US embassy. Rashid stared into space, saying nothing. A nearby system operator looked at him as the chatter over the radio frequencies diminished, then everything was silent. Rashid called the mission off and ordered the team to stand down and return to headquarters. He retreated to his office with his tail between his legs. He was tired, beaten, hungry and frustrated. He looked at his watch as he climbed a set of stairs. He wanted to go home to a hot shower, a warm meal, a warm bed, his wife and his two children. But there was still much to do. He contemplated visiting his mistress, only a ten-minute drive from his building, but thought better of it. He didn't have the will to stay up all night to please the woman. He needed rest, though his mind was still cranking at 10,000 rpm.

His actions to this point had a dual purpose. First, he knew he had to protect the ISI. Their links to Khalid Sheik Mohammed would have serious repercussions around the world if found out. Since time was not on his side, he could not speak with his superiors to address the issue and come up with a viable strategy to deal with the terrorist. He once again thought of the raid in Quetta and how much easier for everyone it would have been if the terrorist had perished. In that scenario, the ISI could maintain their nefarious dealings with al-Qaeda, and the CIA and the world's opinions would not matter, as a high-profile target was no more. His second purpose, however, was that he needed to warn the al-Qaeda operative of the impending betrayal from his friend.

Time and again, the senior leadership within the ranks of the ISI, the "Old Guard" had been content with al-Qaeda activities in the global sphere, and their sturdy links to the Afghanistan Taliban. It suited the ISI and their somewhat erstwhile backers, the Russians, that the Americans could get bogged down in another protracted, Vietnam-style conflict across the border in Afghanistan. The same way they did when they invaded in 1979. Everyone in the region was happy to see the Americans bleed, and if Osama bin Laden provided tools to draw that blood, then senior members of the Pakistan ISI would not stand in their way. Countermanding this approach, however, was the President of Pakistan, but after much discussion with al-Qaeda, Khalid Sheik Mohammed had a plan to silence the conservative leader. The ISI needed the terrorist alive, and his organization fully functional. It was a knife-edge dilemma. Have the terrorist killed, silencing the detractors of ISI policies; or save the man so he could continue his terrorist activities, enabling Pakistan's influence in the region?

The problem was Rashid knew not where Khalid was. Nor did he know the whereabouts of Wahid, his rat on the inside of the terror organization. The only tentative link to finding Khalid was Mahmoud al Mouhammed, who was now slipping further into the clutches of the Americans. He wondered that if his surveillance mission failed, how else would he be able to stop the American asset from revealing the location of Khalid before he could warn him? His troubled, bouncing mind clouded his judgment as he envisioned himself trying his best to plant daisies in a tornado.

"Before you take a shit down my neck, I spotted surveillance, and I used our backup plan. We discussed this before—"

Jon didn't let Chris finish. "—You're talking out of your ass again. I spotted nothing; we should have proceeded to the safe house. That villa was clean, we have never used that place before, there's no way we were compromised." Jon was getting flushed. "What the hell are we going to do now, what the fuck were you thinking?"

Chris wanted to get back into Jon's face and defend his position, but he caught a look from Alex, who was shaking his head in warning. Chris took a breath and let his thought remain in his brain, not falling off his tongue. *Fucking dickhead, it was those waiters who you let into the place that compromised us; it's you that put us in this position. Be thankful that we didn't lose the asset in the fucking process.* He was about to open his mouth, but Alex beat him to it.

"I've got to back Chris on this one, Jon. I spotted something as well. It was the right move coming here. We are safe. We could have easily compromised the safe house by going there. This was the best outcome."

Jon didn't like the odds. Two against one wasn't a fair fight. He had to accept he was in a safe area and the asset was still under their control. The three men were standing out of earshot of Mahmoud, who was still sitting in one of the Toyotas, in a corner of the parking lot at the embassy. Jon stood with his hands on his hips, waiting impatiently. He looked at the two men standing before him, calculating how to get the mission back on track. Nobody uttered a word, but someone needed to say something. He watched Chris look around and saw that something caught his eye. Jon followed his gaze.

"The Marine House." Chris gestured to a squat, two-story building a hundred yards away, within the perimeter of the embassy grounds.

"What about it?"

"We're not going to find anywhere else more secure tonight, Jon. How about we see if they have a bunk or two free? We bed him down for tonight, reconvene in the morning, and work out a new plan?"

Alex nodded; he liked the idea. He looked over at Jon, who seemed conflicted, nervously looking at his watch once, twice, then a third time in a matter of seconds. Though tense and pissed off with the situation, Jon had to admit it was a swift compromise, and the best he could hope for under the circumstances. "Fine," he grumbled, fed up with someone else driving the decision making. "You go find the Gunny, see if he can help. He's your baby for tonight, but tomorrow, it's my orders you'll follow. I don't want anymore bullshit from you Chris, but you left me with no choice."

Oh, fuck off you stupid twat, like it's my fault.

"I'm going to see what's going on in ICE CAVE," Jon concluded. "I'll find a cot and crash for the what's left of the night. One of you needs to be with him the whole time he's here. We don't want any of the locals giving him a queer look, so keep him indoors. The Marines we can trust, but nobody else. Understood?"

So now all of a sudden you're taking security seriously? It's about time, asshole. Chris wanted to put him in his place, but reined himself in. "Sure Jon, excellent idea."

Jon didn't catch Chris's sarcastic tone, but Alex did. His eyes widened, pleading for Chris to wind down. "I'll come look for you in the morning Jon," Alex offered as the senior officer turned to leave.

Both SAD officers waited a few more minutes before making any further comments. Once Jon was out of earshot Chris spoke first. "That guy is a complete wanker. We wouldn't be here if we listened to him. I don't know what you saw, but my gut was telling me we had a bunch of people on us; you?"

"Yeah, I lost count too. You were right to split us up, you did the right thing Chris, but don't let him push your buttons, he's not worth it."

"I know, I know, but can you imagine that prick leading the charge to get KSM? It's fucking ridiculous Alex. I just hope our asset hasn't lost confidence in us. This whole gig could fall apart and we'll be back to square one before we know it."

"One step at a time. Let's get him settled for the night. We'll have to tackle what we can in the morning. I just hope you haven't pissed Jon off enough for you to be sidelined again."

———————— ∞∞∞ ————————

Mary Wright sat at her desk a few doors down from ICE CAVE. She was flipping through her large photo album, trying to identify an early morning walk-in to the embassy, but she was coming up dry. Placed in a small office, near Marine Post One, the entry to the chancery, the man was questioned for a few minutes by security, had his photograph taken, and was told to wait until they found the right person to talk with him. Under normal circumstances, a case officer from the CIA station would handle all walk-ins, as usually the visitors to the embassy wanted something such as political asylum, a green card, money, or something that would make their lives better in some fashion in exchange for information that they had. Information that the United States could not live without, according to the informers. In this case, however, after the CIA had conducted an initial interview, it deemed the subject to be a genuine asset, and had some interesting information to share. But the CIA needed the help of the FBI before they could proceed further. They contacted Mary, as her photo album was developing into the working bible of images that everyone used to identify suspects. With a CIA officer standing over her shoulder, Mary looked at the photo taken by the security staff, and flipped through her album to find a match.

Halfway through her book, she stopped and stared at the man's image once again. She thought she recognized him, but wasn't sure. "What's this guy's story again?"

"He says that he knows about the laptop we retrieved in Quetta."

"Really?"

"That's why we're talking to you. The FBI logged it in as evidence.

We don't have access to it. I thought you might be able to ID him for us. See if there's anything in a file somewhere."

Mary was curious. She was aware of the raid and she had seen some material retrieved and bagged for the diplomatic pouch, ready for shipment to the lab in Quantico. "What's his name?"

"He just says Wahid. Won't give us more than that."

"What does he want?"

"Green card."

"For what?" she asked, not knowing the relevance of it all.

"We don't know. We just did an initial interview with him to figure out if he's some wack job. He passed the sniff test; we just need to identify him now and take it from there. See what information he really has."

Mary continued to flip through the photographs, but came up empty. However, by the time she got to the end of her stash, she was even more convinced that she had seen the man before. "I can't find him, that only means he is not in my book . . . but I think I may have seen him before."

"Here at the embassy?" The CIA officer asked.

"No, Karachi maybe—but it was dark, we had someone else in custody, our focus was elsewhere. I'm not sure, but do you mind if I tag along? Perhaps something will jog my memory?"

"Sure, whatever floats your boat, every pair of friendly eyeballs helps."

Mary gathered up her things and made her way out of her office, only to bump into a tall man in the corridor. "Alex, shit, you almost gave me a heart attack."

"Hey Mary, nice to see you again. How ya doin'?"

"I'm good, good, kinda busy, but if you're here for a while let's catch up." She motioned to her office behind her. "This is my home for now—come by later."

"Sure, will do . . . if I get the chance, you know how it is."

"Okay, got to run." She turned to catch up with the CIA case officer, but then she stopped mid-stride. "Alex, hold up." Alex obeyed the order and marched back towards the FBI agent. She put a photo in his face. "Do you recognize this guy . . . from Karachi, maybe?"

Alex took the photo and studied it for a few seconds. "Isn't that the guy we saw being stuffed into a car the night we took that Nabeel guy? The one we had trouble restraining?"

"Yes, yes, I knew I had seen him before! He's downstairs, wants a green card for some intel. I'm about to go interview him."

"Alex!" Came a shout from down the corridor. It was a busy morning already in the vicinity of the ICE CAVE; Alex couldn't see who was doing the shouting. He turned back to Mary, but she had disappeared. Gene Brooks stuck his head out of a doorway further down the hallway. He was waving his hand above his head, trying to get his attention. Alex stepped over to meet his boss, but Gene rushed towards him. As soon as they were close, Gene whispered, "Chris is in the field, you don't know where he is. Nod that you understand." Confused, he did as he was told. Gene then spoke louder, "Alex, this way buddy, I have some people who would like a chat."

Alex followed Gene into an office where two men were sitting at a small round table: notebooks out, pens at the ready, recording devices set—and eyeing the body language of the tall SAD officer as he entered. "Alex, may I introduce Sean and Danny, Office of the Inspector General's office. They would like to talk to you about an ongoing investigation."

***

Mary Wright stood at the back of the room, silent and leaning into one corner. With her arms crossed in front of her, she had her eyes fixated on Wahid sitting at the desk opposite the CIA officer. She let the agency officer do all the talking. After a few minutes of establishing bona fides and general information about who he was, where he was from and so forth, the officer dug in.

"Tell me more about this laptop."

"I left it in Quetta for you to find."

"Why? What is on there that is so important?"

"The image of a man that works for the Pakistan Government."

"Okay, so what?"

"There is also a voice recording of a conversation that I had with him in Karachi."

"I still don't see what the relevance is, Wahid. You need to give me something worth our time. You need to give me details. Who is this man?"

"You must promise me I can go to America. Until I have assurances, I will say no more."

"Wahid . . . you must understand our position here. We have many people who come here with stories just like yours. We have to ask a lot of questions, and most of the time the information that people bring, it's just not worth our time."

"I called you," Wahid implored as he leaned forward at the desk, his hands and fingers outstretched, begging to be believed. "I called you about Quetta." He could tell that the CIA officer wasn't buying the story. He carried on, trying to win their confidence. "It was me who told you that Mukhtar was in Quetta."

The CIA officer, thrown off a little by the mention of the name, didn't show surprise. He played dumb. "Who is Mukhtar, Wahid?"

"You know exactly who he is . . . Khalid Sheik Mohammed."

"Ah, yes, you must have seen the wanted pictures, you are here for the reward. All you want is money, isn't that right?"

"No, no . . . you are not listening." He was getting flustered. "I called you, I left the laptop for you. I placed an image and voice recording on the device." He paused and looked up at the silent lady in the corner, hoping that she was an ally. "You have to believe me. I want to go to America; my life is in danger here. They will come for me." He pleaded, his eyes welling up, a trickle of sweat beading on his forehead.

Sensing distress, Mary asked, "Who is Nabeel, Wahid?"

Wahid reeled back in his chair at the name. He sucked in a hefty chunk of invisible air. "What?" he stammered. "What?"

"Nabeel, I know that you know him," she bluffed.

Wahid stood quickly. She had stirred an involuntary reaction from him. He thought he would never hear that name again. He looked over to the door, seeking an escape. The CIA officer, while glad he had some support in the interview, wasn't about to let the prospect go. He tried to act as coolly as he could. He needed to win some confidence; he suspected there was more to the youthful man than he originally thought.

"Wahid, sit. Please sit down. You are safe here. Nobody can harm you now. Tell me, tell me your story. What is your connection to Mukhtar?"

Wahid was still standing, stiff as a board. "You must promise me first that I can go to America!"

"I can't promise anything. It is a complicated process, but we can get things moving in the right direction if you can provide me with something I can take to my superiors. I don't make these decisions; you can understand that. But please sit. Let's talk this through and we can see if you have a case that I can take to my boss. Okay?"

Wahid reluctantly sat down. It took him a while to compose himself, and his eyes darted across the desk from one side of the other, looking for answers as if he was reading invisible ink. He rubbed his face and took a deep breath. "I work for Khalid Sheik Mohammed. I am his IT specialist." He let the news settle. He was hoping for a reaction from the two Americans, but was getting none. He spoke calmly, more in control, a wave of relief finally reaching him. "The image and voice recording of the man on the computer is of Colonel Rashid Ghazini from the ISI. He wanted me to betray Mukhtar to him, but he is a liar. He is corrupt; he too works for Mukhtar."

"You need to explain that more for me, Wahid. What do you mean?" the CIA man asked.

"The laptop has a GPS device on it. Rashid made me upload the program onto the device so that when I used it, he would know where Mukhtar was. He said that the ISI created the program, and that I could not disable it."

"Did you?"

"Yes."

The CIA officer knew that was all interesting stuff, but he needed to focus on the big elephant in the room. If the man sitting before him was telling the truth, this could be the win of the century for the CIA. Stoked, but disciplined enough not to show it, he cautiously asked one of the most important questions of his career. "So where is Mukhtar now?"

The question from the CIA officer made Mary twitch. She stood up straight from her slouched position, took a step forward and relaxed her arms. Her pulse raced, her mouth was dry, she swallowed hard.

"I am to meet him in Rawalpindi."

"When?"

"I don't know. He calls me in advance. I usually go to an address that he gives me, setup his computer needs, and when I am ready, I send him an email. Then he arrives, sometimes the same day, sometimes the next. I never know."

Rashid rested his head on his folded arms on his desk. His burning, tired eyes were shut, but he was not sleeping. Anyone passing his office door would have remarked that the senior officer was a slouch and showed no respect for his organization by snoozing while supposedly working, but he was deep in thought and needed some peace. So much had happened in the last few days and weeks. His head filled with multiple scenarios, with multiple outcomes. He needed to close his eyes just long enough to clear out some cobwebs and focus on the immediate tasks at hand. He looked up briefly from the small nest he had created to look at the clock on the wall. It was nearing midday. He placed his head back down and surmised that he would formulate a plan after lunch and perhaps a shot of brandy that he had secreted in his locked desk draw. Before he could mentally draw up the first action item on his list, his office phone rang. He raised his heavy head.

"Yes."

"Sir, this is Lieutenant Panwar with Signals Intelligence. Your GPS signal has been activated." Rashid didn't say a word. He stared blankly at the wall before him. "I just thought you would like to know, sir." The colonel still did reply. "Sir?"

"I'll be right there. I need to know exactly where that signal is coming from."

"From the American embassy . . . Sir, are you still there?"

Rashid was not as he bustled his way through the corridors and headed downstairs to the Directorate of Signals Intelligence. It took him three minutes to get there. "Who is Panwar?" he announced when he entered the Signals department. He received a few head bobs from the cubicle farm, and one man in a far corner stood up and waved his hand. Rashid marched over to him and pulled up a chair. "Sit, tell me what have you found."

"Sir the signal is coming from the American embassy here in Islamabad." He pointed to the screen, wondering if the colonel didn't understand where the embassy was.

Rashid rocked back in his chair; this was not the news he wanted to hear. "How long has it been active?"

"Eight minutes and twenty-one seconds."

"Check your diagnostics. I need 100 percent confirmation of that location."

"Yes, sir."

The junior officer continued with his tasks, clicking icons and filling out fields in various forms, finally hitting a "start scan" button. Within three minutes the system popped up a colorful screen showing that all systems on the program were functioning as programmed. Rashid stared at the computer, not saying anything. For all the worst-case scenarios he could think of, this was one that he hadn't thought of. He leaned forward in his chair, his arms resting on his lap, his hands wrangling backward and forward as if he was washing his hands without water.

The lieutenant saw that the senior officer looked pained. "Sir, is there anything else I can help you with?"

Rashid ignored the offer. He continued to look at the image on the screen. His mind whirred like a Swiss watch calculating atmospherics and the depth of a nearby ocean. He forced himself to concentrate on a plan. This was a setback, but he needed to do something with the information before him. He grabbed a notepad from Panwar's desk and scribbled his cell phone number. "Take this," he ordered. "It is my personal phone number. I need to know if that signal changes location or is turned off. I need you—and I mean *you*, lieutenant—to monitor this system around the clock. This is now your prime task. Drop everything else that you are working on and do exactly what I say. I need your undivided attention for this task. Do you understand?"

"Sir, my shift ends—"

"—Your shift ends when I tell you, lieutenant; find someone you can trust to relieve you for momentary breaks, but I need that signal on your screen at all times." Rashid stood to walk away. "I will call you for a status in one hour, but if there is a change, call me, interrupt me—but you must find me."

Bearded Jon, Mary, the CIA case officer, an NSA communications officer and an FBI computer programmer were all looking at the now-active laptop seized in Quetta. On receiving the intelligence from Wahid and the password for the device, Mary and the case officer left him to sweat in the interview room on the ground floor, while they hurriedly put together a meeting of individuals who needed to be in the know, to plan next steps. Unconvinced that Wahid was telling the truth, Jon inserted himself into a second interview to verify the story that was being pedaled. Not only was this time-consuming, but it was a bureaucratic slap in the face for the case officer and Mary, who were in effect told that the story was too good to be true. Mary took the news on the chin. Satisfied that what she heard and saw was high quality, she was feeling confident enough that she could take what she had learned to the FBI for further investigations. She was unoffended by Jon's meddling; but she could tell that he wasn't flavor of the month with his own CIA colleagues at the embassy.

They all saw the image of Rashid Ghazini on the screen, and they all heard the voice recording. Though poor, it was enough to convince the team that Wahid was telling the truth. The FBI programmer beavered away at the GPS program that Wahid had tried to circumvent.

"Whatever he did to disable the system, it's now live," he announced.

"Meaning what?" Jon asked.

"Meaning whoever was monitoring this is now aware that it is here."

Jon looked at the screen deep in thought, but everyone was waiting for an order, or at least a discussion of which direction they would take next. He turned to the NSA man. "Can your agency track this system?"

"Sure, what do you have in mind?"

Jon didn't answer straightaway, but looked at the FBI computer expert. "Can you clone this program onto another computer?"

"Yes, and no. If I can find a computer exactly like this one, this model with the same BIOS settings and it has the right drivers, then we should be okay. If there isn't one here in the embassy, then we have to either get one shipped in, or we will have to buy one locally. Whatever we do, it could take a while."

Jon contemplated the news. He looked back at the NSA man. "So, I guess for now it's up to you guys. If this system stays on, the NSA can track it. If it is off, we are done. Am I right?"

There were nods around the room. There was a little more discussion with the tech guys, but Jon had hit the nail on the head. However, nobody really knew what he had in mind. He let the shoe drop when there was a lull in the conversation. "What I want to do is cut Wahid loose," he announced. Mary was about to say something, but Jon continued before she could utter a word. "Let's try to clone this thing, give it back to Wahid and let him lead us to KSM. We hold on to him for as long as we can while we set things up, and in the meantime, we can set up a surveillance package and a raid team. Rawalpindi isn't far from here, so it's not going to be that much of a stretch."

The group bounced around a few more questions, but a consensus was forming. Mary wasn't exactly happy with the situation, and was sucked in slightly by Wahid's woeful predicament. She wanted to keep him at the embassy for further interrogation, but that was her FBI instinct coming out. Even if she objected to the plan, she didn't have any cards to play. This was now a CIA operation and she would be happy if she could observe from afar—or even better, be part of the raid team.

Jon finally announced that he would confer with other members of the CIA team in the embassy, and also get a blessing from CIA headquarters in Langley to proceed. The meeting was over. However, he'd kept his silver bullet in his ammunition belt, and withheld Asset X's potential participation in his next move. He left the room with a smile.

That was more than could be said for Alex, who was storming out of an office with a scowl on his face. The look Jon was receiving told him to walk the other way, but there was still work to do. "Hey Alex, you headed back to the Marine House?" Jon asked softly. Alex nodded, saying nothing. "We need to move our asset to Rawalpindi; can you arrange that and let me know where you are? I want to leave it up to you guys to take care of—you don't need me messing up the dinner party again. Right?"

"Sure Jon, how soon?"

Jon wondered if he should include Alex and Chris in the Wahid plan, but decided against telling Alex everything. Asset X would be his backup plan should the Wahid angle fail. "It's possible that KSM will be in Rawalpindi. We're still working through some new intel, so things are up in the air. I just need to have Mahmoud lie low until we have some more concrete information. Okay?"

Alex was still angry, and the best makeup artist couldn't paint a smiling face on him to hide his rage. "Sure, I'll get right on it. Excuse me." He brushed passed Jon and headed down the corridor for the bank of elevators. With his head dipped slightly and his arms bowed outward as if he was carrying two kegs of beer under each, he stormed away. Jon didn't know what to make of the scene. He scurried off, the plans in his mind coming together as he searched for a secure telephone line to Langley.

Alex arrived back at the Marine House within ten minutes after he talked to Jon. As he stormed over to the building, he calmed down a bit, but he was still seething. His meeting with the OIG had not gone well. He found Chris playing cards with Mahmoud in the cafeteria-style galley the Marines had constructed to make their lives a little more comforting, a respite from the hostile anti-American environment outside the embassy walls.

Chris stopped what he was doing when Alex showed up. He dropped his cards on the table. He was about to rib his friend for showing up late, but he had known the man for long enough to know when he was serious about something. "Hey," he greeted his friend.

"We need to talk . . . outside," Alex responded glumly.

Chris stood up. He looked down at Mahmoud and let him know that they'd be just outside and would be back in a few minutes. Neither man spoke until they were a short distance away from the Marine House.

"What's wrong, Alex?"

"Before I go there, I have to tell you I bumped into Jon on the way down here. We need to move him to Rawalpindi." Chris knew he was talking about relocating Mahmoud. "It's only about 30-40 minutes from here, but we need to organize it ourselves. I think he's learned his lesson, and he's leaving us alone. We can call him when we get there, wherever that is. I'll talk to Gene about finding us a safe place."

"How soon?"

"Now."

"Okay, but that's not what's pissing you off. What's going on?"

Alex stared at Chris. He stuck his hands in his pockets and shifted on his feet. A little too often for Chris's liking. "I've just been grilled by two goons from the Inspector General's Office."

"The OIG? What the hell are they doing here?"

"You need to get the fuck out of dodge, buddy."

"What the hell has their shit got to do with me?"

"They are investigating an incident of something that happened in Afghanistan." Alex paused; Chris wanted to say something to fill the gap, but let his friend carry on.

"The Army CID has a guy in custody, some Staff Sergeant Hansen from TF-160, the Nightstalkers. Turns out they caught this limp dick running some heavy drugs out of Afghanistan. Heroin, etcetera. Sounds like he had been doing it for a while, and they think he's just the tip of the iceberg. Anyway, this piece of shit is trying to bargain his way out of a lengthy prison sentence and is ready to give someone up to save his own butt."

Chris frowned; he still wasn't able to connect the dots. He waited patiently for Alex to spill the beans but couldn't hold back. "What's that got to do with the price of sausages, Alex?"

"He says that he saw some CIA officer throw a civilian off a helicopter on a secret mission last year. Your name was mentioned as being part of the operation; so was mine."

"Fuck!"

Though Alex continued to talk, it was Chris's turn to pace. His head hurt and things were getting mushy between his ears; he couldn't focus on what Alex was saying. He needed to concentrate, he needed to slow his heart down a notch or two. He stopped moving and took a few lengthy breaths, in through the nose, out through the mouth. Alex placed a hand on his friend's shoulder. "You okay?"

"Yeah, yeah. I'll be all right. It's not every day I get kicked in the balls."

"I hear you. But did you hear me?"

"What?"

"Gene is stalling them. He told them you're out in the field and he isn't sure when you'll be back. He told them that the KSM operation is taking precedence over everything right now, so they'll have to wait to talk to you."

"Gene is here?"

"Yeah, he's got your back Chris. He wants to help you. But you can't hang around here."

Chris changed subjects. He didn't doubt that his friend was supporting him, but he wanted to make sure they were on the same page. "What did you tell the OIG . . . about the Chinook ride?"

"I told them the truth. I was looking after the wounded. I didn't see what was happening at the back."

Chris knew that wasn't true. Alex saw everything. "What about the Green Berets; have they been interviewed yet?"

"I don't know. But what I do know is that Stone, the captain of the team, an IED took him out in Kandahar a few months back."

Saddened by the news, Chris shook his head. "So, it's just a matter of time before the OIG gets to the rest of them. I'm guessing they're not going to question the Afghans we had on board." An image of Terry flashed before him, his missing eye, his broken teeth, the prison tattoos. His heart raced, scared of becoming the same. He trembled. Prison was the last place he wanted to go. He needed to find a way out of the mess. "Fuck Alex, this is bullshit."

"Tell me about it. But listen, I heard the army isn't going for a plea deal with the prick. They're taking him down." Alex could see there was a glimmer of hope in his friend's eyes. He hated to burst his bubble, but he had to be honest with him. "The OIG, they won't let it go. They will come after you Chris." He let the news sink in, but he didn't want his partner to wallow in self-pity. "We need to get you out of here. Create some distance from this place. Jon doesn't know about this shit, and we need to keep it that way."

"The less that knucklehead knows, the better," Chris agreed. "He would give me up for a peck on the cheek and a dollar bill, that one."

"Our man here doesn't need to know either, but let's get him thinking about the mission. Let's ask him why KSM is going to Rawalpindi. Maybe it'll take our minds off things. Who knows? We might end up catching the bastard, and all this stuff with the OIG will disappear."

"You smoking crack, or what? I may end up on the way to jail by the time the day is out!"

CHAPTER FOURTEEN

Islamabad, Pakistan

CHRIS, ALEX AND ASSET X were on the move. The trio were sitting out of sight on the hard floor of the black panel van as it left the confines of the US embassy. They were heading towards the city based on a call the asset had made late in the evening the night before. The asset, still a popular figure in underground business circles, had been feverishly phoning a host of former business contacts in the Islamabad and Rawalpindi areas, garnering invitations to meetings for coffee, lunch or dinner to re-establish ties. Even though he'd been absent from Pakistan for several years, it seemed to Chris and Alex that Mahmoud was still in demand, and his reputation in the community allowed him a measure of respect. It was therefore fortunate for the CIA that when he called a friend or associate for a meeting, he usually got what he wanted. Now, with a schedule to keep, and the first meeting less than an hour away, the small group ventured out from the safety of the American complex and hit the streets, hoping to find a person who could tell them where to find Khalid Sheik Mohammed.

Bearded Jon was at first reluctant to conduct a parallel operation. It would have suited him if his Wahid plan worked, thus saving the US government $25 million, and it was unusual to have two sources with the same potential focusing on the same target. He would have to walk a thin line in recruiting more American assets, both human and technological, to support these dual attempts to track down the mastermind of 9/11. Once he gained more assets, he then would have to divide them up to support either the Wahid or Asset X portion of the hunt.

Ramping up his efforts, Jon assembled a large force of CIA officers from his agency and others. Jon would only allow Mahmoud out in the field if the American intelligence community and the protective shield of SAD operators supported him. By assigning Chris and Alex to play the asset's minders and support the armed officers surrounding them, it freed him up to focus on what he deemed as his favored outcome—Wahid's betrayal of KSM. However, Jon was still the officer in charge, and he needed to keep the small team of "freelancers" on a tight leash.

Though Chris and Alex tried to keep things low key, lest they spook the asset, Jon's insistence that they follow strict check-in procedures and live monitoring—via tracking devices, cell phones and radios—hamstrung them to the point of frustration.

Both operators hated the thought of such restrictions and preferred the freedom to make their own decisions, but had no choice. The United States government had not ever been this close to catching the architect of the Big Wedding, and nobody, from the Director of the CIA down, wanted to lose the opportunity. From this point onwards, it would be a massive team effort.

The black van carrying the trio of Alex, Chris and the asset zipped through the quiet, dark streets without so much as a glance in their direction. Four miles outside the embassy, the van quietly pulled to the side of the road in a subdued part of Islamabad. The driver turned to the three men in back and nodded. Chris, Alex and Mahmoud exited the vehicle, slowly and without slamming doors, and made their way to a white Daihatsu Hijet van. Emblazoned on the rear window of the vehicle were two Pepsi logos. The *si* part, however, was missing from the lower sticker. Chris smiled. He'd been in the van before, in Peshawar, just before he headed into Afghanistan on a fateful covert mission to find and rescue his boss, Richard Nash. That mission seemed like an eon ago. The memory was bittersweet. He achieved his goal, but the consequence of his actions came back to haunt him. He needed to push Alex's warning about the OIG out of his mind and focus on what lay ahead.

As planned, Chris got in the front passenger seat. He looked over to the Pakistani driver and recognized him, though he couldn't remember his name. It mattered not. He sat there in silence, waiting patiently for Alex and Mahmoud to get in and settle down. Chris had his right hand on the grip of his Makarov 9mm pistol underneath his wool shawl, a part of the disguise that both Americans were wearing, hoping to blend into their new environment. Once the van's sliding door closed, Chris turned on his radio and reported that they were mobile once again. Four teams of SAD operators, all at separate locations within two miles of the asset vehicle, heard the transmission but did not respond. A fifth vehicle, operating as command and control, noted the time and position. The satellite, sailing way above their heads, triggered the GPS coordinates and pushed the live data back to the Counterterrorism Center in Langley. The screen watchers observed the red dots on the display impassively, not able to personalize the information, as all they saw were assets and tags.

Chris, trying his best to look like a native in a dirty shalwar kameez, his wool shawl, and Chitrali cap, fitted in well enough. Aiding his costume, his already scraggy, well grown-out beard, face and hands were cosmetically altered to make his complexion appear darker and more aged. Alex sported a similar look, both hoping that if they encountered hostiles, they could fool a casual glance—as long as they didn't have to speak. However, that plan relied on Mahmoud bailing them out with his language skills, and there lay the danger in the entire operation. Neither SAD operator knew Mahmoud well enough to trust him fully. He'd already fooled Chris once, and he was a man motivated by money, a lot of money.

Before the mission got underway, Alex discussed with Chris the possibility of the asset betraying them. But his friend assured him that without a doubt he would throw Mahmoud off a helicopter if it meant that they could both go home in one piece. Though the threat was merely rhetorical, they both knew they had to be careful with how they moved and acted. It was at first a serious conversation, but as they talked, the mere suggestion of a helicopter ride, and Alex sharing a cell with Chris, began a banter and fun-poking session that lasted ten minutes, with both men laughing at whatever misgivings one could throw against the other. But that was over two hours ago. The two men were now in full mission mode. No banter, no witticisms, no bullshit. The game was on. Chris had a broad smile on his face.

⸻ ∞∞∞ ⸻

Wahid left the embassy with his laptop bag strapped across his shoulder. He swallowed hard and his eyes danced furtively in what felt like twenty-five directions at once, scared that all the world was watching what he had just done, or what he was about to do. He wasn't happy being "released back into the wild" by the Americans, but they convinced him it was the only course of action they could viably take to get him to the United States. Even though they believed his story, they'd interrogated him throughout the day, the questions relentless. He'd dealt mainly with the man they called Jon, and the FBI woman whose name he never knew. She was the more relaxed of the two, but they both wanted the same thing. They simply wanted Wahid to meet with Mukhtar, and they would do the rest.

As he strode away, his doubts festered. He feared his immediate surroundings and the shadows of the early evening, which could camouflage the assassins he knew lay in wait. As he moved each few steps, his head turned around to look for a watcher, a follower, someone who wished him harm. But he was also dubious of his new paymasters and their intentions. Once again, he was being used by a government agency—but this one wielded greater power and authority. He tried his best to figure out what was happening to him; what would happen to him.

Striding along at a quick pace, the weight of his actions pushed down on him. His brain was conflicted about telling him what to prioritize first: his present perceived danger, or the upcoming meeting with a terror mastermind? The mixed messages dragged his focus inward; his mind and body almost willing a protective shell to shroud him from impending doom. Thus, instead of using his intellect and savvy to look up and around for danger, his focus was now downward, on the dust and debris of the pavement.

He marched on, wondering if he had made the right decision. What had started out as a fool's errand to confront Nabeel had now turned into a game of betrayal. He knew that Rashid was using him, but he thought his actions to circumvent the GPS program would buy him the time he needed to run to the safety of the Americans. He naively thought exposing the ISI officer would be enough to grant him the pass he needed to get out of Pakistan, but, to his dismay, it was not enough. He faulted himself for opening Pandora's box by not informing Mukhtar of Rashid's deviousness. If only he had confided in his leader at the onset of his problems with his uncle trying to hold him back, he might now feel more secure, safe in the world of al-Qaeda, safe following the true path of Islam.

But it was now the Americans' turn to betray him. His intent was to stay at the embassy. He stupidly thought he could remain in the confines of the grounds there, patiently waiting for a plane ticket and a visa while the Americans dealt with Rashid, but it had turned out much more complicated than he envisioned. Once again, his scrambled mind searched for the right data output. As an IT geek, he sought linear solutions, bits and bytes of code that were easy to follow, easy to hack, easy to manipulate—but such common sense now eluded him.

He adjusted the straps on his laptop bag, more out of nervousness than need. He wiped his sweaty brow with his sleeve, his eyes still spinning in their sockets, probing for something untoward. As his adrenalin pumped, his analytical mind labored away, chomping lines of code. But while his brain continued to adjust to the adverse environment, his body was trying to tell him something else. He dug deep for an answer, but as he did, he tripped on a loose paving stone.

He recovered quick enough, before he stumbled to the ground, but then a delayed reaction came to the fore. He raised his head in confidence as an idea materialized: the Americans might have him in their claws, but he had the know-how to deceive them. He would once again hack into the GPS program and forget his passage to America. He would return to the organization and the safety net of the celebrated architect of 9/11. He would put all of it behind him and move on.

With a sparkle in his eye, he smiled to himself, confident of his plan. He didn't hear the running feet behind him. His computer-like brain humming away inside of him was focused only on forward-facing logical tasks, and not his surroundings. His internal computer chip-like functions only malfunctioned when he felt his wrists being restrained, a hood being placed over his head and a cattle prod being stuck between his ribs.

Rashid looked into the rear of the blue canvas covered Isuzu utility truck and saw the hapless figure of Wahid sitting on the floor cross-legged, handcuffed and gagged, flanked by four of the ISI colonel's best men. "Laptop?" he asked curtly. One of his men produced Wahid's bag. Rashid did not inspect it but handed it off to another member of his team standing next to him, who threw the bag over his shoulder. "Go to the airport, wait two hours," he instructed the man. "Then go to the Margalla Hills and wait. Report your location to the office, then someone will be in contact with you in the next two days. Go. Go now." The man nodded in compliance, then mounted a motorcycle and sped away in a cloud of dust.

Rashid climbed into the back of the truck and sat down on the side bench. "Cell phone?" He asked nobody in particular. Without a word being uttered, the device appeared and was handed over to the senior officer. Rashid flipped it open to see if it was functioning, then tucked it away in his pocket. Satisfied the phone had enough power, he looked down at Wahid but said nothing. Wahid looked back at Rashid and held back a whine. With his precious laptop gone, and his only means of communication now in the firm grasp of the cunning ISI man, he was lost. Wahid thought that maybe he could talk his way out of the situation, but he was out of his depth. He was a nerd, a geek, not used to socializing or negotiating. He wanted to speak to his defense, but this was not a computer game, it was real. He didn't know if in the next few minutes if he would live or die, and if there was anything he could do about it. But before he could come up with something to say, Rashid spoke up, calmly asking one of his men, "Is the doctor waiting?"

"Yes, sir," came the reply.

A cold chill ran through Wahid's body. He desperately wanted to ask, *"Doctor? Doctor? Why a doctor? What . . . what is going on?"* He tried to will his voice to say something, anything, but he was mute. Instead he pissed himself. Rashid saw the mess, then barked an order to the driver to get moving.

The bumpy, quiet ride to a farm in the southeastern suburbs of Islamabad took forty-five minutes. When they finally stopped, the ISI officers blindfolded Wahid. The Isuzu tailgate dropped, and Rashid jumped out first, and marched into the farmhouse without looking around him. He knew where he was going, and he knew that his men would bring the prisoner along at their own pace. Rashid found the interrogation room, greeted the waiting doctor and then inspected Wahid's phone. Dragged into the room a few minutes later, Wahid was not faring well. After Rashid exited the vehicle, the ISI officers had picked Wahid up under his armpits, carried him to the edge of the tailgate, and let him drop. He broke his shoulder as he hit the hard cobblestone courtyard. Now placed in a chair in the middle of the room, Rashid could hear he was in distress from the muffled groans, but paid him no attention. He continued to peruse the phone.

The ISI officers stripped Wahid of all his clothes. While still bound, gagged and blindfolded the doctor gave a cursory inspection of his wounds.

"He has a broken scapula, and some scratches on his head and face from his fall. I have morphine for the shoulder if you wish," he whispered to Rashid. The ISI colonel felt no remorse. It was a tactic he approved of. Cause the prisoner some form of physical discomfort to gain submissiveness, then offer medical help to gain his confidence and obedience.

"Remove his gag," he ordered one of the two men standing behind the prisoner.

Wahid heaved and spat upon removal of the cloth. He wanted to scream, but his body forced him to pant, begging for more air, more out of panic than pain, as his adrenalin disallowed him to feel the true injury. He knew something was wrong with his body, but he didn't know how bad it was. The real pain had not yet begun.

"Wahid, Rashid began." You fell out of the truck. How careless of you."

Wahid was still gasping for air, globs of spit flying out of his mouth. He had no immediate response; he was still trying to grasp the gravity of his situation. He blindly looked around in vain to figure out where Rashid was, hoping his blindfold would slip away. He heard his voice, but it was coming from all directions. He was experiencing sensory overload.

"Do you require medical help?" Rashid continued, feigning genuine concern.

Wahid didn't answer. The doctor approached and poked the young man's shoulder. He screamed at the touch.

"I can help you Wahid, but you must give me something in return," Rashid stated bluntly.

Wahid shook his head; he could take the throbbing discomfort for the moment. A young man of no physical talents or experience, this was the first time he had broken a bone. He was once again showing his naivety by not understanding that soon the actual pain would begin.

The doctor stepped back and pulled up a chair in a corner of the room, waiting patiently for Rashid to give him a direction.

Rashid looked on. He studied Wahid in the dim light of the decrepit room that once was used to slaughter sheep and goats. Wahid sat on a steel chair conveniently placed above a drain, making the cleaning up of bodily fluids that much easier—though clean the room was not and never would be at the hands of the ISI torturers. The colonel placed Wahid's phone on a desk in front of him and lit up a cigarette. As he smoked, a haze enveloped his face. He wondered how much time he had. He needed to warn Mukhtar how close the Americans were to capturing him. Disposing of the laptop was a good first move, which he had used as a method to divert the Americans from Wahid—and thus Mukhtar. By sending his man to the hills outside the capital, he hoped he could win some time by dispatching the Americans' efforts elsewhere, giving him more time to come up with a new strategy. Part one of this plan was now complete; finding out where Mukhtar was would be Part two.

Part three, however, was dealing with the new threat of Mahmoud al Mouhammed. He didn't know where the trader was, or what his alliances were. Rashid had his spies scouring Islamabad for the man, but so far, his agents and informers were coming up empty. Until he could find the traitor, he could not implement Part four of his plan, and take him off the chessboard.

A restless Wahid halted his thought process.

"What is wrong with you, Wahid? Are you in pain?" Rashid didn't need to know the answer. He could see it in the man's pallor, which was changing from flushed redness to white. The pain was coming to life.

Wahid remained silent, battling the unknown force that was making him shudder. He willed himself to hold his tongue and not ask for anything. But the pain was getting intense. He tried to shake his misery away.

"You need to go to the hospital, you know that?"

Wahid nodded.

"But I will not allow that," Rashid said, then paused, letting the news sink in. He wanted Wahid to feel trapped, which didn't take much. "I will ease your pain though . . . if you help me."

Wahid finally found something to say. "I have nothing for you! Why can't you understand that? I don't know what you want from me."

It was what Rashid was waiting for, an opening. The prisoner was talking. "Let's talk about that in a minute. Doctor, please help our young friend here . . . I believe you have some morphine." He held up his index finger and thumb to instruct the physician to only administer a small dose. The doctor reached into his bag of tricks, produced a vial of the painkiller, and injected the narcotic as ordered.

Rashid allowed Wahid to enjoy the sensation for a few minutes before continuing on. He looked at his watch. He didn't want to be there all night; however, he knew he could not rush things. He needed Wahid lucid, and aware enough so he could talk to Mukhtar if he needed to. If Mukhtar were to call Wahid now, then having a scared man answer would warn the terrorist. However, Rashid needed to tell Mukhtar about the steps the Americans were taking and the need for him to go into hiding or leave the country. If he heard danger in Wahid's voice, it could have the unintended consequence of scaring him off completely, not knowing how close things were. If Rashid were to answer Wahid's phone, it could spook him into hanging up immediately without any explanation. "Where is Mukhtar, Wahid?"

"I don't know," he feebly replied. Even a small dose was causing him to relax. Rashid could see the effects of the drug working its magic.

"I have a hundred questions for you regarding your behavior, Wahid. For example, why did you go to the Americans when I told you not to?"

"I . . . I," he stammered in reply.

"—You don't need to answer, idiot. What has happened is in the past. We cannot undo it. You are now safe here with us. I don't know what the Americans promised you, but whatever it was, is now gone. You understand that . . . yes?"

Wahid let his head drop almost to his chest. He was dejected, worn down and still in pain.

"Give me one reason why I should not kill you, Wahid."

Wahid sobbed; he didn't know what to say. He pissed himself again.

Rashid could see that his prisoner was feeling at odds and defeated. But he still needed him. "But I am not that callous, my young friend." He let the statement sink in. "I think you and I have the same goals . . . now. Don't you think so? We can overlook your inexperience with strategy and tactics and perhaps look on this one day as a learning experience."

Wahid questioned why Rashid was playing nice. He picked up on the phrase "one day as a learning experience." It gave him hope. "What do you want me to say, Rashid? I don't know where he is. All I know is that he will be in Rawalpindi."

Rashid perked up. This was news to him; it threw his practiced script out the window. His mind jerked into overdrive. It put a new spin on things, knowing that Mukhtar could be so close. "When?"

"He doesn't tell me. He told me a week ago to be here, and when he arrives, he tells me in an email, a phone call or a text message where to meet him. That is all. I never know, Rashid. You must believe me."

And you set up his network, Rashid mused. *It makes sense not to trust the IT man fully. He is careful. That damn laptop . . . now he can't see an email if Mukhtar sends one. I could not have foreseen that; or should I have?* Suddenly his thoughts were a jumbled mess. *Now we only have the phone. I need this idiot more than I thought!*

Rashid caught the attention of the doctor and gave him a sign to give Wahid a little more morphine. He picked up Wahid's cell phone to look at the signal strength. It was poor. *I may get lucky and receive a text*, he considered, *and there will be no need to talk to him. I can meet him and warn him.*

But the permutations were now mounting. He needed to think things through. He stared at the phone, but then his eyes widened in horror. *What if the Americans can track this phone; is that even possible?* He dropped the phone like it had an infectious disease. His ignorance of modern technology had come back to haunt him. He wasn't sure what to do. Diverting the laptop to the outer hills of Islamabad had been in his mind a good move, but now in retrospect he regretted his decision as, besides the lack of email access, it was now separated from the phone. He didn't know if the Americans and their know-how would spot that Wahid's technology tethers were now in two different places, and if they did, what action they would take. He wondered if it was too late to recall his man with the laptop. He grabbed Wahid's phone and took a risk. He turned off the device.

"The phone is down," reported an analyst from ICE CAVE.

Jon hurried across to the man who made the announcement. "Where was the last signal coming from?" The analyst typed a few commands and brought up a map showing the location of a farm in the southeastern suburbs of Islamabad, near the Rawat Fort. Jon studied the map for a minute. He sensed something was wrong. He pointed to a red dot on the screen. It was miles away from the farm. "And this is the laptop?"

"Yes, it's mobile, has been for about three hours now. It was at the airport for a while, but is now heading north."

"They should be together. How long does the feed take to refresh itself?"

"Fifteen seconds."

"Shit, then there's no need for them to have separate signals. This guy is either fucking with us, or our billion-dollar satellites are worthless. Fuck!" Jon had hoped that his strategy was working. Seeing the static signal at the international airport gave him faith that Wahid had received a call or a message to meet with KSM, and that they were together, potentially heading to a hideout in the hills above the city. While watching the signal move away from Islamabad, Jon was mentally preparing his forces to take down the terrorist. "Fuck!" he shouted again.

Gene Brooks heard the commotion and made his way slowly over to Jon's side. He studied the screen over the operations officer's shoulder, and he too made the same assessment: things were going sideways. He raised his eyebrows, trying to interpret the development. Not one for relying on signal intelligence, or SIGINT, Gene was old school and preferred good old human spies—HUMINT. He sauntered back to his side of the room and counted the red dots on his screen. He suppressed a smile. Everyone was still in play, and no reports were coming in.

Gene looked at two red dots and a bright blue one, almost all meshed together. He knew it was the asset, Alex and Chris. He stared at the screen a few minutes more. He wondered how much longer he could keep Chris out of the clutches of the OIG. He'd bought his friend some time, but before long they'd start berating him for obstruction. He needed this operation to go well, not only for the CIA, but for Chris—and for himself. Though he'd admonished his subordinate for his actions leading up to the asset being delivered to the Salt Pit, he had to admit, nobody knew at the time how valuable that lead could be. If things were going wrong with Jon's primary focus, then Asset X could be the only chance they had to find the terror mastermind. The CIA would have to be grateful to Chris for that.

It was still quiet on his side of the house—no radio traffic, no messages, just dedicated, highly trained professionals going about their work without complaint or concern. He loved this part of 'The Game'. He glanced back at Jon, who was still doing a song and dance with his analyst about the missing technology he needed to do his job. Whatever his misgivings for the senior operations officer were, they still had a common worry. Nobody knew where Khalid Sheik Mohammed was.

"You need to give me more room, Chris."

"What do you mean?"

"You and your team, you are getting too close. I need my freedom to meet my associates. I understand you are trying to protect me, but I can't do my job if you are over my shoulder all the time. People will suspect something is wrong."

They were sitting in the back of the Pepsi van, considering their next move, when Mahmoud voiced his fear. Alex was still monitoring the surrounding area, hiding in an alleyway, watching for any movement that could mature into a threat. Chris nodded when Mahmoud spoke; he understood the concern. The golden rule of surveillance was not to stand out and to have a reason for being in a place. It was no good pretending to be a bird-watcher at night while roaming the dark streets, bird book and camera in hand. You had to have a valid reason for being where you were, and your story had to be solid enough, disguise or not, to convince even your grandmother.

Even under the mantle of the night, with poor lighting and the plentiful shadows to hide in, he and Alex were living on borrowed time. Until now, one or the other always had eyes on the asset when he was meeting with someone. But it would only take one concerned citizen to shout an obscenity at them or cause a ruckus because they were hiding in a doorway or just being in the way of someone's daily business—thus drawing undue attention to themselves. If Mahmoud was getting close, if he were meeting members of criminal organizations, then there was a good chance those ne'er-do-wells would have a security contingent nearby who'd react to an encounter—which could also scupper their entire enterprise.

Chris looked at the asset. He was trying to figure out a course of action. It was late, this was the third meeting of the evening, and there was still one more coffee invitation to attend. He wanted to give Mahmoud some leeway, but wasn't sure how much. He wondered what would happen at the next rendezvous; what if the next character were to invite Mahmoud to his home, or elsewhere, for the rest of the night? The list of what-ifs scared him. The information Asset X was bringing back from his intelligence gatherings was promising—though it wasn't enough though to stop a wave of pessimism from washing over Chris. He wasn't sure if he was overthinking the situation or just being too cautious, but he began wondering, *What if he's playing us again? What if he's planning to dump our asses here in the jungle, or get us killed?* He still hadn't answered Mahmoud's request. He looked at the man, hard. *What if he's trying to warn KSM, for his own safety? He won't wear a tracker. How the hell are we supposed to trust this guy?*

Mahmoud wanted an answer. "You need to let me go, Chris. I can be in contact with you over the phone."

"You need to wear a tracker," Chris countered.

"No. I will not. If I find him, his men will search me. And then what?"

Chris was in a bind. They needed a decision. But the repercussions of letting the asset loose could be massive. He sat in silence, taking turns between gazing into the eyes of the asset and peering outside the van windows. He still couldn't see Alex, but he knew his friend was out there; he wondered what he would do. Chris weighed his options, trying to rationalize his thoughts. *He's right, we've been out here too long. We can't sustain this much longer, especially when the sun comes up. We have his phone.*

We can trace him and keep mobile with the van . . . Wait, who the hell is that? He's getting too close to the van, he needs to fuck off . . . keep moving Patel, go on, fuck off. He grabbed his pistol under his shawl, glaring at the man, who was just ambling along without a care in the world and looked interested in the van for no real reason. Chris watched the man he called Patel, walk silently by, another non-issue to dump into his memory bank.

He needed to get his thoughts in order. *We'll keep the teams at a safe distance and they can follow us, not him.* He sighed, then rubbed his eyes. They were burning. He didn't need a mirror to tell him what shade of red his whites were. His inner voice was working hard. *I will not ask that dipshit Jon for permission; we need an in-the-field decision.* He spotted Alex coming around a corner. "Stay here," he ordered the asset.

Chris walked slowly to meet his friend, and stopped him about fifty feet away from the van. "I'm making an executive decision," he began.

Stumped and surprised, Alex didn't know what Chris had in mind. He'd already broken protocol by leaving the asset alone with the driver. He thought something must have happened while he did his security sweep. "What's up, Chris?"

Chris outlined his plan by beginning with, "This is all my decision Alex; you don't need to be involved—you keep sightseeing and I will take care of this."

Alex shuddered at the statement, thinking, *What the hell has he done now?* He waited for Chris to finish before saying something. He had to admit there was some merit to his friend's logic, after he'd heard his plan. Alex didn't enjoy circumventing the chain of command, but he also knew that Mahmoud needed to gain some momentum, and having two boat anchors chained to his legs prevented that. Besides, waiting for the powers-that-be to make a final decision on releasing him under his own steam could cost them the entire operation by waiting hours—or even days—for an approval, or a denial. Alex asked several questions about logistics and maintaining control of the asset, which Chris answered with well thought out solutions. The more they talked, the more the idea was firming up.

Chris saw an opening when Alex, who wasn't saying anything, dug at his dirty fingernails. "I'm calling this in, Alex," he said.

"Hang on, this is *our* decision. There's no need for you to take all the heat on this."

"Alex, mate, this has to be me . . . my career is already over. As soon as we find this fucker, I'm done. Gene and I have had this conversation already—there's no place for me at the CIA." He paused a few beats. "I think we're close in finding this asswipe, so there's no point in me giving a shit anymore. You, on the other hand, should take a stroll with the asset, get him moving down the road a bit, get him up to speed on how we'll handle things from here on out. Establish check-in times, waypoints, passwords, abort codes, you know the drill. While you do that, I'll make the call, nobody will be able to reach you—and that will be that. I'll tell them this was all my idea, and I took the opportunity while you were doing a security sweep."

"Don't be an idiot, Chris. If we don't get the target after all of this, they'll crucify you."

"I don't want you near me if that happens, Alex. There's no need for both of us to sink. If I don't get fired, then the OIG will grab me by the balls and anyone close to me will get the same treatment. And even if I get canned, the OIG will still want to drag me over the coals. I'm fucked either way. Let me at least go out with something . . . something I can honestly say I tried my best at." Chris looked at his friend; he wanted to protect him from the potential fallout, but he wanted to try one last time to do something to be proud of. "Let me do this, Alex."

Alex ruminated for a minute, but finally relented. "Use the term 'exigent circumstances,' they'll like that legal bullshit."

Chris smiled. "Thanks buddy, you might want to take him for a stroll. You don't want to hear my next phone call." Both men returned to the van and brought the asset up to speed. Mahmoud got out and took off with Alex. Chris jumped in the vehicle and pulled out his cell phone. He asked the driver to take a short walk then made his call. He dialed Gene's number and watched the asset talk to Alex while they both ambled down the street. While waiting for his boss to answer, he wondered if this would be the last time he would see the asset; he also wondered if Mahmoud was still playing a game and he himself was just another sacrificial pawn.

Gene had worked a form of magic by providing the SAD teams a safe house, which was more of a forward base of operations, so his men could get some downtime and their faces off the streets. When Chris called in the change of strategy, it caused a stink that reached all the way from Pakistan to the United States. Bandied around in the halls of the CIA, Chris's name was accompanied by disparaging insults, name-calling and genuine disgust. The moan-and-groan sessions hadn't made their way up the ladder to the senior echelons of the CIA hierarchy, but still, those involved in the bowels of the operation saw only doom on the horizon. Everyone who had an opinion aired it. Everyone who wanted some gossip got it. If Chris Morehouse wanted a career in the CIA after today, he would not get it. Everyone who wanted someone to blame now had a target.

Gene remained in ICE CAVE as his team members got together in the ramshackle house, near a military hospital in Rawalpindi. He supplied the place with the basics of food and water, communications, cots, and a roof that didn't leak—but not much else. It was very temporary and probably would be vacated in less than twenty-four hours.

Chris entered first, followed closely by Alex. If there was a piano man playing, he would have stopped. If there was beer to be had, the drinking would have ceased. All eyes were pinned on the Brit who'd made the lives of the SAD operators that much harder to deal with now that they had nobody to watch, no target in their sights. Alex stood by his partner's side. He gave the room a deathly stare, daring—hoping—that someone would offer a foul word, but he was pleased that none came. Though the tension in the room was high, none of the SAD operators were about to go off on Chris or Alex. The professionals were in a field operational environment and had no time for petty skirmishes or office politics. They were all there to do a job and were used to working on the fly. It was their job to be flexible.

Alex made for a stash of water bottles in a corner. He grabbed four, handed two to Chris and slugged away half a bottle without saying a word. Chris popped the lid on one and chugged away, reading the room as he slurped. There were still a few hard stares from the team, but mostly the mood was somber. The others who weren't staring at him were nodding off on a cot or in a chair, following standard soldier procedure: sleep when you're doing nothing, not knowing when you'll get another chance. Chris moved to one of the house's free corners and made himself comfortable on the ground. He loosened his clothing and relaxed. Alex mingled for a minute or two, speaking with some of his colleagues. He soon plonked down next to Chris, with nothing much to say. It felt like lead weights were pushing down on Chris's eyelids. He didn't fight back, letting sleep take over to ease his troubled mind.

Chris wasn't sure how long he had been out. He woke to the sound of a commotion and raised voices. He cracked one eyelid open, saw Jon, then closed it again. *If I pretend I'm still asleep, maybe he'll go away; maybe he has a heart and will leave me and my tired bones alone. Or perhaps the prick won't recognize me.* A kick on the bottom of his foot squashed his dreams. *Oh, sod off tosser,* he groaned to himself.

"Hey, hey, wake up, I need to talk to you," Jon said as he kicked him again. "Hey! Wake up! I'm talking to you."

Chris slowly opened his eyes. He wanted to tell him to go forth and multiply, but held back his curse. He looked up and saw the senior CIA officer standing right in front of him, flanked by one of his flunkies and a Pakistan ISI officer. "Jon, what can I do for you?" he coolly asked.

"Where is he?"

Chris was still sitting in the corner, arms folded across his chest, legs stretched out before him. He didn't budge when Jon finally dropped to his level expecting an answer.

"I don't know," he said looking at his watch, trying to calculate how much time had passed since he let the asset walk. "We let him go about eight . . . eight and a half hours ago."

"When was the last contact?"

"I haven't had any. I've been catching some Zs and my phone hasn't been ringing, so my guess he's still out there meeting sources. Why aren't you tracking his phone? I called this in last night and I told ICE CAVE to track him; what's changed?"

Jon ground his teeth. He wanted to scream but held on to his thin veil of composure. "His phone is off, you dick."

Oops, that wasn't supposed to happen, Chris thought as he scrambled for something to hold on to before things really split sideways. "He thought he might have to do that. He was worried that someone—" *Someone like you, butt-munch.* "—may try to call at the wrong time. Part of his briefing was to call or text as soon he was free of scrutiny. I'm assuming you read the notes I gave to the ICE CAVE last night?"

Unimpressed with the answer, Jon had read the report but skimmed over some finer details. He too was feeling the pressure of little sleep and gut rot. He kneeled closer into Chris's comfort zone. "You know you are finished," he whispered. Chris stared at him, uncomfortable with him being so close. He could smell his bad breath and see the boogers up his nose. He quickly made a plan for how to strike him and hurt him. He kept his arms folded, blood pressure under control and eyes fixated on the blue eyes of the interloper. His mouth was shut tight as a drum. He tried to look bored and nonthreatening.

"I just had an interesting meeting with the OIG," he continued; his voice was still low. He was trying to get a rise from the Brit, but wasn't getting anything in return. "You're an interesting guy, Chris, a tough guy. You might think you are a man of steel or some other bullshit, but you are as dumb as a rock. We don't need people like you in this agency." He was getting perturbed because the Brit looked back at him with utter vacancy. He pushed on, hoping for a confrontation, an excuse to have Chris removed and out of his operation. "I knew Richard Nash. I knew he took a chance on you—but he was a dinosaur; his way of thinking was archaic, Cold War stuff. We are in a new era now, and he didn't belong, nor do you. Look around this room. These are smart, dedicated men, not knuckle-dragging apes who speak with their fists. Men that I can rely on to follow orders. If I had my way, you wouldn't be in the country, let alone on this operation." Chris still didn't budge, didn't say a word, and didn't acknowledge the affront, which only pissed Jon off more. "Are you hearing me? Are you fucking deaf?" His voice bounded up an octave. "Say something you idiot."

"Why Jon, you're doing such an outstanding job, carry on," Chris replied nonchalantly. Alex overheard the comment and rolled his eyes.

Jon briefly contemplated grabbing Chris by the scruff and throttling him. He had the advantage of being physically above him, after all; but he thought better of it after seeing Alex nearby. "If we don't find the asset soon, you are fucked. I'll take you back to the embassy myself and turn you over to OIG. You can thank Gene for going to bat for you to keep you out here, and to keep the OIG from talking to you. But I can guarantee that if things go sideways out here, he will suffer too. He's another one that needs to go out to pasture. His career will go down the drain because of you—but it won't be a significant loss." The last comment stung Chris. He felt a little warmth under his armpits, his face flushed slightly. He didn't know his unintended actions would have such far-reaching results. He worried for his friend; he didn't want that for him, regardless of their recent disagreements.

"As soon as this is over—and thanks to your shenanigans last night, it may be over before we know it—you're done, you piece of shit."

Alex caught the last part of the conversation and desperately wanted Chris to keep his mouth shut, but it wasn't to be.

"Why is that ISI officer here?" the Brit piped up.

The question flummoxed Jon. It was as if he'd just wasted his breath berating Chris. "What?" he asked.

"The ISI guy, the one you brought with you, why is he here? This is a forward operating base—a fuckin' FOB—you know the rules Jon— he shouldn't be here."

Jon stood up and shook his head in disbelief. He thought maybe Chris was too stupid to comprehend the repercussions of his actions; or perhaps he was just being a smart-ass who was just trying to show his disrespect and deflect the entire problem.

"You're a piece of work . . . I've never met such an asshole."

"Get in line Jon. There are plenty more who have the same ideas."

"Okay, okay, enough, enough," Alex interjected by walking over to the two antagonists. "We've all thrown our binkies around so let's see if we can be adults now. Jon, have a nice day. Chris, shut the fuck up."

Rashid felt his phone ring. "Hello."

"Colonel Ghazini sir, this is Captain Machi."

"Yes captain, what can I do for you?"

"Sir, I have found the CIA forward operating base."

"Good, tell me, give me details."

The captain did as he was told. He was out of earshot of Jon and the other CIA operatives. He had just witnessed an altercation between the Americans, which he explained to his superior. Although the argument intrigued Rashid, he was more interested in the location and makeup of the team at the CIA base. After being given more details, he hung up the phone. He now knew that Mahmoud was still in play, but was out of communication with his handlers. He saw this development as an advantage to his strategy. If the Americans were in discord, then he may move quicker, without hindrance. He also now knew which part of Rawalpindi the Americans were concentrating their efforts on, alleviating him of having to cast such a wide net. Keeping his man embedded with the Americans would also speed up the flow of information to him, but he wondered how much time he had. He looked at his watch, then smiled to himself as, unlike the Americans, he still had a source that could provide Mukhtar's location. Things were looking up.

CHAPTER FIFTEEN

Rawalpindi, Pakistan

RASHID HADN'T BEEN IDLE. KNOWING where the Americans were focusing their efforts in Rawalpindi had proved to be an enormous advantage. Having an officer embedded with the CIA, one who reported directly to him, was also favorable. However, the onus of preventing the Americans from capturing Khalid Sheik Mohammed was on him. Despite the early morning hour, he had conferred with some of his superiors, who were adamant that the terrorist not be captured by the Americans. From his conversations with some members of the Old Guard he learned that the terrorist had visited Abbottabad to discuss a plan to kill the Pakistani president, and while the plot was still in its infancy, it was gaining support from others in the government.

The discussions, however, came with a warning. There were moderates in the ruling party, the ISI, and the military who saw benefits in ridding Pakistan of the scourge of al-Qaeda. Rashid had to walk a fine line and use his resources wisely. Learning from his previous failed surveillance mission of Mahmoud, he gathered enough competent men, those who were loyal to him, to be at his beck and call. His skill, however, was in marshalling his trusted team, while still being cognizant of the opposing ISI officers who were legitimately assisting the Americans.

He was happy to hear of the discord amongst the CIA, but he was more wary of the deep divide in his own organization. What he didn't want was for Pakistani people to suffer in any crossfire. He hoped that this would not come down to a shooting match amongst his people, as he wasn't comfortable issuing an order to kill his fellow officers or citizens to save a terrorist. Not one to work off flimsy by-the-seat-of-your-pants plans, he preferred well thought out scenarios with fallback strategies and contingencies to achieve his aims. But this time he *was* flying by the seat of his pants. Things were fluid and developing quickly. Knowing that Mahmoud was roaming solo added to his consternation; he feared the trader would reach Mukhtar before he did. He therefore had to rely on Captain Machi to give him the updates he needed, and he hoped he had enough men in the right places and times to jump ahead of the Americans.

He looked at his watch. He'd been at the farmhouse through the night, catching a few moments of sleep here and there while he made his phone calls and paced around, desperately trying to figure things out. He returned to the room where Wahid, still bound to a chair, had his head on his chest. He was asleep.

Rashid wanted to leave him be, but he needed the young man. He needed him to be a team player and answer the phone if Mukhtar called. But after that, he was expendable, a casualty of war.

One of his men was directly behind him, waiting for a command. Rashid spoke delicately. "Unbind him. Clean him up, give him a shower, find some clothes and feed him. Find the doctor, tell him to give aid to this man's needs. We will leave within the hour."

Rashid was about to leave the room, but then he paused. He looked down at Wahid's phone, which he was carrying, as well as the laptop he'd re-diverted back to the farmhouse. He powered up the phone to see at how much battery charge it had. It was not enough. He quickly rummaged through Wahid's laptop bag and found the charger. Plugging it in, he worried that he was making a mistake, but the pros outweighed the cons. He didn't want to use Wahid's phone or his laptop, fearing they may be being tracked, but he had no choice; he needed to communicate with Mukhtar somehow.

"Someone get Jon, the phone is up," reported an analyst from ICE CAVE.

Jon scurried back into ICE CAVE upon hearing the news. He looked at the screen. "Where?"

"Same place as last night, the farm in the southeast of Islamabad."

Jon's face turned into a scowl. "What the hell is going on?"

"The laptop is on, same place," the analyst commented further.

Jon was perturbed, momentarily pissed off with relying on the highly vaunted CIA technology systems, though he knew it was a necessary evil. "Let me get this right. The phone was turned off, not long after he left here. Then the laptop he was carrying, which should have been off, still emitted a signal to us and was headed north. Now, the phone is on and the laptop is off and we're still receiving a signal?" He looked around the room for answers, but all he received were blank looks in return. "Anybody? Anyone want to guess what the hell is happening?"

One of the older, seasoned CIA officers threw out the first pitch. "What if he went to this farmhouse, then got news he had to travel north? He takes off, halfway up the road, he figures out he left his phone behind and skittered back for it?"

Jon groaned. It was a slim possibility, but he didn't like it. "How far are we talking about?" he asked nobody in particular.

"About twenty-five miles, give or take a few," the response came back.

"And it took him all night to go back for it? I don't like it." He stood with his hands on his hips, looking at the screens in front of him. Perplexed, he wasn't sure how to proceed. He looked to another screen that showed the location of the FOB. "How far from the FOB to the farmhouse?"

"About twelve miles, Jon."

"Do we have any eyes on yet?" He responded.

"Key Hole is due in about eleven hours."

Jon let out a huge sigh, rolled his eyes and looked up at the ceiling, he urged himself to calm down and focus. "Anything else?"

"We have a Viewpoint team in the area but it's a farm, there's a lot of ground to cover. It's going to take some time to get a clear picture of the day-to-day there. Viewpoint are not equipped for a long-term surveillance operation like this. Someone is going to have to dig a hole and live in a field for a while, and that means SAD or Special Forces."

Jon was agitated, he wanted to kick a trash can, but calmed himself. He went silent, *we don't have days, I need eyes now! Fuck!*

His mind whirred away as he thought about sending a few SAD men to give him an actual read on the location. He wanted eyeballs on the farmhouse, but knew the operators would not see too much without knocking on the front door. He contemplated splitting his force, but he didn't want to blow their cover over a flimsy possibility. He wondered if he should take the chance that the terrorist had already arrived, but Wahid had not passed on the confirmation code over his phone, nor his laptop. He wanted to act; he wanted to do something with the information. His mind bounced around sending a US Special Forces team into the farm, but that was complex, and nor was it a speedy deployment. He needed to hash the idea out, he needed to think things through. He needed to talk to the embassy military attaché, or at least someone with a detailed tactical mind. "Keep me posted," was all he could muster, then rushed out the room.

"Was that him?"

"Yeah, on time," Chris said, closing his flip phone. "Nothing to report, but he's going to lunch with Gupta, Gopal, Gunga Din, or somebody whose name starts with a G."

Alex shook his head; he didn't need Chris to have short-timer's disease now. "That's really precise, Chris. I'll let you explain that one to Jon."

"Put it down to a poor connection with the phone. How many names have we heard from him in the last twenty-four hours? Can you keep track of it?"

"We should be trying. Did he at least say where?"

"Not exactly, just a district." Chris pulled out a map and shared it with his friend. "Here . . ." He pointed with his pen. "Westridge."

"He's getting a little too far away from us," Alex noted. "Do you want to move up? Close in a little tighter?"

"Think so; what about the rest of the gang?"

Alex knew he was talking about the SAD team milling around the FOB. The two men were unimpressed with the expanding number of people coming and going. It should have been a low-key affair, but it was slowly becoming like Piccadilly Circus, "This place needs to close," Alex answered. "Let me call Gene, see if he has a new location for us. But I'm going to recommend that we go alone again . . . get as close as we can to Westridge."

"Sounds like a plan. But if he sets up a new place for us, ask him for some chocolate. I could murder a piece right now."

Alex gave a little chuckle. "I now understand why Gene always shakes his head when he talks about you. You never know what's going to come out of your mouth. Sometimes it's shit, sometimes . . . chocolate, really, Chris?"

"I wouldn't have survived this long by being predictable, Alex."

Alex held back his retort. *If this thing goes south on us, neither of us will survive.* "Let me go find a quiet spot; I'll call Gene and get us rolling out of here."

"Make that mint, if he's got any!" Chris shouted at Alex's back as he was walking away. The comment drew a few curious glances from the CIA crew, but Chris buried himself in a corner again, pretending to be a tortoise hiding in his shell.

The Isuzu utility truck pulled into the courtyard of the Rawalpindi Military Veterinary Hospital in the center of the city. The vehicle backed into one of the disused barns at the small complex. Rashid and his driver parked their car nearby, while the ISI officers lowered Wahid gently from the truck's tailgate—this time taking care not to injure the man again. They moved him to a horse stall and placed him in a wooden chair. They removed his handcuffs, but two ISI officers held on to his arms firmly and raised them slightly, causing him to scream into the cloth bound around his mouth. They secured a belt around his waist and the chair. The same was done to his legs. Once the officers had completed the task, they placed a small desk in front of him and the two officers lowered his hands to the top, where a large belt secured his wrists flat down onto the surface. They removed his blindfold but kept the gag on his mouth.

Wahid blinked a hundred times, trying to figure out where he was and what was going on. He looked down at his bound arms and writhed in vain, attempting to break free. He knew not why, but all his instincts were telling him he was in mortal danger. His thrashing around brought no relief, only more pain to his throbbing shoulder. He was grateful for the aid he had received from Rashid at the farmhouse. It even buoyed his confidence somewhat. He was alive.

But then Rashid entered the stall and gave him a stone-cold look; he now wondered if that had all been a ploy to soften him up. When Rashid removed a blanket from the top of a nearby table, he knew he was right. He saw the long blade of a knife, a pair of pliers, a small bolt cutter, a hammer. He swallowed hard, struggling to maintain what little composure he had left. Petrified at the sight of the tools, tears ran down his face.

Rashid placed the phone and the laptop next to the implements and let Wahid gain control of his now labored breathing and his weepy eyes. "I will remove your binding, but when I do, please do not scream. Nobody will hear you. If they do, they will not care." He paused a moment to let Wahid slow his heart rate; he could see the blood vessels in the young man's forehead, popping out under the strain. He needed not to see that. It was a man not in control of his faculties and would do or say anything to get out of a predicament. Rashid needed him calm and under control. But first he needed to show dominance. "Remove his shirt," he ordered.

The two ISI officers standing behind Wahid weren't gentle in carrying out the command. They ripped at the material, then tossed it to the side and stood back to await the next order. Rashid had to wait another few minutes for the prisoner to further calm down.

"Wahid, listen to me. We both know why you are here. You have information that I need. But you must remember, we both have the same goal you and I. We need to warn Mukhtar of the Americans."

Wahid only stared back, his eyes the size of dinner plates.

"Wahid, I need the password to your laptop, and you will tell me how to navigate to get to your email." The young IT geek didn't submit. He didn't even acknowledge the request. Rashid now saw the defiance in his eyes. "I can see that you don't trust me, Wahid. Let me put this to you differently." He looked over at the tools on the table, then back at his prisoner. Wahid followed his gaze. "I know how much you rely on your fingers to play with your precious computers; how would that work when you are missing one or two?" his jailer asked.

Wahid shook his head vigorously from side to side. His livelihood was in his fingers. His body was warning him of an issue; there was sharp burning pain in his broken shoulder, but he feared more. His peripheral vision caught the sight of a needle in the doctor's hands. He retched uncontrollably; his neck and facial muscles contorting. Rashid ordered the gag removed. Wahid sucked in the stale air of the stall and hyperventilated. Rashid allowed him to breathe and gather himself. He wanted to rush things, but he also needed Wahid to be in control of himself, still worried that Mukhtar would call the young man on the phone.

"Wahid, my friend. I have told you this before. I wish you no harm. As soon as we have contacted him, we can put this behind us. You will be free to go back to him if you so desire. But we must warn him . . . Now, guide me through this laptop of yours."

"Jon, the laptop is live . . . and the phone!" shouted the analyst at ICE CAVE. Jon strode into the room from the corridor, glancing at the large screen on the wall. "He's in the center of the city, close to the Rawalpindi Golf Club—the Shaheed Officer's Colony. I can give you exact coordinates if you want?"

"Yes, and forward that to the FOB."

"FOB is no longer there. They've gone mobile, heading into the center of the city. No known location," the analyst responded without looking up from his computer.

"Shit, why didn't anyone tell me? Do they have anything new from the asset?"

"Not that I know of. The two SAD guys on the ground are out of communication."

"Those assholes. Anyone seen Gene?"

"He was in the cafeteria last time I saw him," someone in the room chimed in.

Jon needed to find his counterpart and rip him a new one for not keeping him in the loop. But as he stormed off, he analyzed his predicament. Wahid had been on the move, his laptop now live. His phone active. If nothing of substance was coming from the asset, should he pool all his resources towards finding Wahid? Whatever his decision, he needed the SAD to help him out. He needed boots on the ground ready to go at his command if, and when, Wahid gave him the confirmation that he was with KSM.

The dirty white Pepsi van pulled over to the side of the road outside the Westridge Shopping Complex. Chris, sitting in the passenger seat, had his right hand on his Makarov pistol under his wool shawl. Alex was in the van's rear, monitoring the radio and waiting for the asset to call. They had been at the side of the road only for a few moments when Mahmoud phoned to let them know he would join them. On hearing the news, Alex exited the vehicle to conduct a security sweep, while Chris contacted the SAD mobile command post to inform them where they were—and they were meeting the asset.

Chris got out of the vehicle and wandered slowly around, looking for the trap his inner voice was telling him was surely there. It was the middle of the day with lots to see, lots to process. *Speeding two-wheeler, two guys, one eyeballing me . . . tangos?* He watched the men, waiting for something else to pique his interest, hand still holding his hidden gun. *Keep rolling turd-balls, nothing to see here.* The men were not a threat. He mentally photographed an image of the two, then looked around for the next potential tango. *White car, three guys, one old, two young, windows open . . . windows open—hope it's because someone farted in there. Show me your hands, show me your hands . . . nothing . . . good, moving on.*

He used his internal radar to scan all around him, trying his best to look nonchalant to the casual passersby, each time focusing on the next potential scumbag who crossed his path. It was draining. His eyes saw everything, his ears heard everything. Sometimes his attention on one thing was focused too much, sometimes it was not enough. He knew his time in this mode was finite; he needed to relax his brain for a few seconds now and then in order to maintain his vigilance long-term. But he continued to scope out the area, until he saw Mahmoud approach and Alex in the distance, leaning up against a wall as if just watching the day go by. The asset showed no concern and entered the van without saying a word, Chris followed suit, and within thirty seconds, Alex mounted up. The driver then pulled away.

Mahmoud knew the drill. The two CIA officers preferred not to speak immediately to him as they were conducting their safety drills, scanning this, checking that, seeing suspects here, there and everywhere. It would take another ten minutes before they were comfortable enough to engage in conversation.

Mahmoud couldn't wait. "I think we may be in luck," he started.

Chris turned around in the passenger seat to look at the asset. He was smiling. "What's going on? What did you find out?"

"He is in Westridge. Not far from here, or so I am told."

"But it sounds like you haven't confirmed this yourself; you have heard it from someone else?" Chris asked. He was excited, but still cautious.

"Yes, there is an army officer, Major Adil Qadoos. He is a supporter of al-Qaeda. He has a home here in the district. I had lunch with him earlier, and dinner at his house last night. I have met this man many times over the years. He is well connected in the city with businessmen like myself, as well as politicians, civil servants. For a military man, he is quite wealthy."

"Black market?" Alex supposed.

"Yes, mainly arms, some logistics and training."

"Things you didn't want to get involved with," Chris asked, still skeptical on hearing the news.

"Yes, but he thinks I am now interested in supporting the cause. He doesn't know of my past, but I have reconfirmed my commitment. He's a greedy man. He only sees dollar signs. He has Swiss bank accounts, many properties in Pakistan. He wants to expand his business with me, and eventually support al-Qaeda from overseas. He will retire soon from the military."

"That's fine, Mahmoud, but what about Khalid? Is he there now, at this major's house?" Chris pushed.

"I don't know. I am to go there tonight; I am his guest and I will stay the night. There is a small party."

"Pull over," Alex ordered the driver. "Where is the party?"

"Nisar Road, it is about two, two and a half kilometers from where you picked me up."

Alex and Chris were exchanging glances, reading each other's minds. They were close, really close. This could be the big break they were looking for. Alex, however, wanted to get all his ducks in a row. If this information was accurate, or not, the operation could end by the middle of the night. He for one needed details before they committed to the next part of the mission. There would be a paper chain after all was said and done, and before he signed off on his report, he wanted the skinny on everything. He took out a notepad. "Okay, we need to go through this from top to bottom. Start with the time we left the embassy. Who did you meet first, where did you go, where did you sleep? All of it."

The large belt was still bound around Wahid's arms. The leather straps holding his feet in place chafed his skin, the belt around his waist put pressure on his stomach. He wanted to pee; he wanted to shit. He could do neither.

Rashid had placed the laptop in front of his prisoner with the email page open, but Wahid decided naively to play a game. He didn't know if Rashid or his men were clever enough to notice, though in his mind it was rudimentary, but he could see that there was no Internet service in the barn. He kept his mouth shut, looking at the small struck-through Internet icon at the bottom corner of the screen, while trying to buy time and seek a way out of the mess. Wahid was winning his little game. He could see Rashid's frustration mounting as his lack of basic computer knowledge forced him to pace around, smoke, make calls that Wahid could hear in the distance, coming back only to smoke and pace some more. But he thought the more time Rashid wasted doing that, the more time he had to live. He rationalized that the only way Mukhtar would contact him was over his phone, and if he did, he would not risk a voice call. It would be a text message. Every time Rashid appeared; Wahid averted his eyes from his phone. He wondered if Rashid had the volume turned back up. Wahid had set it to silent when he left the embassy.

As he was pondering the what-ifs, an overhead light came on; the sunlight of the day had disappeared. He was getting hungry and contemplated asking Rashid for food. They had only hurt him once since being in the stall, but apart from the discomfort of his straps, he was doing relatively okay. His shoulder pain had subsided some, but he knew that could change in an instant if the mysterious doctor crept up behind him. He closed his eyes for a minute, but they sprang open the second he heard the phone beep.

Rashid, wandering around outside, ran into the stall. He picked up the phone and read the text. *'82 Atta Road, Westridge'*. He smiled. *At last*, he thought. Digesting the information, he put the phone back on the table. As he did it beeped again. He read the next text: *'18a Nisar Road, Westridge'*.

"What does this mean, Wahid? Why is he sending two addresses?"

Wahid shrugged, saying nothing.

Rashid suddenly lost his cool. It was unusual of him to do so, but he was at a loss. He uncharacteristically panicked and shoved the phone in his prisoner's face. "What is this Wahid? Is this a code?" he screamed. "Why is he sending two addresses? What is going on Wahid? Tell me! How are you supposed to respond?"

"I don't know."

Rashid slapped him across his face. "Don't lie to me. Tell me what is going on."

Wahid remained staunch; he knew that Rashid needed him. He knew, or at least he thought he knew, his tormentor couldn't hurt him that much.

Rashid picked up the hammer from the table and smashed it down, perilously close to Wahid's right hand. Wahid tried to retract from the blow but couldn't budge an inch. "Tell me!" he shouted again. This time he was screaming within a hairsbreadth distance of the prisoner's face. Wahid remained silent. Rashid grabbed his injured shoulder and squeezed. Wahid screamed at the top of his voice. Rashid stood back.

"Talk to me. Tell me what these messages mean."

Wahid finally relented. "He wants me to go to both locations!"

"What is the response code? How do you tell him you understand the order?"

"You have to let me go."

Rashid slapped him in the face again. He grabbed his shoulder again. "Talk you fool!"

"Stop, stop, please . . . there is no code, I don't need to respond. I just need to go there."

Rashid took a step back. He contemplated what the young man was saying. "Which house first?"

"I don't know, it doesn't matter. I just need to go to both places; I need to setup his Internet connection. When it is done, I will wait for him. If he is not there, he will call for me if he needs me. Perhaps he will change his mind and go elsewhere . . . it happens."

Rashid paced, needing time to think. Worrying that if there was no text confirmation from the terrorist's order, then how would he know that his bidding was complete?

"You must let me go; you must let me warn Mukhtar."

"Don't be so stupid boy! You are not going anywhere. I will take care of this." He dialed the number on the screen. He waited for a response—only to receive a recording from a woman saying the number was no longer in service.

Chris and Mahmoud strolled along the path of the Sikander Shaheed Park as if they were old friends catching up on old times. They paused at a five-way intersection and stood motionless for a while. Mahmoud had his back to the house he would visit later in the evening; he was describing to Chris the layout of number 18a Nisar Road. They were standing roughly five hundred feet from the house and Chris was looking over the asset's shoulder, trying his best to take in all he could see. It took him about thirty seconds to have a fair understanding of the location, but he dared not get any closer. The pair, though concealed by the trees in the park and the lack of natural light, ambled along, chatting quietly as if they had not a care in the world.

The duo split up at an intersection with Marble Road, where Alex was waiting with the Pepsi van. Mahmoud got in and they pulled away. Chris continued to circle the block onto Street 1 where he came upon another intersection, where he could see number 18a again from a different angle. However, the distance was greater this time from where he was standing. Once again, he took in all the mental images he could before he moved on. The roads were dark, the suburban streets were quiet, the well-to-do inhabitants were getting ready to settle in for the evening. He rambled on, keeping his head down and shuffling from time to time to give any onlooker a nonthreatening appearance. He found the path that led from Street 1 to the rear of the houses along Nisar Road. It wasn't much of a walkway. It was pitch black and Chris was dubious about what he would find if he ventured into it. He held back. He was too close to the target house to make a mistake now. He didn't know if KSM was in the home he was looking at, but he was sure that if the man were there, even the smallest ruckus would spook the terrorist and they would be back to square one. But a reconnaissance of the neighborhood had to happen; the operational team would create a plan for a raid based on the intelligence gathered by his observations. He meandered slowly on, finding a large open field flanked on three sides by squat housing. It reminded him of the disused barracks he found once upon a time long ago in Afghanistan.

Mahmoud stated that the military had a presence in the area, so he wondered if these buildings were housing for soldiers. It added another dimension to their plans, not knowing if the military were hiding KSM in plain sight. Chris snapped a picture with his mind and moved off. He continued his act for another ten minutes. When was relatively comfortable with what he saw, he made his way to the rendezvous point with Alex and the van, at the Sacred Heart Church.

Chris hastily sketched on a notepad the layout of the house and its surroundings. Mahmoud, who had visited the dwelling, provided a detailed picture of the rooms, hallways, stairs, and more. The trio then dissected the motions of who would do what, where and when. The bones of the operation to capture Khalid Sheik Mohammed were finally coming together. Ideally, a raid of such magnitude would take days, if not weeks, of detailed planning. Unfortunately, the SAD team did not have that luxury; they were working on limited intelligence. But both Chris and Alex had faith in the asset, and the CIA were ready to go all in. With all the makings of a best-case-scenario plan, Chris and Alex reluctantly let Mahmoud go. The first part of Operation Ball was set in motion as soon as the asset got out of the van. Part two would be for Chris and Alex to meet at the mobile FOB with other SAD assets, brief them on the information they had gathered, then wait.

The Isuzu utility truck pulled into the parking lot of the Maryam Memorial Hospital on the Peshawar Road. Wahid sat dejected and handcuffed on the floor, flanked by two ISI goons. Rashid sat next to one of his men, while holding onto Wahid's phone and his laptop.

When the vehicle finally came to a stop, Rashid began making calls on his personal cell phone, starting to marshal his troops into place. After thirty frustrating minutes of outgoing calls, he finally received an incoming call from his embedded ISI officer with the CIA. "Tell me, captain, what news is there?"

"Sir, the Americans have split up their force. The man they call Jon is leading one element, but the other is static."

"Where is Jon now?"

"Sir, I believe they are following the signal from the laptop and phone."

Rashid cringed and almost crushed his phone in his hands. He rubbed his forehead hard, trying to process the news. "What of the other element? Where are they now?"

"Sir, I believe they—"

"—FACTS captain . . . I want facts, not your beliefs!" Rashid spat as he interrupted the report.

"Sir . . . the second element is stationary at a parking area on the Zahid Baig Road, near the Saint Mary Church.

"Why aren't you with them, you fool?"

"I am following Jon, sir."

"Go back! Go back now to the second element. Report to me from there, stay close to them."

The captain wanted to respond to the order, but the line was dead.

Rashid stared at the phone and contemplated what he needed to do. The Americans were on the move, toward him. He needed to shake them, but he needed to find Mukhtar—though he wasn't sure which house to go to. A salient thought crossed his mind. *If the Americans are following the laptop and the phone, then they may not have confidence in their informer.* He smirked slightly. He gazed down at his prisoner and dwelled on other information that needed processing. He gave the young man a curious look, as if trying to solve a complex mathematical problem. *That laptop, his phone . . . damn, damn, damn. Curse that swine, I should have dealt with him earlier . . . differently.* He got out of the back of the truck to clear his mind; he could not look at the wimpy Wahid any longer.

He walked away from the vehicle and toyed with his phone. His mind was trying to find its top gear, he needed to be at his best. Things were transpiring quickly and he had to be up to speed, not lagging behind. He processed what was forefront in his mind. The residence on Atta Road was the closest, only ten minutes away, and the other was at least three kilometers north from his location. *We should go to Atta Road first. If Mukhtar is there we can exit quickly and be on our way . . . Wahid and his equipment can stay . . . as a decoy. The Americans will be wary of approaching and will take their time if they observe a static signal. They lack the will to act decisively . . . an advantage.* As solutions became clearer so did his pace while marching in circles around the hospital parking lot. *I need another vehicle, more men at the rear of the house. If he is not there . . . then Nisar Road.*

Another benefit that would help his cause was the late hour. It had long since passed midnight and there were few vehicles on the roads, making his speedy interventions much easier. His thought process was becoming less cloudy, though there were still many players in the game. Wahid sitting silently in the pickup, forlorn, unsure, in pain and looking for sympathy. Mukhtar, in one of two houses in the city, or not at all. The Americans and their insurmountable resources; the greediness of the traitor Mahmoud. His loyal ISI officers looking to him for direction, commands, wise tactical decisions. The pressure of it all was pounding his head like an incessant pile driver at a construction site. He knew he had found a course of action, but he also knew that things could draw to a close for him—and not pleasantly—if he were not careful. Before he issued any orders, he dissected his plan and self-brainstormed potential obstacles. Upmost in his mind, however, was his fear of the capture of the master terrorist, as it would not be long thereafter that the long, boney fingers of authority would poke at his own chest. Satisfied with his strategy, he made some calls, then got into the front of the utility truck. "Atta Road, now!"

The driver started the vehicle and did as he was told.

"He must be about half a mile from you, ICE BEAR. Heading northeast up the Peshawar Road, looks like he just pulled out of a hospital parking lot."

"Roger that ICE CAVE. Keep this line open, I need a minute-by-minute play," Jon responded. He was riding shotgun in an SUV with one SAD officer driving, and another sitting in the rear next to an ISI officer who was also coordinating the Pakistan effort to follow the signal the Americans were monitoring. ICE BEAR's SUV led a small convoy of similar vehicles. The four SUVs that followed contained a mixture of heavily armed SAD operators and Pakistan Special Forces.

"Drop your speed, ICE BEAR, you will be in his rearview any minute."

Jon acknowledged with a simple "10-4" and ordered the driver to slow down.

The CIA analyst at ICE CAVE continued the play-by-play, directing raid team Alpha down the same streets the target was traversing.

"Slow down ICE BEAR . . . slow, crawl, crawl . . . stop."

There was silence over the radio waves; no one spoke, no one dared even breathe. Jon stared out the window in front of him, wishing he had X-ray eyes.

"He's on foot ICE BEAR, 300 feet to your front, right side of the street; stand by for house number."

Jon maintained radio silence. He fidgeted in his seat. Though he didn't show it, his heart was working hard trying to break free of his chest. A sliver of sweat gave away his efforts to control his emotions. He knew the CIA hadn't been this close to such an important target in its entire history. If they could capture Khalid Sheik Mohammed alive, the next step would be Osama bin Laden. The enormity of the moment was almost overwhelming. His eyes were almost popping out of his head as he desperately tried to see exactly what was going on, and who was in the house the target had just entered. He willed himself to be quiet and not push ICE CAVE for information. He had been on enough operations to know what it was like on both ends of the line. Mostly quarterbacking missions from afar, he occasionally got his feet wet in order to garner fame and potential fortune. But this was different. He knew that the giant machine back at ICE CAVE and at the Counterterrorism Center in the United States were dissecting tons of data to provide the decision makers a solution to scenarios from both tactical and strategic angles. Truth be told, he would rather have been calling the shots from the safety of a command center and letting the SAD make the dangerous capture, but his ego demanded that he be in the field, and the one to kick in the door that would lead to the man's capture. He knew that this would be the pinnacle of his career, and it had to go right.

"Target is static, ICE BEAR. Number 82, second floor. Stand by for tactical orders."

"Negative ICE CAVE, we will mobilize; we are the closet to the target."

"Negative ICE BEAR, I repeat, negative. Wait for a tactical solution. The decision to deploy will come from CTC."

"ICE CAVE, please inform CTC that I am proceeding. I believe that our target is in that house and we cannot wait until they decide from overseas."

"ICE BEAR I have a direct communication from CTC. Stand by, I repeat stand by."

Jon reluctantly complied with the last order. He sat and stewed for a few minutes before deciding on a course of action. He turned to the SAD officer sitting behind him. "Get your boys and the Special Forces team to come up with a plan to take that house." He pointed down the street. "Number 82, second floor. We are going in . . . in ten minutes."

"CTC wants us to stand by Jon."

"Fuck that! I am not losing this opportunity. I am ordering you to prepare to raid that house. Do you understand?"

The SAD officer tried to argue with Jon, but could see it wasn't getting him anywhere; they were only losing time. He unenthusiastically left the vehicle to confer with his team and the Pakistani commandos about how best to proceed. Ten minutes was nowhere near enough to create a plan to raid a house they had not even seen before, with no intelligence about the layout or the makeup of the occupants. He strung out the planning for as long as he could, hoping that someone with a sound mind could guide them better than the ill-prepared operations officer making the calls.

Jon didn't see the blue utility vehicle pull away from the curb. He was busy on his phone, dialing his allies in Washington DC to garner support for his impending success. After finishing his last call he looked at his watch: 0130 hours.

Ten minutes turned into forty. However, the order from CTC to move in was finally given and the two teams of specialists deployed to attack the target.

The Pakistan Special Forces used a battering ram to smash the front door of the residence. The large man who had wielded the ram then stood to one side as his team rushed through the door, weapons raised, laser beams leading the way. The first five-man "stick" team deployed to the ground floor, and the second "stick" to the first floor. The teams encountered no resistance. Nor were they greeted with any vocal protestations. By the time the SAD team entered the property, with Jon in the lead, the commandos had retraced their steps to the front hallway to report to Jon that nobody was in the house. Nobody alive, at least. They led Jon to the first-floor bathroom, where he saw a body on the floor. A damaged laptop and phone were lying next to the corpse.

"His neck is broken; his shoulder is also damaged," a soldier reported.

Jon looked down at the lifeless Wahid. He felt a moment of sadness, but it didn't last long. "Did you do this?" he asked the soldier.

The man clad in black didn't reply; he simply looked at the American with disdain. He wanted to spit at the arrogant officer. He brushed passed him without looking at him further.

Jon looked back down at the young man on the floor and realized that the soldiers could not know who he was. To them he was just a source. There would have been no need for them to kill him. However, it opened up a new set of questions. Who killed Wahid? Was it Mukhtar?

Alex checked his watch, it was almost 0200 hours. He stifled a yawn. His body was telling him he should rest, he should have taken a shower, he should have eaten. He should have been a thousand different places other than down the end of a dark alleyway waiting for the asset to message him, but he wouldn't have it any other way.

Unlike raid team Alpha, his team Bravo were on strict radio silence. Standing by at the church of Saint Mary, the same compliment of forces as team Alpha were sitting in running vehicles, waiting for a signal from a SAD operator who was as close to the target as one could be without sitting at the target's kitchen table.

Alex had been sitting in the alleyway for almost an hour, waiting for something to happen. The plan was to wait until everyone in the target house was asleep before raid team Bravo hit the location; everyone expected that would be around 0100 hours. Allowing the residents of the house to unwind and get into a good sleep pattern was crucial to the element of surprise. However, the team still didn't know if KSM was even in the house. The longer the silence, the greater the chance of him not being there, and everyone, including the asset, was in fact asleep. Alex felt a vibration in his pocket; his phone was notifying him of a message. He shielded its light with the palms of his hands and read the message.

"I am with KSM."

Alex involuntarily swallowed. *Goddamm! It's on.* He didn't reply to the message but instead whispered into his radio. "Viper, Viper, Viper. Go, go, go."

Chris received the radio message and acknowledged the transmission. He turned to the two civilian-clothed Pakistan Special Forces soldiers. "Viper," he stated quietly. The three men left the cover of the small group of vehicles, as they were doing so, the remainder of the men that composed the raid team sauntered casually over to the front door of number 18a Nisar Road after them. Chris gripped his silenced 9mm Makarov pistol with his right hand, covered by his wool shawl.

He was third in line, behind the two soldiers who were both carrying H&K MP5SD machine guns, also hidden from view. The trio clambered gently over a low wall and avoided the gate that led directly to the front door. As soon as the men crossed the threshold, they produced their weapons and aimed their barrels at the main entry, as well as the windows to their left and front. Though they were the closest to the house, two teams of snipers also covered the men and focused on the same door and windows.

"Sir the Americans are moving forward; they are at the house on Nisar Road," the captain reported.

Rashid gritted his teeth. He'd missed one opportunity, and now it looked like his gamble didn't pay off. He'd bet on the wrong house. "Keep me informed, captain." He replied, his heart was in his mouth. He wasn't sure if he should proceed to Nisar Road, or run in the other direction.

Still undetected, one Pakistani soldier slung his MP5 around his back, took a knee, then produced a lock pick. He donned his night-vision goggles, and his two compatriots did the same. Chris covered the window nearest the door while the other soldier covered the front entrance. The kneeling soldier worked quietly, yet feverishly on the lock, and within a minute he defeated it. Without opening the door, the kneeling soldier raised himself up and readied his weapon.

The motion of his body set the rest of the raid team into action. Silently, more members of the Special Forces team lined themselves up to breach the target. The lead soldier at the front door grasped the door handle. He paused. He tried his best to listen for a movement—a scrape of a chair, a voice, something that would prevent his silent entry. There was nothing. He held his breath; the trickiest and most dangerous part of the operation was now his to make. He didn't know if there was a man standing guard on the other side of the door, if it would blow up at the slightest of movements, or an alarm was ready to howl. He turned the handle and nudged the door gently open. He praised his God that the door didn't creak or moan. He took two steps inside, bringing his weapon up to his shoulder, and scanned the area slowly for threats, a laser beam on the front of his barrel leading the way.

While the three-man team entered the foyer, the rest of the Special Forces team crept into position and held post outside the door, ready to sprint inside and kill any combatants who dared pose a threat. Chris waited patiently for his two comrades to make the next move; he covered the stairs while they scoured the downstairs for signs of life. There were none.

There were still no words spoken. Before the lead soldier returned to Chris's position, he motioned for the rest of his team to enter the premises and showed them he wanted them to stage on the stairway. He then moved stealthily up the stairs, weapon at the ready, its trusty red beam leading the way. At the top of the landing, he led Chris down the corridor, then both men halted at a door. They kneeled in position and waited for the rest of the team to move quietly into place. Eight men crouched in the hallway, two to each bedroom door. Everyone waited for Chris and the team lead to enter the bedroom where they thought their target was. It was the second time the group leader hesitated. The entire team could be in great peril at this moment. The same scenario he envisioned at the front door again entered his mind: was there a man waiting, were there explosives, was there an alarm?

He turned the door's knob and nuzzled it open. He spotted a lump of a figure on the bed, laying on his side, facing away from the door. Once more he prayed to his God that this was the target. He got up from his kneeling position. Chris did the same. Both men moved silently and slowly to the bed, weapons aimed at the figure's head. Chris made it to the bed frame first. The soldier next to him whispered, "Khalid . . . Khalid."

Chris leaned forward, within arm's reach of the man sleeping comfortably like a baby on the bed. "Khalid . . . Khalid, Chris softly said. The man on the bed rolled slightly on hearing the name, but he didn't wake up. Chris quickly checked the room for weapons, then made his way to the other side of the bed to face the sleeping man. He got close enough to put the barrel of the gun on the sleeper's forehead. "Khalid!" he said forcefully.

Khalid heard his name being called, but he was so far into his slumber he couldn't tell if it was real or a dream. He stirred slightly on the second call, but his eyes remained shut, oblivious to any problem. Between the time he heard the second call and the third, he realized that there was nothing delightful accompanying his name. There was no magic unicorn or gentle streams or beautiful women. His mind was void of anything so sublime. The piece of metal that he felt on his forehead was real. He rolled over on his back wanting to swat it away, but he opened his eyes first. His entrancing dream was turning into a nightmare. He blinked his eyes, only to see a demon shape above him with three green eyes. He pulled himself back and grabbed at the bedclothes, in defense of the monster, but then he saw a red beam dance in front of his belly, stopping at his heart. He looked to his left and saw another three-eyed demon.

"Khalid! Khalid!" one creature shouted. "Wake up, wake up!"

He still wasn't sure this was really happening, but then he heard the noises coming from elsewhere in the house, his mind catching up to the surreal experience playing out in front of him. The demons ripped the bedclothes from him, and the bedroom light came on. It was then he realized this was no dream, nor even a nightmare—it was real.

Chris removed his night-vision goggles and the Pakistani soldier did the same. Two more soldiers appeared at the foot of the bed. Chris holstered his pistol, grabbed KSM by his tousled hair, and pulled him off the bed. He slammed him to the ground and searched his body for weapons. All he found was moisture from the terrorist's sweat glands. The thought momentarily disgusted him and he wiped his hands clean with KSM's nightclothes. The lead soldier then cuffed the terrorist who was lying face down on the floor. Satisfied he was no longer a threat, they brought him to his knees. They left him in that pose until the ruckus in the house dissipated.

Chris stared at him the whole time. He couldn't believe that this wild-haired, greasy, slovenly looking man, dressed in striped pajama pants and dirty wife beater tank top, was the revered hero of al-Qaeda. He wanted to spit in his face, stab him in the heart, put a bullet in his head. Anything but allow him to live.

KSM could tell that the man staring at him wanted to do him harm. He spouted off to the Pakistani soldiers in the room. Chris couldn't make heads or tails of what he was saying, but the captive continued to rant. His voice was getting louder and Chris was contemplating punching him in the mouth—but he held back. He had only completed Phase 1 of the mission; there was still another part to play.

But he could daydream. By the time Chris had gotten to number eighteen on the list of his favored ways to kill a man—especially this man—Gene entered the room, flanked by some senior ISI officers. Gene walked over to the captive. "Khalid Sheik Mohammed?" he asked.

The terrorist didn't answer. Instead he turned to his Pakistani captors. "Why are you doing this for the Americans? If it's money, I will give you what you want." But the men were unmoved. The ISI offered a translation to Gene, who only shook his head. He turned to Chris, "Everything is set; you ready?"

Chris nodded, then grabbed a blanket off the bed and threw it over KSM's head. He dragged him into the hallway, and was met by three more blanketed prisoners being shuffled down the stairs by some of his SAD colleagues. Chris joined the troupe, pulling KSM with him. However, when they reached the bottom of the stairs, there was a brief scuffle between the prisoners and the SAD officers. Fists flew, accompanied by shoves and kicks intended to maintain order. In the brief fracas, the order of the prisoners got mixed up. Chris grabbed the last man in the train and herded him away from the group, out the kitchen door and into the backyard. The opposite direction of the others.

Alex, waiting in the shadows for Chris, called out "Viper!" in the darkness. Chris headed toward the sound, his prisoner in tow. Alex led the way through the rough brush and into the pathway behind the houses. After a short while, the three men ended up on Street 1, just a short distance away from the waiting Pepsi van.

———∞∞∞———

Rashid halted the Isuzu at the intersection of Nisar Road and Street 1. He got out of the vehicle, looked up the road and witnessed the spectacle of three men being ushered into different SUVs. He studied the commotion as best as he could, but with the lack of decent street lighting and the blankets placed over the men's heads, he couldn't tell who the detainees or the captors were—but he knew he was too late. Thoughts of defeat, and indeed retreat, entered his mind.

He brushed the negativity away for a moment and concentrated on the road in front of him, but he didn't notice the white Daihatsu van sitting at the curb nearby. He only paid it attention when he heard the engine start. The driver of the vehicle got out, paid him no regard, and opened the vehicle's sliding door.

Rashid wondered what was going on. He shimmied to the side of the truck and tapped the side, expecting his men to exit and join him on the street. His heart skipped a beat when he saw three men approach from a pathway. The first man looked like a local, and so did the third. But the man in the middle did not belong. He was bent over and had a blanket covering his head.

Mukhtar?

Chris saw the utility truck first. It didn't belong. He stared closely at the man who was standing next to it, and saw that he was soon joined by two beefier men. Chris knew the tall one was an authority figure, but he didn't know who for. *Who the fuck are these Muppets?* He wanted to keep an eye on his new audience, but his head spun around, looking for other potential threats. His driver was where he wanted him to be, behind the wheel, engine running. He looked back at the tallest of the three men who approached his group. Alex also spotted the unknown visitors. He conducted the same exercise as Chris, but was also looking behind him, back down the path from where they came, seeking a threat.

Rashid saw the two men's posture changing, but it was the look in their eyes that set his warning bells off. *These are not Pakistani . . . Americans?* He neared the group. He needed to assert his authority and take charge of whatever activity was playing out before him.

Chris spotted the mood change in the tallest man of the group. He reached back and grabbed the prisoner's shackles to drag him closer with his left hand, while his right reached for his Makarov. Alex saw the movement and closed in. He placed his left hand on the prisoner's shoulder, his right on his concealed pistol.

"Gentlemen, this way please, this is your transport vehicle," Rashid bluffed.

Like fuck it is, Chris thought. "No thanks, we're good here. If you don't mind moving your truck out of the way, that would be great."

"But I insist," Rashid pestered. "Jon asked me to assist you."

Chris was surprised by the mention of Jon's name. This was not part of the plan, nor was it a contingency. The situation stunk. Chris was still moving toward the van and had roughly thirty feet to go before they were inside.

"Colonel Rashid, ISI," whispered Alex.

"Don't give a flying fuck, we're not going with him."

"Concur."

Rashid moved closer. "The prisoner is to come with me. He is a Pakistan citizen; he must not leave this country—we will take him into custody." Chris and Alex tried to keep moving, but Rashid had moved to block their path.

Chris was having none of it. "Not today, boss," he said. "We have somewhere else to be, so if you don't mind getting out of our way, that would be nice."

Rashid's voice turned to one used to having his orders followed without question. "But I insist," he repeated. "You must hand him over to me." He raised his right hand as he spoke. His men behind him drew their concealed pistols and readied them at their sides.

"Look," Chris started, his hand grasped firmly around his pistol. *Colonel shit for brains is not armed. Good. Alex will move the prisoner to cover. I will take out Laurel and Hardy. Kick the colonel in the nuts, then get in the van.* "I've been nice to you and I politely asked you to get out of my way,"

Chris continued, "We are not going with you so *fuck off*—and it's my turn to insist."

"Mukhtar! Mukhtar!" Rashid screamed and reached for the prisoner.

The lunge didn't surprise Chris; he saw the tell. The body tensing, the deep intake of breath, the narrowing of the eyes. Chris saw an opening as the officer leaned over and reached with his left arm. He let go of his pistol in his waistband as well as the prisoner, then grabbed the colonel's arm and punched him hard in the ribs with his right. He kept ahold of the officer's arm and punched him two more times.

Alex shielded his prisoner with his body and tried to rush him to the van, but the struggle between Chris and Rashid was in his way. Out of the corner of his eye he saw the two ISI goons move in, weapons aimed at the small scrum. He pushed the prisoner to the ground and drew, aimed and shot his gun. The first round hit one man in the neck, the second shot his right shoulder, the third, his heart.

Chris was still engaged with Rashid, who was falling over. He pushed him down all the way to the ground as the first rounds of fire flew above their heads. Though one ISI officer was down, the second one, and the driver of the truck, joined the fight. The driver was armed with an Uzi, and he sprayed fire over the tops of everyone's heads. Chris dove into the van for cover; as he did rounds peppered the inside of the vehicle, killing his driver. Alex was still returning fire and covering the prisoner. The two men who were shooting at him stopped and ran for cover.

The brief lull was the opportunity Chris needed. He drew his weapon, leaned out of the van and provided cover for Alex and the prisoner. He couldn't see exactly who he was shooting at, but it made the attackers pause before continuing the fight.

"Get in! Get in!" he screamed at Alex.

Rashid scrambled away, into the alleyway where he'd first spotted the Americans and their prisoner. He came very close to being shot by his own men, but survived by scampering away on all fours. When he looked back at the van, he saw one of the Americans shooting at his men, and the other trying to stuff Mukhtar into the vehicle. The shots continued to fly between his men and the Americans, and it gave him an opportunity to run back to his vehicle.

Alex hadn't had time to close the vehicle's sliding door, and he struggled to climb forward into the driver's seat. He knew he had to get them moving if they were to survive. Chris was still providing the cover he needed to get things done.

Rashid stumbled over the dead body of one of his men and fell flat on his face. He recovered in time to look up and see that the Americans were about to get away with the prisoner. He found his dead colleague's gun and made a quick decision. With one American shooting at his men, the other struggling to get the dead driver out of the driver's seat, he saw a gap. He moved forward slowly, approaching the Daihatsu from the flank, the blind side of the American who was reloading his weapon. He raised his pistol and saw the cocky CIA officer in his sights. He tried to pull the trigger but his vision went black, his fingers limp.

Chris spun around at the sound of a weapon being fired from behind him to his left. The sight shocked him. Jawad was aiming a gun at the now-prone Colonel Rashid, blood pumping out of his head. He didn't have long to think about what he was looking at, as he searched for the remaining two ISI officers. But a shout from Alex, who was now in the driver's seat, also didn't give him any time.

"Shut the goddam door!"

Chris complied with the order, and the van screeched away. Chris looked out the rear window expecting more shots, but none came. All he could see was Jawad, hustling into a car, with Guy Trimble waiting in the driver's seat.

"Chris, you okay? Chris!" Alex shouted from behind the wheel.

What the hell just happened . . . Jawad?

"Chris!"

"I'm good, Alex. I'm okay, you?"

"Yeah, yeah, check on our boy."

Chris removed the blanket from Mahmoud's head. "Are you okay? Are you hit?"

"No, but please take these off me," he pleaded, showing Chris the handcuffs.

Chris called Gene as they were barreling down the Airport Road. Before Chris used his phone, both he and Alex agreed that they would not delay in getting their charge onto the waiting airplane. Gene tried his best to convince them otherwise, by redirecting them to another safe house, due to the circumstances of the attack by Colonel Rashid. Chris mentioned the death of Rashid, but left out the sudden appearance of Jawad and Guy. Chris was thrown for a loop when he saw them, but he resolved himself to keeping that nugget away from Gene, just in case his boss thought he had something to do with them being there. He would have to dissect the incident later; it was another complication he didn't need, although it helped him to make a decision.

He pushed Gene for a directive; the boss only relented when he found out that a small crowd had shown up at 18a Nisar Road demanding that the authorities had the wrong man, and Khalid Sheik Mohammed was not a terrorist. Chris didn't care which rent-a-mob was on the streets; he knew he would only feel safe when he had Mahmoud on a plane and out of the country. All Gene had to do was grease the skids with airport security and ask them to ignore a shot-up Daihatsu van when it showed up at the gates of the Chaklala Airport.

True to form, Gene had once again worked his magic. Alex steered the van past the waving, smiling security guard and onto the Rawalpindi Flying Club & School apron. He slowed the vehicle down, looking for the Gulfstream IV. Chris spotted it first. "Two o'clock, five hundred feet."

"Seen," Alex replied as he pushed on slowly towards the waiting aircraft. He stopped well enough away of any potential prop wash.

Chris opened the sliding door. "Stay here," he ordered Mahmoud. He then tapped on Alex's shoulder. "You want to keep it running buddy? I'll go see if we're on."

"Sure. Make it snappy. We're running out of gas, and we still need to get back to the embassy."

Chris nodded and dashed over to the aircraft. He stood outside the plane and looked up at the cockpit; he got the pilot's attention. The man got out of his seat, opened the cabin door and lowered the steps. Chris returned to the van after a brief conversation with the pilot, and assured Alex and Mahmoud the plane was ready. Mahmoud exited the van, and Chris asked Alex to back the vehicle up closer to the building, explaining that the pilot thought it was too close. He complied with the request as Mahmoud and Chris walked towards the aircraft and up the stairs.

Alex parked the vehicle and turned off the engine. He exited and made his way to meet Chris at the foot of the stairs leading into the cabin. Halfway to the jet, Chris came back to meet him.

"He's left his passport in the van; can you go get it? I'll stick with him, he's nervous as fuck, he doesn't think he's getting out of here."

"Passport? What the hell Chris. I don't recall seeing any passport."

"I don't know either, can you check? I'll go hold his hand."

Alex jogged back to the van and began his search. He rummaged around, and after a few minutes of finding nothing he turned to go back to the Gulfstream and saw Chris waving from the top of the stairs.

Chris saw him approaching. He wanted to talk to him, wanted to tell him what he was doing, but he couldn't. *Sorry mate, I'm not letting you fall with me*, he told his friend silently. *I need to lay low for a while. The OIG can go fuck themselves.*

Alex squinted his eyes; he had a sickly feeling in his stomach. He picked up his pace a little, and shouted, "Chris, what are you doing?!" knowing that Chris couldn't hear him over the plane's engines. He stopped dead in his tracks as Chris raised the steps and locked the door in place. He looked on in disbelief as the plane taxied away, but couldn't hold back the smile that crept across his face as he thought *Clever bastard. See you next time, mate.*

END

EPILOGUE

US Army 121st General Hospital, Yongsan, South Korea

RESTRAINED BY HIS WRISTS AND ankles, all Staff Sergeant Troy Hansen could do was move his head from one side to the other. As a patient in the psychiatric ward of the base hospital, they left him in a room by himself. Although it was the middle of the night, he was wide awake when a man entered the room dressed in hospital scrubs. The man carried a tray with two small cups. He held one to the patient's lips.

Troy balked. "I'm not taking anything."

"It's to help you sleep, it's just a sedative."

"I don't need shit. Leave me alone."

"You don't have a choice. If you don't take the pill, we will just inject it. You lost all your privileges when you overdosed."

He turned his face away from the orderly. "Get the fuck out of here, I don't need anything from you."

The man in the scrubs lay the tray down on a nearby table. "Fine," he said as he moved to the end of bed and uncovered the patient's feet. He produced a needle from his pocket, grabbed the patient's right foot firmly, and injected a colorless substance in between the big and second toe. He stood back and ignored the soldier's protestations, then looked at his watch and counted down the seconds. As the chemicals streamed through the patient's body, he could tell it wouldn't be long before the man's entire nervous system would shut down. It was the panic in the eyes that gave the first tell. He waited for the neck muscles to strain, then he slinked away.

Jefferson County, Washington State

Chris Morehouse pulled into the gravel driveway that led up to the farm he'd once called home. As he drove in, he spotted a blue Ford pickup truck with a large Seattle Seahawks sticker plastered across the rear window. He frowned, not knowing who the truck's owner was. He spotted Sandy's red Jeep Wrangler parked nearby. As he got out, he looked across the pasture. The horses weren't there. He moved toward the house, taking it all in, scanning for what was in its right place, searching for something that wasn't. He hadn't been to his home in almost a year, and while his memories of the place were good, he still had to remind himself that he didn't need to feel threatened. He tried the kitchen door; it was locked. He was relieved knowing that Sandy wasn't there. Then he put two and two together and surmised she was out riding her horse with someone else.

He found the spare key secreted inside a small box wedged in an overhead truss. He let himself in. As he did, he received a loud greeting from Mango, Sandy's cat, who took umbrage to being rudely awakened by the intruder. He gave the cat a brief pat on the head, then headed upstairs to the spare bedroom. Chris pulled out one of his trusty kit bags and stuffed in what belongings he still had to his name. He filled one, then grabbed another to complete the task. As soon as he finished, he found his binoculars on his desk and made for the balcony. He opened the door but didn't step out. He scanned the open fields and tree lines, hoping to glimpse Sandy. It took a few minutes, but he finally spotted what he was looking for. Sandy and a tall man, holding hands, leading the horses and walking back towards the house. He placed the binoculars down, took in a large breath of air, then made a quick guesstimate. If the couple were just sauntering, they would be back at the farm in thirty minutes, if they rode it'd be less than ten. He wasn't mad, nor upset, just a little disappointed—not in her; in himself.

Chris grabbed both his bags and his binoculars and headed back to his car. He dropped all his belongings in the trunk, then headed for the kitchen once more. He found the cookie jar and stuck his hand in to retrieve a few. He munched on them for a short while, then shuffled around to see if any letters or bills were waiting for him. Finding nothing of interest, he stroked Mango once again and said his good-byes. He exited the kitchen just in time to spot Sandy and tall boy nearing the main house. They hadn't seen him, even though he wasn't trying to hide. He strolled casually over to his car and stopped at the driver's-side door. Tall boy and Sandy finally saw Chris. She dropped her new man's hand, then moved quickly between him and Chris. It was an instinctive defensive move on her part. Chris understood what she was doing.

"Sandy. Don't worry, I'm not going to do what you think I'm going to do."

"Chris—"

"I've just come to pick up a few things and to say goodbye. I'm sorry it turned out this way Sandy; it's not your fault. I guess we had different paths after all."

"Chris, you—" She struggled to find the words; it surprised her to see him there after all this time without a word. She didn't even know if he was still alive. Didn't know what he was doing or where he had been. "—Where have you been?" she began.

Chris smiled without answering. He got in the car and pulled away slowly. He looked in the rearview mirror and saw her standing there, her hands on her hips. Tall boy was making his move to comfort her.

Chris loaded the *Certa Cito* with what meager possessions he had. He'd stopped off at the local QFC supermarket on the way to the marina, and grabbed as many essentials as he could for his next adventure. His friend Patrick had been maintaining, stocking and sailing the boat while he was away, and according to the old Irishman, it was more than seaworthy.

"Permission to come aboard?" someone called out from the dock.

Chris almost bumped his head on the bulkhead when he heard the voice. *Jesus Christ, what now?* He made his way up from the cabin into the cockpit and saw a familiar face. "Sure Gene," he said with a grin, "but don't be surprised if you turn into a boat anchor."

"You're a funny guy, Chris. Nice boat, by the way."

How the hell did he know I was here? Chris pondered, but didn't want to dwell on it. "I've got little to offer. Sit down if you want; but speak now or forever hold your peace. I'm about to leave."

"Where you headed?"

"Normally I would say, 'I'll tell you when I get there.' But I won't."

"There's no need to be like that, Chris. You've no need to worry. I'm not going to ask you for anything."

"Are you sure? Or did someone send you to come get me?"

"Nobody sent me Chris. I'm here on my own accord."

"Speaking of which," he interjected. "How did you know I was back?"

Gene looked up over the cockpit toward the restaurant on the shoreline. He waved to someone Chris couldn't see until he stood up. The old Irishman was waving back. "Patrick Mooney and I go way back. He was in Vietnam with me, and then the NSA. We've been friends for a very long time. I asked him to keep me in the loop a little."

"I thought we were finished, you and I. We agreed that as soon as KSM was captured I was done. I'm holding up my end of the deal. So what do you want?"

"I want nothing from you Chris. I just didn't want us to end on bad terms. I still would like to consider you a friend."

"That's not what you told me in Paris."

Gene slowly nodded and looked down on the deck. "I know, I know. Sorry, I was under a lot of pressure."

"Everyone was Gene, but I'm not coming back."

"I'm not asking you to. I just wanted to let you know that I'm out. I retired."

Chris bore a wide, genuine smile. "I'm happy for you Gene, really! You've earned it, especially after Pakistan. Congratulations."

"Thanks."

"But you didn't need to come all this way to tell me that. What's going on?"

"That thing with the OIG, the investigation. It's gone away."

Chris's mood was getting better by the minute. He was happy that Gene would finally take things easy, pleased that he'd left on a high, and relieved his old boss wasn't asking him to go to some God-awful hellhole for another assignment. But the icing on the cake was that the OIG were no longer interested in talking to him; it was a tremendous weight off his mind. "What happened to that guy from the army?"

"I don't know. I guess something changed his mind. I was told it was no longer an issue."

Chris looked at Gene and tried to read his face and his body language, but he was getting nothing. He pottered around the boat a little, trying to take his mind off things. He didn't really want to think about his previous employment, but he was still curious. "What about KSM? He was all over the news for a while there?"

"That dirtbag screamed like a little girl when they showed him the hot water bottle and the jumpsuit. I heard that he didn't need it anyway, he shit himself. The guys let him stew in it for hours. Last I heard he was at the Salt Pit; he's not going anywhere. They're going to drag every last ounce of information out of him. He won't see the light of day for a long, long time, or ever, really." Chris smiled at the image of the terrorist, the infamous architect of 9/11, wallowing in his own filth. "You need to give yourself credit, Chris. You were an integral part of bringing him in—"

"—But I'm still an obnoxious ass."

"There's no need to go there, Chris. I didn't come here to lecture you on your attitude or what's been said and done. You are who you are, only you can change, and I certainly can't make you something else."

Chris was content with the honest words. Gene had read him right. He wouldn't change who he was for someone else. It was something that he needed to do for himself. He reached up to grab the mainsheet tackle lines and tighten them. Not because there was a need, it was just something to keep his hands and mind busy. He appreciated the kind words, but he didn't want to get all touchy feely.

Gene saw that his friend wasn't about to get too personal with him, which he thought was fine, though he still had one more thing to say. "You probably haven't heard this very often, Chris, but thank you. Thank you for your service. You have my gratitude . . . and that of every other American who needed this. You should be proud of yourself."

Chris squirmed and grabbed another line to tighten on the boat. He wasn't used to taking praise or thanks; however, it was a pleasant change. But he kept his mouth shut. He didn't want any counter-cliches ruining the moment. They both stared at each other for a minute, neither saying anything.

Gene finally asked, "So, where are you going Chris?"

"I'll tell you when I get there."

—⊸∞⊶—

THE END

AUTHOR'S NOTE

The preceding work is of course fictional . . . for the most part. Khalid Sheik Mohammed, aka., KSM, aka., Mukhtar, aka., Bojenga, the architect of 9/11 was captured at 18a Nisar Road, Westridge, Rawalpindi, Pakistan in February 2003. As of this writing he is a prisoner of the US Government in Guantanamo Bay awaiting trial.

Asset X exists, and was awarded $25 million for his part in the capture of KSM. He is now a resident of the United States. He was nowhere near Nisar Road when the capture of the terrorist occurred.

ABOUT THE AUTHOR

David A. Davies is an independent security consultant with experience in executive protection, investigations, and physical security design. He has been engaged in the security industry in both the public and private sectors for more than twenty years. David resides with his family in the greater Seattle area. For more information about his books, or you if wish to contact him directly, you can find him at:
www.davidadaviesauthor.com.

PLEASE REVIEW THIS BOOK!

Thank you for picking up a copy of Asset X, I have but one small request. Reviews help authors more than you might think. If you enjoyed this book, please consider leaving a review at Amazon, Goodreads or your favorite review/purchase site. Any and all feedback would be greatly appreciated.

www.ingramcontent.com/pod-product-compliance
Lightning Source LLC
Chambersburg PA
CBHW060156260626
47160CB00001B/294